THE SECOND DELUGE

"THEY MEANT TO CARRY THE ARK WITH A RUSH" [Page 106]

THE
SECOND DELUGE

By

GARRETT P. SERVISS

Author of

Moon Metal, A Columbus of Space,
Astronomy with the Naked Eye, etc.

ILLUSTRATIONS BY

GEORGE VARIAN

WITH A NEW INTRODUCTION BY

JOSEPH WRZOS

HYPERION PRESS, INC.

WESTPORT, CONNECTICUT

Library of Congress Cataloging in Publication Data

Serviss, Garrett Putman, 1851-1929.
    The second deluge.

    Reprint of the 1912 ed. published by McBride,
Nast, New York.
    Includes bibliographical references.
    I. Title.
PZ3.S4925Se20   [PS3537.E68]   813'.4   73-13266
ISBN 0-88355-120-9
ISBN 0-88355-149-7 (pbk.)

Published in 1912
by McBride, Nast & Company, New York
Copyright 1912
by McBride, Nast & Company

Copyright © 1974 by Hyperion Press, Inc.

Hyperion reprint edition 1974

Library of Congress Catalogue Number 73-13266

ISBN 0-88355-120-9 (cloth ed.)
ISBN 0-88355-149-7 (paper ed.)

Printed in the United States of America

THE SECOND DELUGE:
Serviss's Masterwork

*By Joseph Wrzos**

Over the centuries a good many authors have borrowed — for their own special literary purposes — the widely circulated Biblical story of Noah and the Flood. In the nineteenth century, for example, there was Mark Twain's eruptive "Letters from the Earth" (posthumous publication of which his daughter blocked, judging the text atypical of her father's true beliefs, but finally relenting in 1962), in which Satan — corresponding with some archangel friends — charges the Creator with apparently not having the foggiest notion of how to construct a practical ark ("It had no rudder ... no sails ... no compass," etc.) and with leaving the refinements to Noah, who knowing even less about such matters, understandably made a botch of it. Warming to his subject, Satan goes on to accuse God of sparing the patriarch and his family (all of them "full to the eyebrows" with microbes) not because of Noah's righteousness but just to make sure that future generations of mankind would not be spared the debilitating effects of disease.

With no trace of Twain's vitriol but with equal ingenuity, Edward Page Mitchell (1852-1927), an editor of the New York *Sun* and occasional contributor of anonymous science fiction to its pages, also made good use of the Noachic account. According to the Mitchell version, "The Story of the Deluge" (New York *Sun*, April 28, 1875)[1], Noah kept a log, recently translated, in which he laments some of the trials of life aboard an ark. One entry reveals that the last pterodactyl had been eaten the day before; another, that the bitter ale and mastodons

*Joseph Wrzos was formerly the editor of *Amazing Stories* and *Fantastic Science Fiction*. He also edited the book, *Best of Amazing* published by Doubleday & Co. Mr. Wrzos is currently Chairman of the English Department at Millburn Senior High School in Millburn, New Jersey.

[1]Recently reprinted in *The Crystal Man, Landmark Science Fiction*, by Edward Page Mitchell, collected and with a biographical perspective by Sam Moskowitz (Garden City, N.Y., Doubleday and Co., 1973).

were now also all gone — such references to now extinct species slyly twitting the authenticity of the original account. However, since the piece was intended for a newspaper audience presumably much more interested in the political fauna of its own day than in deluvian speculations, Mitchell also provides a few subtle barbs for the then Senator from Maine, the Honorable Hannibal Hamlin (Lincon's running mate in 1860). According to the startling revelations in "The Story of the Deluge," the Senator could apparently trace his ancestry back to one of the passengers on the ark, Habl Hamin, a victim of scurvy so severe that Noah had to put him ashore in the vicinity of what is now Maine, where he could seek some relief by subsisting on huckleberries. After a period of convalescense, the castaway went inland, founded a village (naming it after himself), and immediately ran for some public office. His descendants, presumably, have been doing the same ever since.

Although — as both Twain and Mitchell showed — the story of the Flood could be used with telling effect, at least in the short narrative, either to challenge faith (by juxtaposing Darwinian theory and Scriptural claim) or to jibe at local politicians, by 1911 the basic idea of a deluge mighty enough to engulf the entire world, not just — as legend had it — such relatively limited areas as the Mediterranean valley or Georgia and the Caspian region,[2] would receive what some consider to be, at least so far, its definitive treatment in science fiction. For in that year astronomer, journalist, lecturer and science-fiction novelist Garrett P. Serviss's The Second Deluge began to run serially in Frank A. Munsey's Cavalier magazine.

By the time Serviss began writing The Second Deluge, it was c. 1910, the same year which saw both the death of Mark Twain and the passage of earth through the tail of Halley's Comet, accompanied by sensational but — as it turned out — unfounded predictions of cosmic doom disseminated by the press. None of these lurid accounts could have come from the Serviss pen, since he was too well qualified to confuse journalistic fancy with scientific fact.

Born on March 24, 1851, in Sharon Springs, N.Y. (and

[2] H. G. Wells, The Outline of History (N.Y., Macmillan Co., 1927), p. 248.

descended from a long line of prerevolutionary settlers in the Mohawk valley), Garrett Putnam Serviss was educated both at Cornell and Columbia University receiving from the latter the degree of LL.B. But young Serviss never practiced law, preferring journalism and science instead, particularly astronomy, a boyhood passion that he apparently developed while going out to bring in the cows beneath the starry — still unpolluted — skies above his father's farm. Both of these interests he combined by writing popular articles on astronomy and other scientific subjects, first for the New York *Tribune*, then for the New York *Sun*, where he served (between 1882 and 1892) as editorial writer and night editor at the same time that E.P. Mitchell, a long-time friend, was employed as editor and occasional contributor of seminal science fiction.

So popular did his astronomy articles become — they were published anonymously, a policy which occasioned much reader speculation as to the true identity of the "*Sun*'s Astronomer" — that by 1892, then in his forties, Serviss decided to give up the steady grind of journalistic deadlines for the more lucrative pace of the lecture platform, where (with the aid of elaborate lantern slides) he proved to be equally effective at popularizing the study of astronomy across the land. At the same time he managed to find time to make several trips to Europe (echoes of which can be detected in the "Paris Under the Sea" and the "French Pyrenees" sections of *The Second Deluge*), to continue writing articles and books (primarily on astronomy), to teach an astronomy course evenings in the public schools of New York, and — with the aid of S.V. White, a fellow enthusiast — to found the American Astronomical Society, whose initial members sometimes met at the Serviss home to peer through the telescope he had installed for study of the stars.

Much more significantly, by the turn of the century Serviss began adapting his considerable imaginative gifts and scientific interests to purely fictional forms, to what is now called *science fiction* but which Serviss himself probably thought of as *scientific romances*. In *Other Worlds*[3] (one of his more popular works on astronomy,

[3] Garrett P. Perviss, *Other Worlds* (N.Y., D. Appleton and Co., 1901), p. 2.

still in print as late as 1932), he revealed that he was thoroughly familiar with much of the science fiction available in his own day, both the "classics" such as Lucian and the "moderns" such as H.G. Wells, for whose *War of the Worlds* (1897) Serviss wrote his own sequel,[4] in which earth strikes back at the Red Planet before it can mount a second invasion force and finish what it had started on its first strike at our world. He also disclosed some of his own theories on what made for good science fiction, the writer's ability to make effective use of the hints provided by modern science to serve as a guide to his speculations and to lend verisimilitude to his narrative.[5]

Serviss continued to make good use of the hints afforded by science whenever he again turned his pen to a new piece of science fiction. In *The Moon Metal* (1900), for example, the basic premise is that to replace gold (suddenly *too* plentiful) as a standard of international currency, artemisium, a new metal, is secretly beamed down from the moon (by means of a matter-transmission device) but, in turn, loses its value when too many learn the same process and flood the market. In *A Columbus of Space* (1909), even more originative, an *atomic*-powered spaceship reaches Venus and finds two humanoid cultures, the one on the light-side going mad once in a lifetime when the cloudy atmosphere thins enough to admit the full force of the sun's high-intensity rays — a theme foreshadowing the basic concept in Isaac Asimov's brilliant novelet, "Nightfall" (*Astounding Science Fiction*, September, 1941).

Innovative and convincing as his earlier science fiction was, in *The Second Deluge* (1911) Serviss, nearing the end of his career as a science-fiction writer at least, turned to what he might well have thought of as his *magnum opus*, the *big* novel into which he could infuse all his passion for astronomy, all his faith in reason and science, and — in the course of developing the narrative — all his criticisms of the world in which he lived. He does so not by "retelling" (humorously and anachronistically) — as

---

4 Garrett P. Serviss, *Edison's Conquest of Mars*, published serially in The New York *Evening Journal*, January 12 - February 10, 1898, and subsequently in book form by Carcosa House (Los Angeles, 1947).

5 Serviss, *Other Worlds*, p. 2.

did Twain, Mitchell and, most likely, a host of others — the story of Noah's ordeal, but by asking himself a question which few, if any, have asked before him: Assuming the First Deluge to have been worldwide instead of local and historically exaggerated, when the Lord caused all the "fountains of the great deep" to break up and "the windows of heaven" to open, a directive resulting in forty days and forty nights of continuous rain, precisely *where* did all that water really come from and precisely how much of it must have fallen to drown the world?

Instead of speculating on that question from a *terrestrial* viewpoint, it was typical of Serviss, oriented toward the starry skies and the future shocks in store for man, to hypothesize on a cosmic scale, to consider the possibility that the enormous quantities of water required to do a thorough job ("quintrillions of tons" of it, as Cosmo Versal, Serviss's Scientist-as-Noah, estimates) might have come from the depths of space in the form of a giant spiral nebula consisting of watery vapor on a collision course with earth. And if — at the Lord's behest or through the vagaries of an indifferent universe — such a catastrophe had indeed occurred 6,000 years ago, could it not conceivably happen once again, perhaps on an even greater scale? If so, despite the Lord's covenant never again to "curse the ground any more for man's sake" (even deity can have a change of heart) the next time there might be absolutely *no* warning to anyone at all!

As a scientist, Serviss would, of course, have admitted the possibility of a nebular flood or some such similar catastrophe looming suddenly into earth's pathway through space. (Fresh in his thoughts, at the time he was working on the story, must have been the sight of Halley's Comet fanning out across the evening sky, amid all the hue and cry from press and public.) He would also have recognized that in the case of a watery nebula, invisible to the naked eye and to telescopic observation, the only kind of man who could be on guard against such an impending cataclysm would be the scientist, not the Establishment professional, who tends to see the past in the future, but the maverick (someone like Cosmo Versal or Serviss himself), who tries to glimpse the *future* in the future.

Besides recognizing that the story of a truly cosmic deluge, one still allowing for the possibility of survival by the few, would best be unfolded in a future setting, Serviss — like most visionaries — probably could not resist opting for tomorrow because it also allowed him to express, by indirection, some of his discontent with his own time, a period for the most part no more partial to reason and science than our own. True, in his portrait of tomorrow (c. A.D. 2000), he does foresee *some* progress, mostly technological, such as the attempts to set limits for weapons of war. (Submarines, for instance, have been outlawed as too destructive for conventional warfare, and the dropping of explosive bombs by aerial navies has been prohibited by international agreement.) It is also a time of high-speed travel by giant and small-scale "aeros" that fly swiftly between the great cities of the globe. Genetics has also made some significant advances in the production of experimental breeds of kingsize livestock such as the great Australian rabbit (edible) and the giant California cow, which yields twenty times the quantity and equal the quality of the best milk produced by any of our own breeds. And in the Sahara the percentage of the world's arable land has been increased considerably by the reclamation of large areas converted into viable farming communities.

Offsetting these signs of progress, however, are some disturbing indications that it is also a time of backsliding. In the earlier part of the century, a "Second Revolution" had swept away rampant capitalism and corrupt government, establishing — in their place — "reforms in business methods and social ideals." But on the eye of the Great Nebula's arrival, the pendulum had begun to swing back, with monopoly burgeoning once more, with laxity settling into "high places," and with a never quite satisfied itch to revive full-scale wars that really meant business. Worst of all — from the viewpoint of Cosmo Versal (and Serviss) — in the very teeth of the scientific evidence that Doom was upon them, the great majority of mankind — despite the scares engendered by the Three Signs of the approaching flood (heat, storm, darkness), all predicted by Versal — persisted in taking their cue from bewildered and frightened world leaders, who publicly advocated calm but privately made secret preparations, just in case. As for Cosmo Versal and his nagging predictions, obviously the man, though brilliant in his way, on the question of the nebula was something of a fool, a fit subject for burlesque in the music halls. In the world of tomorrow, then — in the Serviss view — prophets will still be without honor, even on their own planet.

It is *this* world that Serviss, somewhat like his predecessor (if we think of the creator of fictional worlds as a kind of demigod in his own right), chooses to wipe out, except for about three million Americans (he can be forgiven his touch of chauvinsim) who are spared when Pike's Peak and vicinity are thrust above the rising flood by subterranean activity (the batholite, as Professor Pludder, Serviss's stereotype for the Establishment scientist, explains it). These survivors, however, are leavened by the hand-picked thousand Versal set out with in his ark, though the number aboard the ship had been slightly augmented by the addition of some "undesirables" whom the great scientist, humane beyond his genius, could not consign to doom.

In this respect, the tempering of genius with compassion, the readiness to adapt to the realities of changing circumstance, particularly when brought about by the unexpected intrusion of random *human* factors, Cosmo Versal (who *did*, after all, spare the corrupt industrialist, Amos Blank, when he had it in his power not to) is somewhat like his creator, a man of continued creativity even into his final years, Versal helping to establish his New America on Pike's Peak, Serviss continuing to write to the end — and both of them lived a long life. For when Serviss was 77 (he was to die a year later, on May 25, 1929), he granted reporters an interview just before sailing, once again, to the Europe he must have loved. In response to their need for a story, the veteran journalist gladly obliged by speculating on the possibility of utilizing dirigible balloons to place huge telescopes at altitudes sufficient to reduce atmospheric interference with astronomical observation. If he had been alive twenty years ago and still granting interviews, he probably would have substituted the term *satellite* for dirigible balloon. If he were living today and speculating under similar circumstances (perhaps on television), he would certainly not even mention the subject, since we have already placed large telescopes in orbit, but — considering his track record — he would probably come up with some other completely original proposal for getting even closer to the stars, something that most of us couldn't even begin to guess at. For that is the fundamental difference between foresight on the genius level and the hindsight of those who miss the Ark in every age.

FOREWORD

WHAT is here set down is the fruit of long and careful research among disjointed records left by survivors of the terrible events described. The writer wishes frankly to say that, in some instances, he has followed the course which all historians are compelled to take by using his imagination to round out the picture. But he is able conscientiously to declare that in the substance of his narrative, as well as in every detail which is specifically described, he has followed faithfully the accounts of eyewitnesses, or of those who were in a position to know the truth of what they related.

CONTENTS

ILLUSTRATIONS

THE SECOND DELUGE

THE SECOND DELUGE

CHAPTER I

COSMO VERSÁL

AN undersized, lean, wizen-faced man, with an immense bald head, as round and smooth and shining as a giant soap-bubble, and a pair of beady black eyes, set close together, so that he resembled a gnome of amazing brain capacity and prodigious power of concentration, sat bent over a writing desk with a huge sheet of cardboard before him, on which he was swiftly drawing geometrical and trigonometrical figures. Compasses, T-squares, rulers, protractors, and ellipsographs obeyed the touch of his fingers as if inspired with life.

The room around him was a jungle of terrestrial and celestial globes, chemists' retorts, tubes, pipes, and all the indescribable apparatus that modern science has invented, and which, to the uninitiated, seems as incomprehensible as the ancient paraphernalia of alchemists and astrologers. The walls were lined with book shelves, and adorned along the upper portions with the most extraordinary photo-

3

graphs and drawings. Even the ceiling was covered with charts, some representing the sky, while many others were geological and topographical pictures of the face of the earth.

Beside the drawing-board lay a pad of paper, and occasionally the little man nervously turned to this, and, grasping a long pencil, made elaborate calculations, covering the paper with a sprinkling of mathematical symbols that looked like magnified animalcula. While he worked, under a high light from a single window placed well up near the ceiling, his forehead contracted into a hundred wrinkles, his cheeks became feverous, his piercing eyes glowed with inner fire, and drops of perspiration ran down in front of his ears. One would have thought that he was laboring to save his very soul and had but a few seconds of respite left.

Presently he threw down the pencil, and with astonishing agility let himself rapidly, but carefully, off the stool on which he had been sitting, keeping the palms of his hands on the seat beside his hips until he felt his feet touch the floor. Then he darted at a book-shelf, pulled down a ponderous tome, flapped it open in a clear space on the floor, and dropped on his knees to consult it.

After turning a leaf or two he found what he was after, read down the page, keeping a finger on the lines, and, having finished his reading, jumped to his feet and hurried back to the stool, on which he mounted so quickly that it was impossible to see how he managed it- without an upset. Instantly he made a new diagram, and then fell to figuring furiously on the pad, making his pencil gyrate so fast that its upper end vibrated like the wing of a dragon-fly.

At last he threw down the pencil, and, encircling his knees with his clasped arms, sank in a heap on the stool. The lids dropped over his shining eyes, and he became buried in thought.

When he reopened his eyes and unbent his brows, his gaze happened to be directed toward a row of curious big photographs which ran like a pictured frieze round the upper side of the wall of the room. A casual observer might have thought that the little man had been amusing himself by photographing the explosions of fireworks on a Fourth of July night; but it was evident by his expression that these singular pictures had no connection with civic pyrotechnics, but must represent something of incomparably greater importance, and, in fact, of stupendous import.

The little man's face took on a rapt look, in which wonder and fear seemed to be blended. With a sweep of his hand he included the whole series of photographs in a comprehensive glance, and then, settling his gaze upon a particularly bizarre object in the center, he began to speak aloud, although there was nobody to listen to him.

" My God! " he said. " That's it! That Lick photograph of the Lord Rosse Nebula is its very image, except that there's no electric fire in it. The same great whirl of outer spirals, and then comes the awful central mass—and we're going to plunge straight into it. Then quintillions of tons of water will condense on the earth and cover it like a universal cloudburst. And then good-by to the human race—unless—unless—I, Cosmo Versál, inspired by science, can save a remnant to repeople the planet after the catastrophe."

Again, for a moment, he closed his eyes, and puckered his hemispherical brow, while, with drawn-up knees, he seemed perilously balanced on the high stool. Several times he slowly shook his head, like a dreaming owl, and when his eyes reopened their fire was gone, and a reflective film covered them. He began to speak, more deliberately than before, and in a musing tone:

"What can I do? I don't believe there is a mountain on the face of the globe lofty enough to lift its head above that flood. Hum, hum! It's no use thinking about mountains! The flood will be six miles deep—six miles from the present sea-level; my last calculation proves it beyond all question. And that's only a minimum—it may be miles deeper, for no mortal man can tell exactly what'll happen when the earth plunges into a nebula.

"We'll have to float; that's the thing. I'll have to build an ark. I'll be a second Noah. But I'll advise the whole world to build arks.

" Millions might save themselves that way, for the flood is not going to last forever. We'll get through the nebula in a few months, and then the waters will gradually recede, and the high lands will emerge again. It'll be an awful long time, though; I doubt if the earth will ever be just as it was before. There won't be much room, except for fish—but there won't be many inhabitants for what dry land there is."

Once more he fell into silent meditation, and while he mused there came a knock at the door. The little man started up on his seat, alert as a squirrel, and turned his eyes over his shoulder, listening intently. The knock was repeated—three quick sharp raps. Evidently he at once recognized them.

" All right," he called out, and, letting himself down, ran swiftly to the door and opened it.

A tall, thin man, with bushy black hair, heavy eyebrows, a high, narrow forehead, and a wide, clean shaven mouth, wearing a solemn kind of smile, entered and grasped the little man by both hands.

" Cosmo," he said, without wasting any time on preliminaries, " have you worked it out?"

" I have just finished."

" And you find the worst?"

" Yes, worse than I ever dreamed it would be. The waters will be six miles deep."

" Phew!" exclaimed the other, his smile fading. " That is indeed serious. And when does it begin?"

" Inside of a year. We're within three hundred

million miles of the watery nebula now, and you
know that the earth travels more than that distance
in twelve months."

" Have you seen it? "

" How could I see it—haven't I told you it is
invisible? If it could be seen all these stupid astronomers would have spotted it long ago. But I'll tell
you what I *have* seen."

Cosmo Versál's voice sank into a whisper, and
he shuddered slightly as he went on:

" Only last night I was sweeping the sky with the
telescope when I noticed, in Hercules and Lyra, and
all that part of the heavens, a dimming of some of
the fainter stars. It was like the shadow of the
shroud of a ghost. Nobody else would have noticed
it, and I wouldn't if I had not been looking for it.
It's knowledge that clarifies the eyes and breeds
knowledge, Joseph Smith. It was not truly visible,
and yet I could see that it was there. I tried to
make out the shape of the thing—but it was too
indefinite. But I know very well what it is. See
here "—he suddenly broke off—" Look at that photograph." (He was pointing at the Lord Rosse
Nebula on the wall). " It's like that, only it's coming edgewise toward us. We may miss some of the
outer spirals, but we're going smash into the center."

With fallen jaw, and black brows contracted,
Joseph Smith stared at the photograph.

" It doesn't shine like that," he said at last.

The little man snorted contemptuously.

"What have I told you about its invisibility?" he demanded.

"But how, then, do you know that it is of a watery nature?"

Cosmo Versál threw up his hands and waved them in an agony of impatience. He climbed upon his stool to get nearer the level of the other's eyes, and fixing him with his gaze, exclaimed:

"You know very well how I know it. I know it because I have demonstrated with my new spectroscope, which analyzes extra-visual rays, that all those dark nebulæ that were photographed in the Milky Way years ago are composed of watery vapor. They are far off, on the limits of the universe. This one is one right at hand. It's a little one compared with them—but it's enough, yes, it's enough! You know that more than two years ago I began to correspond with astronomers all over the world about this thing, and not one of them would listen to me. Well, they'll listen when it's too late perhaps.

"They'll listen when the flood-gates are opened and the inundation begins. It's not the first time that this thing has happened. I haven't a doubt that the flood of Noah, that everybody pretends to laugh at now, was caused by the earth passing through a watery nebula. But this will be worse than that; there weren't two thousand million people to be drowned then."

For five minutes neither spoke. Cosmo Versál swung on the stool, and played with an ellipsograph; Joseph Smith dropped his chin on his breast and nervously fingered the pockets of his long vest. At last he raised his head and asked, in a low voice:

" What are you going to do, Cosmo? "

" I'm going to get ready," was the short reply.

" How? "

" Build an ark."

" But will you give no warning to others? "

" I'll do my best. I'll telephone to all the officials, scientific and otherwise, in America, Europe, Africa, Asia, and Australia. I'll write in every language to all the newspapers and magazines. I'll send out circulars. I'll counsel everybody to drop every other occupation and begin to build arks—but nobody will heed me. You'll see. My ark will be the only one, but I'll save as many in it as I can. And I depend upon you, Joseph, to help me. From all appearances, it's the only chance that the human race has of survival.

" If I hadn't made this discovery they would all have been wiped out like miners in a flooded pit. We may persuade a few to be saved—but what an awful thing it is that when the truth is thrust into their very faces people won't believe, won't listen, won't see, won't be helped, but will die like dogs in their obstinate ignorance and blindness."

plan, and trust to the buoyant power of water. I fully expect that when the deluge begins people will flock to the high-lands and the mountains in air-ships —but alas! that won't save them. Remember what I have told you—this flood is going to be six miles deep!"

The second morning after the conversation between Cosmo Versál and Joseph Smith, New York was startled by seeing, in huge red letters, on every blank wall, on the bare flanks of towering sky-scrapers, on the lofty stations of aeroplane lines, on bill-boards, fences, advertising-boards along suburban roads, in the Subway stations, and fluttering from strings of kites over the city, the following announcement:

THE WORLD IS TO BE DROWNED!

Save Yourselves While It Is Yet Time!
Drop Your Business: It Is of No Consequence!
Build Arks: It Is Your Only Salvation!
The Earth Is Going To Plunge into a Watery
Nebula: There Is No Escape!
Hundreds of Millions Will Be Drowned: You Have
Only a Few Months To Get Ready!
For Particulars Address: Cosmo Versál,
3000 Fifth Avenue.

CHAPTER II

MOCKING AT FATE

WHEN New York recovered from its first astonishment over the extraordinary posters, it indulged in a loud laugh. Everybody knew who Cosmo Versál was. His eccentricities had filled many readable columns in the newspapers. Yet there was a certain respect for him, too. This was due to his extraordinary intellectual ability and unquestionable scientific knowledge. But his imagination was as free as the winds, and it often led him upon excursions in which nobody could follow him, and which caused the more steady-going scientific brethren to shake their heads. They called him able but flighty. The public considered him brilliant and amusing.

His father, who had sprung from some unknown source in southeastern Europe, and, beginning as a newsboy in New York, had made his way to the front in the financial world, had left his entire fortune to Cosmo. The latter had no taste for finance or business, but a devouring appetite for science, to which, in his own way, he devoted all his powers, all his time, and all his money. He never married, was

16

never seen in society, and had very few intimates—
but he was known by sight, or reputation, to everybody. There was not a scientific body or association of any consequence in the world of which he
was not a member. Those which looked askance at
his bizarre ideas were glad to accept pecuniary aid
from him.

The notion that the world was to be drowned
had taken possession of him about three years before
the opening scene of this narrative. To work out
the idea, he built an observatory, set up a laboratory,
invented instruments, including his strange spectroscope, which was scoffed at by the scientific world.

Finally, submitting the results of his observations
to mathematical treatment, he proved, to his own
satisfaction, the absolute correctness of his thesis that
the well-known " proper motion of the solar system "
was about to result in an encounter between the
earth and an invisible watery nebula, which would
have the effect of inundating the globe. As this
startling idea gradually took shape, he communicated
it to scientific men in all lands, but failed to find a
single disciple, except his friend Joseph Smith, who,
without being able to follow all his reasonings, accepted on trust the conclusions of Cosmo's more
powerful mind. Accordingly, at the end of his investigation, he enlisted Smith as secretary, propa-
gandist, and publicity agent.

New York laughed a whole day and night at the

warning red letters. They were the talk of the town. People joked about them in cafés, clubs, at home, in the streets, in the offices, in the exchanges, in the street-cars, on the Elevated, in the Subways. Crowds gathered on corners to watch the flapping posters aloft on the kite lines. The afternoon newspapers issued specials which were all about the coming flood, and everywhere one heard the cry of the newsboys: "*Extra-a-a! Drowning of a Thousand Million people! Cosmo Versál predicts the End of the World!*" On their editorial pages the papers were careful to discount the scare lines, and terrific pictures, that covered the front sheets, with humorous jibes at the author of the formidable prediction.

The Owl, which was the only paper that put the news in half a column of ordinary type, took a judicial attitude, called upon the city authorities to tear down the posters, and hinted that "this absurd person, Cosmo Versál, who disgraces a once honored name with his childish attempt to create a sensation that may cause untold harm among the ignorant masses," had laid himself open to criminal prosecution.

In their latest editions, several of the papers printed an interview with Cosmo Versál, in which he gave figures and calculations that, on their face, seemed to offer mathematical proof of the correctness of his forecast. In impassioned language, he implored the public to believe that he would not mislead them, spoke of the instant necessity of constructing arks of safety, and averred that the presence of the terrible nebula that was so soon to drown the world was already manifest in the heavens.

Some readers of these confident statements began to waver, especially when confronted with mathematics which they could not understand. But still, in general, the laugh went on. It broke into boisterousness in one of the largest theaters where a bright-witted " artist," who always made a point of hitting off the very latest sensation, got himself up in a life-like imitation of the well-known figure of Cosmo Versál, topped with a bald head as big as a bushel, and sailed away into the flies with a pretty member of the ballet, whom he had gallantly snatched from a tumbling ocean of green baize, singing at the top of his voice until they disappeared behind the proscenium arch:

> " Oh, th' Nebula is coming
>   To drown the wicked earth,
> With all his spirals humming
>   'S he waltzes in his mirth.

> *Chorus*
>   " Don't hesitate a second,
>   Get ready to embark,
>   And skip away to safety
>   With Cosmo and his ark.

> " Th' Nebula is a direful bird
>   'S he skims the ether blue!
> He's angry over what he's heard,
>   'N's got his eye on you.

Chorus
"Don't hesitate a second, etc.

"When Nebulas begin to pipe
   The bloomin' O. H. 2
Y'bet yer life the time is ripe
   To think what you will do.

Chorus
"Don't hesitate a second, etc.

"He'll tip th' Atlantic o'er its brim,
   And swamp the mountains tall;
He'll let the broad Pacific in,
   And leave no land at all.

Chorus
"Don't hesitate a second, etc.

"He's got an option on the spheres;
   He's leased the Milky Way;
He's caught the planets in arrears,
   'N's bound to make 'em pay.

Chorus
"Don't hesitate a second, etc."

The roars of laughter and applause with which this effusion of vaudeville genius was greeted, showed the cheerful spirit in which the public took the affair. No harm seemed to have come to the " ignorant masses " yet.

But the next morning there was a suspicious change in the popular mind. People were surprised to see new posters in place of the old ones, more lurid in letters and language than the original. The morning papers had columns of description and comment, and some of them seemed disposed to treat the prophet and his prediction with a certain degree of seriousness.

The savants who had been interviewed overnight, did not talk very convincingly, and made the mistake of flinging contempt on both Cosmo and " the gullible public."

Naturally, the public wouldn't stand for that, and the pendulum of opinion began to swing the other way. Cosmo helped his cause by sending to every newspaper a carefully prepared statement of his observations and calculations, in which he spoke with such force of conviction that few could read his words without feeling a thrill of apprehensive uncertainty. This was strengthened by published dispatches which showed that he had forwarded his warnings to all the well-known scientific bodies of the world, which, while decrying them, made no effective response.

And then came a note of positive alarm in a double-leaded bulletin from the new observatory at Mount McKinley, which affirmed that during the preceding night *a singular obscurity* had been suspected in the northern sky, seeming to veil many stars below the twelfth magnitude. It was added that the phenomenon was unprecedented, but that the observation was both difficult and uncertain.

Nowhere was the atmosphere of doubt and mystery, which now began to hang over the public, so remarkable as in Wall Street. The sensitive currents there responded like electric waves to the new influence, and, to the dismay of hard-headed observers, the market dropped as if it had been hit with a sledge-hammer. Stocks went down five, ten, in some cases twenty points in as many minutes.

The speculative issues slid down like wheat into a bin when the chutes are opened. Nobody could trace the exact origin of the movement, but selling-orders came tumbling in until there was a veritable panic.

From London, Paris, Berlin, Vienna, St. Petersburg, flashed dispatches announcing that the same unreasonable slump had manifested itself there, and all united in holding Cosmo Versál solely responsible for the foolish break in prices. Leaders of finance rushed to the exchanges trying by arguments and expostulations to arrest the downfall, but in vain.

In the afternoon, however, reason partially resumed its sway; then a quick recovery was felt, and many who had rushed to sell all they had, found cause to regret their precipitancy. The next day all was on the mend, as far as the stock market was concerned, but among the people at large the poison of awakened credulity continued to spread, nourished by fresh announcements from the fountain head.

Cosmo issued another statement to the effect that he had perfected plans for an ark of safety, which

he would begin at once to construct in the neighborhood of New York, and he not only offered freely
to give his plans to any who wished to commence
construction on their own account, but he urged them,
in the name of Heaven, to lose no time. This produced a prodigious effect, and multitudes began to
be infected with a nameless fear.

Meanwhile an extraordinary scene occurred, behind
closed doors, at the headquarters of the Carnegie Institution in Washington. Joseph Smith, acting under
Cosmo Versál's direction, had forwarded an elaborate *précis* of the latter's argument, accompanied with
full mathematical details, to the head of the institution. The character of this document was such that
it could not be ignored. Moreover, the savants com-
posing the council of the most important scientific
association in the world were aware of the state of
the public mind, and felt that it was incumbent upon
them to do something to allay the alarm. Of late
years a sort of supervisory control over scientific
news of all kinds had been accorded to them, and they
appreciated the fact that a duty now rested upon
their shoulders.

Accordingly, a special meeting was called to consider the communication from Cosmo Versál. It was
the general belief that a little critical examination
would result in complete proof of the fallacy of all
his work, proof which could be put in a form that
the most uninstructed would understand.

But the papers, diagrams, and mathematical formulæ had no sooner been spread upon the table under the knowing eyes of the learned members of the council, than a chill of conscious impuissance ran through them. They saw that Cosmo's mathematics were unimpeachable. His formulæ were accurately deduced, and his operations absolutely correct.

They could do nothing but attack his fundamental data, based on the alleged revelations of his new form of spectroscope, and on telescopic observations which were described in so much detail that the only way to combat them was by the general assertion that they were illusory. This was felt to be a very unsatisfactory method of procedure, as far as the public was concerned, because it amounted to no more than attacking the credibility of a witness who pretended to describe only what he himself had seen— and there is nothing so hard as to prove a negative.

Then, Cosmo had on his side the whole force of that curious tendency of the human mind which habitually gravitates toward whatever is extraordinary, revolutionary, and mysterious.

But a yet greater difficulty arose. Mention has been made of the strange bulletin from the Mount McKinley observatory. That had been incautiously sent out to the public by a thoughtless observer, who was more intent upon describing a singular phenomenon than upon considering its possible effect on the popular imagination. He had immediately received an expostulatory dispatch from headquarters which henceforth shut his mouth—but he had told the simple truth, and how embarrassing that was became evident when, on the very table around which the savants were now assembled, three dispatches were laid in quick succession from the great observatories of Mount Hekla, Iceland, the North Cape, and Kamchatka, all corroborating the statement of the Mount McKinley observer, that an inexplicable veiling of faint stars had manifested itself in the boreal quarter of the sky.

When the president read these dispatches—which the senders had taken the precaution to mark " confidential "—the members of the council looked at one another with no little dismay. Here was the most unprejudiced corroboration of Cosmo Versál's assertion that the great nebula was already within the range of observation. How could they dispute such testimony, and what were they to make of it?

Two or three of the members began to be shaken in their convictions.

" Upon my word," exclaimed Professor Alexander Jones, " but this is very curious! And suppose the fellow should be right, after all? "

" Right! " cried the president, Professor Pludder, disdainfully. " Who ever heard of a watery nebula? The thing's absurd! "

" I don't see that it's absurd," replied Professor

Jones. "There's plenty of proof of the existence of hydrogen in some of the nebulæ."

"So there is," chimed in Professor Abel Able, "and if there's hydrogen there may be oxygen, and there you have all that's necessary. It's not the idea that a nebula may consist of watery vapor that's absurd, but it is that a watery nebula, large enough to drown the earth by condensation upon it could have approached so near as this one must now be without sooner betraying its presence."

"How so?" demanded a voice.

"By its attraction. Cosmo Versál says it is already less than three hundred million miles away. If it is massive enough to drown the earth, it ought long ago to have been discovered by its disturbance of the planetary orbits."

"Not at all," exclaimed Professor Jeremiah Moses. "If you stick to that argument you'll be drowned sure. Just look at these facts. The earth weighs six and a half sextillions of tons, and the ocean one and a half quintillions. The average depth of the oceans is two and one-fifth miles. Now —if the level of the oceans were raised only about 1,600 feet, practically all the inhabited parts of the world would be flooded. To cause that increase in the level of the oceans only about one-eighth part would have to be added to their total mass, or, say, one-seventh part, allowing for the greater surface to be covered. That would be one thirty-thousandth

of the weight of the globe, and if you suppose that
only one-hundredth of the entire nebula were condensed on the earth, the whole mass of the nebula
would not need to exceed one three-hundredth of
the weight of the earth, or a quarter that of the
moon—and nobody here will be bold enough to say
that the approach of a mass no greater than that
would be likely to be discovered through its attraction
when it was three hundred million miles away."

Several of the astronomers present shook their
heads at this, and Professor Pludder irritably declared that it was absurd.

" The attraction would be noticeable when it was
a thousand millions of miles away," he continued.

" Yes, ' noticeable ' I admit," replied Professor
Moses, " but all the same you wouldn't notice it,
because you wouldn't be looking for it unless the
nebula were visible first, and even then it would
require months of observation to detect the effects.
And how are you going to get around those bulletins ?
The thing is beginning to be visible now, and I'll
bet that if, from this time on, you study carefully
the planetary motions, you will find evidence of the
disturbance becoming stronger and stronger. Versál
has pointed out that very thing, and calculated the
perturbations. This thing has come like a thief in
the night."

" You'd better hurry up and secure a place in the
ark," said Professor Pludder sarcastically.

"I don't know but I shall, if I can get one," returned Professor Moses. "You may not think this is such a laughing matter a few months hence."

"I'm surprised," pursued the president, "that a man of your scientific standing should stultify himself by taking seriously such balderdash as this. I tell you the thing is absurd."

"And I tell you, *you* are absurd to say so!" retorted Professor Moses, losing his temper. "You've got four of the biggest telescopes in the world under your control; why don't you order your observers to look for this thing?"

Professor Pludder, who was a very big man, reared up his rotund form, and, bringing his fist down upon the table with a resounding whack, exclaimed:

"I'll do nothing so ridiculous! These bulletins have undoubtedly been influenced by the popular excitement. There has possibly been a little obscurity in the atmosphere—cirrus clouds, or something—and the observers have imagined the rest. I'm not going to insult science by encouraging the proceedings of a mountebank like Cosmo Versál. What we've got to do is to prepare a dispatch for the press reassuring the populace and throwing the weight of this institution on the side of common sense and public tranquillity. Let the secretary indite such a dispatch, and then we'll edit it and send it out."

Professor Pludder, naturally dictatorial, was sometimes a little overbearing, but being a man of great

ability, and universally respected for his high rank
in the scientific world, his colleagues usually bowed
to his decisions. On this occasion his force of character sufficed to silence the doubters, and when the
statement intended for the press had received its final
touches it contained no hint of the seeds of discord
that Cosmo Versál had sown among America's foremost savants. The next morning it appeared in all
the newspapers as follows:

Official Statement from the Carnegie Institution

In consequence of the popular excitement caused by the sensational utterance of a notorious pretender to scientific knowledge in
New York, the council of this institution authorizes the statement
that it has examined the alleged grounds on which the prediction of
a great flood, to be caused by a nebula encountering the earth, is
based, and finds, as all real men of science knew beforehand, that
the entire matter is simply a canard.

The nebulæ are not composed of water; if they were composed
of water they could not cause a flood on the earth; the report that
some strange, misty object is visible in the starry heavens is based
on a misapprehension; and finally, the so-called calculations of the
author of this inexcusable hoax are baseless and totally devoid
of validity.

The public is earnestly advised to pay no further attention to the
matter. If there were any danger to the earth—and such a thing is
not to be seriously considered—astronomers would know it long in
advance, and would give due and official warning.

Unfortunately for the popular effect of this pro-
nouncement, on the very morning when it appeared
in print, thirty thousand people were crowded
around the old aviation field at Mineola, excitedly

watching Cosmo Versál, with five hundred workmen, laying the foundations of a huge platform, while about the field were stretched sheets of canvas displaying the words:

THE ARK OF SAFETY
Earnest Inspection Invited by All
Attendants will Furnish Gratis Plans for Similar Constructions
Small Arks Can Be Built for Families
Act While There Is Yet Time

The multitude saw at a glance that here was a work that would cost millions, and the spectacle of this immense expenditure, the evidence that Cosmo was backing his words with his money, furnished a silent argument which was irresistible. In the midst of all, flying about among his men, was Cosmo, impressing every beholder with the feeling that intellect was in charge.

Like the gray coat of Napoleon on a battlefield, the sight of that mighty brow bred confidence.

CHAPTER III

THE FIRST DROPS OF THE DELUGE

THE utterance of the Carnegie Institution indeed fell flat, and Cosmo Versál's star reigned in the ascendent. He pushed his preparations with amazing speed, and not only politics, but even the war that had just broken out in South America was swallowed up in the newspapers by endless descriptions of the mysterious proceedings at Mineola. Cosmo still found time every day to write articles and to give out interviews; and Joseph Smith was kept constantly on the jump, running for street-cars or trains, or leaping, with his long coat flapping, into and out of elevators on ceaseless missions to the papers, the scientific societies, and the meetings of learned or unlearned bodies which had been persuaded to investigate the subject of the coming flood. Between the work of preparation and that of proselytism it is difficult to see how Cosmo found time to sleep.

Day by day the Ark of Safety rose higher upon its great platform, its huge metallic ribs and broad, bulging sides glinting strangely in the unbroken sunshine—for, as if imitating the ominous quiet before an earthquake, the July sky had stripped itself of all clouds. No thunder-storms broke the serenity of the long days, and never had the overarching heavens seemed so spotless and motionless in their cerulean depths.

All over the world, as the news dispatches showed, the same strange calm prevailed. Cosmo did not fail to call attention to this unparalleled repose of nature as a sure prognostic of the awful event in preparation.

The heat became tremendous. Hundreds were stricken down in the blazing streets. Multitudes fled to the seashore, and lay panting under umbrellas on the burning sands, or vainly sought relief by plunging into the heated water, which, rolling lazily in with the tide, felt as if it had come from over a boiler.

Still, perspiring crowds constantly watched the workmen, who struggled with the overpowering heat, although Cosmo had erected canvas screens for them and installed a hundred immense electric fans to create a breeze.

Beginning with five hundred men, he had, in less than a month, increased his force to nearer five thousand, many of whom, not engaged in the actual construction, were preparing the materials and bringing them together. The ark was being made of pure levium, the wonderful new metal which, although already employed in the construction of aeroplanes and the framework of dirigible balloons, had not before been used for shipbuilding, except in the case of a few small boats, and these used only in the navy.

For mere raw material Cosmo must have expended an enormous sum, and his expenses were quadrupled by the fact that he was compelled, in order to save time, practically to lease several of the largest steel plants in the country. Fortunately levium was easily rolled into plates, and the supply was sufficient, owing to the discovery two years before of an expeditious process of producing the metal from its ores.

The wireless telegraph and telephone offices were besieged by correspondents eager to send inland, and all over Europe and Asia, the latest particulars of the construction of the great ark. Nobody followed Cosmo's advice or example, but everybody was intensely interested and puzzled.

At last the government officials found themselves forced to take cognizance of the affair. They could no longer ignore it after they discovered that it was seriously interfering with the conduct of public business. Cosmo Versál's pressing orders, accompanied by cash, displaced or delayed orders of the government commanding materials for the navy and the air fleet. In consequence, about the middle of July he received a summons to visit the President of the United States. Cosmo hurried to Washington on the given date, and presented his card at the White

House. He was shown immediately into the President's reception-room, where he found the entire Cabinet in presence. As he entered he was the focus of a formidable battery of curious and not too friendly eyes.

President Samson was a large, heavy man, more than six feet tall. Every member of his Cabinet was above the average in avoirdupois, and the heavyweight president of the Carnegie Institution, Professor Pludder, who had been specially invited, added by his presence to the air of ponderosity that characterized the assemblage. All seemed magnified by the thin white garments which they wore on account of the oppressive heat. Many of them had come in haste from various summer resorts, and were plainly annoyed by the necessity of attending at the President's command.

Cosmo Versál was the only cool man there, and his diminutive form presented a striking contrast to the others. But he looked as if he carried more brains than all of them put together.

He was not in the least overawed by the hostile glances of the statesmen. On the contrary, his lips perceptibly curled, in a half-disdainful smile, as he took the big hand which the President extended to him. As soon as Cosmo Versál had sunk into the embrace of a large easy chair, the President opened the subject.

" I have directed you to come," he said in a

majestic tone, " in order the sooner to dispel the effects of your unjustifiable predictions and extraordinary proceedings on the public mind—and, I may add, on public affairs. Are you aware that you have interfered with the measures of this government for the defense of the country? You have stepped in front of the government, and delayed the beginning of four battleships which Congress has authorized in urgent haste on account of the threatening aspect of affairs in the East? I need hardly say to you that we shall, if necessary, find means to set aside the private agreements under which you are proceeding, as inimical to public interests, but you have already struck a serious blow at the security of your country."

The President pronounced the last sentence with oratorical unction, and Cosmo was conscious of an approving movement of big official shoulders around him. The disdain deepened on his lips.

After a moment's pause the President continued:

" Before proceeding to extremities I have wished to see you personally, in order, in the first place, to assure myself that you are mentally responsible, and then to appeal to your patriotism, which should lead you to withdraw at once an obstruction so dangerous to the nation. Do you know the position in which you have placed yourself ? "

Cosmo Versál got upon his feet and advanced to the center of the room like a little David. Every eye was fixed upon him. His voice was steady, but intense with suppressed nervousness.

"Mr. President," he said, "you have accused me of obstructing the measures of the government for the defense of the country. Sir, I am trying to save *the whole human race* from a danger in comparison with which that of war is infinitesimal—a danger which is rushing down upon us with appalling speed, and which will strike every land on the globe simultaneously. Within seven months not a warship or any other existing vessel will remain afloat."

The listeners smiled, and nodded significantly to one another, but the speaker only grew more earnest.

"You think I am insane," he said, "but the truth is you are hoodwinked by official stupidity. That man," pointing at Professor Pludder, "who knows me well, and who has had all my proofs laid before him, is either too thick-headed to understand a demonstration or too pig-headed to confess his own error."

"Come, come," interrupted the President sternly, while Professor Pludder flushed very red, "this will not do! Indulge in no personalities here. I have strained a point in offering to listen to you at all, and I have invited the head of the greatest of our scientific societies to be present, with the hope that here before us all he might convince you of your folly, and thus bring the whole unfortunate affair promptly to an end."

"*He* convince *me!*" cried Cosmo Versál disdainfully. "He is incapable of understanding the A, B, C of my work. But let me tell you this, Mr. President—there are men in his own council who are not so blind. I know what occurred at the recent meeting of that council, and I know that the ridiculous announcement put forth in its name to deceive the public was whipped into shape by him, and does not express the real opinion of many of the members."

Professor Pludder's face grew redder than ever.

"Name one!" he thundered.

"Ah," said Cosmo sneeringly, "that hits hard, doesn't it? You want me to name *one;* well, I'll name *three.* What did Professor Alexander Jones and Professor Abel Able say about the existence of watery nebulæ, and what was the opinion expressed by Professor Jeremiah Moses about the actual approach of one out of the northern sky, and what it could do if it hit the earth? What was the unanimous opinion of the entire council about the correctness of my mathematical work? And what," he continued, approaching Professor Pludder and shaking his finger up at him—"*what have you done with those three dispatches from Iceland, the North Cape, and Kamchatka, which absolutely confirmed my announcement that the nebula was already visible?*"

Professor Pludder began stammeringly:

"Some spy——"

"Ah," cried Cosmo, catching him up, "*a spy,* hey? Then, you admit it! Mr. President, I beg

you to notice that he admits it.   Sir, this is a conspiracy to conceal the truth.   Great Heaven, the
world is on the point of being drowned, and yet the
pride of officialism is so strong in this plodder—
Pludder—and others of his ilk that they'd sooner
take the chance of letting the human race be destroyed than recognize the truth!"

Cosmo Versál spoke with such tremendous concentration of mental energy, and with such evident
sincerity of conviction, and he had so plainly put
Professor Pludder to rout, that the President, no
less than the other listening statesmen, was thrown
into a quandary.

There was a creaking of heavily burdened chairs,
a ponderous stir all round the circle, while a look of
perplexity became visible on every face.   Professor
Pludder's conduct helped to produce the change of
moral atmosphere.   He had been so completely surprised by Cosmo's accusation, based on facts which
he had supposed were known only to himself and
the council, that he was unable for a minute to speak
at all, and before he could align his faculties his
triumphant little opponent renewed the attack.

" Mr. President," he said, laying his hand on the
arm of Mr. Samson's big chair, which was nearly
on a level with his breast, and speaking with persuasive earnestness, " you are the executive head of
a mighty nation—the nation that sets the pace for
the world.   It is in your power to do a vast, an

incalculable, service to humanity. One official word from you would save millions upon millions of lives. I implore you, instead of interfering with my work, to give instant order for the construction of as many arks, based upon the plans I have perfected, as the navy yard can possibly turn out. Issue a proclamation to the people, warning them that this is their only chance of escape."

By a curious operation of the human mind, this speech cost Cosmo nearly all the advantage that he had previously gained. His ominous suggestion of a great nebula rushing out of the heavens to overwhelm the earth had immensely impressed the imagination of his hearers, and his uncontradicted accusation that Professor Pludder was concealing the facts had almost convinced them that he was right. But when he mentioned " arks," the strain was relieved, and a smile broke out on the broad face of the President. He shook his head, and was about to speak, when Cosmo, perceiving that he had lost ground, changed his tactics.

" Still you are incredulous! " he exclaimed. " But the proof is before you! Look at the blazing heavens! The annals of meteorology do not record another such summer as this. The vanguard of the fatal nebula is already upon us. The signs of disaster are in the sky. But, note what I say—this is only the *first* sign. There is another following on its heels which may be here at any moment. To heat will succeed cold, and as we rush through the tenuous outer spirals the earth will alternately be whipped with tempests of snow and sleet, and scorched by fierce outbursts of solar fire. For three weeks the atmosphere has been heated by the inrush of invisible vapor—but look out, I warn you, for the change that is impending! "

These extraordinary words, pronounced with the wild air of a prophet, completed the growing conviction of the listeners that they really had a madman to deal with, and Professor Pludder, having recovered his self-command, rose to his feet.

" Mr. President," he began, " the evidence which we have just seen of an unbalanced mind——"

He got no further. A pall of darkness suddenly dropped upon the room. An inky curtain seemed to have fallen from the sky. At the same time the windows were shaken by tremendous blasts of wind, and, as the electric lights were hastily turned on, huge snowflakes, intermingled with rattling hailstones, were seen careering outside. In a few seconds several large panes of glass were broken, and the chilling wind, sweeping round the apartment, made the teeth of the thinly clad statesmen chatter, while the noise of the storm became deafening. The sky lightened, but at the same moment dreadful thunderpeals shook the building. Two or three trees in the White House grounds were struck by the bolts, and their broken branches were driven through the air and carried high above the ground by the whirling winds, and one of them was thrown against the building with such force that for a moment it seemed as if the wall had been shattered.

After the first stunning effect of this outbreak of the elements had passed, everybody rushed to the windows to look out—everybody except Cosmo Versál, who remained standing in the center of the room.

" I told you ! " he said; but nobody listened to him. What they saw outside absorbed every faculty. The noise was so stunning that they could not have heard him.

We have said that the air lightened after the passage of the first pall of darkness, but it was not the reappearance of the sun that caused the brightening. It was an awful light, which seemed to be born out of the air itself. It had a menacing, coppery hue, continually changing in character. The whole upper atmosphere was choked with dense clouds, which swirled and tumbled, and twisted themselves into great vortical rolls, spinning like gigantic millshafts. Once, one of these vortexes shot downward, with projectile speed, rapidly assuming the terrible form of the trombe of a tornado, and where it struck the ground it tore everything to pieces—trees, houses, the very earth itself were ground to powder and then whirled aloft by the resistless suction.

Occasionally the darkness returned for a few minutes, as if a cover had been clapped upon the sky, and then, again, the murk would roll off, and the reddish gleam would reappear.   These swift alternations of impenetrable gloom and unearthly light shook the hearts of the dumfounded statesmen even more than the roar and rush of the storm.

A cry of horror broke from the onlookers when a man and a woman suddenly appeared trying to cross the White House grounds to reach a place of comparative safety, and were caught up by the wind, clinging desperately to each other, and hurled against a wall, at whose base they fell in a heap.

Then came another outburst of lightning, and a vicious bolt descended upon the Washington Monument, and, twisting round it, seemed to envelop the great shaft in a pulsating corkscrew of blinding fire. The report that instantly followed made the White House dance upon its foundations, and, as if that had been a signal, the flood-gates of the sky immediately opened, and rain so dense that it looked like a solid cataract of water poured down upon the earth. The raging water burst into the basement of the building, and ran off in a shoreless river toward the Potomac.

The streaming rain, still driven by the wind, poured through the broken windows, driving the President and the others to the middle of the room, where they soon stood in rills of water soaking the thick carpet.

They were all as pale as death.   Their eyes sought one another's faces in dumb amazement.   Cosmo Versál alone retained perfect self-command.   In spite of his slight stature he looked their master. Raising his voice to the highest pitch, in order to be heard, he shouted:

" These are the first drops of the Deluge!   Will you believe now? "

CHAPTER IV

THE WORLD SWEPT WITH TERROR

THE tempest of hail, snow, lightning, and rain, which burst so unexpectedly over Washington, was not a local phenomenon. It leveled the antennæ of the wireless telegraph systems all over the world, cutting off communication everywhere. Only the submarine telephone cables remained unaffected, and by them was transmitted the most astonishing news of the ravages of the storm. Rivers had careered over their banks, low-lying towns were flooded, the swollen sewers of cities exploded and inundated the streets, and gradually news came in from country districts showing that vast areas of land had been submerged, and hundreds drowned.

The downfall of rain far exceeded everything that the meteorological bureaus had ever recorded.

The vagaries of the lightning, and the frightful power that it exhibited, were especially terrifying.

In London the Victoria Tower was partly dismantled by a bolt.

In Moscow the ancient and beautiful Church of St. Basil was nearly destroyed.

The celebrated Leaning Tower of Pisa, the wonder of centuries, was flung to the ground.

The vast dome of St. Peter's at Rome was said to have been encased during three whole minutes with a blinding armor of electric fire, though the only harm done was the throwing down of a statue in one of the chapels.

But, strangest freak of all, in New York a tremendous bolt, which seems to have entered the Pennsylvania tunnel on the Jersey side, followed the rails under the river, throwing two trains from the track, and, emerging in the great station in the heart of the city, expanded into a rose-colored sphere, which exploded with an awful report, and blew the great roof to pieces.   And yet, although the fragments were scattered a dozen blocks away, hundreds of persons who were in the stations suffered no other injury than such as resulted from being flung violently to the floor, or against the walls.

Cosmo Versál's great ark seemed charmed.   Not a single discharge of lightning occurred in its vicinity, a fact which he attributed to the dielectric properties of levium.   Nevertheless, the wind carried away all his screens and electric fans.

If this storm had continued the predicted deluge would unquestionably have occurred at once, and even its prophet would have perished through having begun his preparations too late.   But the disturbed elements sank into repose as suddenly as they had broken out with fury. The rain did not last, in most places, more than twenty-four hours, although the atmosphere continued to be filled with troubled clouds for a week. At the end of that time the sun reappeared, as hot as before, and a spotless dome once more over-arched the earth; but from this time the sky never resumed its former brilliant azure—there was always a strange coppery tinge, the sight of which was appalling, although it gradually lost its first effect through familiarity.

The indifference and derision with which Cosmo's predictions and elaborate preparations had hitherto been regarded now vanished, and the world, in spite of itself, shivered with vague apprehension. No reassurances from those savants who still refused to admit the validity of Cosmo Versál's calculations and deductions had any permanent effect upon the public mind.

With amusing inconsequence people sold stocks again, until all the exchanges were once more swept with panic—and then put the money in their strong boxes, as if they thought that the mere possession of the lucre could protect them. They hugged the money and remained deaf to Cosmo's reiterated advice to build arks with it.

After all, they were only terrified, not convinced, and they felt that, somehow, everything would come out right, now that they had their possessions well in hand.

For, in spite of the scare, nobody really believed that an actual deluge was coming. There might be great floods, and great suffering and loss, but the world was not going to be drowned! Such things only occurred in early and dark ages.

Some nervous persons found comfort in the fact that when the skies cleared after the sudden downpour brilliant rainbows were seen. Their hearts bounded with joy.

" The ' Bow of Promise ! ' " they cried. " Behold the unvarying assurance that the world shall never again be drowned."

Then a great revival movement was set on foot, starting in the Mississippi valley under the leadership of an eloquent exhorter, who declared that, although a false prophet had arisen, whose delusive prediction was contrary to Scripture, yet it was true that the world was about to be punished in unexpected ways for its many iniquities.

This movement rapidly spread all over the country, and was taken up in England and throughout Protestant Europe, and soon prayers were offered in thousands of churches to avert the wrath of Heaven. Multitudes thus found their fears turned into a new direction, and by a strange reaction, Cosmo Versál came to be regarded as a kind of Antichrist who was seeking to mislead mankind.

Just at this juncture, to add to the dismay and uncertainty, a grand and fearful comet suddenly appeared. It came up unexpectedly from the south, blazed brightly close beside the sun, even at noonday, and a few nights later was visible after sunset with an immense fiery head and a broad curved tail that seemed to pulsate from end to end. It was so bright that it cast shadows at night, as distinct as those made by the moon. No such cometary monster had ever before been seen. People shuddered when they looked at it. It moved with amazing speed, sweeping across the firmament like a besom of destruction. Calculation showed that it was not more than 3,000,000 miles from the earth.

But one night the wonder and dread awakened by the comet were magnified a hundredfold by an occurrence so unexpected and extraordinary that the spectators gasped in amazement.

The writer happens to have before him an entry in a diary, which is, probably, the sole contemporary record of this event. It was written in the city of Washington by no less a person than Professor Jeremiah Moses, of the Council of the Carnegie Institution. Let it tell its own story:

" A marvelous thing happened this night. I walked out into the park near my house with the intention of viewing the great comet. The park on my side (the west), is bordered with a dense screen of tall trees, and I advanced toward the open place in the center in order to have an unobstructed sight of the flaming stranger. As I passed across the edge of the shadow of the trees—the ground ahead being brilliantly illuminated by the light of the comet—I suddenly noticed, with an involuntary start, that I was being preceded by a *double shadow,* with a black center, which forked away from my feet.

"I cast my eyes behind me to find the cause of the phenomenon, and saw, to my inexpressible amazement, that *the comet had divided into two.* There were two distinct heads, already widely separated, but each, it seemed to me, as brilliant as the original one had been, and each supplied with a vast plume of fire a hundred degrees in length, and consequently stretching far past the zenith. The cause of the double shadow was evident at once—but what can have produced this sudden disruption of the comet? It must have occurred since last evening, and already, if the calculated distance of the comet is correct, the parts of the severed head are 300,000 miles asunder!"

Underneath this entry was scribbled:

"Can this have anything to do with Cosmo Versál's flood?"

Whether it had anything to do with the flood or not, at any rate the public believed that it had. People went about with fear written on their faces.

The double shadows had a surprising effect. The phantasm was pointed out, and stared at with superstitious terror by thousands every night. The fact that there was nothing really mysterious about it made no difference. Even those who knew well that it was an inevitable optical result of the division of the bright comet were thrilled with instinctive dread when they saw that forked umbra, mimicking their every movement. There is nothing that so upsets the mind as a sudden change in the aspect of familiar things.

The astronomers now took their turn. Those who

were absolutely incredulous about Cosmo's prediction, and genuinely desirous of allaying the popular alarm, issued statements in which, with a disingenuousness that may have been unintentional, they tried to sidetrack his arguments.

Professor Pludder led the way with a pronunciamento declaring that "the absurd vaporings of the modern Nostradamus of New York" had now demonstrated their own emptiness.

"A comet," said Professor Pludder, with reassuring seriousness, "cannot drown the earth. It is composed of rare gases, which, as the experience of Halley's comet many years ago showed, are unable to penetrate the atmosphere even when an actual encounter occurs. In this case there cannot even be an encounter; the comet is now moving away. Its division is not an unprecedented occurrence, for many previous comets have met with similar accidents. This comet happened to be of unusual size, and the partition of the head occurred when it was relatively nearby—whence the startling phenomena observed. There is nothing to be feared."

It will be remarked that Professor Pludder entirely avoided the real issue. Cosmo Versál had never said that the comet would drown the earth. In fact, he had been as much surprised by its appearance as everybody else. But when he read Professor Pludder's statement, followed by others of similar import, he took up the cudgels with a vengeance. All over the world, translated into a dozen languages, he scattered his reply, and the effect was startling.

" My fellow-citizens of the world in all lands, and of every race," he began, " you are face to face with destruction! And yet, while its heralds are plainly signaling from the sky, and shaking the earth with lightning to awaken it, blind leaders of blind try to deceive you!

" They are defying science itself!

" They say that the comet cannot touch the earth. That is true. It is passing away. I myself did not foresee its coming. It arrived by accident, *but every step that it has made through the silent depths of space has been a proclamation of the presence of the nebula,* which is the real agent of the perdition of the world!

" Why that ominous redness which overcasts the heavens? You have all noticed it. Why that blinding brightness which the comet has displayed, exceeding all that has ever been beheld in such visitors. The explanation is plain: the comet has been feeding on the substance of the nebula, which is rare yet because we have only encountered some of its outlying spirals.

" But it is coming on with terrible speed. In a few short months we shall be plunged into its awful center, and then the oceans will swell to the mountain-tops, and the continents will become the bottoms of angry seas.

" When the flood begins it will be too late to save yourselves.   You have already lost too much precious time.   I tell you solemnly that not one in a million can now be saved.   Throw away every other consideration, and try, try desperately, to be of the little company of those who escape!

" Remember that your only chance is in building arks—arks of levium, the metal that floats.   I have sent broadcast plans for such arks.   They can be made of any size, but the larger the better.   In my own ark I can take only a selected number, and when the complement is made up not another soul will be admitted.

" I have established all my facts by mathematical proofs.   The most expert mathematicians of the world have been unable to detect any error in my calculations.   They try to dispute the data, but the data are already before you for your own judgment. The heavens are so obscured that only the brightest stars can now be seen."   (This was a fact which had caused bewilderment in the observatories.)   " The recent outburst of storms and floods was the second sign of the approaching end, and the third sign will not be long delayed—*and after that the deluge!*"

It is futile to try to describe the haunting fear and horror which seized upon the majority of the millions who read these words.   Business was paralyzed, for men found it impossible to concentrate their minds upon ordinary affairs. Every night the twin comets, still very bright, although they were fast retreating, brandished their fiery scimitars in the sky—more fearful to the imagination now, since Cosmo Versál had declared that it was the nebula that stimulated their energies. And by day the sky was watched with anxious eyes striving to detect signs of a deepening of the menacing hue, which, to an excited fancy, suggested a tinge of blood.

Now, at last, Cosmo's warnings and entreaties bore practical fruit. Men began to inquire about places in his ark, and to make preparations for building arks of their own.

He had not been interfered with after his memorable interview with the President of the United States, and had pushed his work at Mineola with redoubled energy, employing night gangs of workmen so that progress was continuous throughout the twenty-four hours.

Standing on its platform, the ark, whose hull was approaching completion, rose a hundred feet into the air. It was 800 feet long and 250 broad—proportions which practical ship-builders ridiculed, but Cosmo, as original in this as in everything else, declared that, taking into account the buoyancy of levium, no other form would answer as well. He estimated that when its great engines were in place, its immense stores of material for producing power, its ballast, and its supplies of food stowed away, and its cargo of men and animals taken aboard, it would not draw more than twenty feet of water.

Hardly a day passed now without somebody coming to Cosmo to inquire about the best method of constructing arks. He gave the required information, in all possible detail, with the utmost willingness. He drew plans and sketches, made all kinds of practical suggestions, and never failed to urge the utmost haste. He inspired every visitor at the same time with alarm and a resolution to go to work at once.

Some did go to work. But their progress was slow, and as days passed, and the comets gradually faded out of sight, and then the dome of the sky showed a tendency to resume its natural blueness, the enthusiasm of Cosmo's imitators weakened, together with their confidence in his prophetic powers.

They concluded to postpone their operations until the need of arks should become more evident.

As to those who had sent inquiries about places in Cosmo's ark, now that the danger seemed to be blowing away, they did not even take the trouble to answer the very kind responses that he had made.

It is a singular circumstance that not one of these anxious inquirers seemed to have paid particular attention to a very significant sentence in his reply. If they had given it a little thought, it would probably have set them pondering, although they might have been more puzzled than edified. The sentence ran as follows:

"While assuring you that my ark has been built for the benefit of my fellow men, I am bound to tell you that I reserve absolutely the right to determine who are truly representative of *homo sapiens.*"

The fact was that Cosmo had been turning over in his mind the great fundamental question which he had asked himself when the idea of trying to save the human race from annihilation had first occurred to him, and apparently he had fixed upon certain principles that were to guide him.

Since, when the mind is under great strain through fear, the slightest relaxation, caused by an apparently favorable change, produces a rebound of hope, as unreasoning as the preceding terror, so, on this occasion, the vanishing of the comets, and the fading of the disquieting color of the sky, had a wonderful effect in restoring public confidence in the orderly procession of nature.

Cosmo Versál's vogue as a prophet of disaster was soon gone, and once more everybody began to laugh at him. People turned again to their neglected affairs with the general remark that they "guessed the world would manage to wade through."

Those who had begun preparations to build arks looked very sheepish when their friends guyed them about their childish credulity.

Then a feeling of angry resentment arose, and one

day Cosmo Verṣál was mobbed in the street, and the gamins threw stones at him.

People forgot the extraordinary storm of lightning and rain, the split comet, and all the other circumstances which, a little time before, had filled them with terror.

But they were making a fearful mistake!

With eyes blindfolded they were walking straight into the jaws of destruction.

Without warning, and as suddenly almost as an explosion, the *third sign* appeared, and on its heels came a veritable Reign of Terror!

CHAPTER V

THE THIRD SIGN

I N the middle of the night, at New York, hundreds
of thousands simultaneously awoke with a feeling of suffocation.

They struggled for breath as if they had suddenly
been plunged into a steam bath.

The air was hot, heavy, and terribly oppressive.

The throwing open of windows brought no relief.
The outer air was as stifling as that within.

It was so dark that, on looking out, one could
not see his own doorsteps. The arc-lamps in the
street flickered with an ineffective blue gleam which
shed no illumination round about.

House lights, when turned on, looked like tiny
candles inclosed in thick blue globes.

Frightened men and women stumbled around in
the gloom of their chambers trying to dress themselves.

Cries and exclamations rang from room to room;
children wailed; hysterical mothers ran wildly hither
and thither, seeking their little ones. Many fainted,
partly through terror and partly from the difficulty of
breathing. Sick persons, seized with a terrible op-

pression of the chest, gasped, and never rose from their beds.

At every window, and in every doorway, throughout the vast city, invisible heads and forms were crowded, making their presence known by their voices —distracted householders striving to peer through the strange darkness, and to find out the cause of these terrifying phenomena.

Some managed to get a faint glimpse of their watches by holding them close against lamps, and thus noted the time. It was two o'clock in the morning.

Neighbors, unseen, called to one another, but got little comfort from the replies.

" What is it?   In God's name, what has happened? "

" I don't know.   I can hardly breathe."

" It is awful!   We shall all be suffocated."

" Is it a fire? "

" No!   No!   It cannot be a fire."

" The air is full of steam.   The stones and the window-panes are streaming with moisture."

" Great Heavens, how stifling it is! "

Then, into thousands of minds at once leaped the thought of *the flood!*

The memory of Cosmo Versál's reiterated warnings came back with overwhelming force.   It must be the *third sign* that he had foretold.   *It had really come!*

Those fateful words—" the flood " and " Cosmo Versál "—ran from lip to lip, and the hearts of those who spoke, and those who heard, sank like lead in their bosoms.

He would be a bold man, more confident in his powers of description than the present writer, who should attempt to picture the scenes in New York on that fearful night.

The gasping and terror-stricken millions waited and longed for the hour of sunrise, hoping that then the stygian darkness would be dissipated, so that people might, at least, see where to go and what to do. Many, oppressed by the almost unbreathable air, gave up in despair, and no longer even hoped for morning to come.

In the midst of it all a collision occurred directly over Central Park between two aero-expresses, one coming from Boston and the other from Albany. (The use of small aeroplanes within the city limits had, for some time, been prohibited on account of the constant danger of collisions, but the long-distance lines were permitted to enter the metropolitan district, making their landings and departures on specially constructed towers.) These two, crowded with passengers, had, as it afterward appeared, completely lost their bearings—the strongest electric lights being invisible a few hundred feet away, while the wireless signals were confusing—and, before the danger was apprehended, they crashed together.

The collision occurred at a height of a thousand feet, on the Fifth Avenue side of the park. Both of the airships had their aeroplanes smashed and their decks crumpled up, and the unfortunate crews and passengers were hurled through the impenetrable darkness to the ground.

Only four or five, who were lucky enough to be entangled with the lighter parts of the wreckage, escaped with their lives. But they were too much injured to get upon their feet, and there they lay, their sufferings made tenfold worse by the stifling air, and the horror of their inexplicable situation, until they were found and humanely relieved, more than ten hours after their fall.

The noise of the collision had been heard in Fifth Avenue, and its meaning was understood; but amid the universal terror no one thought of trying to aid the victims. Everybody was absorbed in wondering what would become of himself.

When the long attended hour of sunrise approached, the watchers were appalled by the absence of even the slightest indication of the reappearance of the orb of day. There was no lightening of the dense cloak of darkness, and the great city seemed dead.

For the first time in its history it failed to awake after its regular period of repose, and to send forth its myriad voices. It could not be seen; it could not be heard; it made no sign. As far as any outward

indication of its existence was concerned the mighty
capital had ceased to be.

It was this frightful silence of the streets, and of
all the outer world, that terrified the people, cooped
up in their houses, and their rooms, by the walls of
darkness, more than almost any other circumstance;
it gave such an overwhelming sense of the universality
of the disaster, whatever that disaster might be. Except where the voices of neighbors could be heard,
one could not be sure that the whole population, outside his own family, had not perished.

As the hours passed, and yet no light appeared,
another intimidating circumstance manifested itself.
From the start everybody had noticed the excessive
humidity of the dense air. Every solid object that
the hands came in contact with in the darkness was
wet, as if a thick fog had condensed upon it. This
supersaturation of the air (a principal cause of the
difficulty experienced in breathing) led to a result
which would quickly have been foreseen if people
could have had the use of their eyes, but which,
coming on invisibly, produced a panic fear when at
last its presence was strikingly forced upon the attention.

The moisture collected on all exposed surfaces—
on the roofs, the walls, the pavements—until its
quantity became sufficient to form little rills, which
sought the gutters, and there gathered force and volume. Presently the streams became large enough to

create a noise of flowing water that attracted the attention of the anxious watchers at the open windows. Then cries of dismay arose. If the water had been visible it would not have been terrible.

But, to the overstrained imagination, the bubbling and splashing sound that came out of the darkness was magnified into the rush of a torrent. It seemed to grow louder every moment. What was but a murmur on the ear-drum became a roar in the excited brain-cells.

Once more were heard the ominous words, " The flood! "

They spread from room to room, and from house to house. The wild scenes that had attended the first awakening were tame in comparison with what now occurred. Self-control, reason—everything—gave way to panic.

If they could only have *seen* what they were about!

But then they would not have been about it. Then their reason would not have been dethroned.

Darkness is the microscope of the imagination, and it magnifies a million times!

Some timorously descended their doorsteps, and feeling a current of water in the gutter, recoiled with cries of horror, as if they had slipped down the bank of a flooded river. As they retreated they believed that the water was rising at their heels!

Others made their way to the roofs, persuaded that

the flood was already inundating the basements and the lower stories of their dwellings.

Women wrung their hands and wept, and children cried, and men pushed and stumbled about, and shouted, and would have done something if only they could have seen what to do. That was the pity of it! It was as if the world had been stricken blind, and then the trump of an archangel had sounded, crying: " Fly! Fly! for the Avenger is on your heels!" How could they fly?

This awful strain could not have lasted. It would have needed no deluge to finish New York if that maddening pall of darkness had remained unbroken a few hours longer. But, just when thousands had given up in despair, there came a rapid change.

At the hour of noon light suddenly broke overhead. Beginning in a round patch inclosed in an iridescent halo, it spread swiftly, seeming to melt its way down through the thick, dark mass that choked the air, and in less than fifteen minutes New York and all its surroundings emerged into the golden light of noonday.

People who had expected at any moment to feel the water pitilessly rising about them looked out of their windows, and were astonished to see only tiny rivulets which were already shriveling out of sight in the gutters. In a few minutes there was no running water left, although the dampness on the walls and walks showed how great the humidity of the air had been.

At the same time the oppression was lifted from the respiratory apparatus, and everybody breathed freely once more, and felt courage returning with each respiration.

The whole great city seemed to utter a vast sigh of relief.

And then its voice was heard, as it had never been heard before, rising higher and louder every moment. It was the first time that morning had ever broken at midday.

The streets became filled, with magical quickness, by hundreds of thousands, who chattered, and shouted, and laughed, and shook hands, and asked questions, and told their experiences, and demanded if anybody had ever heard of such a thing before, and wondered what it could have been, and what it meant, and whether it would come back again.

Telephones of all kinds were kept constantly busy. Women called up their friends, and talked hysterically; men called up their associates and partners, and tried to talk business.

There was a rush for the Elevated, for the Subways, for the street auto-cars. The great arteries of traffic became jammed, and the noise rose louder and louder.

Belated aero-expresses arrived at the towers from East and West, and their passengers hurried down to join the excited multitudes below.

In an incredibly brief time the newsboys were out

with extras. Then everybody read with the utmost avidity what everybody knew already.

But before many hours passed there was real news, come by wireless, and by submarine telephone and telegraph, telling how the whole world had been swept by the marvelous cloak of darkness.

In Europe it had arrived during the morning hours; in Asia during the afternoon.

The phenomena had varied in different places. In some the darkness had not been complete, but everywhere it was accompanied by extraordinary humidity, and occasionally by brief but torrential rains. The terror had been universal, and all believed that it was the *third sign* predicted by Cosmo Versál.

Of course, the latter was interviewed, and he gave out a characteristic manifesto.

"One of the outlying spirals of the nebula has struck the earth," he said. "But do not be deceived. It is nothing in comparison with what is coming. *And it is the* LAST WARNING *that will be given!* You have obstinately shut your eyes to the truth, *and you have thrown away your lives!*"

This, together with the recent awful experience, produced a great effect. Those who had begun to lay foundations for arks thought of resuming the work. Those who had before sought places with Cosmo called him up by telephone. But only the voice of Joseph Smith answered, and his words were not reassuring.

" Mr. Versál," he said, " directs me to say that at present he will allot no places. He is considering whom he will take."

The recipients of this reply looked very blank. But at least one of them, a well-known broker in Wall Street, was more angered than frightened:

" Let him go to the deuce! " he growled; " him and his flood together! "

Then he resolutely set out to bull the market.

It seems incredible—but such is human nature—that a few days of bright sunshine should once more have driven off the clouds of fear that had settled so densely over the popular mind. Of course, not everybody forgot the terrors of the *third sign*—they had struck too deep, but gradually the strain was relaxed, and people in general accepted the renewed assurances of the savants of the Pludder type that nothing that had occurred was inexplicable by the ordinary laws of nature. The great darkness, they averred, differed from previous occurrences of the kind only in degree, and it was to be ascribed to nothing more serious than atmospheric vagaries, such as that which produced the historic Dark Day in New England in the year 1780.

But more nervous persons noticed, with certain misgivings, that Cosmo Versál pushed on his operations, if possible more energetically than before. And there was a stir of renewed interest when the announcement came out one day that the ark was finished. Then thousands hurried to Mineola to look upon the completed work.

The extraordinary massiveness of the ark was imposing. Towering ominously on its platform, which was so arranged that when the waters came they should lift the structure from its cradle and set it afloat without any other launching, it seemed in itself a prophecy of impending disaster.

Overhead it was roofed with an oblong dome of levium, through which rose four great metallic chimneys, placed above the mighty engines. The roof sloped down to the vertical sides, to afford protection from in-bursting waves. Rows of portholes, covered with thick, stout glass, indicated the location of the superposed decks. On each side four gangways gave access to the interior, and long, sloping approaches offered means of entry from the ground.

Cosmo had a force of trained guards on hand, but everybody who wished was permitted to enter and inspect the ark. Curious multitudes constantly mounted and descended the long approaches, being kept moving by the guards.

Inside they wandered about astonished by what they saw.

The three lower decks were devoted to the storage of food and of fuel for the electric generators which Cosmo Versál had been accumulating for months.

Above these were two decks, which the visitors were informed would be occupied by animals, and by boxes of seeds and prepared roots of plants, with which it was intended to restore the vegetable life of the planet after the water should have sufficiently receded.

The five remaining decks were for human beings. There were roomy quarters for the commander and his officers, others for the crew, several large saloons, and five hundred sets of apartments of various sizes to be occupied by the passengers whom Cosmo should choose to accompany him. They had all the convenience of the most luxurious staterooms of the trans. oceanic liners. Many joking remarks were exchanged by the visitors as they inspected these rooms.

Cosmo ran about among his guests, explaining everything, showing great pride in his work, pointing out a thousand particulars in which his foresight had been displayed—but, to everybody's astonishment, he uttered no more warnings, and made no appeals. On the contrary, as some observant persons noticed, he seemed to avoid any reference to the fate of those who should not be included in his ship's company.

Some sensitive souls were disturbed by detecting in his eyes a look that seemed to express deep pity and regret. Occasionally he would draw apart, and gaze at the passing crowds with a compassionate expression, and then, slowly turning his back, while his fingers worked nervously, would disappear, with downcast head, in his private room.

The comparatively few who particularly noticed

this conduct of Cosmo's were deeply moved—more than they had been by all the enigmatic events of the past months. One man, Amos Blank, a rich manufacturer, who was notorious for the merciless methods that he had pursued in eliminating his weaker competitors, was so much disturbed by Cosmo Versál's change of manner that he sought an opportunity to speak to him privately. Cosmo received him with a reluctance that he could not but notice, and which, somehow, increased his anxiety.

" I—I—thought," said the billionaire hesitatingly, " that I ought—that is to say, that I might, perhaps, inquire—might inform myself—under what conditions one could, supposing the necessity to arise, obtain a passage in your—in your ark. Of course the question of cost does not enter in the matter—not with *me.*"

Cosmo gazed at the man coldly, and all the compassion that had recently softened his steely eyes disappeared. For a moment he did not speak. Then he said, measuring his words and speaking with an emphasis that chilled the heart of his listener:

" Mr. Blank, *the necessity has arisen.*"

" So you say—so you say——" began Mr. Blank.

" So I say," interrupted Cosmo sternly, " and I say further that this ark has been constructed to save those who are worthy of salvation, in order that all that is good and admirable in humanity may not perish from the earth."

" Exactly, exactly," responded the other, smiling, and rubbing his hands. " You are quite right to make a proper choice. If your flood is going to cause a general destruction of mankind, of course you are bound to select the best, the most advanced, those who have pushed to the front, those who have means, those with the strongest resources. The masses, who possess none of these qualifications and claims——"

Again Cosmo Versál interrupted him, more coldly than before:

" It *costs nothing* to be a passenger in this ark. Ten million dollars, a hundred millions, would not purchase a place in it! Did you ever hear the parable of the camel and the needle's eye? The price of a ticket here is *an irreproachable record!* "

With these astonishing words Cosmo turned his back upon his visitor and shut the door in his face.

The billionaire staggered back, rubbed his head, and then went off muttering:

" An idiot! A plain idiot! There will be no flood."

CHAPTER VI

SELECTING THE FLOWER OF MANKIND

AFTER a day or two, during which the ark was left open for inspection, and was visited by many thousands, Cosmo Versál announced that no more visitors would be admitted. He placed sentinels at all entrances, and began the construction of a shallow ditch, entirely inclosing the grounds. Public curiosity was intensely excited by this singular proceeding, especially when it became known that the workmen were stringing copper wires the whole length of the ditch.

" What the deuce is he up to now? " was the question on everybody's lips.

But Cosmo and his employees gave evasive replies to all inquiries. A great change had come about in Cosmo's treatment of the public. No one was any longer encouraged to watch the operations.

When the wires were all placed and the ditch was finished, it was covered up so that it made a broad flat-topped wall, encircling the field.

Speculation was rife for several days concerning the purpose of the mysterious ditch and its wires, but no universally satisfactory explanation was found.

One enterprising reporter worked out an elaborate scheme, which he ascribed to Cosmo Versál, according to which the wired ditch was to serve as a cumulator of electricity, which would, at the proper moment, launch the ark upon the waters, thus avoiding all danger of a fatal detention in case the flood should rise too rapidly.

This seemed so absurd on its face that it went far to quiet apprehension by reawakening doubts of Cosmo's sanity—the more especially since he made no attempt to contradict the assertion that the scheme was his.

Nobody guessed what his real intention was; if people had guessed, it might have been bad for their peace of mind.

The next move of Cosmo Versál was taken without any knowledge or suspicion on the part of the public. He had now established himself in his apartments in the ark, and was never seen in the city.

One evening, when all was quiet about the ark, night work being now unnecessary, Cosmo and Joseph Smith sat facing one another at a square table lighted by a shaded lamp. Smith had a pile of writing paper before him, and was evidently prepared to take copious notes.

Cosmo's great brow was contracted with thought, and he leaned his cheek upon his hand. It was clear that his meditations were troublesome. For at least ten minutes he did not open his lips, and Smith watched him anxiously. At last he said, speaking slowly:

" Joseph, this is the most trying problem that I have had to solve. The success of all my work depends upon my not making a mistake now.

" The burden of responsibility that rests on my shoulders is such as no mortal has ever borne. It is too great for human capacity—and yet how can I cast it off?

" I am to decide who shall be saved! *I, I* alone, *I,* Cosmo Versál, hold in my hands the fate of a race numbering two thousand million souls!—the fate of a planet which, without my intervention, would become simply a vast tomb. It is for *me* to say whether the *genus homo* shall be perpetuated, and in what form it shall be perpetuated. Joseph, this is terrible! These are the functions of deity, not of man."

Joseph Smith seemed no longer to breathe, so intense was his attention. His eyes glowed under the dark brows, and his pencil trembled in his fingers. After a slight pause Cosmo Versál went on:

" If I felt any doubt that Providence had foreordained me to do this work, and given me extraordinary faculties, and extraordinary knowledge, to enable me to perform it, I would, this instant, blow out my brains."

Again he was silent, the secretary, after fidgeting about, bending and unbending his brows, and tapping nervously upon the table, at last said solemnly:

" Cosmo, you *are* ordained; you must *do the work*."

" I must," returned Cosmo Versál, " I know that; and yet the sense of my responsibility sometimes covers me with a cloud of despair. The other day, when the ark was crowded with curiosity seekers, the thought that not one of all those tens of thousands could escape, and that hundreds of millions of others must also be lost, overwhelmed me. Then I began to reproach myself for not having been a more effective agent in warning my fellows of their peril. Joseph, I have miserably failed. I ought to have produced universal conviction that I was right, and I have not done it."

" It is not your fault, Cosmo," said Joseph Smith, reaching out his long arm to touch his leader's hand. " It is an unbelieving generation. They have rejected even the signs in the heavens. The voice of an archangel would not have convinced them."

" It is true," replied Cosmo. " And the truth is the more bitter to me because I spoke in the name of science, and the very men who represent science have been my most determined opponents, blinding the people's eyes—after willfully shutting their own."

" You say you have been weak," interposed Smith, " which you have not been; but you would be weak if you now shrank from your plain duty."

" True! " cried Cosmo, in a changed voice. " Let us then proceed. I had a lesson the other day. Amos Blank came to me, puffed with his pillaged millions.

I saw then what I had to do.   I told him plainly that
he was not among the chosen.   Hand me that book
over there."

The secretary pushed a large volume within Cosmo's reach.   He opened it.   It was a " Year-Book
of Science, Politics, Sociology, History, and Government."

Cosmo ran over its pages, stopping to read a few
lines here and there, seeming to make mental notes.
After a while he pushed the book aside, looked at his
companion thoughtfully, and began:

" The trouble with the world is that morally and
physically it has for thousands of years grown more
and more corrupt.   The flower of civilization, about
which people boast so much, nods over the stagnant
waters of a moral swamp and draws its perilous
beauty from the poisons of the miasma.

" The nebula, in drowning the earth, brings opportunity for a new birth of mankind.   You will remember, Joseph, that the same conditions are said to have
prevailed in the time of Noah.   There was no science
then, and we do not know exactly on what principles
the choice was made of those who should escape; but
the simple history of Noah shows that he and his
friends represented the best manhood of that early
age.

" But the seeds of corruption were not eliminated,
and the same problem recurs to-day.

" I have to determine whom I will save.   I attack

the question by inquiring who represent the best elements of humanity? Let us first consider men by classes."

" And why not by races? " asked Smith.

" I shall not look to see whether a man is black, white, or yellow; whether his skull is brachycephalic or dolichocephalic," replied Cosmo. " I shall look inside. No race has ever shown itself permanently the best."

" Then by classes you mean occupations? "

" Well, yes, for the occupation shows the tendency, the quintessence of character. Some men are born rulers and leaders; others are born followers. Both are necessary, and I must have both kinds."

" You will begin perhaps with the kings, the presidents? "

" Not at all. I shall begin with the men of science. They are the true leaders."

" But they have betrayed you—they have shut their eyes and blindfolded others," objected Joseph Smith, as if in extenuation.

" You do not understand me," said Cosmo, with a commiserating smile. " If my scientific brethren have not seen as clearly as I have done, the fault lies not in science, but in lack of comprehension. Nevertheless, they are on the right track; they have the gist of the matter in them; they are trained in the right method. If I should leave them out, the regenerated world would start a thousand years behind time. Besides, many of them are not so blind; some of them have got a glimpse of the truth."

"Not such men as Pludder," said Smith.

"All the same, I am going to save Pludder," said Cosmo Versál.

Joseph Smith fairly jumped with astonishment.

"You—are—going—to—save—Pludder," he faltered. "But he is the worst of all."

"Not from my present view-point. Pludder has a good brain; he can handle the tools; he is intellectually honest; he has done great things for science in the past. And, besides, I do not conceal from you the fact that I should like to see him convicted out of his own mouth."

"But," persisted Smith, "I have heard you say that he was——"

"No matter what you have heard me say," interrupted Cosmo impatiently. "I say now that he shall go with us. Put down his name at the head of the list."

Dumfounded and muttering under his breath, Smith obeyed.

"I can take exactly one thousand individuals, exclusive of the crew," continued Versál, paying no attention to his confidant's repeated shaking of his head. "Good Heavens, think of that! One thousand out of two thousand millions! But so be it. Nobody would listen to me, and now it is too late. I must fix the number for each class."

"There is one thing—one curious question—that occurs to me," put in Smith hesitatingly. "What about families?"

"There you've hit it," cried Cosmo. "That's exactly what bothers me. There must be as many women as men—that goes without saying. Then, too, the strongest moral element is in the women, although they don't weigh heavily for science. But the aged people and the children—there's the difficulty. If I invite a man who possesses unquestionable qualifications, but has a large family, what am I to do? I can't crowd out others as desirable as he for the sake of carrying all of his stirpes. The principles of eugenics demand a wide field of selection."

Cosmo Versál covered his eyes, rested his big head on his hands, and his elbows on the table. Presently he looked up with an air of decision.

"I see what I must do," he said. "I can take only four persons belonging to any one family. Two of them may be children—a man, his wife, and two children—no more."

"But that will be very hard lines for them——" began Joseph Smith.

"Hard lines!" Cosmo broke in. "Do you think it is easy lines for *me?* Good Heavens, man! I am *forced* to this decision. It rends my heart to think of it, but I can't avoid the responsibility."

Smith dropped his eyes, and Cosmo resumed his reflections. In a little while he spoke again:

"Another thing that I must fix is an age limit. But that will have to be subject to certain exceptions. Very aged persons in general will not do—they could not survive the long voyage, and only in the rare instances where their experience of life might be valuable would they serve any good purpose in reëstablishing the race. Children are indispensable—but they must not be too young—infants in arms would not do at all. Oh, this is sorry work! But I must harden my heart."

Joseph Smith looked at his chief, and felt a twinge of sympathy, tempered by admiration, for he saw clearly the terrible contest in his friend's mind and appreciated the heroic nature of the decision to which the inexorable logic of facts had driven it.

Cosmo Versál was again silent for a long time. Finally he appeared to throw off the incubus, and, with a return of his ordinary decisiveness, exclaimed:

"Enough. I have settled the general principle. Now to the choice."

Then, closing his eyes, as if to assist his memory, he ran over a list of names well known in the world of science, and Smith set them down in a long row under the name of "Abiel Pludder," with which he had begun.

At last Cosmo Versál ceased his dictation.

"There," he said, "that is the end of that category. I may add to or subtract from it later. According to probability, making allowance for bache-

lors, each name will represent three persons; there
are seventy-five names, which means two hundred and
twenty-five places reserved for science. I will now
make a series of other categories and assign the number of places for each."

He seized a sheet of paper and fell to work, while
Smith looked on, drumming with his fingers and con-
torting his huge black eyebrows. For half an hour
complete silence reigned, broken only by the gliding
sound of Cosmo Versál's pencil, occasionally em-
phasized by a soft thump. At the end of that time
he threw down the pencil and held out the paper to
his companion.

"Of course," he said, "this is not a complete list
of human occupations. I have set down the principal
ones as they occurred to me. There will be time to
correct any oversight. Read it."

Smith, by force of habit, read it aloud:

Occupation	No. of Names	Probable No. of Places
Science (already assigned)	75	225
Rulers	15	45
Statesmen	10	30
Business magnates	10	30
Philanthropists	5	15
Artists	15	45
Religious teachers	20	60
School-teachers	20	60
Doctors	30	90
Lawyers	1	3
Writers	6	18
Editors	2	6
Players	14	42

Occupation	No. of Names	Probable No. of Places
Philosophers	1	3
Musicians	12	36
Speculative geniuses	3	9
"Society"	0	0
Agriculture and mechanics	90	270
Totals	329	987
Special reservations		13
Grand total, places		1,000

Several times while Joseph Smith was reading he raised his eyebrows, as if in surprise or mental protest, but made no remark.

"Now," resumed Cosmo when the secretary had finished, "let us begin with the rulers. I do not know them as intimately as I know the men of science, but I am sure I have given them places enough. Suppose you take this book and call them over to me."

Smith opened the "year-book," and began:

"George Washington Samson, President of the United States."

"He goes. He is not intellectually brilliant, but he has strong sense and good moral fiber. I'll save him if for no other reason than his veto of the Antarctic Continent grab bill."

"Shen Su, Son of Heaven, President-Emperor of China."

"Put him down. I like him. He is a true Confucian."

Joseph Smith read off several other names at which Cosmo shook his head. Then he came to:

"Richard Edward, by the grace of God, King of Great——"

"Enough," broke in Cosmo; "we all know him—the man who has done more for peace by putting half the British navy out of commission than any other ruler in history. I can't leave him out."

"Achille Dumont, President of the French republic."

"I'll take him."

"William IV, German Emperor."

"Admitted, for he has at last got the war microbe out of the family blood."

Then followed a number of rulers who were not lucky enough to meet with Cosmo Versál's approval, and when Smith read:

"Alexander V, Emperor of all the Russias," the big head was violently shaken, and its owner exclaimed:

"There will be many Russians in the ark, for tyranny has been like a lustration to that people; but I will carry none of its Romanoff seeds to my new world."

The selection was continued until fifteen names had been obtained, including that of the new, dark-skinned President of Liberia, and Cosmo declared that he would not add another one.

Then came the ten statesmen who were chosen with utter disregard to racial and national lines.

In selecting his ten business magnates, Cosmo stated his rule:

" I exclude no man simply because he is a billionaire. I consider the way he made his money. The world must always have rich men. How could I have built the ark if I had been poor? "

" Philanthropists," read Smith.

" I should have taken a hundred if I could have found them," said Cosmo. " There are plenty of candidates, but these five [naming them] are the only genuine ones, and I am doubtful about several of them. But I must run some chances, philanthropy being indispensable."

For the fifteen representatives of art Cosmo confined his selection largely to architecture.

" The building instinct must be preserved," he explained. " One of the first things we shall need after the flood recedes is a variety of all kinds of structures. But it's a pretty bad lot at the best. I shall try to reform their ideas during the voyage. As to the other artists, they, too, will need some hints that I can give them, and that they can transmit to their children."

Under the head of religious teachers, Cosmo remarked that he had tried to be fair to all forms of genuine faith that had a large following. The school-teachers represented the principal languages, and

Cosmo selected the names from a volume on " The Educational Systems of the World," remarking that he ran some risk here, but it could not easily be avoided.

" Doctors—they get a rather liberal allowance, don't they? " asked Smith.

" Not half as large as I'd like to have it," was the response. " The doctors are the salt of the earth. It breaks my heart to have to leave out so many whose worth I know."

" And only one lawyer! " pursued Joseph. " That's curious."

" Not in the least curious. Do you think I want to scatter broadcast the seeds of litigation in a regenerated world? Put down the name of Chief Justice Good of the United States Supreme Court. He'll see that equity prevails."

" And only six writers," continued Smith.

" And that's probably too many," said Cosmo. " Set down under that head Peter Inkson, whom I will engage to record the last scenes on the drowning earth; James Henry Blackwitt, who will tell the story of the voyage; Jules Bourgeois, who can describe the personnel of the passengers; Sergius Narishkoff, who will make a study of their psychology; and Nicolao Ludolfo, whose description of the ark will be an invaluable historic document a thousand years hence."

" But you have included no poets," remarked Smith.

" Not necessary," responded Cosmo. " Every human being is a poet at bottom."

" And no novelists," persisted the secretary.

" They will spring up thicker than weeds before the waters are half gone—at least, they would if I let one aboard the ark."

" Editors—two ? "

" That's right. And two too many, perhaps. I'll take Jinks of the *Thunderer,* and Bullock of the *Owl.*"

" But both of them have persistently called you an idiot."

" For that reason I want them. No world could get along without some real idiots."

" I am rather surprised at the next entry, if you will permit me to speak of it," said Joseph Smith. "Here you have forty-two places reserved for players."

" That means twenty-eight adults, and probably some youngsters who will be able to take parts," returned Cosmo, rubbing his hands with a satisfied smile. " I have taken as many players as I con-scientiously could, not only because of their future value, but because they will do more than anything else to keep up the spirits of everybody in the ark. I shall have a stage set in the largest saloon."

Joseph Smith scowled, but held his peace. Then, glancing again at the paper, he remarked that there was but one philosopher to be provided for.

"It is easy to name him," said Cosmo. "Kant Jacobi Leergeschwätz."

"Why he?"

"Because he will harmlessly represent the metaphysical *genus,* for nobody will ever understand him."

"Musicians twelve?"

"Chosen for the same reason as the players," said Cosmo, rapidly writing down twelve names because they were not easy to pronounce, and handing them to Smith, who duly copied them off.

When this was done Cosmo himself called out the next category—"'speculative geniuses.'"

"I mean by that," he continued, "not Wall Street speculators, but foreseeing men who possess the gift of looking into the 'seeds of time,' but who never get a hearing in their own day, and are hardly ever remembered by the future ages which enjoy the fruits whose buds they recognized."

Cosmo mentioned two names which Joseph Smith had never heard, and told him they ought to be written in golden ink.

"They are *sui generis,* and alone in the world. They are the most precious cargo I shall have aboard," he added.

Smith shrugged his shoulders and stared blankly at the paper, while Cosmo sank into a reverie. Finally the secretary said, smiling with evident approval this time:

"'Society' zero."

" Precisely, for what does ' society ' represent except its own vanity? "

" And then comes agriculture and mechanics."

For this category Cosmo seemed to be quite as well prepared as for that of science. He took from his pocket a list already made out and handed it to Joseph Smith. It contained forty names marked " cultivators, farmers, gardeners," and fifty " mechanics."

" At the beginning of the twentieth century," he said, " I should have had to reverse that proportion—in fact, my entire list would then have been top-heavy, and I should have been forced to give half of all the places to agriculture. But thanks to our scientific farming, the personnel employed in cultivation is now reduced to a minimum while showing maximum results. I have already stored the ark with seeds of the latest scientifically developed plants, and with all the needed agricultural implements and machinery."

" There yet remain thirteen places ' specially reserved,' " said Smith, referring to the paper.

" I shall fill those later," responded Cosmo, and then added with a thoughtful look, " I have some humble friends."

" The next thing," he continued, after a pause, " is to prepare the letters of invitation. But we have done enough for to-night. I will give you the form to-morrow."

And all this while half the world had been peacefully sleeping, and the other half going about its business, more and more forgetful of recent events, and if it had known what those two men were about it would probably have exploded in a gust of laughter.

CHAPTER VII

THE WATERS BEGIN TO RISE

COSMO VERSÁL had begun the construction of his ark in the latter part of June. It was now the end of November. The terrors of the *third sign* had occurred in September. Since then the sky had nearly resumed its normal color, there had been no storms, but the heat of summer had not relaxed. People were puzzled by the absence of the usual indications of autumn, although vegetation had shriveled on account of the persistent high temperature and constant sunshine.

"An extraordinary year," admitted the meteorologists, "but there have been warm falls before, and it is simply a question of degree. Nature will restore the balance and in good time, and probably we shall have a severe winter."

On the 31st of November, the brassy sky at New York showed no signs of change, when the following dispatch, which most of the newspapers triple-leaded and capped with stunning headlines, quivered down from Churchill, Keewatin:

During last night the level of the water in Hudson Bay rose fully nine feet. Consternation reigned this morning when ship-owners found their wharves inundated, and vessels straining at short cables. The ice-breaker "Victoria" was lifted on the back of a sandy bar, having apparently been driven by a heavy wave, which must have come from the East. There are other indications that the mysterious rise began with a "bore" from the eastward. It is thought that the vast mass of icebergs set afloat on Davis's Strait by the long continued hot weather melting the shore glaciers, has caused a jam off the mouth of Hudson Strait, and turned the Polar current suddenly into the bay. But this is only a theory. A further rise is anticipated.

Startling as was this news, it might not, by itself, have greatly disturbed the public mind if it had not been followed, in a few hours, by intelligence of immense floods in Alaska and in the basin of the Mackenzie River.

And the next day an etherogram from Obdorsk bordered on the grotesque, and filled many sensitive readers with horror.

It is said that in the vast tundra regions of Northern Siberia the frozen soil had dissolved into a bottomless slough, from whose depths uprose prehistoric mammoths, their long hair matted with mud, and their curved tusks of ivory gleaming like trumpets over the field of their resurrection. The dispatch concluded with a heart-rending account of the loss of a large party of ivory hunters, who, having ventured too far from the more solid land, suddenly found the ground turning to black ooze beneath their feet, and, despite their struggles, were all engulfed within sight of their friends, who dared not try to approach them.

Cosmo Versál, when interviewed, calmly remarked that the flood was beginning in the north, because it was the northern part of the globe that was nearest the heart of the nebula. The motion of the earth being northward, that end of its axis resembled the prow of a ship.

"But this," he added, "is not the true deluge. The Arctic ice-cap is melting, and the frozen soil is turning into a sponge in consequence of the heat of friction developed in the air by the inrush of nebulous matter. The aqueous vapor, however, has not yet touched the earth. It will begin to manifest its presence within a few days, and then the globe will drink water at every pore. The vapor will finally condense into falling oceans."

"What would you advise people to do?" asked one of the reporters.

The reply was given in a perfectly even voice, without change of countenance:

"*Commit suicide!* They have practically done that already."

It was nearly two weeks later when the first signs of a change of weather were manifested in middle latitudes. It came on with a rapid veiling of the sky, followed by a thin, misty, persistent rain. The heat grew more oppressive, but the rain did not become heavier, and after a few days there would be, for several consecutive hours, a clear spell, during which the sun would shine, though with a sickly, pallid light.

There was a great deal of mystification abroad, and nobody felt at ease. Still, the ebullitions of terror that had accompanied the earlier caprices of the elements were not renewed. People were getting used to these freaks.

In the middle of one of the clear spells a remarkable scene occurred at Mineola.

It was like a panorama of the seventh chapter of Genesis.

It was the procession of the beasts.

Cosmo Versál had concluded that the time was come for housing his animals in the ark. He wished to accustom them to their quarters before the voyage began. The resulting spectacle filled the juvenile world with irrepressible joy, and immensely interested their elders.

No march of a menagerie had ever come within sight of equaling this display. Many of the beasts were such as no one there had ever seen before. Cosmo had consulted experts, but, in the end, he had been guided in his choice by his own judgment. Nobody knew as well as he exactly what was wanted. He had developed in his mind a scheme for making the new world that was to emerge from the waters better in every respect than the old one.

Mingled with such familiar creatures as sheep, cows, dogs, and barn-yard fowls, were animals of the past, which the majority of the onlookers had only read about or seen pictures of, or perhaps, in a few cases, heard described in childhood, by grandfathers long since sleeping in their graves.

Cosmo had rapidly collected them from all parts of the world, but as they arrived in small consignments, and were carried in closed vans, very few persons had any idea of what he was doing.

The greatest sensation was produced by four beautiful horses, which had been purchased at an enormous price from an English duke, who never would have parted with them—for they were almost the last living representatives of the equine race left on the earth— if financial stress had not compelled the sacrifice.

These splendid animals were dapple gray, with long white tails, and flowing manes borne proudly on their arching necks, and as they were led at the head of the procession, snorting at the unwonted scene about them, their eyes bright with excitement, prancing and curvetting, cries of admiration and rounds of applause broke from the constantly growing throngs of spectators.

Those who had only known the horse from pictures and sculptures were filled with astonishment by its living beauty. People could not help saying to themselves:

" What a pity that the honking auto, in its hundred forms of mechanical ugliness, should have driven these beautiful and powerful creatures out of the world! What could our forefathers have been thinking of? "

A few elephants, collected from African zoölogical gardens, and some giraffes, also attracted a great deal of attention, but the horses were the favorites with the crowd.

Cosmo might have had lions and tigers, and similar beasts, which had been preserved in larger numbers than the useful horse, but when Joseph Smith suggested their inclusion he shook his head, declaring that it was better that they should perish. As far as possible, he averred, he would eliminate all carnivores.

In some respects, even more interesting to the onlookers than the animals of the past, were the animals of the future that marched in the procession. Few of them had ever been seen outside the experimental stations where they had been undergoing the process of artificial evolution.

There were the stately white Californian cattle, without horns, but of gigantic stature, the cows, it was said, being capable of producing twenty times more milk than their ancestral species, and of a vastly superior quality.

There were the Australian rabbits, as large as Newfoundland dogs, though short-legged, and furnishing food of the most exquisite flavor; and the Argentine sheep, great balls of snowy wool, moving smartly along on legs three feet in length.

The greatest astonishment was excited by the " grand astoria terrapin," a developed species of dia-

mond-back tortoise, whose exquisitely sculptured convex back, lurching awkwardly as it crawled, rose
almost three feet above the ground; and the "new
century turkey," which carried its beacon head and
staring eyes as high as a tall man's hat.

The end of the procession was formed of animals
familiar to everybody, and among them were cages
of monkeys (concerning whose educational development Cosmo Versál had theories of his own) and a
large variety of birds, together with boxes of insect
eggs and chrysalids.

The delight of the boys who had chased after the
procession culminated when the animals began to ascend the sloping ways into the ark.

The horses shied and danced, making the metallic
flooring resound like a rattle of thunder; the elephants trumpeted; the sheep baaed and crowded themselves into inextricable masses against the guard-rails;
the huge new cattle moved lumberingly up the slope,
turning their big white heads inquiringly about; the
tall turkeys stretched their red coral necks and gobbled
with Brobdingnagian voices; and the great terrapins
were ignominiously attached to cables and drawn up
the side of the ark, helplessly waving their immense
flappers in the air.

And when the sensational entry was finished, the
satisfied crowd turned away, laughing, joking, chattering, with never a thought that it was anything more
than the most amusing exhibition they had ever seen!

But when they got back in the city streets they met a flying squadron of yelling newsboys, and seizing the papers from their hands read, in big black letters:

"AWFUL FLOOD IN THE MISSISSIPPI!

Thousands of People Drowned!

THE STORM COMING THIS WAY!"

It was a startling commentary on the recent scene at the ark, and many turned pale as they read.

But the storm did not come in the way expected. The deluging rains appeared to be confined to the Middle West and the Northwest, while at New York the sky simply grew thicker and seemed to squeeze out moisture in the form of watery dust. This condition lasted for some time, and then came what everybody, even the most skeptical, had been secretly dreading.

The ocean began to rise!

The first perception of this startling fact, according to a newspaper account, came in a very strange, roundabout way to a man living on the outskirts of the vast area of made ground where the great city had spread over what was formerly the Newark meadows and Newark Bay.

About three o'clock in the morning, this man, who it appears was a policeman off duty, was awakened by scurrying sounds in the house. He struck a light, and seeing dark forms issuing from the cellar, went down to investigate. The ominous gleam of water, reflecting the light of his lamp, told him that the cellar was inundated almost to the top of the walls.

"Come down here, Annie!" he shouted to his wife. "Sure 'tis Coshmo Versá-al is invadin' the cellar with his flood. The rats are lavin' us."

Seeing that the slight foundation walls were crumbling, he hurried his family into the street, and not too soon, for within ten minutes the house was in ruins.

Neighbors, living in equally frail structures, were awakened, and soon other undermined houses fell. Terror spread through the quarter, and gradually half the city was aroused.

When day broke, residents along the water-front in Manhattan found their cellars flooded, and South and West Streets swimming with water, which was continually rising. It was noted that the hour was that of flood-tide, but nobody had ever heard of a tide so high as this.

Alarm deepened into terror when the time for the tide to ebb arrived and there was no ebbing. On the contrary, the water continued to rise. The government observer at the Highlands telephoned that Sandy Hook was submerged. Soon it was known that Coney Island, Rockaway, and all the seaside places along the south shore of Long Island were under water. The mighty current poured in through the

Narrows with the velocity of a mill-race. The Hudson, set backward on its course, rushed northward with a raging bore at its head that swelled higher until it licked the feet of the rock chimneys of the Palisades.

But when the terror inspired by this sudden invasion from the sea was at its height there came unexpected relief. The water began to fall more rapidly than it had risen. It rushed out through the Narrows faster than it had rushed in, and ships, dragged from their anchorage in the upper harbor, were carried out seaward, some being stranded on the sandbanks and shoals in the lower bay.

Now again houses standing on made ground, whose foundations had been undermined, fell with a crash, and many were buried in the ruins.

Notwithstanding the immense damage and loss of life, the recession of the waters immediately had a reassuring effect, and the public, in general, was disposed to be comforted by the explanation of the weather officials, who declared that what had occurred was nothing more than an unprecedentedly high tide, probably resulting from some unforeseen disturbance out at sea.

The phenomenon had been noted all along the Atlantic coast. The chief forecaster ventured the assertion that a volcanic eruption had occurred somewhere on the line from Halifax to Bermuda. He thought that the probable location of the upheaval had been at Munn's Reef, about halfway between those points, and the more he discussed his theory the readier he became to stake his reputation on its correctness, for, he said, it was impossible that any combination of the effects of high and low pressures could have created such a surge of the ocean, while a volcanic wave, combining with the regular oscillation of the tide, could have done it easily.

But Cosmo Versál smiled at this explanation, and said in reply:

"The whole Arctic ice-cap is dissolved, and the condensation of the nebula is at hand. But there is worse behind. When the wave comes back it will rise higher."

As the time for the next flood-tide grew near, anxious eyes were on the watch to see how high the water would go. There was something in the mere manner of its approach that made the nerves tingle.

It speeded toward the beaches, combing into rollers at an unwonted distance from shore; plunged with savage violence upon the sands of the shallows, as if it would annihilate them; and then, spreading swiftly, ran with terrific speed up the strand, seeming to devour everything it touched. After each recoil it sprang higher and roared louder and grew blacker with the mud that it had ground up from the bottom. Miles inland the ground trembled with the fast-repeated shocks.

Again the Hudson was hurled backward until a

huge bore of water burst over the wharves at Albany. Every foot of ground in New York less than twenty feet above the mean high tide level was inundated. The destruction was enormous, incalculable. Ocean liners moored along the wharves were, in some cases, lifted above the level of the neighboring streets, and sent crashing into the buildings along the water-front.

Etherograms told, in broken sentences, of similar experiences on the western coasts of Europe, and from the Pacific came the news of the flooding of San Francisco, Los Angeles, Portland, Tacoma, Seattle, and, in fact, every coast-lying town. On the western coast of South America the incoming waves broke among the foothills of the Andes.

It was as if the mighty basins of the world's two greatest oceans were being rocked to and fro, sending the waters spinning from side to side.

And to add to the horror of the situation, every volcano on the globe seemed to burst simultaneously into activity, probably through the effects of the invasion of sea water into the subterranean fire, while the strain of the unwonted weight thrown upon the coasts broke open the tectonic lines of weakness in the earth's crust, causing the most terrible earthquakes, which destroyed much that the water could not reach.

From Alaska to Patagonia, from Kamchatka through Japan to the East Indies, from Mount Hecla to Vesuvius, Etna, and Teneriffe, the raging oceans were bordered with pouring clouds of volcanic smoke, hurled upward in swift succeeding puffs, as if every crater had become the stack of a stupendous steam-engine driven at its maddest speed; while immense rivers of lava flamed down the mountain flanks and plunged into the invading waters with reverberated roarings, hissings, and explosions that seemed to shake the framework of the globe.

During the second awful shoreward heave of the Atlantic a scene occurred off New York Bay that made the stoutest nerves quiver. A great crowd had collected on the Highlands of the Navesink to watch the ingress of the tidal wave.

Suddenly, afar off, the smoke of an approaching ocean liner was seen. It needed but a glance to show that she was struggling with tremendous surges. Sometimes she sank completely out of sight; then she reappeared, riding high on the waves. Those who had glasses recognized her. Word ran from mouth to mouth that it was the great *Atlantis,* the mightiest of the ocean monarchs, of a hundred thousand tons register, coming from Europe, and bearing, without question, many thousands of souls.

She was flying signals of distress, and filling the ether with her inarticulate calls for help, which quavered into every radiograph station within a radius of hundreds of miles.

But, at the same time, she was battling nobly for herself and for the lives of her passengers and crew.

From her main peak the Stars and Stripes streamed in the tearing wind. There were many in the watching throngs who personally knew her commander, Captain Basil Brown, and who felt that if any human being could bring the laboring ship through safely, he could. Aid from land was not to be thought of for a moment.

As she swiftly drew nearer, hurled onward by the resistless surges with the speed of an express train, the captain was recognized on his bridge, balancing himself amid the lurches of the vessel; and even at that distance, and in those terrible circumstances, there was something in his bearing perceptible to those who breathlessly watched him, through powerful glasses, which spoke of perfect self-command, entire absence of fear, and iron determination to save his ship or die with her under his feet.

It could be seen that he was issuing orders and watching their execution, but precisely what their nature was, of course, could only be guessed. His sole hope must be to keep the vessel from being cast ashore. There was no danger from the shoals, for they were by this time deeply covered by the swelling of the sea.

Slowly, slowly, with a terrific straining of mechanic energies, which pressed the jaws of the watchers together with spasmodic sympathy, as if their own nervous power were coöperating in the struggle, the gallant ship bore her head round to face the driving waves.   From the ten huge, red stacks columns of inky black smoke poured out as the stokers crammed the furnaces beneath.   It was man against nature, human nerve and mechanical science against blind force.

It began to look as if the *Atlantis* would win the battle.   She was now fearfully close to the shore, but her bow had been turned into the very eye of the sea, and one could almost feel the tension of her steel muscles as she seemed to spring to the encounter.   The billows that split themselves in quick succession on her sharp stem burst into shooting geysers three hundred feet high.

The hearts of the spectators almost ceased to beat. Their souls were wrapped up with the fate of the brave ship.   They forgot the terrors of their own situation, the peril of the coming flood, and saw nothing but the agonized struggle before their eyes.   With all their inward strength they prayed against the ocean.

Such a contest could not last long.   Suddenly, as the *Atlantis* swerved a little aside, a surge that towered above her loftiest deck rushed upon her.   She was lifted like a cockleshell upon its crest, her huge hull spun around, and the next minute, with a crash that resounded above the roar of the maddened sea, she was dashed in pieces.

At the very last moment before the vessel disappeared in the whirling breakers, to be strewed in broken and twisted bits of battered metal upon the pounding sands, Captain Basil Brown was seen on the commander's bridge.

No sooner had this tragedy passed than the pent-up terror broke forth, and men ran for their lives, ran for their homes, ran to *do something*—something, but what?—to save themselves and their dear ones.

For now, at last, they *believed!*

CHAPTER VIII

STORMING THE ARK

THERE was to be no more respite now. The time of warnings was past. The "signs" had all been shown to a skeptical and vacillating world, and at last the fulfillment was at hand.

There was no crying of "extras" in the streets, for men had something more pressing to think of than sending and reading news about their distresses and those of their fellow-men. Many of the newspapers ceased publication; every business place was abandoned; there was no thought but of the means of escape.

But how should they escape? And whither should they fly?

The lower lying streets were under water. The Atlantic still surged back and forth as if the ocean itself were in agony. And every time the waves poured in they rose higher. The new shores of the bay, and the new coasts of Long Island and New Jersey, receding inward hour by hour, were strewn with the wrecks of hundreds of vessel of all kinds which had been caught by the surges and pitilessly hurled to destruction.

Even if men did not yet fully believe in Cosmo Versál's theory of a whelming nebula, they were terrified to the bottom of their souls by the conviction, which nobody could resist, that the vast ice-fields of the north, the glaciers of Greenland, the icy mountains of Alaska, had melted away under the terrible downpour of heat, and were swelling the oceans over their brims. And then a greater fear dropped like a blanket upon them. Some one thought of the *antarctic ice*.

The latest dispatches that had come, before the cessation of all communication to the newspapers, had told of the prevalence of stifling heat throughout the southern hemisphere, and of the vast fleets of antarctic icebergs that filled the south seas. The mighty deposits of ice, towering to mountain heights, that stretched a thousand miles in every direction around the south pole were melting as the arctic ice had melted, and, when the water thus formed was added to the already overflowing seas, to what elevation might not the flood attain!

The antarctic ice was known to be the principal mass of frozen water on the globe. The frigid cap of the north was nothing in comparison with it. It had long been believed that that tremendous accumulation unbalanced the globe and was the principal cause of the unsteadiness of the earth's axis of rotation.

Every fresh exploration had only served to magnify the conception of the incredible vastness of that deposit. The skirts of the Antarctic Continent had proved to be rich in minerals wherever the rocks could find a place to penetrate through the gigantic burden of ice, and the principal nations had quarreled over the possession or control of these protruding bits of wealth-crammed strata. But behind the bordering cliffs of ice, rising in places a thousand feet above the level of the sea, and towering farther inland so high that this region was, in mean elevation, the loftiest on the planet, nothing but ice could be seen.

And now that ice was dissolving and flowing into the swollen oceans, adding billions of tons of water every minute!

Men did not stop to calculate, as Cosmo Versál had done, just how much the dissolution of all the ice and permanent snow of the globe would add to the volume of the seas. He knew that it would be but a drop in the bucket—although sufficient to start the flood—and that the great thing to be feared was the condensation of the aqueous nebula, already beginning to enwrap the planet in its stifling folds.

The public could understand the melting ice, although it could not fully understand the nebula; it could understand the swelling sea, and the raging rivers, and the lakes breaking over their banks—and the terror and despair became universal.

But what should they *do?*

Those who had thought of building arks hurried

to see if the work might not yet be completed, but most of them had begun their foundations on low land, which was already surmerged.

Then a cry arose, terrible in its significance and in its consequences—one of those cries that the vanished but unconquerable god Pan occasionally sets ringing, nobody can tell how:

"Cosmo's ark! Get aboard! Storm it!"

And thereupon there was a mighty rush for Mineola. Nobody who caught the infection stopped to reason. Some of them had to wade through water, which in places was knee-deep. They came from various directions, and united in a yelling mob. They meant to carry the ark with a rush. They would not be denied. As the excited throngs neared the great vessel they saw its huge form rising like a mount of safety, with an American flag flapping over it, and they broke into a mighty cheer. On they sped, seized with the unreason of a crowd, shouting, falling over one another, struggling, fighting for places, men dragging their wives and children through the awful crush, many trampled helpless under the myriads of struggling feet—driving the last traces of sanity from one another's minds.

The foremost ranks presently spied Cosmo Versál, watching them from an open gangway sixty feet above their heads. They were dismayed at finding the approaches gone. How should they get into the ark? How could they climb up its vertical sides?

But they would find means. They would re-erect the approaches. They would *get in somehow.*

Cosmo waved them off with frantic gesticulations; then, through a trumpet, he shouted in a voice audible above the din:

" Keep back, for your lives! "

But they paid no attention to him; they rushed upon the raised wall, surrounding the field where Cosmo had buried his mysterious lines of wire. Then the meaning of that enigmatical work was flashed upon them.

As the first to arrive laid their hands upon the top of the low wall they fell as if shot through the brain, tumbling backward on those behind. Others pushed wildly on, but the instant they touched the wall they too collapsed. Wicked blue-green sparks occasionally flashed above the struggling mass.

The explanation was clear. Cosmo, foreseeing the probability of a despairing attack, had surrounded the ark with an impassable electric barrier. The sound of a whirring dynamo could be heard. A tremendous current was flowing through the hidden wires and transmitting its paralyzing energy to the metallic crest of the wall.

Still those behind pushed on, until rank after rank had sunk helpless at the impregnable line of defense. They were not killed—at least, not many—but the shock was so paralyzing that those who had experienced its effects made no further attempts to cross

the barrier. Many lay for a time helpless upon the
sodden ground.

Cosmo and Joseph Smith, who had now appeared
at his side, continued to shout warnings, which began
to be heeded when the nature of the obstacle became
known. The rush was stopped, and the multitude
stood at bay, dazed, and uncertain what to do. Then
a murmur arose, growing louder and more angry and
threatening, until suddenly a shot was heard in the
midst of the crowd, and Cosmo was seen to start
backward, while Joseph Smith instantly dodged out
of sight.

A cry arose:

" Shoot him! That's right! Shoot the devil!
He's a witch! He's drowning the world! "

They meant it—at least, half of them did. It
was the logic of terror.

Hundreds of shots were now fired from all quarters,
and heads that had been seen flitting behind the various portholes instantly disappeared. The bullets rat-
tled on the huge sides of the ark, but they came from
small pistols and had not force enough to penetrate.

Cosmo Versál alone remained in sight. Occasionally a quick motion showed that even his nerves were
not steady enough to defy the whistling of the bullets
passing close; but he held his ground, and stretched
out his hand to implore attention.

When the fusillade ceased for a moment he put his
trumpet again to his lips and shouted:

"I have done my best to save you, but you would not listen. Although I know that you must perish, I would not myself harm a hair of your heads. Go back, I implore you. You may prolong your lives if you will fly to the highlands and the mountains— but here you cannot enter. *The ark is full.*"

Another volley of shots was the only answer. One broad-shouldered man forced his way to the front, took his stand close to the wall, and yelled in stentorian tones:

"Cosmo Versál, listen to me! You are the curse of the world! You have brought this flood upon us with your damnable incantations. Your infernal nebula is the seal of Satan! Here, beast and devil, here at my feet, lies my only son, slain by your hellish device. By the Eternal I swear you shall go back to the pit!"

Instantly a pistol flashed in the speaker's hand, and five shots rang in quick succession. One after another they whistled by Cosmo's head and flattened themselves upon the metal-work behind. Cosmo Versál, untouched, folded his arms and looked straight at his foe. The man, staring a moment confusedly, as if he could not comprehend his failure, threw up his arms with a despairing gesture, and fell prone upon the ground.

Then yells and shots once more broke out. Cosmo stepped back, and a great metallic door swung to, closing the gangway.

But three minutes later the door opened, and the mob saw two machine-guns trained upon them.

Once more Cosmo appeared, with the trumpet.

" If you fire again," he cried, " I shall sweep you with grapeshot. I have told you how you can prolong your lives. Now go! "

Not another shot was fired. In the face of the guns, whose terrible power all comprehended, no one dared to make a hostile movement.

But, perhaps, if Cosmo Versál had not set new thoughts running in the minds of the assailants by telling them there was temporary safety to be found by seeking high ground, even the terror of the guns would not have daunted them. Now their hopefulness was reawakened, and many began to ponder upon his words.

" He says we must perish, and yet that we can find safety in the hills and mountains," said one man. " I believe half of that is a lie. We are not going to be drowned. The water won't rise much higher. The flood from the south pole that they talk about must be here by this time, and then what's left to come? "

" The nebula," suggested one.

" Aw, the nebula be hanged! There's no such thing! I live on high ground; I'm going to keep a sharp outlook, and if the water begins to shut off Manhattan I'll take my family up the Hudson to the Highlands. I guess old Storm King'll keep his head above. That's where I come from—up that way. I used to hear people say when I was a boy that New York was bound to sink some day. I used to laugh at that then, but it looks mighty like it now, don't it?"

"Say," put in another, "what did the fellow mean by saying the ark was *full?* That's funny, ain't it? Who's he got inside, anyway?"

"Oh, he ain't got nobody," said another.

"Yes, he has. I seen a goodish lot through the portholes. He's got somebody, sure."

"A lot of fools like himself, most likely."

"Well, if he's a fool, and they's fools, what are *we,* I'd like to know? What did you come here for, hey?"

It was a puzzling question, and brought forth only a sheepish laugh, followed by the remark:

"I guess we fooled ourselves considerable. We got scared too easy."

"Maybe you'll feel scared again when you see the water climbing up the streets in New York. I don't half like this thing. I'm going to follow his advice and light out for higher ground."

Soon conversation of this sort was heard on all sides, and the crowd began to disperse, only those lingering behind who had friends or relatives that had been struck down at the fatal wall. It turned out that not more than one or two had been mortally shocked. The rest were able to limp away, and many had fully recovered within five minutes after suffering the shock. In half an hour not a dozen persons were in sight from the ark.

But when the retreating throngs drew near the shores of the Sound, and the East River, which had expanded into a true arm of the sea, and found that there had been a perceptible rise since they set out to capture the ark, they began to shake their heads and fear once more entered their hearts.

Thousands then and there resolved that they would not lose another instant in setting out for high land, up the Hudson, in Connecticut, among the hills of New Jersey. In fact, many had already fled thither, some escaping on aeros; and hosts would now have followed but for a marvelous change that came just before nightfall and prevented them.

For some days the heavens had alternately darkened and lightened, as gushes of mist came and went, but there had been no actual rain. Now, without warning, a steady downpour began. Even at the beginning it would have been called, in ordinary times, a veritable cloudburst; but it rapidly grew worse and worse, until there was no word in the vernacular or in the terminology of science to describe it.

It seemed, in truth, that " all the fountains of the great deep were broken up, and the windows of heaven were opened." The water thundered upon the roofs, and poured off them in torrents. In five minutes every sloping street had become an angry river, and every level place a swelling lake. People

caught out of doors were almost beaten to the ground
by the force of the water falling upon them as if they
had been standing under a cataract.

In a short time every cellar and every basement
was filled to overflowing, and in the avenues the
flood, lapping every instant higher upon the doorsteps and the walls, rushed by with frightful roarings,
bearing in its awful embrace pieces of furniture,
clothing, bedding, washed out of ground-floor rooms
—and, alas! human beings; some motionless, already
mercifully deprived of life, but others struggling and
shouting for aid which could not be given.

So terrible a spectacle no one had ever looked upon,
no one had ever imagined. Those who beheld it
were too stunned to cry out, too overwhelmed with
terror and horror to utter a word. They stood, or fell
into chairs or upon the floor, trembling in every limb,
with staring eyes and drooping jaws, passively await-
ing their fate.

As night came on there was no light. The awful
darkness of the *third sign* once more settled upon
the great city, but now it was not the terror of indefinite expectation that crushed down the souls of
men and women—it was the weight of doom accom-
plished!

There was no longer any room for self-deception;
every quaking heart felt now that the nebula had
come. *Cosmo Versál had been right!*

After the water had attained a certain height in

the streets and yards, depending upon the ratio between the amount descending from the sky and that
which could find its way to the rivers, the flood for
the time being rose no higher. The actual drowning
of New York could not happen until the Hudson and
the East River should become so swollen that the
water would stand above the level of the highest
buildings, and turn the whole region round about,
as far as the Orange hills, the Ramapo Mountains,
the Highlands, and the Housatonic hills, into an inland sea.

But before we tell that story we must return to
see what was going on at Mineola. Cosmo Versál,
on that awful night when New York first knew beyond the shadow of a doubt, or the gleam of a hope,
that it was doomed, presided over a remarkable assembly in the grand saloon of his ark.

CHAPTER IX

THE COMPANY OF THE REPRIEVED

HOW did it happen that Cosmo Versál was able to inform the mob when it assailed the ark that he had no room left?

Who composed his ship's company, whence had they come, and how had they managed to embark without the knowledge of the public?

The explanation is quite simple. It was all due to the tremendous excitement that had prevailed ever since the seas began to overflow. In the universal confusion people had to think of other things nearer their doors than the operations of Cosmo Versál. Since the embarkation of the animals the crowds had ceased to visit the field at Mineola, and it was only occasionally that even a reporter was sent there. Accordingly, there were many hours every day when no curiosity-seekers were in sight of the ark, and at night the neighborhood was deserted; and this state of affairs continued until the sudden panic which led to the attack that has been described.

Cosmo Versál, of course, had every reason to conceal the fact that he was carefully selecting his company. It was a dangerous game to play, and he knew it. The consequence was that he enjoined secrecy upon his invited guests, and conducted them, a few at a time, into the ark, assuring them that their lives might be in peril if they were recognized. And once under the domain of the fear which led them to accept his invitation, they were no less anxious than he to avoid publicity. Some of them probably desired to avoid recognition through dread of ridicule; for, after all, the flood might not turn out to be so bad as Cosmo had predicted.

So it happened that the ark was filled, little by little, and the public knew nothing about it.

And who composed the throng which, while the awful downpour roared on the ellipsoidal cover of the ark, and shook it to its center and while New York, a few miles away, saw story after story buried under the waters, crowded Cosmo's brilliantly lighted saloon, and raised their voices to a high pitch in order to be heard?

Had all the invitations which he dictated to Joseph Smith after their memorable discussion, and which were sent forth in the utmost haste, flying to every point of the compass, been accepted, and was it the famous leaders of science, the rulers and crowned heads who had passed his critical inspection that were now knocking elbows under the great dome of levium? Had kings and queens stolen incognito under the shelter of the ark, and magnates of the financial world hidden themselves there?

It would have been well for them all if they had been there. But, in fact, many of those to whom the invitations had gone did not even take the trouble to thank their would-be savior. A few, however, who did not come in person, sent responses. Among these was the President of the United States. Mr. Samson's letter was brief but characteristic. It read:

To Cosmo Versál, Esq.
Sir:
The President directs me to say that he is grateful for your invitation, and regrets that he cannot accept it. He is informed by those to whose official advice he feels bound to listen, that the recent extraordinary events possess no such significance as you attach to them.

Respectfully,   FOR THE PRESIDENT,
JAMES JENKS, Secretary.

It must be remembered that this letter was written before the oceanic overflow began. After that, possibly, the President and his advisers changed their opinion. But then communication by rail was cut off, and as soon as the downpour from the sky commenced the aero express lines were abandoned. The airships would have been deluged, and blown to destruction by the tremendous gusts which, at intervals, packed the rain-choked air itself into solid billows of water.

None of the rulers of the old world responded, but about half the men of science, and representatives of the other classes that Cosmo had set down on his

list, were wise enough to accept, and they hurried to
New York before the means of transit by land and
sea were destroyed.

Among these were Englishmen, Frenchmen, Ital-
ians, Spaniards, Germans, Austrians, Poles, people
from the Balkan states, Swedes, Danes, Russians, and
a few from India, China, and Japan. The clatter
of their various tongues made a very Babel inside the
ark, when they talked to one another in groups, but
nearly all of them were able to speak English, which,
after many years of experiment, had been adopted
as the common language for transacting the world's
affairs.

There was another letter, which Cosmo read with
real regret, although hardly with surprise. It was
from Professor Pludder. Instead of expressing gratitude for the invitation, as the President, trained in
political blandiloquence, had done, Professor Pludder indulged in denunciation.

"You are insane," he said. "You do not know
what you are talking about. Your letter is an insult
to science. These inundations" (this, too, was written before the sky had opened its flood-gates) "are
perfectly explicable by the ordinary laws of nature.
Your talk of a nebula is so ridiculous that it deserves
no reply. If any lunatic accepts your absurd invitation, and goes into your 'ark,' he will find himself in
Bedlam, where he ought to be."

"I guess you were right," Cosmo remarked to

Joseph Smith, after reading this outburst. Pludder would not contribute to the regeneration of mankind. We are better off without him."

But Cosmo Versál was mistaken in thinking he had heard the last of Abiel Pludder. The latter was destined to show that he was hardly a less remarkable speciment of *homo sapiens* than the big-headed prophet of the second deluge himself.

As soon as it became evident that there would be room to spare in the ark, Cosmo set at work to fill up the list. He went over his categories once more, but now, owing to the pressure of time, he was obliged to confine his selections to persons within easy reach. They came, nearly all, from New York, or its vicinity; and since these last invitations went out just on the eve of the events described in the last two chapters, there was no delay in the acceptances, and the invitees promptly presented themselves in person.

Cosmo's warning to them of the necessity of secrecy was superfluous, for the selfishness of human nature never had a better illustration than they afforded. The lucky recipients of the invitations stole away without a word of farewell, circumspectly disappearing, generally at night, and often in disguise; and when the attack occurred on the ark, there were, behind the portholes, many anxious eyes cautiously staring out and recognizing familiar faces in the mob, while the owners of those eyes trembled in their shoes lest their friends might succeed in forcing an entrance. After all, it was to be doubted if Cosmo Versál, with all his vigilance, had succeeded in collecting a company representing anything above the average quality of the race.

But there was one thing that did great credit to his heart. When he found that he had room unoccupied, before adding to his lists he consented to take more than two children in a family. It was an immense relief, for—it must be recorded—there were some who, in order to qualify themselves, had actually abandoned members of their own families! Let it also be said, however, that many, when they found that the conditions imposed were inexorable, and that they could only save themselves by leaving behind others as dear to them as their own lives, indignantly refused, and most of these did not even reply to the invitations.

It was another indication of Cosmo's real humanity, as well as of his shrewdness, that, as far as they were known, and could be reached, the persons who had thus remained true to the best instincts of nature were the first to receive a second invitation, with an injunction to bring their entire families. So it happened that, after all, there were aged men and women, as well as children in arms, mingled in that remarkable assemblage.

It will be recalled that thirteen places had been specially reserved, to be filled by Cosmo Versál's personal friends. His choice of these revealed another pleasing side of his mind. He took thirteen men and women who had been, in one capacity or another, employed for many years in his service. Some of them were old family servants that had been in his father's house.

"Every one of these persons," he said to Joseph Smith, "is worth his weight in gold. Their disinterested fidelity to duty is a type of character that almost became extinct generations ago, and no more valuable leaven could be introduced into the society of the future. Rather than leave them, I would stay behind myself."

Finally there was the crew. This comprised one hundred and fifty members, all of them chosen from the body of engineers, mechanics, and workmen who had been employed in the construction of the ark. Cosmo himself was, of course, the commander, but he had for his lieutenants skilled mariners, electrical and mechanical engineers, and men whom he himself had instructed in the peculiar duties that would fall to them in the navigation and management of the ark, every detail of which he had laboriously worked out with a foresight that seemed all but superhuman.

All of the passengers and crew were aboard when the baffled mob retreated from Mineola, and some, when that danger was past, wished to descend to the ground, and go and look at the rising waters, which had not yet invaded the neighborhood. But Cosmo absolutely forbade any departures from the ark. The condensation of the nebula, he declared, was likely to begin any minute, and the downpour would be so fierce that a person might be drowned in the open field.

It came even sooner than he had anticipated, with the results that we have already noted in New York. At first many thought that the ark itself would be destroyed, so dreadful was the impact of the falling water. The women and children, and some of the men, were seized with panic, and Cosmo had great difficulty in reassuring them.

" The flood will not reach us for several hours yet," he said. " The level of the water must rise at least a hundred feet more before we shall be afloat. Inside here we are perfectly safe. The ark is exceedingly strong and absolutely tight. You have nothing to fear."

Then he ordered an ingenious sound-absorbing screen, which he had prepared, to be drawn over the great ceiling of the saloon, the effect of which was to shut out the awful noise of the water roaring upon the roof of the ark. A silence that was at first startling by contrast to the preceding din prevailed as soon as the screen was in place.

Amid a hush of expectancy, Cosmo now mounted a dais at one end of the room. Never before had the intellectual superiority of the man seemed so evident. His huge " dome of thought," surmounting his slight body, dominated the assembly like the front of Jove. Chairs near him were occupied by Professor Jeremiah Moses, Professor Abel Able, Professor Alexander Jones, and the two " speculative geniuses " whom he had named to Joseph Smith. These were Costaké Theriade, of Rumania, a tall, dark, high-browed thinker, who was engaged in devising ways to extract and recover interatomic energy; and Sir Wilfred Athelstone, whose specialty was bio-chemistry, and who was said to have produced amazing results in artificial parthenogenesis and the production of new species.

As soon as attention was concentrated upon him, Cosmo Versál began to speak.

" My friends," he said, " the world around us is now sinking beneath a flood that will not be arrested until America, Europe, Africa, Asia, and Australia have disappeared. We stand at the opening of a new age. You alone who are here assembled, and your descendants, will constitute the population of the new world that is to be.

" In this ark, which owes its existence to the fore-seeing eye of science, you will be borne in safety upon the bosom of the battling waters, and we will disembark upon the first promising land that reappears, and begin the plantation and development of a new society of men and women, which, I trust, will afford a practical demonstration of the principles of eugenics.

" I have, as far as possible, and as far as the pitiful blindness of mankind permitted me to go, selected and assembled here representatives of the best tendencies of humanity. You are a chosen remnant, and the future of this planet depends upon you.

" I have been fortunate in securing the companionship of men of science who will be able to lead and direct. The ark is fully provisioned for a period which must exceed the probable duration of the flood. I have taken pains not to overcrowd it, and every preparation has been made for any contingencies which may arise.

" It is inexpressibly sad to part thus with the millions of our fellow-beings who would not heed the warnings that were lavished upon them; but, while our hearts may be rent with the thought, it is our duty to cast off the burden of vain regrets and concentrate all our energies upon the great work before us.

" I salute," he continued, raising his voice and lifting a glass of wine from the little table before him, " the world of the past—may its faults be forgotten —and the world of the future—may it rise on the wings of science to nobler prospects! "

He poured out the wine like a libation; and as his voice ceased to echo, and he sank into his seat, an uncontrollable wave of emotion ran over the assembly. Many of the women wept, and the men conversed in whispers. After a considerable interval, during which no one spoke above his breath, Professor Able Abel arose and said:

" The gratitude which we owe to this man "—indicating Cosmo Versál—"can best be expressed, not in words, but by acts. He has led us thus far; he must continue to lead us to the end. We were blind, while he was full of light. It will become us hereafter to heed well whatever he may say. I now wish to ask if he can foresee where upon the re-emerging planet a foothold is first likely to be obtained. Where lies our land of promise? "

" I can answer that question," Cosmo replied, " only in general terms. You are all aware that the vast table-land of Tibet is the loftiest region upon the globe. In its western part it lies from fourteen to seventeen or eighteen thousand feet above the ordinary level of the sea. Above it rise the greatest mountain peaks in existence. Here the first considerable area is likely to be uncovered. It is upon the Pamirs, the ' Roof of the World,' that we shall probably make our landing."

" May I ask," said Professor Abel Able, " in what manner you expect the waters of the flood to be withdrawn, after the earth is completely drowned? "

" That," was the reply, " was one of the fundamental questions that I examined, but I do not care to enter into a discussion of it now. I may simply say that it is not only upon the disappearance of the waters that our hopes depend, but upon circumstances that I shall endeavor to make clear hereafter. The new cradle of mankind will be located near the old one, and the roses of the Vale of Cashmere will canopy it."

Cosmo Versál's words made a profound impression upon his hearers, and awoke thoughts that carried their minds off into strange reveries. No more questions were asked, and gradually the assemblage broke up into groups of interested talkers.

It was now near midnight. Cosmo, beckoning Professor Abel Able, Professor Alexander Jones, and Professor Jeremiah Moses to accompany him, made his way out of the saloon, and, secretly opening one of the gangway doors, they presently stood, sheltering themselves from the pouring rain, in a position which enabled them to look toward New York.

Nothing, of course, was visible through the downpour; but they were startled at hearing fearful cries issuing out of the darkness. The rural parts of the city, filled with gardens and villas, lay round within a quarter of a mile of the ark, and the sound, accelerated by the water-charged atmosphere, struck upon their ears with terrible distinctness. Sometimes, when a gust of wind blew the rain into their faces, the sound deepened into a long, despairing wail, which seemed to be borne from afar off, mingled with the roar of the descending torrent—the death-cry of the vast metropolis!

" Merciful Heaven, I cannot endure this ! " cried Professor Moses.

" Go to my cabin," Cosmo yelled in his ear, " and

take the others with you. I will join you there in a little while. I wish to measure the rate of rise of the water."

They gladly left him, and fled into the interior of the ark. Cosmo procured an electric lamp; and the moment its light streamed out he perceived that the water had already submerged the great cradle in which the ark rested, and was beginning to creep up the metallic sides. He lowered a graduated tape into it, provided with an automatic register. In a few minutes he had completed his task, and then he went to rejoin his late companions in his cabin.

"In about an hour," he said to them, "we shall be afloat. The water is rising at the rate of one-thirtieth of an inch per second."

"No more than that?" asked Professor Jones with an accent of surprise.

"That is quite enough," Cosmo replied. "One-thirtieth of an inch per second means two inches in a minute, and ten feet in an hour. In twenty-four hours from now the water will stand two hundred and forty feet above its present level, and then only the tallest structures in New York will lift their tops above it, if, indeed, they are not long before overturned by undermining or the force of the waves."

"But it will be a long time before the hills and highlands are submerged," suggested Professor Jones. "Are you perfectly sure that the flood will cover them?"

Cosmo Versál looked at his interlocutor, and slowly shook his head.

"It is truly a disappointment to me," he said at length, "to find that, even now, remnants of doubt cling to your minds. I tell you that the nebula is condensing at its maximum rate. It is likely to continue to do so for at least four months. In four months, at the rate of two inches per minute, the level of the water will rise 28,800 feet. There is only one peak in the world which is surely known to attain a slightly greater height than that—Mount Everest, in the Himalayas. Even in a single month the rise will amount to 7,200 feet. That is 511 feet higher than the loftiest mountain in the Appalachians. In one month, then, there will be nothing visible of North America east of the Rockies. And in another month *they* will have gone under."

Not another word was said. The three professors sat, wide-eyed and open-mouthed, staring at Cosmo Versál, whose bald head was crowned with an aureole by the electric light that beamed from the ceiling, while, with a gold pocket pencil, he fell to figuring upon a sheet of paper.

CHAPTER X

THE LAST DAY OF NEW YORK

WHILE Cosmo Versál was calculating, from the measured rise of the water, the rate of condensation of the nebula, and finding that it added twenty-nine trillion two hundred and ninety billion tons to the weight of the earth every minute—a computation that seemed to give him great mental satisfaction—the metropolis of the world, whose nucleus was the island of Manhattan, and every other town and city on the globe that lay near the ordinary level of the sea, was swiftly sinking beneath the swelling flood.

Everywhere, over all the broad surface of the planet, a wail of despair arose from the perishing millions, beaten down by the water that poured from the unpitying sky. Even on the highlands the situation was little better than in the valleys. The hills seemed to have been turned into the crests of cataracts from which torrents of water rushed down on all sides, stripping the soil from the rocks, and sending the stones and bowlders roaring and leaping into the lowlands and the gorges. Farmhouses, barns, villas, trees, animals, human beings—all were swept away together.

Only on broad elevated plateaus, where higher
points rose above the general level, were a few of
the inhabitants able to find a kind of refuge. By
seeking these high places, and sheltering themselves
as best they could among immovable rocks, they succeeded, at least, in delaying their fate. Notwithstanding the fact that the atmosphere was filled with
falling water, they could yet breathe, if they kept the
rain from striking directly in their faces. It was
owing to this circumstance, and to some extraordinary occurrences which we shall have to relate, that
the fate of the human race was not precisely that
which Cosmo Versál had predicted.

We quitted the scene in New York when the
shadow of night had just fallen, and turned the
gloom of the watery atmosphere into impenetrable
darkness. The events of that dreadful night we shall
not attempt to depict. When the hours of daylight
returned, and the sun should have brightened over
the doomed city, only a faint, phosphorescent luminosity filled the sky. It was just sufficient to render
objects dimly visible. If the enclosing nebula had
remained in a cloud-like state it would have cut off
all light, but having condensed into raindrops, which
streamed down in parallel lines, except when sudden
blasts of wind swept them into a confused mass, the
sunlight was able to penetrate through the interstices,
aided by the transparency of the water, and so a slight
but variable illumination was produced.

In this unearthly light many tall structures of the metropolis, which had as yet escaped the effects of undermining by the rushing torrents in the streets, towered dimly toward the sky, shedding streams of water from every cornice. Most of the buildings of only six or eight stories had already been submerged, with the exception of those that stood on the high grounds in the upper part of the island, and about Spuyten Duyvil.

In the towers and upper stories of the lofty buildings still standing in the heart of the city, crowds of unfortunates assembled, gazing with horror at the spectacles around them, and wringing their hands in helpless despair. When the light brightened they could see below them the angry water, creeping every instant closer to their places of refuge, beaten into foam by the terrible downpour, and sometimes, moved by a mysterious impulse, rising in sweeping waves which threatened to carry everything before them.

Every few minutes one of the great structures would sway, crack, crumble, and go down into the seething flood, the cries of the lost souls being swallowed up in the thunder of the fall. And when this occurred within sight of neighboring towers yet intact, men and women could be seen, some with children in their arms, madly throwing themselves from windows and ledges, seeking quick death now that hope was no more!

Strange and terrible scenes were enacted in the

neighborhood of what had been the water-fronts. Most of the vessels moored there had been virtually wrecked by the earlier invasion of the sea. Some had been driven upon the shore, others had careened and been swamped at their wharves. But a few had succeeded in cutting loose in time to get fairly afloat. Some tried to go out to sea, but were wrecked by running against obstacles, or by being swept over the Jersey flats. Some met their end by crashing into the submerged pedestal of the Statue of Liberty. Others steered up the course of the Hudson River, but that had become a narrow sea, filled with floating and tossing débris of every sort, and all landmarks being invisible, the luckless navigators lost their way, and perished, either through collisions with other vessels, or by driving upon a rocky shore.

The fate of the gigantic building containing the offices of the municipal government, which stood near the ancient City Hall, and which had been the culminating achievement of the famous epoch of " skyscrapers," was a thing so singular, and at the same time dramatic, that in a narrative dealing with less extraordinary events than we are obliged to record it would appear altogether incredible.

With its twoscore lofty stories, and its massive base, this wonderful structure rose above the lower quarter of the city, and dominated it, like a veritable Tower of Babel, made to defy the flood. Many thousands of people evidently regarded it in that very light, and they had fled from all quarters, as soon as the great downpour began, to find refuge within its mountainous flanks. There were men—clerks, merchants, brokers from the downtown offices—and women and children from neighboring tenements.

By good chance, but a few weeks before, this building had been fitted with a newly invented system of lighting, by which each story was supplied with electricity from a small dynamo of its own, and so it happened that now the lamps within were all aglow, lightening the people's hearts a little with their cheering radiance.

Up and up they climbed, the water ever following at their heels, from floor to floor, until ten of the great stages were submerged. But there were more than twice as many stages yet above, and they counted them with unexpiring hope, telling one another, with the assurance of desperation, that long before the flood could attain so stupendous an altitude the rain would surely cease, and the danger, as far as they were concerned, would pass away.

" See! See! " cries one. " It is stopping! It is coming no higher! I've been watching that step, and the water has stopped! It hasn't risen for ten minutes! "

" Hurrah! Hurrah! " yells the crowd behind and above. And the glad cry is taken up and reverberated from story to story until it bursts wildly out into the rain-choked air at the very summit.

"Hurrah! Hurrah! We are saved! The flood has stopped!"

Men madly embrace each other. Women burst into tears and hug their children to their breasts, filled with a joy and thankfulness that can find no expression in words.

"You are wrong," says another man, crouching beside him who first spoke. "It has not stopped— it is still rising."

"*What!* I tell you it *has* stopped," snaps the other. "Look at that step! It stopped right below it."

"*You've been watching the wrong step.* It's rising!"

"You fool! Shut your mouth! I say it has *stopped.*"

"No, it has not."

"*It has! It has!*"

"Look at *that* step, then! See the water just now coming over it."

The obstinate optimist stares a moment, turns pale, and then, with an oath, strikes his more clear-headed neighbor in the face! And the excited crowd behind, with the blind instinctive feeling that, somehow, he has robbed them of the hope which was but now as the breath of life to them, strike him and curse him, too.

But he had seen only too clearly.

With the steady march of fate—two inches a min-

ute, as Cosmo Versál had accurately measured it—
the water still advances and climbs upward.

In a little while they were driven to another story,
and then to another. But hope would not down.
They could not believe that the glad news, which
had so recently filled them with joy, was altogether
false. The water *must* have stopped rising *once;* it
had been *seen.* Then, it would surely stop *again,* stop
to rise no more.

Poor deluded creatures! With the love of life
so strong within them, they could not picture, in their
affrighted minds, the terrible consummation to which
they were being slowly driven, when, jammed into
the narrow chambers at the very top of the mighty
structure, their remorseless enemy would seize them
at last.

But they were nearer the end than they could have
imagined even if they had accepted and coolly rea-
soned upon the facts that were so plain before them.
And, after all, it was not to come upon them only
after they had fought their way to the highest loft
and into the last corner.

A link of this strange chain of fatal events now
carries us to the spot where the United States Navy
Yard in Brooklyn once existed. That place was sunk
deep beneath the waters. All of the cruisers, battleships, and other vessels that had been at anchor or
at moorings there had gone under. One only, the
boast of the American navy, the unconquerable *Uncle*

Sam, which, in the last great war that the world had known, had borne the starry flag to victories whose names broke men's voices and filled their eyes with tears of pride, had escaped, through the incomparable seamanship of Captain Robert Decatur, who had been her commander for thirty years.

But though the *Uncle Sam* managed to float upon the rising flood, she was unable to get away because of the obstructions lodged about the great bridges that spanned the East River. A curious eddy that the raging currents formed over what was once the widest part of that stream kept her revolving round and round, never departing far in any direction, and, with majestic strength, riding down or brushing aside the floating timbers, wooden houses, and other wreckage that pounded furiously against her mighty steel sides.

Just at the time when the waters had mounted to the eighteenth story of the beleaguered Municipal Building, a sudden change occurred in these currents. They swept westward with resistless force, and the *Uncle Sam* was carried directly over the drowned city. First she encountered the cables of the Manhattan Bridge, striking them near the western tower, and, swinging round, wrenched the tower itself from its foundations and hurled it beneath the waters.

Then she rushed on, riding with the turbid flood high above the buried roofs, finding no other obstruction in her way until she approached the Municipal

" THE GREAT BATTLESHIP . . . CRASHED, PROW ON, INTO
THE STEEL-RIBBED WALLS "

Building, which was stoutly resisting the push of the waves.

Those who were near the windows and on the balconies, on the eastern side of the building, saw the great battleship coming out of the gray gloom like some diluvian monster, and before they could comprehend what it was, it crashed, prow on, into the steel-ribbed walls, driving them in as if they had been the armored sides of an enemy.

So tremendous was the momentum of the striking mass that the huge vessel passed, like a projectile, through walls and floors and partitions. But as she emerged in the central court the whole vast structure came thundering down upon her, and ship and building together sank beneath the boiling waves.

But out of the awful tangle of steel girders, that whipped the air and the water as if some terrible spidery life yet clung to them, by one of those miracles of chance which defy all the laws of probability and reason, a small boat of levium, that had belonged to the *Uncle Sam,* was cast forth, and floated away, half submerged but unsinkable; and clinging to its thwarts, struggling for breath, insane with terror, were two men, the sole survivors of all those thousands.

One of them was a seaman who had taken refuge, with a crowd of comrades, in the boat before the battleship rushed down upon the building. All of his comrades had been hurled out and lost when the blow came, while his present companion was swept in and lodged against the thwarts. And so those two waifs drove off in the raging waves. Both of them were bleeding from many wounds, but they had no fatal hurts.

The boat, though filled with water, was so light that it could not sink. Moreover, it was ballasted, and amid all its wild gyrations it kept right side up. Even the ceaseless downpour from the sky could not drive it beneath the waves.

After a while the currents that had been setting westward changed their direction, and the boat was driven toward the north. It swept on past toppling skyscrapers until it was over the place where Madison Square once spread its lawns, looked down upon by gigantic structures, most of which had now either crumbled and disappeared or were swaying to their fall. Here there was an eddy, and the boat turned round and round amid floating débris until two other draggled creatures, who had been clinging to floating objects, succeeded by desperate efforts in pulling themselves into it. Others tried but failed, and no one lent a helping hand. Those who were already in the boat neither opposed nor aided the efforts of those who battled to enter it. No words were heard in the fearful uproar—only inarticulate cries.

Suddenly the current changed again, and the boat, with its dazed occupants, was hurried off in the direction of the Hudson. Night was now beginning once more to drop an obscuring curtain over the scene, and under that curtain the last throes of drowning New York were hidden. When the sun again faintly illuminated the western hemisphere the whole Atlantic seaboard was buried under the sea.

As the water rose higher, Cosmo Versál's Ark at last left its cradle, and cumbrously floated off, moving first eastward, then turning in the direction of Brooklyn and Manhattan. Cosmo had his engines in operation, but their full power was not developed as soon as he had expected, and the great vessel drifted at the will of the currents and the wind, the latter coming now from one side and now from another, rising at times to hurricane strength and then dying away until only a spanking breeze swept the ever-falling rain into swishing sheets. Occasionally the wind failed entirely, and for many minutes at a time the water fell in vertical streams.

At length the motive power of the Ark was developed, and it began to obey its helm. From the shelter of a " captain's bridge," constructed at the forward end of the huge levium dome that covered the vessel, Cosmo Versál, with Captain Arms, a liberally bewhiskered, veteran navigator in whose skill he confided, peered over the interminable waste of waters. There was nothing in sight except floating objects that had welled up from the drowned city and the surrounding villages. Here and there the body of an animal or a human being was seen in the tossing waves, and Cosmo Versál sadly shook his head as he pointed them out, but the stout mariner at his side chewed his tobacco, and paid attention only to his duties, shouting orders from time to time through a speaking-tube, or touching an electric button.

Cosmo Versál brought a rain-gage and again and again allowed it to fill itself. The story was always the same—two inches per minute, ten feet per hour, the water mounted.

The nebula had settled down to regular work, and, if Cosmo's calculations were sound, there would be no intermission for four months.

After the power of the propellers had been developed the Ark was steered southeastward. Its progress was very slow. In the course of eight hours it had not gone more than fifty miles. The night came on, and the speed was reduced until there was only sufficient way to insure the command of the vessel's movements. Powerful searchlights were employed as long as the stygian darkness continued.

With the return of the pallid light, at what should have been daybreak, Cosmo and his navigator were again at their post. In fact, the former had not slept at all, keeping watch through the long hours, with Captain Arms within easy call.

As the light became stronger, Cosmo said to the captain:

" Steer toward New York. I wish to see if the last of the tall buildings on the upper heights have gone under."

" It will be very dangerous to go that way," objected Captain Arms. " There are no landmarks, and we may strike a snag."

" Not if we are careful," replied Cosmo. " All but the highest ground is now buried very deep."

" It is taking a fool's risk," growled Captain Arms, through his brush, but nevertheless he obeyed.

It was true that they had nothing to go by. The air was too thick with water, and the light too feeble for them to be able to lay their course by sighting the distant hills of New Jersey which yet remained above the level of the flood. Still, by a kind of seaman's instinct, Captain Arms made his way, until he felt that he ought to venture no farther. He had just turned to Cosmo Versál with the intention of voicing his protest, when the Ark careened slightly, shivered from stem to stern, and then began a bumping movement that nearly threw the two men from their feet.

" We are aground! " cried the captain, and instantly turned a knob that set in motion automatic machinery which cut off the engines from the propellers, and at the same time slowed down the engines themselves.

CHAPTER XI

" A BILLION FOR A SHARE "

THE Ark had lodged on the loftiest part of the Palisades. It was only after long and careful study of their position, rendered possible by occasional glimpses of the Orange Hills and high points further up the course of the Hudson, that Cosmo Versál and Captain Arms were able to reach that conclusion. Where New York had stood nothing was visible but an expanse of turbid and rushing water.

But suppose the hard trap rocks had penetrated the bottom of the Ark! It was a contingency too terrible to be thought of. Yet the facts must be ascertained at once.

Cosmo, calling Joseph Smith, and commanding him to go among the frightened passengers and assure them, in his name, that there was no danger, hurried, with the captain and a few trusty men, into the bowels of the vessel. They thoroughly sounded the bottom plates. No aperture and no indentation was to be found.

But, then, the bottom was double, and the outer plates might have been perforated. If this had happened the fact would reveal itself through the leakage of water into the intervening space. To ascertain if that had occurred it was necessary to unscrew the covers of some of the manholes in the inner skin of levium.

It was an anxious moment when they cautiously removed one of these covers. At the last turns of the screw the workman who handled it instinctively turned his head aside, and made ready for a spring, more than half expecting that the cover would be driven from his hands, and a stream of water would burst in.

But the cover remained in place after it was completely loosened, and until it had been lifted off. A sigh of relief broke from every breast. No water was visible.

" Climb in there, and explore the bottom," Cosmo commanded.

There was a space of eighteen inches between the two bottoms, which were connected and braced by the curved ribs of the hull. A man immediately disappeared in the opening and began the exploration. Cosmo ordered the removal of other covers at various points, and the exploration was extended over the whole bottom. He himself passed through one of the manholes and aided in the work.

At last it was determined, beyond any doubt, that even the outer skin was uninjured. Not so much as a dent could be found in it.

" By the favor of Providence," said Cosmo Versál, as his great head emerged from a manhole, " the Ark has touched upon a place where the rocks are covered with soil, and no harm has come to us. In a very short time the rising water will lift us off."

" And, with my consent, you'll do no more navigating over hills and mountains," grumbled Captain Arms. " The open sea for the sailor."

The covers were carefully replaced, and the party, in happier spirits, returned to the upper decks, where the good news was quickly spread.

The fact was that while the inspection was under way the Ark had floated off, and when Cosmo and the captain reached their bridge the man who had been left in charge reported that the vessel had swung halfway round.

" She's headed for the old Atlantic," sung out Captain Arms. " The sooner we're off the better."

But before the captain could signal the order to go ahead, Cosmo Versál laid his hand on his arm and said:

" Wait a moment; listen."

Through the lashing of the rain a voice penetrated with a sound between a call and a scream. There could be no doubt that it was human. The captain and Cosmo looked at one another in speechless astonishment. The idea that any one outside the Ark could have survived, and could now be afloat amid this turmoil of waters, had not occurred to their minds. They experienced a creeping of the nerves. In a few minutes the voice came again, louder than before, and the words that it pronounced being now clearly audible, the two listeners could not believe their ears.

"Cosmo Versál!" it yelled. "Cosmo-o-o Ver-sá-al! A billion for a share! A *billion*, I say, a *bil-li-on* for a share!"

Then they perceived a little way off to the left something which looked like the outline of a boat, sunk to the gunwales, washed over by every wave; and standing in it, up to their waists in water, were four men, one of whom was gesticulating violently, while the others seemed dazed and incapable of voluntary movement.

It was the boat of levium that had been thrown out of the wreckage when the battleship ran down the Municipal tower, and we must now follow the thread of its adventures up to the time of its encounter with the Ark.

As the boat was driven westward from the drowned site of Madison Square it gradually freed itself from the objects floating around, most of which soon sunk, and in an hour or two its inmates were alone—the sole survivors of a dense population of many millions.

Alone they were in impenetrable darkness, for, as we have said, night had by this time once more fallen.

They floated on, half drowned, chilled to the bone, not trying to speak, not really conscious of one another's presence. The rain beat down upon them, the waves washed over them, the unsinkable boat sluggishly rose and fell with the heaving of the water, and occasionally they were nearly flung overboard by a sudden lurch—and yet they clung with desperate tenacity to the thwarts, as if life were still dear, as if they thought that they might yet survive, though the world was drowned.

Thus hours passed, and at last a glimmer appeared in the streaming air, and a faint light stole over the face of the water. If they saw one another, it was with unrecognizing eyes. They were devoured with hunger, but they did not know it.

Suddenly one of them—it was he who had been so miraculously thrown into the boat when it shot out of the tangle of falling beams and walls—raised his head and threw up his arms, a wild light gleaming in his eyes.

In a hoarse, screaming voice he yelled:

" Cosmo Versál! "

No other syllables that the tongue could shape would have produced the effect of that name. It roused the three men who heard it from their lethargy of despair, and thrilled them to the marrow. With amazed eyes they stared at their companion. He did not look at them, but gazed off into the thick rain. Again his voice rose in a maniacal shriek:

" Cosmo Versál! Do you hear me? Let me in! A billion for a share!"

The men looked at each other, and, even in their desperate situation, felt a stir of pity in their hearts. They were not too dazed to comprehend that their companion had gone mad. One of them moved to his side, and laid a hand upon his shoulder, as if he would try to soothe him.

But the maniac threw him off, nearly precipitating him over the side of the submerged boat, crying:

" What are *you* doing in my boat? Overboard with you! I am looking for Cosmo Versál! He's got the biggest thing afloat! Securities! Securities! Gilt-edged! A *billion*, I tell you! Here I have them —look! Gilt-edged, every one!" and he snatched a thick bundle of papers from his pocket and waved them wildly until they melted into a pulpy mass with the downpour.

The others now shrank away from him in fear. Fear? Yes, for still they loved their lives, and the staggering support beneath their feet had become as precious to them as the solid earth. They would have fought with the fury of madmen to retain their places in that half-swamped shell. They were still capable of experiencing a keener fear than that of the flood. They were as terrified by the presence of this maniac as they would have been on encountering him in their homes.

But he did not attempt to follow them. He still

looked off through the driving rain, balancing himself to the sluggish lurching of the boat, and continuing to rave, and shout, and shake his soaked bundle of
papers, until, exhausted by his efforts, and half-choked
by the water that drove in his face, he sank helpless
upon a thwart.

Then they fell back into their lethargy, but in a
little while he was on his feet again, gesticulating and
raging—and thus hours passed on, and still they were
afloat, and still clinging to life.

Suddenly, looming out of the 'strange gloom, they
perceived the huge form of the Ark, and all struggled
to their feet, but none could find voice but the maniac.

As soon as he saw the men, Cosmo Versál had
run down to the lowest deck, and ordered the opening of a gangway on that side. When the door swung
back he found himself within a few yards of the
swamped boat, but ten feet above its level. Joseph
Smith, Professor Moses, Professor Jones, Professor
Able, and others of the passengers, and several of the
crew, hurried to his side, while the rest of the passengers crowded as near as they could get.

The instant that Cosmo appeared the maniac redoubled his cries.

"Here they are," he yelled, shaking what remained of his papers. "A billion—all gilt-edged!
Let me in. But shut out the others. They're only
little fellows. They've got no means. They can't

float an enterprise like this. Ah, you're a bright
one! You and me, Cosmo Versál—we'll squeeze 'em
all out. I'll give you the secrets. We'll own the
earth! I'm *Amos Blank!*"

Cosmo Versál recognized the man in spite of the
dreadful change that had come over him. His face
was white and drawn, his eyes staring, his head bare,
his hair matted with water, his clothing in shreds—
but it was unmistakably Amos Blank, a man whose
features the newspapers had rendered familiar to
millions, a man who had for years stood before the
public as the unabashed representative of the system
of remorseless repression of competition, and shame-
less corruption of justice and legislation. After the
world, for nearly two generations, had enjoyed the
blessings of the reforms in business methods and social
ideals that had been inaugurated by the great uprising
of the people in the first quarter of the twentieth
century, Amos Blank, and lesser men of his ilk, had
swung back the pendulum, and re-established more
firmly than ever the reign of monopoly and iniquitous
privilege.

The water-logged little craft floated nearer until
it almost touched the side of the Ark directly below
the gangway. The madman's eyes glowed with eagerness, and he reached up his papers, continually yelling
his refrain: " A billion! Gilt-edged! Let me in!
Don't give the rabble a show!"

Cosmo made no reply, but gazed down upon the

man and his bedraggled companions with impassive features, but thoughtful eyes. Any one who knew him intimately, as Joseph Smith alone did, could have read his mind. He was asking himself what he ought to do. Here was the whole fundamental question to be gone over again. To what purpose had he taken so great pains to select the flower of mankind? Here was the head and chief of the offense that he had striven to eliminate appealing to him to be saved under circumstances which went straight to the heart and awoke every sentiment of humanity.

Presently he said in as low a voice as could be made audible:

" Joseph, advise me. What should I do? "

" You were willing to take Professor Pludder," replied Smith evasively, but with a plain leaning to the side of mercy.

" You know very well that that was different," Cosmo returned irritably. " Pludder was not morally rotten. He was only mistaken. He had the fundamental scientific quality, and I'm sorry he threw himself away in his obstinacy. But this man——"

" Since he is *alone*," broke in Joseph Smith with a sudden illumination, " he could do no harm."

Cosmo Versál's expression instantly brightened.

" You are right! " he exclaimed. " By himself he can do nothing. I am sure there is no one aboard who would sympathize with his ideas. Alone, he is innocuous. Besides, he's insane, and I can't leave him to drown in that condition. And I must take the others, too. Let down a landing stage," he continued in a louder voice, addressing some members of the crew.

In a few minutes all four of the unfortunates, seeming more dead than alive, were helped into the Ark.

Amos Blank immediately precipitated himself upon Cosmo Versál, and, seizing him by the arm, tried to lead him apart, saying in his ear, as he glared round upon the faces of the throng which crowded every available space:

"Hist! Overboard with 'em! What's all this trash? Shovel 'em out! They'll want to get in with us; they'll queer the game!"

Then he turned furiously upon the persons nearest him, and began to push them toward the open gangway. At a signal from Cosmo Versál, two men seized him and pinioned his arms. At that his mood changed, and, wrenching himself loose, he once more ran to Cosmo, waving his bedraggled bundle, and shouting:

"A billion! Here's the certificates—gilt-edge! But," he continued, with a cunning leer, and suddenly thrusting the sodden papers into his pocket, "you'll make out the receipts first. I'll put in *five* billions to make it a sure go, if you won't let in another soul."

Cosmo shook off the man's grasp, and again calling the two members of the crew who had before pinioned his arms, told them to lead him away, at the same time saying to him:

"You go with these men into my room. I'll see you later."

Blank took it in the best part, and willingly accompanied his conductors, only stopping a moment to wink over his shoulder at Cosmo, and then he was led through the crowd, which regarded him with unconcealed astonishment, and in many cases with no small degree of fear. As soon as he was beyond earshot, Cosmo directed Joseph Smith to hurry ahead of the party and conduct them to a particular apartment, which he designated at the same time, saying to Smith:

"Turn the key on him as soon as he's inside."

Amos Blank, now an insane prisoner in Cosmo Versál's Ark, had been the greatest financial power in the world's metropolis, a man of iron nerve and the clearest of brains, who always kept his head and never uttered a foolish word. It was he who had stood over the flight of steps in the Municipal Building, coolly measuring with his eye the rise of the water, exposing the terrible error that sent such a wave of unreasoning joy through the hearts of the thousands of refugees crowded into the doomed edifice, and receiving blows and curses for making the truth known.

He had himself taken refuge there, after visiting

his office and filling his pockets with his most precious papers. How, by a marvelous stroke of fate, he became one of the four persons who alone escaped from New York after the downpour began is already known.

The other men taken from the boat were treated like rescued mariners snatched from a wreck at sea. Every attention was lavished upon them, and Cosmo Versál did not appear to regret, as far as they were concerned, that his ship's company had been so unexpectedly recruited.

CHAPTER XII

THE SUBMERGENCE OF THE OLD WORLD

WE now turn our attention for a time from the New World to the Old. What did the throng-ing populations of Europe, Africa, and Asia do when the signs of coming disaster chased one on another's heels, when the oceans began to burst their bonds, and when the windows of the firmament were opened?

The picture that can be drawn must necessarily be very fragmentary, because the number who escaped was small and the records that they left are few.

The savants of the older nations were, in general, quite as incredulous and as set in their opposition to Cosmo Versál's extraordinary outgivings as those of America. They decried his science and denounced his predictions as the work of a fool or a madman. The president of the Royal Astronomical Society of Great Britain proved to the satisfaction of most of his colleagues that a nebula could not possibly contain enough water to drown an asteroid, let alone the earth.

" The nebulæ," said this learned astronomer, amid the plaudits of his hearers, " are infinitely rarer in composition than the rarest gas left in the receiver of an exhausted air-pump. I would undertake to swallow from a wineglass the entire substance of any nebula that could enter the space between the earth and the sun, if it were condensed into the liquid state."

" It might be intoxicating," called out a facetious member.

" Will the chair permit me to point out," said another with great gravity, " that such a proceeding would be eminently rash, for the nebulous fluid might be highly poisonous." [" Hear! Hear!" and laughter.]

" What do you say of this strange darkness and these storms?" asked an earnest-looking man. (This meeting was held after the terrors of the *third sign* had occurred.)

" I say," replied the president, " that that is the affair of the Meteorological Society, and has nothing to do with astronomy. I dare say that they can account for it."

" And I dare say they can't," cried a voice.

" Hear! Hear!" " Who are you?" " Put him out!" " I dare say he's right!" " Cosmo Versál!" Everybody was talking at once.

" Will this gentleman identify himself?" asked the president. " Will he please explain his words?"

" That I will," said a tall man with long whiskers, rising at the rear end of the room. " I am pretty well known. I——"

" It's Jameson, the astrologer," cried a voice.
" What's *he* doing here? "

" Yes," said the whiskered man, " it's Jameson,
the astrologer, and he has come here to let you know
that Cosmo Versál was born under the sign Cancer,
the first of the watery triplicity, and that Berosus, the
Chaldean, declared——"

An uproar immediately ensued; half the members
were on their feet at once; there was a scuffle in the
back part of the room, and Jameson, the astrologer,
was hustled out, shouting at the top of his voice:

" Berosus, the Chaldean, predicted that the world
would be drowned when all the planets should assemble in the sign Cancer—*and where are they now?*
Blind and stupid dolts that you are—*where are they
now?* "

It was some time before order could be restored,
and a number of members disappeared, having followed Jameson, the astrologer, possibly through sympathy, or possibly with a desire to learn more about
the prediction of Berosus, the father of astrology.

When those who remained, and who constituted the
great majority of the membership, had quieted down,
the president remarked that the interruption which
they had just experienced was quite in line with all
the other proceedings of the disturbers of public tranquillity who, under the lead of a crazy American
charlatan, were trying to deceive the ignorant multitude. But they would find themselves seriously in

error if they imagined that their absurd ideas were going to be " taken over " in England.

" I dare say," he concluded, " that there is some *scheme* behind it all."

" Another American ' trust '! " cried a voice.

The proceedings were finally brought to an end, but not before a modest member had risen in his place and timidly remarked that there was one question that he would like to put to the chair—one thing that did not seem to have been made quite clear—" Where *were* the planets now? "

A volley of hoots, mingled with a few " hears! " constituted the only reply.

Scenes not altogether unlike this occurred in the other great learned societies—astronomical, meteorological, and geological. The official representatives of science were virtually unanimous in condemnation of Cosmo Versál, and in persistent assertion that nothing that had occurred was inexplicable by known laws. But in no instance did they make it clear to anybody precisely what were the laws that they invoked, or how it happened that Cosmo Versál had been able to predict so many strange things which everybody knew really had come to pass, such as the sudden storms and the great darkness.

We are still, it must not be forgotten, dealing with a time anterior to the rising of the sea.

The Paris Academy of Sciences voted that the subject was unworthy of serious investigation, and similar action was taken at Berlin, St. Petersburg, Vienna, and elsewhere.

But among the people at large universal alarm prevailed, and nothing was so eagerly read as the dispatches from New York, detailing the proceedings of Cosmo Versál, and describing the progress of his great levium ark. In England many procured copies of Cosmo's circulars, in which the proper methods to be pursued in the construction of arks were carefully set forth. Some set to work to build such vessels; but, following British methods of construction, they doubled the weight of everything, with the result that, if Cosmo had seen what they were about he would have told them that such arks would go to the bottom faster than to the top.

In Germany the balloon idea took full possession of the public mind. Germany had long before developed the greatest fleet of dirigible balloons in existence, preferring them to every other type of flying apparatus. It was reported that the Kaiser was of the opinion that if worst came to worst the best manner of meeting the emergency would be by the multiplication of dirigibles and the increase of their capacity.

The result was that a considerable number of wealthy Germans began the construction of such vessels. But when interviewed they denied that they were preparing for a flood. They said that they simply wished to enlarge and increase the number of their pleasure craft, after the example of the Kaiser. All this was in contemptuous defiance of the warning which Cosmo Versál had been careful to insert in his circulars, that " balloons and aeros of all kinds will be of no use whatever; the only safety will be found in arks, and they must be provisioned for at least five years."

The most remarkable thing of all happened in France. It might naturally have been expected that a Frenchman who thought it worth his while to take any precautions against the extinction of the human race would, when it became a question of a flood, have turned to the aero, for from the commencement of aerial navigation French engineers had maintained an unquestionable superiority in the construction and perfection of that kind of machine.

Their aeros could usually fly longer and carry more dead weight than those of any other nation. In the transoceanic aero races which occasionally took place the French furnished the most daring and the most frequently successful competitors.

But the French mind is masterly in appreciation of details, and Cosmo Versál's reasons for condemning the aero and the balloon as means of escaping the flood were promptly divined. In the first place it was seen that no kind of airship could be successfully provisioned for a flight of indefinite length, and in the second place the probable strength of the winds, or the crushing weight of the descending water, in case, as Cosmo predicted, a nebula should condense upon the earth, would either sweep an aero or a balloon to swift destruction, or carry it down into the waves like a water-soaked butterfly.

Accordingly, when a few Frenchmen began seriously to consider the question of providing a way of escape from the flood—always supposing, for the sake of argument, that there would be a flood—they got together, under the leadership of an engineer officer named Yves de Beauxchamps, and discussed the matter in all its aspects. They were not long in arriving at the conclusion that the best and most logical thing that could possibly be done would be to construct a *submarine.*

In fact, this was almost an inevitable conclusion for them, because before the abandonment of submarines in war on account of their *too* great powers of destruction—a circumstance which had also led to the prohibition of the use of explosive bombs in the aerial navies—the French had held the lead in the construction and management of submersible vessels, even more decisively than in the case of aeros.

"A large submarine," said De Beauxchamps, "into whose construction a certain amount of levium entered, would possess manifest advantages over Versál's Ark. It could be provisioned to any extent desired, it would escape the discomforts of the waves, winds, and flooding rain, and it could easily rise to the surface whenever that might be desirable for change of air. It would have all the amphibious advantages of a whale."

The others were decidedly of De Beauxchamps's opinion, and it was enthusiastically resolved that a vessel of this kind should be begun at once.

" If we don't need it for a flood," said De Beauxchamps, " we can employ it for a pleasure vessel to visit the wonders of the deep. We will then make a reality of that marvelous dream of our countryman of old, that prince of dreamers, Jules Verne."

" Let's name it for him! " cried one.

" Admirable! Charming! " they all exclaimed. *" Vive le ' Jules Verne '! "*

Within two days, but without the knowledge of the public, the keel of the submersible *Jules Verne* was laid. But we shall hear of that remarkable craft again.

While animated, and in some cases violent, discussions were taking place in the learned circles of Europe, and a few were making ready in such manner as they deemed most effective for possible contingencies, waves of panic swept over the remainder of the Old World. There were yet hundreds of millions in Africa and Asia to whom the advantages of scientific instruction had not extended, but who, while still more or less under the dominion of ignorance and superstition, were in touch with the *news* of the whole planet.

The rumor that a wise man in America had dis-

covered that the world was to be drowned was not
long in reaching the most remote recesses of the
African forests and of the boundless steppes of the
greater continent, and, however it might be ridiculed
or received with skeptical smiles in the strongholds of
civilization, it met with ready belief in less enlight-
ened minds.

Then, the three "signs"—the first great heat, the
onslaught of storm and lightning, and the *Noche
Triste,* the great darkness—had been world-wide in
their effects, and each had heightened the terror
caused by its predecessor. Moreover, in the less en-
lightened parts of the world the reassurances of the
astronomers and others did not penetrate at all, or, if
they did, had no effect, for not only does bad news
run while good news walks, but it talks faster.

It will be recalled that one of the most disquieting
incidents in America, immediately preceding the catas-
trophal rising of the oceans, was the melting of the
Arctic snows and ice-fields, with consequent inundations in the north. This stage in the progress of the
coming disaster was accentuated in Europe by the
existence of the vast glaciers of the Alps. The Rocky
Mountains, in their middle course, had relatively little
snow and almost no true glaciers, and consequently
there were no scenes of this kind in the United States
comparable with those that occurred in the heart of
Europe.

After the alarm caused by the great darkness in

September had died out, and the long spell of continuous clear skies began, the summer resorts of Switzerland were crowded as they had seldom been. People were driven there by the heat, for one thing; and then, owing to the early melting of the winter's deposit of snow, the Alps presented themselves in a new aspect.

Mountain-climbers found it easy to make ascents upon peaks which had always hitherto presented great difficulties on account of the vast snow-fields, seamed with dangerous crevasses, which hung upon their flanks. These were now so far removed that it was practicable for amateur climbers to go where always before only trained Alpinists, accompanied by the most experienced guides, dared to venture.

But as the autumn days ran on and new snows fell, the deep-seated glaciers began to dissolve, and masses of ice that had lain for untold centuries in the mighty laps of the mountains, projecting frozen noses into the valleys, came tumbling down, partly in the form of torrents of water and partly in roaring avalanches.

The great Aletsch glacier was turned into a river that swept down into the valley of the Rhône, carrying everything before it. The glaciers at the head of the Rhône added their contribution. The whole of the Bernese Oberland seemed to have suddenly been dissolved like a huge mass of sugar candy, and on the north the valley of Interlaken was inundated, while the lakes of Thun and Brientz were lost in an inland sea which rapidly spread over all the lower lands between the Alps and the Swiss Jura.

Farther east the Rhine, swollen by the continual descent of the glacier water, burst its banks, and broadened out until Strasburg lay under water with the finger of its ancient cathedral helplessly pointing skyward out of the midst of the flood. All the ancient cities of the great valley from Basle to Mayence saw their streets inundated and the foundations of their most precious architectural monuments undermined by the searching water.

The swollen river reared back at the narrow pass through the Taunus range, and formed a huge eddy that swirled over the old city of Bingen. Then it tore down between the castle-crowned heights, sweeping away the villages on the river banks from Bingen to Coblentz, lashing the projecting rocks of the Lorelei, and carrying off houses, churches, and old abbeys in a rush of ruin.

It widened out as it approached Bonn and Cologne, but the water was still deep enough to inundate those cities, and finally it spread over the plain of Holland, finding a score of new mouths through which to pour into the German Ocean, while the reclaimed area of the Zuyder Zee once more joined the ocean, and Amsterdam and the other cities of the Netherlands were buried, in many cases to the tops of the house doors.

West and south the situation was the same. The Mer de Glace at Chamonix, and all the other glaciers of the Mont Blanc range, disappeared, sending floods down to Geneva and over the Dauphiny and down into the plains of Piedmont and Lombardy. The ruin was tremendous and the loss of life incalculable. Geneva, Turin, Milan, and a hundred other cities, were swept by torrents.

The rapidity of this melting of the vast snow-beds and glaciers of the Alps was inconceivable, and the effect of the sudden denudation upon the mountains themselves was ghastly. Their seamed and cavernous sides stood forth, gaunt and naked, a revelation of Nature in her most fearful aspects such as men had never looked upon. Mont Blanc, without its blanket of snow and ice, towered like the blackened ruin of a fallen world, a sight that made the beholders shudder.

But this flood ended as suddenly as it had begun. When the age-long accumulations of snow had all melted the torrents ceased to pour down from the mountains, and immediately the courageous and industrious inhabitants of the Netherlands began to repair their broken dikes, while in Northern Italy and the plains of Southeastern France every effort was made to repair the terrible losses.

Of course similar scenes had been enacted, and on even a more fearful scale, in the plains of India, flooded by the melting of the enormous icy burden that covered the Himalayas, the "Abode of Snow." And all over the world, wherever icy mountains reared themselves above inhabited lands, the same story of destruction and death was told.

Then, after an interval, came the yet more awful invasion of the sea.

But few details can be given from lack of records. The Thames roared backward on its course, and London and all central England were inundated. A great bore of sea-water swept along the shores of the English Channel, and bursting through the Skager Rack, covered the lower end of Sweden, and rushed up the Gulf of Finland, burying St. Petersburg, and turning all Western Russia, and the plains of Pomerania into a sea. The Netherlands disappeared. The Atlantic poured through the narrow pass of the Strait of Gibraltar, leaving only the Lion Rock visible above the waves.

At length the ocean found its way into the Desert of Sahara, large areas of which had been reclaimed, and were inhabited by a considerable population of prosperous farmers. Nowhere did the sudden coming of the flood cause greater consternation than here —strange as that statement may seem. The people had an undefined idea that they were protected by a sort of barrier from any possible inundation.

It had taken so many years and such endless labor to introduce into the Sahara sufficient water to transform its potentially rich soil into arable land that the thought of any sudden superabundance of that element was far from the minds of the industrious agriculturists. They had heard of the inundations caused by the melting of the mountain snows elsewhere, but there were no snow-clad mountains near them to be feared.

Accordingly, when a great wave of water came rushing upon them, surmounted, where it swept over yet unredeemed areas of the desert, by immense clouds of whirling dust, that darkened the air and recalled the old days of the simoom, they were taken completely by surprise. But as the water rose higher they tried valiantly to escape. They were progressive people, and many of them had aeros. Besides, two or three lines of aero expresses crossed their country. All who could do so immediately embarked in airships, some fleeing toward Europe, and others hovering about, gazing in despair at the spreading waters beneath them.

As the invasion of the sea grew more and more serious, this flight by airship became a common spectacle over all the lower-lying parts of Europe, and in the British Isles. But, in the midst of it, the heavens opened their flood-gates, as they had done in the New World, and then the aeros, flooded with rain, and hurled about by contending blasts of wind, drooped, fluttered, and fell by hundreds into the fast mounting waves. The nebula was upon them!

In the meantime those who had provided arks of one kind or another, tried desperately to get them safely afloat. All the vessels that succeeded in leaving their wharves were packed with fugitives. Boats of every sort were pressed into use, and the few that survived were soon floating over the sites of the drowned homes of their occupants.

Before it was too late Yves de Beauxchamps and his friends launched their submarine, and plunged into the bosom of the flood.

CHAPTER XIII

STRANGE FREAKS OF THE NEBULA

WE return to follow the fortunes of Cosmo Versál's Ark.

After he had so providentially picked up the crazed billionaire, Amos Blank, and his three companions, Cosmo ordered Captain Arms to bear away southeastward, bidding farewell to the drowned shores of America, and sailing directly over the lower part of Manhattan, and western Long Island. The navigation was not easy, and if the Ark had not been a marvelously buoyant vessel it would not long have survived. At the beginning the heavy and continuous rain kept down the waves, and the surface of the sea was comparatively smooth, but after a while a curious phenomenon began to be noticed; immense billows would suddenly appear, rushing upon the Ark now from one direction and now from another, canting it over at a dangerous angle, and washing almost to the top of the huge ellipsoid of the dome. At such times it was difficult for anybody to maintain a footing, and there was great terror among the passengers. But Cosmo, and stout Captain Arms, remained at their post, relieving one another at frequent intervals, and never entrusting the sole charge of the vessel to any of their lieutenants.

Cosmo Versál himself was puzzled to account for the origin of the mighty billows, for it seemed impossible that they could be raised by the wind notwithstanding the fact that it blew at times with hurricane force. But at last the explanation came of itself.

Both Cosmo and the captain happened to be on the bridge together when they saw ahead something that looked like an enormous column as black as ink, standing upright on the surface of the water. A glance showed that it was in swift motion, and, more than that, was approaching in a direct line toward the Ark. In less than two minutes it was upon them.

The instant that it met the Ark a terrific roaring deafened them, and the rounded front of the dome beneath their eyes disappeared under a deluge of descending water so dense that the vision could not penetrate it. In another half minute the great vessel seemed to have been driven to the bottom of the sea. But for the peculiar construction of the shelter of the bridge its occupants would have been drowned at their posts. As it was they were soaked as if they had been plunged overboard. Impenetrable darkness surrounded them.

But the buoyant vessel shook itself, rolled from side to side, and rose with a staggering motion until it seemed to be poised on the summit of a watery mountain. Immediately the complete darkness passed, the awful downpour ceased, although the rain still fell in torrents, and the Ark began to glide downward with sickening velocity, as if it were sliding down a liquid slope.

It was a considerable time before the two men, clinging to the supports of the bridge, were able to maintain their equilibrium sufficiently to render it possible to utter a few connected words. As soon as he could speak with reasonable comfort Cosmo exclaimed:

"Now I see what it is that causes the billows, but it is a phenomenon that I should never have anticipated. It is all due to the nebula. Evidently there are irregularities of some kind in its constitution which cause the formation of almost solid masses of water in the atmosphere—suspended lakes, as it were —which then plunge down in a body as if a hundred thousand Niagaras were pouring together from the sky.

"These sudden accessions of water raise stupendous waves which sweep off in every direction, and that explains the billows that we have encountered."

"Well, this nebular navigation beats all my experience," said Captain Arms, wiping the water out of his eyes. "I was struck by a waterspout once in the Indian Ocean, and I thought that that capped the climax, but it was only a catspaw to this. Give me a clear offing and I don't care how much wind blows, but blow me if I want to get under any more lakes in the sky."

"We'll have to take whatever comes," returned Cosmo, "but I don't think there is much danger of running directly into many of these downpours as we did into this one. Now that we know what they are, we can, perhaps, detect them long enough in advance to steer out of their way. Anyhow, we've got a good vessel under our feet. Anything but an ark of levium would have gone under for good, and if I had not covered the vessel with the dome there would have been no chance for a soul in her."

As a matter of fact, the Ark did not encounter any more of the columns of descending water, but the frequent billows that were met showed that they were careering over the face of the swollen sea in every direction.

But there was another trouble of a different nature. The absence of sun and stars deprived them of the ordinary means of discovering their place. They could only make a rough guess as to the direction in which they were going. The gyrostatic compasses gave them considerable assistance, and they had perfect chronometers, but these latter could be of no use without celestial observations of some kind.

At length Cosmo devised a means of obtaining observations that were of sufficient value to partially serve their purpose. He found that while the disk of the sun was completely hidden in the watery sky, yet it was possible to determine its location by means of the varying intensity of the light.

Where the sun was a concentrated glow appeared, shading gradually off on all sides. With infinite pains Cosmo, assisted by the experience of the captain, succeeded in determining the center of the maximum illumination, and, assuming that to represent the true place of the sun, they got something in the nature of observations for altitude and azimuth, and Captain Arms even drew on his chart " Sumner lines " to determine the position of the Ark, although he smiled at the thought of their absurd inaccuracy. Still, it was the best they could do, and was better than nothing at all.

They kept a log going also, although, as the captain pointed out, it was not of much use to know how fast they were traveling, since they could not know the precise direction, within a whole point of the compass, or perhaps several points.

" Besides," he remarked, " what do we know of the currents? This is not the old Atlantic. If I could feel the Gulf Stream I'd know whereabouts I was, but these currents come from all directions, and a man might as well try to navigate in a tub of boiling water."

" But we can, at least, keep working eastward," said Cosmo. " My idea is first to make enough southing to get into the latitude of the Sahara Desert, and then run directly east, so as to cross Africa where there are no mountains, and where we shall be certain of having plenty of water under our keel.

"Then, having got somewhere in the neighborhood of Suez, we can steer down into the region of the Indian Ocean, and circle round south of the Himalayas. I want to keep an eye on those mountains, and stay around the place where they disappear, because that will be the first part of the earth to emerge from the flood and it is there that we shall ultimately make land."

"Well, we're averaging eight knots," said the captain, "and at that rate we ought to be in the longitude of the African coast in about twenty days. How high will the water stand then?"

"My gages show," replied Cosmo, "that the regular fall amounts to exactly the same thing as at the beginning—two inches a minute. Of course the spouts increase the amount locally, but I don't think that they add materially to the general rise of the flood. Two inches per minute means 4,800 feet in twenty days. That'll be sufficient to make safe navigation for us all the way across northern Africa. We'll have to be careful in getting out into the Indian Ocean area, for there are mountains on both sides that might give us trouble, but the higher ones will still be in sight, and they will serve to indicate the location of the lower ranges already submerged, but not covered deeply enough to afford safe going over them."

"All right," said Captain Arms, "you're the com-

modore, but if we don't hang our timbers on the
Mountains of the Moon, or the Alps, or old Ararat,
I'm a porpoise. Why can't you keep circling round
at a safe distance, in the middle of the Atlantic, until
all these reefs get a good depth of water on 'em? "

" Because," Cosmo replied, " even if we keep right
on now it will probably take two months, allowing
for delays in getting round dangerous places, to come
within sight of the Himalayas, and in two months
the flood will have risen nearly 15,000 feet, thus hid-
ing many of the landmarks. If we should hold off
here a couple of months before starting eastward
nothing but the one highest peak on the globe would
be left in sight by the time we arrived there, and that
wouldn't be anything more than a rock, so that with
the uncertainty of our navigation we might not be able
to find it at all. I must know the spot where Tibet
sinks, and then manage to keep in its neighborhood."

That ended the argument.

" Give me a safe port, with lights and bearings,
and I'll undertake to hit it anywhere in the two hemispheres, but blow me if I fancy steering for the top
of the world by dead reckoning, or no reckoning at
all," grumbled the captain.

At night, of course, they had not even the slight
advantage that their observations of the probable
place of the sun gave them when it was above the
horizon. Then they had to go solely by the indications of the compass. Still, they forged steadily

ahead, and when they got into what they deemed the proper latitude, they ran for the site of the drowned Sahara.

After about a week the billowing motion caused by the descent of the " lakes in the sky " ceased entirely, to their great delight, but the lawless nebula was now preparing another surprise for them.

On the ninth night after their departure from their lodgment on the Palisades Cosmo Versál was sleeping in his bunk close by the bridge, where he could be called in an instant, dreaming perhaps of the glories of the new world that was to emerge out of the deluge, when he was abruptly awakened by the voice of Captain Arms, who appeared to be laboring under uncontrollable excitement.

" Tumble up quicker'n you ever did in your life! " he exclaimed, his big brown beard wagging almost in Cosmo's face. " The flood's over! "

Cosmo sprang out of bed and pulled on his coat in a second.

" What do you mean? " he demanded.

" Look for yourself," said the captain, pointing overhead.

Cosmo Versál glanced up and saw the sky ablaze with stars! The rain had entirely ceased. The surface of the sea was almost as smooth as glass, though rising and falling slowly, with a long, rolling motion. The Ark rode steadily, shivering, like an ocean liner, under the impulse of its engines, and the sudden silence, succeeding the ceaseless roar of the downpour, which had never been out of their ears from the start of the voyage, seemed supernatural.

" When did this happen? " he demanded.

" It began not more than five minutes ago. I was just saying to myself that we ought to be somewhere near the center of the old Atlantic as it used to be, and wondering whether we had got our course laid right to go fairly between the Canaries and the Cape de Verdes, for I didn't want to be harpooned by Gogo or the Peak of Teneriffe, when all of a sudden there came a lightening in the nor'east and the stars broke out there.

" I was so set aback that I didn't do anything for two or three minutes but stare at the stars. Then the rain stopped and a curtain seemed to roll off the sky, and in a minute more it was clear down to the horizon all around. Then I got my wits together and ran to call you."

Cosmo glanced around and above, seeming to be as much astonished as the captain had been. He rubbed his huge bald dome and looked all round again before speaking. At last he said:

" It's the nebula again. There must be a hole in it."

" Its whole bottom's knocked out, I reckon," said the captain. " Maybe it's run out of water—sort o' squeezed itself dry."

Cosmo shook his head.

" We are not yet in the heart of it," he said. " It is evident to me now that what I took for the nucleus was only a close-coiled spiral, and we're run out of that, but the worst is yet to come. When we strike the center, then we'll catch it, and there'll be no more intermissions."

" How long will that be? " inquired Captain Arms.

" It may be a week, and it may be a month, though I hardly think it will be so long as that. The earth is going about twelve miles a second—that's more than a million miles a day—directly toward the center of the nebula. It has taken ten days to go through the spiral that we have encountered, making that about ten million miles thick. It's not likely that the gap between this spiral and the nucleus of the nebula is more than thirty million miles across, at the most; so you see we'll probably be in the nucleus within a month, and possibly much less than a month."

Captain Arms took a chew of tobacco.

" We can get our bearings now," he remarked. " Look, there's the moon just rising, and on my word, she is going to occult Aldebaran within an hour. I'll get an observation for longitude, and another on Polaris for latitude. No running on submerged mountains for us now."

The captain was as good as his word, and when his observations had been made and the calculations completed he announced that the position of the Ark was:

Latitude, 16 degrees 10 minutes north; longitude, 42 degrees 28 minutes west.

"Lucky for us," he exclaimed, "that the sky cleared. If we'd kept on as we were going we'd have struck the Cape de Verdes, and if that had happened at night we'd probably have left our bones on a drowning volcano. We ought to have been ten or twelve degrees farther north to make a safe passage over the Sahara. What's the course now? Are you still for running down the Himalaya mountains?"

"I'll decide later what to do," said Cosmo Versál. "Make your northing, and then we'll cruise around a little and see what's best to be done."

When day came on, brilliant with sunshine, and the astonished passengers, hurrrying out of their bunks, crowded about the now opened gangways and the portholes, which Cosmo had also ordered to be opened, and gazed with delight upon the smooth blue sea, the utmost enthusiasm took possession of them.

The flood was over!

They were sure of it, and they shook hands with one another and congratulated themselves and hur-rahed, and gave cheers for the Ark and cheers for Cosmo Versál. Then they began to think of their drowned homes and of their lost friends, and sadness followed joy. Cosmo was mobbed by eager inquiries wherever he made his appearance.

Was it all over for good? Would the flood dry up in a few days? How long would it be before New

York would be free of water? Were they going right back there? Did he think there was a chance that many had escaped in boats and ships? Couldn't they pick up the survivors if they hurried back?

Cosmo tried to check the enthusiasm.

"It's too early for rejoicing," he assured them. It's only a break in the nebula. We've got a respite for a short time, but there's worse coming. The drowning of the world will proceed. We are the only survivors, except perhaps some of those who inhabited the highlands. Everything less than 2,400 feet above the former level of the sea is now under water. When the flood begins again it will keep on until it is six miles deep over the old sea margins."

"Why not go back and try to rescue those who you say may have found safety on the highlands?" asked one.

"I have chosen my company," he said, "and I had good reasons for the choice I made. I have already added to the number, because simple humanity compelled me, but I can take no more. The quantity of provisions aboard the Ark is not greater than will be needed by ourselves. If the rest of the world is drowned it is not my fault. I did my best to warn them. Besides, we could do nothing in the way of rescue even if we should go back for that purpose. We could not approach the submerged plateaus. We would be aground before we got within sight of them."

These words went far to change the current of feeling among the passengers. When they learned that there would be danger for themselves in the course that had been proposed their humanity proved to be less strong than their desire for self-preservation. Nevertheless, as we shall see, the Ark ultimately went back to America, though not for any reason that had yet been suggested.

Meanwhile the unexpected respite furnished by the sudden cessation of the downpour from the sky had other important results, to which we now turn.

CHAPTER XIV

THE ESCAPE OF THE PRESIDENT

WHEN Professor Abiel Pludder indited his savage response to Cosmo Versál's invitation to become one of the regenerators of mankind by embarking in the Ark, he was expressing his professional prejudice rather than his intellectual conviction. As Cosmo had remarked, Pludder had a good brain and great scientific acuteness, and, although he did not believe in the nebular theory of a flood, and was obstinately opposed to everything that was not altogether regular and according to recognized authority in science, yet he could not shut his eyes to the fact that something was going wrong in the machinery of the heavens. But it annoyed him to find that his own explanations were always falsified by the event, while Cosmo Versál seemed to have a superhuman foreglimpse of whatever happened.

His pride would not allow him to recede from the position that he had taken, but he could not free himself from a certain anxiety about the future. After he had refused Cosmo Versál's invitation, the course of events strengthened this anxiety. He found that the official meteorologists were totally unable to account for the marvelous vagaries of the weather.

Finally, when the news came of tremendous floods in the north, and of the overflowing of Hudson Bay, he secretly determined to make some preparations of his own. He still rejected the idea of a watery nebula, but he began to think it possible that all the lowlands of the earth might be overflowed by the sea, and by the melting of mountain snows and glaciers, together with deluging rainfall. After what had passed, he could not think of making any public confession of his change of heart, but his sense of humanity compelled him to give confidential warning to his friends that it would be well to be prepared to get on high ground at a moment's notice.

He was on the point of issuing, but without his signature, an official statement cautioning the public against unprecedented inundations, when the first tidal wave arrived on the Atlantic coast and rendered any utterance of that kind unnecessary. People's eyes were opened, and now they would look out for themselves.

Pludder's private preparations amounted to no more than the securing of a large express aero, in which, if the necessity for suddenly leaving Washington should arise, he intended to take flight, together with President Samson, who was his personal friend, and a number of other close friends, with their families. He did not think that it would be necessary, in any event, to go farther than the mountains of Virginia.

The rising of the sea, mounting higher at each return, at length convinced him that the time had come to get away. Hundreds of air craft had already departed westward, not only from Washington, but from New York, Philadelphia, Baltimore, Boston, and other seaboard cities, before Professor Pludder assembled his friends by telephone on the Capitol grounds, where his aero was waiting.

The lower streets of the city were under water from the overflow of the Potomac, which was backed up by the influx of the Atlantic into Chesapeake Bay, and the most distressing scenes were enacted there, people fleeing in the utmost disorder toward higher ground, carrying their children and some of their household goods, and uttering doleful cries. Many, thinking that the best way to escape, embarked in frail boats on the river, which was running up-stream with frightful velocity, and rising perceptibly higher every second. Most of these boats were immediately overturned or swamped.

If the start had been delayed but a little longer, the aero would have been mobbed by the excited people, who uttered yells of disappointment and rage when they saw it rise from its tower and sail over the city. It was the last airship that left Washington, and it carried the last persons who escaped from the national capital before the downpour from the atmosphere began which put an end to all possibility of getting away.

There were on board, in addition to a crew of three, twenty-two persons. These included President Samson, with his wife and three children, seven other men with their families, making, together, sixteen persons, and Professor Pludder, who had no family.

More because they wished to escape from the painful scenes beneath them than because they deemed that there was any occasion for particular haste, they started off at high speed, and it was probably lucky for them that this speed was maintained after they had left Washington out of sight. They rapidly approached the Blue Ridge in the neighborhood of Luray, and Pludder was about to order a landing there as night was approaching, when with great suddenness the sky filled with dense clouds and a tremendous downpour began. This was the same phenomenon which has already been described as following closely the attack at New York on Cosmo Versál's Ark.

The aero, luckily, was one of the best type, and well covered, so that they were protected from the terrible force of the rain, but in the tumult there could be no more thought of descending. It would have been impossible to make a landing in the midst of the storm and the pouring water, which rushed in torrents down the mountainside. Professor Pludder was a brave man and full of resources when driven into a corner. Being familiar with the construction and management of aeros, for he had been educated as an engineer, he now took charge of the airship.

Within twenty minutes after the sky had opened its batteries—for the rain had almost the force of plunging shot—a mighty wind arose, and the aero, pitching, tossing, and dipping like a mad thing, was driven with frightful speed eastward. This wild rush continued for more than an hour. By this time it was full night, and the pouring rain around them was as impenetrable to the sight as a black wall.

They had their electric lamps inside, and their searchlights, but it was impossible to tell where they were. Pludder turned the searchlight downward, but he could not make out the features of the ground beneath them. It is likely that they were driven at least as far as Chesapeake Bay, and they may have passed directly over Washington.

At last, however, the wind slewed round, and began to blow with undiminished violence from the northeast. Plunging and swerving, and sometimes threatened with a complete somersault, the aero hurried away in its crazy flight, while its unfortunate inmates clung to one another, and held on by any object within reach, in the endeavor to keep from being dashed against the metallic walls.

The crew of the aero were picked men, but no experience could have prepared them for the work which they now had to do. Without the ready brain of Professor Pludder to direct their efforts, and without his personal exertions, their aerial ship would have been wrecked within a quarter of an hour after the storm struck it. He seemed transformed into another person. Hatless and coatless, and streaming with water, he worked like a demon. He was ready at each emergency with some device which, under his direction, had the effect of magic.

A hundred times the aero plunged for the ground, but was saved and turned upward again just as it seemed on the point of striking. Up and down, right and left, it ran and pitched and whirled, like a cork in a whirlpool. Sometimes it actually skimmed the ground, plowing its way through a torrent of rushing water, and yet it rose again and was saved from destruction.

This terrible contest lasted another hour after the turning of the wind, and then the latter died out. Relieved from its pressure, the aero ran on with comparative ease. Professor Pludder, suspecting that they might now be getting into a mountainous district, made every effort to keep the craft at a high elevation, and this, notwithstanding the depressing force of the rain, they succeeded in doing. After the dying out of the wind they kept on, by the aid of their propellers, in the same direction in which it had been driving them, because, in the circumstances, one way was as good as another.

The terrible discomfort of the President and his

companions in the cabin of the aero was greatly relieved by the cessation of the wind, but still they were in a most unfortunate state. The rain, driven by the fierce blasts, had penetrated through every crevice, and they were drenched to the skin. No one tried to speak, for it would have been almost impossible to make oneself heard amid the uproar. They simply looked at one another in dismay and prayed for safety.

Professor Pludder, not now compelled to spend every moment in the management of the craft, entered the cabin occasionally, pressed the hand of the President, smiled encouragingly on the women and children, and did all he could, in pantomime, to restore some degree of confidence. Inside, the lights were aglow, but outside it was as dark as pitch, except where the broad finger of the searchlight, plunging into the mass of tumbling water, glittered and flashed.

The awful night seemed endless, but at last a pale illumination appeared in the air, and they knew that day had come. The spectacle of the skyey deluge was now so terrible that it struck cold even to their already benumbed hearts. The atmosphere seemed to have been turned into a mighty cataract thundering down upon the whole face of the earth. Now that they could see as well as hear, the miracle of the preservation of the aero appeared incredible.

As the light slowly brightened, Professor Pludder, constantly on the outlook, caught a glimpse of a dark, misty object ahead. It loomed up so suddenly, and was already so close, that before he could sufficiently alter the course of the aero, it struck with such violence as to crush the forward end of the craft and break one of the aeroplanes. Everybody was pitched headforemost, those inside falling on the flooring, while Pludder and the three men of the crew were thrown out upon a mass of rocks. All were more or less seriously injured, but none was killed or totally disabled.

Pludder sprang to his feet, and, slipping and plunging amid the downpour, managed to get back to the wreck and aid the President and the others to get upon their feet.

" We're lodged on a mountain ! " he yelled. " Stay inside, under the shelter of the roof ! "

The three men who, together with the professor, had been precipitated out among the rocks, also scrambled in, and there they stood, or sat, the most disconsolate and despairing group of human beings that ever the eye of an overseeing Providence looked down upon.

The President presented the most pitiable sight of all. Like the rest, his garments were sopping, his eyes were bloodshot, his face was ghastly, and his tall silk hat, which he had jammed down upon his brow, had been softened by the water and crushed by repeated blows into the form of a closed accordion. Of the women and children it is needless to speak;

no description could convey an idea of their condition.

In these circumstances, the real strength of Professor Abiel Pludder's mind was splendidly displayed. He did not lose his head, and he comprehended the situation, and what it was necessary to do, in a flash. He got out some provisions and distributed them to the company, in some cases actually forcing them to eat. With his own hands he prepared coffee, with the apparatus always carried by express aeros, and made them drink it.

When all had thus been refreshed he approached President Samson and shouted in his ear:

" We shall have to stay here until the downpour ceases. To guard against the effects of a tempest, if one should arise, we must secure the aero in its place. For that I need the aid of every man in the party. We have, fortunately, struck in a spot on the mountain where we are out of the way of the torrents of water that are pouring down through the ravines on either side. We can make our lodgment secure, but we must go to work immediately."

Stimulated by his example, the President and the others set to work, and with great difficulty, for they had to guard their eyes and nostrils from the driving rain, which, sometimes, in spite of their precautions, nearly smothered them, they succeeded in fastening the aero to the rocks by means of metallic cables taken from its stores. When this work was finished they returned under the shelter of the cabin roof and lay down exhausted. So worn out were they that all of them quickly fell into a troubled sleep.

It would be needless to relate in detail the sufferings, mental and physical, that they underwent during the next ten days. While they were hanging there on the mountain the seaboard cities of the world were drowned, and Cosmo Versál's Ark departed on the remarkable voyage that has been described in a former chapter. They had plenty of provisions, for the aero had been well stored, but partly through precaution and partly because of lack of appetite they ate sparingly. The electric generators of the aero had not been injured in the wreck of the craft, and they were able to supply themselves with sufficient heat, and with light inside the cabin at night.

Once they had a strange visitor—a half-drowned bear, which had struggled up the mountain from its den somewhere below—but that was the only living creature beside themselves that they saw. After gazing wistfully at the aero from the top of a rock the poor bear, fighting the choking rain with its soaked paws, stumbled into one of the torrents that poured furiously down on each side, and was swept from their sight.

Fortunately, the wind that they had anticipated did not come, but frequently they saw or heard the roaring downpours of solid watery columns like those that had so much astonished Cosmo Versál and Captain

Arms in the midst of the Atlantic, but none came very near them.

Professor Pludder ventured out from time to time, clambering a little way up and down the projecting ridge of the mountain on which they were lodged, and at length was able to assure his companions that they were on the northwestern face of Mount Mitchell, the highest peak of the Appalachian range. With the aid of his pocket aneroid, making allowance for the effect of the lifting of the whole atmosphere by the flood, and summoning his knowledge of the locality—for he had explored, in former years, all the mountains in this region—he arrived at the conclusion that their place of refuge was elevated about four thousand feet above the former level of the sea.

At first their range of vision did not allow them to see the condition of the valleys below them, but as the water crept higher it gradually came into view. It rose steadily up the slopes beneath, which had already been stripped of their covering of trees and vegetation by the force of the descending torrents, until on the tenth day it had arrived almost within reach. Since, as has just been said, they were four thousand feet above the former level of the sea, it will be observed that the water must have been rising much more rapidly than the measurements of Cosmo Versál indicated. Its average rate of rise had been three instead of two inches per minute, and the world was buried deeper than Cosmo thought. The cause of his error will be explained later.

The consternation of the little party when they thus beheld the rapid drowning of the world below them, and saw no possibility of escape for themselves if the water continued to advance, as it evidently would do, cannot be depicted. Some of them were driven insane, and were with difficulty prevented by those who retained their senses from throwing themselves into the flood.

Pludder was the only one who maintained a command over his nerves, although he now at last *believed in the nebula*. He recognized that there was no other possible explanation of the flood than that which Cosmo Versál had offered long before it began. In his secret heart he had no expectation of ultimate escape, yet he was strong enough to continue to encourage his companions with hopes which he could not himself entertain.

When, after nightfall on the tenth day, the water began to lap the lower parts of the aero, he was on the point of persuading the party to clamber up the rocks in search of some shelter above, but as he stepped out of the door of the cabin to reconnoiter the way, with the aid of the searchlight which he had turned up along the ridge, he was astonished to find the rain rapidly diminishing in force; and a few minutes later it ceased entirely, and the stars shone out.

The sudden cessation of the roar upon the roof

brought everybody to their feet, and before Professor
Pludder could communicate the good news all were
out under the sky, rejoicing and offering thanks for
their deliverance. The women were especially affected. They wept in one another's arms, or con-
vulsively clasped their children to their breasts.

At length the President found his voice.

"What has happened?" he asked.

Professor Pludder, with the new light that had
come to him, was as ready with an explanation as
Cosmo Versál himself had been under similar circumstances.

"We must have run out of the nebula."

"The nebula!" returned Mr. Samson in surprise.
"Has there been a nebula, then?"

"Without question," was the professor's answer.
"Nothing but an encounter with a watery nebula
could have had such a result."

"But you always said——" began the President.

"Yes," Pludder broke in, "but one may be in
error sometimes."

"Then, Cosmo Versál——"

"Let us not discuss Cosmo Versál," exclaimed
Professor Pludder, with a return of his old dictatorial manner.

CHAPTER XV

PROFESSOR PLUDDER'S DEVICE

MORNING dawned brilliantly on Mount Mitchell and revealed to the astonished eyes of the
watchers an endless expanse of water, gleaming and
sparkling in the morning sunlight. It was a spectacle
at once beautiful and fearful, and calculated to make
their hearts sink with pity no less than with terror.
But for a time they were distracted from the awful
thoughts which such a sight must inspire by anxiety
concerning themselves. They could not drive away
the fear that, at any moment, the awful clouds might
return and the terrible downpour be resumed.

But Professor Pludder, whose comprehension of
the cause of the deluge was growing clearer the more
he thought about it, did not share the anxiety of the
President and the others.

" The brightness of the sky," he said, " shows that
there is no considerable quantity of condensing vapor
left in the atmosphere. If the earth has run out of
the nebula, that is likely to be the end of the thing.
If there is more of the nebulous matter in surrounding space we may miss it entirely, or, if not, a long
time would elapse before we came upon it.

"The gaps that exist in nebulæ are millions of miles across, and the earth would require days and weeks to go such distances, granting that it were traveling in the proper direction. I think it altogether probable that this nebula, which must be a small one as such things go, consists of a single mass, and that, having traversed it, we are done with it. We are out of our troubles."

"Well, hardly," said the President. "Here we are, prisoners on a mountain, with no way of getting down, the whole land beneath being turned into a sea. We can't stay here indefinitely. For how long a time are we provisioned?"

"We have compressed food enough to last this party a month," replied Professor Pludder; "that is to say, if we are sparing of it. For water we cannot lack, since this that surrounds us is not salt, and if it were we could manage to distil it. But, of course, when I said we were out of our troubles I meant only that there was no longer any danger of being swallowed up by the flood. It is true that we cannot think of remaining here. We must get off."

"But how? Where can we go?"

Professor Pludder thought a long time before he answered this question. Finally he said, measuring his words:

"The water is four thousand feet above the former level of the sea. There is no land sufficiently lofty to rise above it this side of the Colorado plateau."

" And how far is that? "

" Not less than eleven hundred miles in an air line."

The President shuddered.

" Then, all this vast country of ours from here to the feet of the Rocky Mountains is now under water thousands of feet deep! "

" There can be no doubt of it. The Atlantic Coast States, the Southern States, the Mississippi Valley, the region of the Great Lakes, and Canada are now a part of the Atlantic Ocean."

" And all the great cities—gone! Merciful Father! What a thought! "

The President mused for a time, and gradually a frown came upon his brow. He glanced at Professor Pludder with a singular look. Then his cheek reddened, and an angry expression came into his eyes. Suddenly he turned to the professor and said sternly:

" You said you did not wish to discuss Cosmo Versál. I should not think you would! Who predicted this deluge? Did *you?* "

" I——" began Professor Pludder, taken aback by the President's manner.

" Oh, yes," interrupted the President, " I know what you would say. You didn't predict it because you didn't see it coming. But *why* didn't you see it? What have we got observatories and scientific societies for if they can't *see* or *comprehend* anything? Didn't Cosmo Versál warn you? Didn't he tell you where to look, and what to look for? Didn't he show you his proofs?"

"We thought they were fallacious," stammered Professor Pludder.

"You *thought* they were fallacious—well, *were* they fallacious? Does this spectacle of a nation drowned look ' fallacious ' to you? Why didn't you study the matter until you understood it? Why did you issue officially, and with my ignorant sanction—may God forgive me for my blindness!— statement after statement, assuring the people that there was no danger—statements that were even abusive toward him who alone should have been heard?

"And yet, as now appears, you knew nothing about it. Millions upon millions have perished through your obstinate opposition to the truth. They might have saved themselves if they had been permitted to listen to the many times reiterated warnings of Cosmo Versál.

"Oh, if *I* had only listened to him, and issued a proclamation as he urged me to do! But I followed *your* advice—*you*, in whose learning and pretended science I put blind faith! *Abiel Pludder, I would not have upon my soul the weight that now rests on yours for all the wealth that the lost world carried down into its watery grave!*"

As the President ceased speaking he turned away and sank upon a rock, pressing his hands upon his throat to suppress the sobs that broke forth despite his efforts. His form shook like an aspen.

The others crowded around excitedly, some of the women in hysterics, and the men not knowing what to do or say. Professor Pludder, completely overwhelmed by the suddenness and violence of the attack, went off by himself and sat down with his head in his hands. After a while he arose and approached the President, who had not moved from his place on the rock.

" George," he said—they had known each other from boyhood—" I have made a terrible mistake. And yet I was not alone in it. The majority of my colleagues were of my opinion, as were all the learned societies of Europe. No such thing as a watery nebula has ever been known to science. It was inconceivable."

" Some of your colleagues did not think so," said the President, looking up.

" But they were not really convinced, and they were aware that they were flying in the face of all known laws."

" I am afraid," said the President dryly, " that science does not know all the laws of the universe yet."

" I repeat," resumed Professor Pludder, " that I made a fearful mistake. I have recognized the truth too late. I accept the awful burden of blame that rests upon me, and I now wish to do everything in my power to retrieve the consequences of my terrible error."

The President arose and grasped the professor's hand.

"Forgive me, Abiel," he said, with emotion, "if I have spoken too much in the manner of a judge pronouncing sentence. I was overwhelmed by the thought of the inconceivable calamity that has come upon us. I believe that you acted conscientiously and according to your best lights, and it is not for any mortal to judge you for an error thus committed. Let us think only of what *we* must do now."

"To that thought," responded Professor Pludder, returning the pressure of the President's hand, "I shall devote all my energy. If I can save only this little party I shall have done something in the way of atonement."

It was a deep humiliation for a man of Professor Pludder's proud and uncompromising nature to confess that he had committed an error more fearful in its consequences than had ever been laid at the door of a human being, but Cosmo Versál had rightly judged him when he assured Joseph Smith that Pludder was morally sound, and, in a scientific sense, had the root of the matter in him. When his mental vision was clear, and unclouded by prejudice, no one was more capable of high achievements.

He quickly proved his capacity now, as he had already proved it during the preceding adventures of the President's party. It was perfectly plain to him that their only chance was in getting to Colorado at the earliest possible moment. The eastern part of the continent was hopelessly buried, and even on the high plains of the Middle West the fury of the downpour might have spread universal disaster and destroyed nearly all the vegetation; but, in any event, it was there alone that the means of prolonging life could be sought.

With the problem squarely before his mind, he was not long in finding a solution. His first step was to make a thorough examination of the aero, with the hope that the damage that it had suffered might be reparable. He had all the tools that would be needed, as it was the custom for express aeros to carry a complete equipment for repairs; but unfortunately one of the planes of the aero was wrecked beyond the possibility of repair. He knew upon what delicate adjustments the safety of the modern airship depended, and he did not dare undertake a voyage with a lame craft.

Then the idea occurred to him of trying to escape by water. The aero was a machine of the very latest type, and made of levium, consequently it would float better than wood.

If the opposition of shipbuilders, incited and backed by selfish interests, had not prevented the employment of levium in marine construction, millions of lives might now have been saved; but, as we have before said, only a few experimental boats of levium had been made.

Moreover, like all aeros intended for long trips, this one had what was called a "boat-bottom," intended to enable it to remain afloat with its burden in case of an accidental fall into a large body of water. Pludder saw that this fact would enable him to turn the wreck into a raft.

It would only be necessary to reshape the craft a little, and this was the easier because the aero was put together in such a manner with screw-bolts and nuts that it could be articulated or disarticulated as readily as a watch. He had entire confidence in his engineering skill, and in the ability of the three experienced men of the crew to aid him. He decided to employ the planes for outriders, which would serve to increase the buoyancy and stability.

As soon as he had completed his plan in his mind he explained his intentions to the President. The latter and the other members of the party were at first as much startled as surprised by the idea of embarking on a voyage of eleven hundred miles in so questionable a craft, but Professor Pludder assured them that everything would go well.

"But how about the propulsion?" asked Mr. Samson. "You can't depend on the wind, and we've got no sails."

"I have thought that all out," said Pludder. "I shall use the engine, and rearrange one of the aerial screws so that it will serve for a propeller. I do not expect to get up any great speed, but if we can make only as much as two miles an hour we shall arrive on the borders of the Colorado upland, five thousand feet above sea, within about twenty-three days. We may be able to do better than that."

Nobody felt much confidence in this scheme except its inventor, but it appeared to be the only thing that could be done, and so they all fell to work, each aiding as best he could, and after four days of hard work the remarkable craft was ready for its adventurous voyage.

Professor Pludder had succeeded even better than he anticipated in transforming one of the aerial screws into a propeller. Its original situation was such that it naturally, as it were, fell into the proper place when the "hull" was partly submerged, and, the blades being made of concentric rows of small plates, there was no difficulty in reducing them to a manageable size. The position of the engine did not need to be be shifted at all.

The "outriders," made up of the discarded planes, promised to serve their purpose well, and the cabin remained for a comfortable "deck-house." A rudder had been contrived by an alteration of the one which had served for guiding the aero in its flights.

The water was close to their feet, and there was no great difficulty in pushing the affair off the rocks and getting it afloat. The women and children were

first put aboard, and then the men scrambled in, and
Pludder set the motors going. The improvised propeller churned and spluttered, but it did its work after
a fashion, and, under a blue sky, in dazzling sunshine,
with a soft southerly breeze fanning the strange sea
that spread around them, they soon saw the bared
rocks and deeply scored flanks of Mount Mitchell
receding behind them.

They were delighted to find that they were making,
at the very start, no less than three miles an hour.
Pludder clapped his hands and exclaimed:

" This is capital! In but little over two weeks we
shall be safe on the great plains. I have good hope
that many have survived there, and that we shall find
a plenty of everything needed. With the instruments
that were aboard the aero I can make observations to
determine our position, and I shall steer for the Pike's
Peak region."

When the party had become accustomed to their
situation, and had gained confidence in their craft
by observing how buoyantly it bore them, they became
almost cheerful in their demeanor. The children
gradually lost all fear, and, with the thoughtless joy
of childhood in the pleasures and wonders of the present moment, amused themselves in the cabin, and
about the deck, which had been surrounded with
guard lines made of wire cable.

The water was almost waveless, and, if no storm
should arise, there appeared to be no reason for

anxiety concerning the outcome of their adventure. But as they drove slowly on over the submerged range of the Great Smokies, and across the valleys of Eastern Tennessee, and then over the Cumberland range, and so out above the lowlands, they could not keep their thoughts from turning to what lay beneath that fearful ocean. And occasionally something floated to the surface that wrenched their heart-strings and caused them to avert their faces.

Professor Pludder kept them informed of their location. Now they were over central Tennessee; now Nashville lay more than three thousand feet beneath their keel; now they were crossing the valley of the Tennessee River; now the great Mississippi was under them, hidden deep beneath the universal flood; now they were over the highlands of southern Missouri; and now over those of Kansas.

" George," said Professor Pludder one day, addressing the President, with more emotion than was often to be detected in his voice, " would you like to know what is beneath us now? "

" What is it, Abiel? "

" Our boyhood home—Wichita."

The President bowed his head upon his hands and groaned.

" Yes," continued Professor Pludder musingly, " there it lies, three thousand feet deep. There is the Arkansas, along whose banks we used to play, with its golden waters now mingling feebly with the mighty flood that covers them. There is the school-house and the sandy road where we ran races barefoot in the hot summer dust. There is your father's house, and mine, and the homes of all our early friends— and where are *they?* Would to God that I had not been so blind!"

"But there was another not so blind," said the President, with something of the condemnatory manner of his former speech.

"I know it—I know it too well now," returned the professor. "But do not condemn me, George, for what I did not foresee and could not help."

"I am sorry," said the President sadly, "that you have awakened these old memories. But I do not condemn you, though I condemn your science—or your lack of science. But we can do nothing. Let us speak of it no more."

The weather was wonderful, considering what had so recently occurred. No clouds formed in the sky, there was only a gentle breeze stirring, at night the heavens glittered with starry gems, and by day the sun shone so hotly that awnings were spread over those whose duties required them to be employed outside the shelter of the cabin. The improvised propeller and rudder worked to admiration, and some days they made as much as eighty miles in the twenty-four hours.

At length, on the fourteenth day of their strange voyage, they caught sight of a curiously shaped "pike" that projected above the horizon far to the west. At the same time they saw, not far away toward the north and toward the south, a low line, like a sea-beach.

"We are getting into shallow water now," said Professor Pludder. "I have been following the course of the Arkansas in order to be sure of a sufficient depth, but now we must be very careful. We are close to the site of Las Animas, which is surrounded with land rising four thousand feet above sea-level. If we should get aground there would be no hope for us. That pike in the distance is Pike's Peak."

"And what is that long line of beach that stretches on the north and south?" asked the President.

"It is the topographic line of four thousand feet," replied the professor.

"And we shall encounter it ahead?"

"Yes, it makes a curve about Las Animas, and then the land lies at an average elevation of four thousand feet, until it takes another rise beyond Pueblo."

"But we cannot sail across this half-submerged area," said the President.

"There are depressions," Professor Pludder responded, "and I hope to be able to follow their traces until we reach land that still lies well above the water."

Near nightfall they got so close to the "beach"

that they could hear the surf, not a thundering sound, but a soft, rippling wash of the slight waves. The water about them was ruddy with thick sediment. Professor Pludder did not dare to venture farther in the coming darkness, and he dropped overboard two of the aero's grapples, which he had heavily weighted and attached to wire cables. They took the ground at a depth of only ten feet. There was no wind and no perceptible current, and so they rode all night at anchor off this strangest of coasts.

At daybreak they lifted their anchors, and went in search of the depressions of which the professor had spoken. So accurate was his topographic knowledge and so great his skill, that late in the afternoon they saw a tall chimney projecting above the water a little ahead.

" There's all that remains of Pueblo," said Professor Pludder.

They anchored again that night, and the next day, cautiously approaching a bluff that arose precipitously from the water, their hearts were gladdened by the sight of three men, standing on a bluff, excitedly beckoning to them, and shouting at the top of their voices.

CHAPTER XVI

MUTINY IN THE ARK

WE left Cosmo Versál and his arkful of the flower of mankind in the midst of what was formerly the Atlantic Ocean, but which had now expanded over so many millions of square miles that had once been the seats of vast empires that to an eye looking at it with a telescope from Mars it would have been unrecognizable.

All of eastern North America, all of South America to the feet of the Andes, all but the highest mountains of Europe, nearly all of Africa, except some of the highlands of the south, all of northern and southwestern Asia, as well as the peninsula of India, all of China and the adjacent lands and islands except the lofty peaks, the whole of Australia, and the archipelagoes of the Pacific, had become parts of the floor of a mighty ocean which rolled unbroken from pole to pole.

The Great Deep had resumed its ancient reign, and what was left of the habitable globe presented to view only far separated islands and the serrated tops of such ranges as the Alps, the Caucasus, the Himalayas, and the Andes. The astonished inhabitants of the ocean depths now swam over the ruins of great cities, and brushed with their fins the chiseled capitals of columns that had supported the proudest structures of human hands.

We have seen how the unexpected arrest of the flood had left Cosmo uncertain as to the course that he ought to pursue. But he did not long remain in doubt. He was sure that the downpour would be resumed after an interval which at the most could not exceed a few weeks, and he resolved to continue his way toward the future land of promise in Asia.

But he thought that he would have time to turn his prow in the direction of Europe, for he felt a great desire to know by actual inspection to what height the water had attained. He was certain that it could not be less than he had estimated—the indications of his rain-gage had been too unvarying to admit of doubt on that point—but he had no means of direct measurement since he could not sound the tremendous depths beneath the Ark.

After long meditation on the probable effects of the descending columns of water which he had seen, he concluded that they might have added more rapidly than he first supposed to the increase of the general level. Besides, he reflected that there was no proof that the general downpour might not have been greater over some parts of the earth than others. All these doubts could be dissipated if he could get a good look at some lofty mountain range, such as the

Sierra Nevada of Spain, or the Pyrenees, or, if he could venture within sight of them, the Alps.

So he said to Captain Arms:

" Steer for the coast of Europe."

The fine weather had produced a good effect upon the spirits of the company. Not only were the ports and the gangways all open, but Cosmo ordered the temporary rèmoval of rows of adjustable plates on the sides of the vessel, which transformed the broad outer gangways, running its whole length, into delightful promenade decks. There, in cozy chairs, and protected with rugs, the passengers sat, fanned by a refreshing breeze, and dazzled by the splendor of the ocean.

They recalled, by their appearance, a shipload of summer tourists bound for the wonders and pleasures of foreign parts. This likeness to a pleasure cruise was heightened by the constant attentions of the crew, under Cosmo's orders, who carried about refreshing drinks and lunches, and conducted themselves like regular ocean " stewards."

It seemed impossible to believe that the world had been drowned, and some almost persuaded themselves that the whole thing was a dream.

It must not be supposed that the thousand-odd persons who composed this remarkable ship's company were so hard-hearted, so selfish, so forgetful, so morally obtuse, that they never thought of the real horror of their situation, and of the awful calamity

that had overwhelmed so many millions of their fel-
low-creatures. They thought of all that only too seriously and in spite of themselves. The women especially were overwhelmed by it. But they did not
wish to dwell upon it, and Cosmo Versál did not wish
that they should.

At night he had musicians play in the grand saloon; he distributed books among the passengers from
a large library which he had selected; and at last he
had the stage set, and invited his friends, the players, to entertain the company.

But he would have no plays but those of Shakespeare.

There were, probably, not half a dozen persons in
the Ark who had ever seen representations of these
great dramas, and very few who had read them, so
that they had the advantage of complete novelty.

The play selected for the first representation was
the tragedy of " King Lear," a strange choice, it
would, at first sight, seem, but Cosmo Versál had a
deep knowledge of human nature. He knew that only
tragedy would be endured there, and that it must be
tragedy so profound and overmastering that it would
dominate the feelings of those who heard and beheld
it. It was the principle of immunizing therapeutics,
where poison paralyzes poison.

It came out as he anticipated. The audience, un-
used to such depth of dramatic passion, for the plays
to which they had been accustomed had been far from

the Shakespearian standard, was wholly absorbed in
the development of the tragedy. It was a complete
revelation to them, and they were carried out of themselves, and found in the sympathy awakened by this
heart-crushing spectacle of the acme of human woe an
unconscious solace for their own moral anguish.

Afterward Cosmo put upon the stage " Hamlet,"
and " Othello," and " Macbeth," and " Coriolanus,"
and " Julius Cæsar," but he avoided, for the present,
the less tragic dramas. And all of them, being new
to the hearers, produced an enormous effect.

On alternate nights he substituted music for the
drama, and, as this was confined to the most majestic
productions of the great masters of the past, many
of whose works, like those of Shakespeare, had long
been neglected if not forgotten, their power over the
spirits of the company was, perhaps, even more pronounced.

Cosmo Versál was already beginning the education
of his chosen band of race regenerators, while he
mused upon the wonders that the science of eugenics
would achieve after the world should have re-
emerged from the waters.

One of the most singular effects of the music was
that produced upon the insane billionaire, Amos
Blank. He had been confined in the room that Cosmo
had assigned to him, and was soothed, whenever
Cosmo could find time to visit him, with pretended
acquiescence in his crazed notion that the trip of the

Ark was part of a scheme to "corner" the resources of the world.

Cosmo persuaded him that the secret was unknown except to themselves, and that it was essential to success that he (Blank) should remain in retirement, and accordingly the latter expressed no desire to leave his place of imprisonment, which he regarded as the headquarters of the combination, passing hours in covering sheets of paper with columns of figures, which he fancied represented the future profits of the enterprise.

One night when a symphony of Beethoven was to be played, Cosmo led Amos Blank through the crowded saloon and placed him near the musicians. He resisted at first, and when he saw the crowd he drew back, exclaiming:

"What? Not overboard yet?"

But Cosmo soothed him with some whispered promise, and he took his seat, glancing covertly around him. Then the instruments struck up, and immediately fixed his attention. As the musical theme developed his eyes gradually lost their wild look, and a softened expression took its place. He sank lower in his seat, and rested his head upon his hand. His whole soul seemed, at last, to be absorbed in the music. When it was finished Blank was a changed man.

Then Cosmo clearly explained to him all that had happened.

After the first overwhelming effect of his reawakening to the realities of his situation had passed, the billionaire was fully restored to all his faculties. Henceforth he mingled with the other passengers and, as if the change that had come over his spirit had had greater results than the simple restoration of sanity, he became one of the most popular and useful members of Cosmo Versál's family of pilgrims.

Among the other intellectual diversions which Cosmo provided was something quite unique, due to his own mental bias. This consisted of "conferences," held in the grand saloon, afternoons, in the presence of the entire company, at which the principal speakers were his two "speculative geniuses," Costaké Theriade and Sir Wilfrid Athelstone. They did not care very much for one another and each thought that the time allotted to the other was wasted.

Theriade wished to talk continuously of the infinite energy stored up in the atoms of matter, and of the illimitable power which the release of that energy, by the system that he had all but completed, would place at the disposition of man; and at the same time Sir Athelstone could with difficulty be held in leash while he impatiently awaited an opportunity to explain how excessively near he had arrived to the direct production of protoplasm from inanimate matter, and the chemical control of living cells, so that henceforth man could people or unpeople the earth as he liked.

One evening, when everybody not on duty was in

bed, Captain Arms, with his whiskers fairly bristling, entered Cosmo's cabin, where the latter was dictating to Joseph Smith, and softly approaching his chief, with a furtive glance round the room, stooped and whispered something in his ear. A startled, though incredulous, expression appeared on Cosmo's face, and he sprang to his feet, but before speaking he obeyed a sign from the captain and told Smith to leave the room. Then he locked the door and returned to his table, where he dropped into a chair, exclaiming in a guarded voice:

"Great Heaven, can this be possible! Have you not make a mistake?"

"No," returned the captain in a stridulous whisper, "I have made no mistake. I'm absolutely sure. If something is not done instantly we are lost!"

"This is terrible!" returned Cosmo, taking his head in his hands. "You say it is that fellow Campo? I never liked his looks."

"He is the ringleader," replied the captain. "The first suspicion of what he was up to came to me through an old sailor who has been with me on many a voyage. He overheard Campo talking with another man and he listened. Trust an old sea dog to use his ears and keep himself out of notice."

"And what did they say?"

"Enough to freeze the marrow in your bones! Campo proposed to begin by throwing 'old Versál' and me into the sea, and then he said, with us gone, and nobody but a lot of muddle-headed scientists to deal with, it would be easy to take the ship; seize all the treasure in her; make everybody who would not join the mutiny walk the plank, except the women, and steer for some place where they could land and lead a jolly life.

"'You see,' says Campo, 'this flood is a fake. There ain't going to be no more flood; it's only a shore wash. But there's been enough of it to fix things all right for us. We've got the world in our fist! There's millions of money aboard this ship, and there's plenty of female beauty, and we've only got to reach out and take it.'"

Cosmo Versál's brow darkened as he listened, and a look that would have cowed the mutineers if they could have seen it came into his eyes. His hand nervously clutched a paper-knife which broke in his grasp, as he said in a voice trembling with passion:

"They don't *know* me—*you* don't know me. Show me the proofs of this conspiracy. Who are the others? Campo and his friend can't be alone."

"Alone!" exclaimed the captain, unconsciously raising his voice. "There's a dozen as black-handed rascals in it as ever went unswung."

"Do you know them?"

"Jim Waters does."

"Why haven't you told me sooner? How long has it been going on?"

"Almost ever since the deluge stopped, I think;

but it was only last night that Waters got on the track of it, and only now that he told me. This fellow that Waters heard Campo talking to is plainly a new recruit. I say there are a dozen, because Waters has found out that number; but I don't know but that there may be a hundred."

"How did these wretches get aboard?" demanded Cosmo, fiercely opening and shutting his fists.

"Excuse me," said the captain, "but that is up to you to say."

"So it is," replied Cosmo, with a grim look; "and it's 'up to me' to say what'll become of them. I see how it is, they must have got in with the last lot that I took—under assumed names, very likely. I've been more than once on the point of calling that man Campo up and questioning him. I was surprised by his hangdog look the first time I saw him. But I have been so busy."

"You'll have to get busy in another sense if you mean to save this ship and your life," said the captain earnestly.

"So I shall. Are you armed? No? Then take these—and use 'em when I give the word."

He handed the captain two heavy automatic pistols, and put a pair in his own side pockets.

"Now," he continued, "the first thing is to make sure that we've got the right men—and *all of them*. Call in Joseph Smith."

The captain went to the door, and as he approached

it there was a knock. He turned the key and cautiously opened a crack to look out. The door was instantly slammed in his face, and six men rushed in, with Campo, a burly, black-browed fellow, at their head. Three of the men threw the captain on his back, and pinioned his hands before he could draw a weapon, while Campo and the others sprang toward Cosmo Versál, Campo pointing a pistol at his head.

"It's all up, Mr. Versál!" cried Campo with a sneer. "I'll take command of this ship, and you'll go fish for nebulas."

Cosmo had one advantage; he was behind his desk, and it was a broad and long one, and placed almost against the wall. They could not get at him without getting round the desk. Campo did not fire, though he might have shot Cosmo in his tracks; but evidently he was nourishing the idea of making him walk the plank. With a sign he commanded his co-conspirators to flank the desk at each end, while he kept Cosmo covered with his pistol.

But with a lightning movement, Cosmo dropped under the desk, and, favored by his slight form and his extreme agility, darted like a cat past Campo's legs, and, almost before the latter could turn round, was out of the open door. Campo fired at the retreating form, but the bullet went wide of the mark. The pistol was practically noiseless, and the sound reached no ears in the staterooms.

It happened that a switch controlling the lights in

the gangway was on the wall by Cosmo's door, and in passing he swiftly reached up and turned it off. Thus he was in complete darkness, and when Campo darted out of the door he could not see the fugitive. He could hear his footsteps, however, and with two of his companions he rushed blindly after him, firing two or three shots at random. But Cosmo had turned at the first cross passage, and then at the next, this part of the Ark being a labyrinth of corridors, and the pursuers quickly lost all trace of him.

Campo and his companions made their way back to Cosmo's cabin, where their fellows were guarding Captain Arms. They found the switch in the passage and turned on the light. They were almost immediately joined by several other conspirators conducting Joseph Smith, bound and gagged. They held a short consultation, and Campo, with many curses, declared that Cosmo Versál must be caught at all hazards.

"The big-headed fiend!" he cried, gnashing his teeth. "Let me get my grippers on him and I'll squelch him like a bug!"

They threw Joseph Smith into the room beside the helpless captain, after taking the latter's pistols, locked the door from the outside, and hurried off on their search. In the passages they encountered several more of their friends. They now numbered fifteen, all armed. This may seem a small number to undertake to capture the Ark; but it must be remembered that among the thousand-odd inmates, exclusive of the crew, only about one in three was a man, and the majority of these were peaceable scientists who, it was to be presumed, had no fight in them.

At any rate, Campo, with the reckless courage of his kind, felt confident that if he could get Cosmo Versál, with the captain and Joseph Smith, out of the way, he could easily overmaster the others. He had not much fear of the crew, for he knew that they were not armed, and he had succeeded in winning over three of their number, the only ones he had thought at all dangerous, because he had read their character. More than half the crew were employed about the engines or on the animal deck, and most of the others were simply stewards who would not stand before the pistols.

But, while the mutineers were hurriedly searching the corridors, Cosmo had run straight to the bridge, where he found two of his men in charge, and whence he sent an electric call to all the men employed in the navigation of the vessel. They came running from various directions, but a dozen of them were caught in the passages by the mutineers and bound before they could comprehend what had happened. Seven, however, succeeded in reaching the bridge, and among these was Jim Waters.

" There's a mutiny," said Cosmo. " We've got to fight for our lives. Have you got arms? "

Not one had a weapon except Waters, who displayed a pistol half as long as his arm.

"Here, Peterson, take this," said Cosmo, handing a pistol to one of the two mariners who had been on the bridge. "They will be here in a minute. If Campo had been a sailor, he'd have had possession here the first thing. I'll turn off all lights."

With that he pressed a button which put out every lamp in the ark. But there was a full moon, and they concealed themselves in the shadows.

Presently they heard the mutineers approaching, stumbling and cursing in the darkness. Cosmo directed Peterson and Waters to place themselves at his side, and told them to fire when he gave the word.

The next instant four men appeared crossing a moonlit place at the foot of the steps on the outside of the dome.

"Wait," whispered Cosmo. "The pistols go at a pull. We can sweep down a dozen in ten seconds. Let them all get in sight first."

Half a minute later there were twelve men climbing the steps and cautiously looking up.

"Fire!" cried Cosmo, setting the example, and three streams of blue flame pulsated from the bridge. The sound of the bullets striking made more noise than the explosions.

Five or six of the men below fell, knocking down their comrades, and a loud curse burst from the lips of Campo, who had a bullet through his arm.

The mutineers tumbled in a heap at the bottom, and instantly Cosmo, switching on all lights, led the way down upon them. His men, who had no arms, seized anything they could get their hands on that would serve to strike a blow, and followed him.

The conspirators were overwhelmed by the suddenness and fury of the attack.

Four of them were killed outright and five were wounded, one so severely that he survived only a few hours.

Cosmo's quick and overwhelming victory was due to the fact that the mutineers, in mounting the steps, could not see him and his men in the shadows, and when the automatic weapons, which fired three shots per second by repeated pressure of the trigger, from a chamber containing twenty-one cartridges, once opened on them they could do nothing in the hail of missiles, especially when crowded together on the steps.

Campo was the only one who had any fight left in him. He struck Cosmo a blow on the head that felled him, and then darted out upon the forepart of the dome, running on the cleats, and made his way to the top.

Cosmo was on his feet in a second and rushing in pursuit, closely followed by Jim Waters. The fugitive ran for the ratlines leading to the lookout on the central mast. He climbed them like a squirrel, and the man in the cro'nest, amazed at the sight below him, stared at the approaching mutineer, unable to utter a cry. Campo, who, as the moonbeams showed, now had a knife in his teeth, rapidly approached, and the lookout shrank in terror. But before Campo could reach the cro'nest, a blinding light dazzled his eyes. Cosmo had shouted an order to Peterson to run back to the bridge and turn a searchlight upon the mast. Then Campo heard a thundering voice below him:

" Take another step and I'll blow you into the sea! "

He glanced below, and saw Cosmo and Waters covering him with their pistols.

" Not another step! " roared Cosmo again. " Come down, and I'll give you a trial for your life."

Campo hesitated; but, seeing that he could be shot down, and finding a gleam of hope in Cosmo's words, he turned and came slowly down. The moment he touched the bottom he was seized by Waters and another man, and, under Cosmo's directions, his hands were bound behind his back.

Ten minutes later the members of the crew who had been caught by the mutineers in the gangways were all unbound, and then Cosmo broke open the door of his cabin, the key having been lost or thrown away by Campo, and the captain and Joseph Smith were released.

" Well, we've got 'em," said Cosmo grimly to the captain. " The mutiny is at an end, and there'll never be another."

In the meantime many of the passengers had been

aroused by the unaccustomed noises, although the pistols had not made enough sound to be heard from the place where they were fired. Nightcapped heads appeared on all sides, and some, in scanty clothing, were wandering in the passageways, demanding what the trouble was. Cosmo, the captain, and Joseph Smith reassured them, saying that there was no danger, and that something had happened which would be explained in the morning.

The prisoners—and the whole fifteen were finally captured—were locked up in a strong room, and a surgeon was sent to dress their wounds. Cosmo Versál and the captain resumed their accustomed places on the bridge, where they talked over the affair, and Cosmo explained his plans for the morrow.

"I'll give him his trial, as I promised," Cosmo said in conclusion, "and you'll see what it will be. *Mutiny aboard this Ark!*" And he struck the rail a violent blow with his fist.

The next morning directly after breakfast Cosmo called all passengers and crew into the grand saloon, where many wondering looks were exchanged and many puzzling questions asked. When the mutineers, with hands tied behind their backs and their many bandages on arms and legs, were led in, exclamations of astonishment were heard, and some of the timid ones shrank away in fear.

Cosmo lost no time with preliminaries.

"These men," he said, taking his stand upon the

platform, "have mutinied and tried to capture the Ark. This fellow "—pointing to Campo—" was the concocter and leader of the plot. He intended to throw me and Captain Arms, and all of you whom he did not wish to retain for his fiendish purposes, into the sea. But Heaven has delivered them into our hands. I have promised them a trial, and they shall have it. But it will be a trial in which justice shall not be cheated. I find that a moral poison has stolen into this selected company, and I will eliminate it for once and all."

The expressions of amazement and alarm redoubled in intensity.

" Professor Abel Able, Professor Jeremiah Moses, Sir Wilfrid Athelstone, Costaké Theriade," Cosmo continued, " you will please come forward to act as members of the jury, of which I name myself also a member. I shall be both judge and juror here, but I will hear what the rest of you may have to say."

The men named stepped forward with some evidences of embarrassment, and Cosmo gravely gave them seats beside him. Then he commanded that the prisoners should confront the jury, and, heavily guarded, they were led to the front.

The brutishness of Campo's face had never struck the passengers who had seen him before as it did now. He looked a veritable jailbird. At the same time he was evidently in terror for his life. He muttered something which nobody understood.

Cosmo, who had informed himself of all the circumstances from Waters, and by privately questioning the others, had satisfied himself that the entire scheme of the mutiny was of Campo's contrivance, and that they had been led into it solely by his persuasion and threats, ordered Waters to speak. The seaman told a straight story of what he had heard and seen. Cosmo himself then related the events of the night. When he had finished he turned to Campo and demanded what he had to say.

Campo again muttered under his breath, but made no attempt to defend himself, simply saying:

" You promised me a trial."

" And haven't I given you a trial? " demanded Cosmo with flashing eyes. " You thought you held the world in your grasp. It is *I* that hold it in *my* grasp, and *you,* too! You were going to make us ' walk the plank.' It is *you* who are going to walk it! Is that the verdict? " (turning to the four jurymen).

Some of them nodded, some simply stared at Cosmo, surprised by the vehemence of his manner.

" Enough," he said. " As to you," addressing the other prisoners, " you have had your lesson; see that you don't forget it! Release them, and lead Campo to the promenade deck."

Nobody thought that Cosmo would literally execute his threat to make the mutineer walk the plank, but, as he had told Captain Arms, they didn't know him. They were about to see that in Cosmo Versál they had not only a prophet, a leader, and a judge, but an inexorable master also.

A plank was prepared and placed sloping from the rail.

" Walk! " said Cosmo firmly.

To everybody's surprise Campo, with blinded eyes, started immediately up the plank, followed its full length with quick, unfaltering step, and plunging from the end, disappeared in the sea.

Many had turned away, unable to look, but many also saw the tragedy to the end. Then a profound sigh was heard from the whole company of the spectators. As they turned away, talking in awed voices, they felt, as never before, that the world had shrunk to the dimensions of the Ark, and that Cosmo Versál was its dictator.

That same afternoon Cosmo arranged one of his " conferences," and nobody dared to be absent, although all minds were yet too much excited to follow the discussions which few could understand. But at length Costaké Theriade concentrated their attention by a wild burst of eloquence about the wonders of the inter-atomic forces. Sir Athelstone, unable to endure the applause that greeted his rival, abruptly sprang to his feet, his round face red with anger, and shouted:

" I say, you know, this is twaddle! "

" Will the Englishman interrupt not? " cried

Theriade, with his eyes ablaze. " Shall I project not
the Sir Englishman to the feeshes? "

He looked as if he were about to try to execute his
threat, and Sir Athelstone assumed a boxing attitude;
but before hostilities could begin a loud shout from
the deck, followed by cries and exclamations, caused
everybody to rush out of the saloon.

Those who succeeded in getting a glimpse over the
shoulders of the members of the crew, who were already lined up along the only portion of the bulwarks
available for seeing the part of the ocean on which
attention seemed to be fixed, stared open-mouthed at
a round-backed mass of shining metal, with a circular aperture on the top, the cover of which was
canted to one side, and there stood a man, waving
a gold-laced red kepi, and bowing and smiling with
great civility.

CHAPTER XVII

THE *JULES VERNE*

THE swell of the sea caused the strange-looking craft to rise and sink a little, and sometimes the water ran bubbling all around the low rim of the aperture, in the center of which the red-capped man stood, resting on some invisible support, repeating his salutations and amicable smiles, and balancing his body to the rocking of the waves with the unconscious skill of a sailor.

The Ark was running slowly, but it would very soon have left the stranger in its wake if he had not also been in motion. It was evident that the object under his feet must be a submersible vessel of some kind, although it was of a type which Captain Arms, standing beside Cosmo on the bridge, declared that he had never set eyes on before. It lay so low in the water that nothing could be seen of its motive machinery, but it kept its place alongside the Ark with the ease of a dolphin, and gradually edged in closer and closer.

When it was so near that he could be heard speaking in a voice hardly raised above the ordinary pitch, the man, first again lifting his cap with an easy gesture, addressed Cosmo Versál by name, using the English language with a scarcely perceptible accent:

" M. Versál, I offer you my felicitations upon the magnificent appearance of your Ark, and I present my compliments to the ladies and gentlemen of your company."

And then he bowed once more to the passengers, who were almost crowding each other over the side in their eagerness to both see and hear.

" Thank you," responded Cosmo, " but who are you?"

" Capitaine Yves de Beauxchamps, of the French army."

" Where's the navy, then?" blurted out Captain Arms.

De Beauxchamps glanced at the speaker a little disdainfully, and then replied gravely:

" Alas! At the bottom of the sea—with all the other navies."

" And how have you escaped?" demanded Cosmo Versál.

" As you see, in a submersible."

" Can it be possible!" exclaimed Cosmo. " And you have been in the sea ever since the beginning of the flood?"

" Since the first rise of the ocean on the coast at Brest."

" Have you no companions?"

" Six—in truth, seven."

"Astonishing!" said Cosmo Versál. "But I heard nothing of the preparation of a submersible. In fact, the idea of such a thing never occurred to me. You must have made your preparations secretly."

"We did. We did not share your certainty, M. Versál, concerning the arrival of a deluge. Even when we embarked we were not sure that it would be more than an affair of the coasts."

"But you must be on the point of starvation by this time. The flood has only begun. This cessation is but for a time, while we are passing a gap in the nebula. You will come aboard the Ark. I had chosen my company, but your gallant escape, and the ability that you have shown, prove that you are worthy to aid in the re-establishment of the race, and I have no doubt that your companions are equally worthy."

The Frenchman bowed politely, and with a slight smile replied:

"I believe, M. Versál, that the *Jules Verne* is as safe and comfortable, and proportionately as well provisioned, as your Ark."

"So you call it the *Jules Verne?*" returned Cosmo, smiling in his turn.

"We were proud to give it that name, and its conduct has proved that it is worthy of it."

"But you will surely come aboard and shake hands, and let us offer you a little hospitality," said Cosmo.

"I should be extremely happy to pay my compliments to the ladies," responded De Beauxchamps, "but I must postpone that pleasure for the present. In the meantime, however, I should be glad if you would lower a landing stage, and permit me to send aboard the seventh member of our party, who, I venture to think, may find the Ark a more comfortable abode than our submersible."

"And who may that person be?"

"*The King of England.*"

Exclamations of surprise and wonder were heard on all sides.

"Yes," resumed the Frenchman, "we picked up his majesty the first day after the deluge began to descend from the sky."

"I will lower a ladder at once," Cosmo called out, and immediately ran down to the lowest deck, commanding his men to make haste.

The *Jules Verne* was skillfully brought close up to the side of the Ark, so that the visible part of her rounded back was nearly in contact with the bottom of the companion-ladder when it had been lowered. The sea was so calm that there was little difficulty in executing this maneuver. De Beauxchamps disappeared in the depths of the submersible, and after a few minutes re-emerged into sight, supporting on his arm a stout, rather short man, whose face, it was evident, had once been full and ruddy, but now it was pale and worn.

"It is he!" exclaimed an English member of Cosmo's company to some of his fellow-countrymen who had forced their way to the front.

"*It is the king!*"

And then occurred a singular thing, inspired by the marvelous circumstances of this meeting of the sovereign of a drowned kingdom, upon the bosom of the waters that had destroyed it, with the mere handful which remained alive out of all the millions of his subjects.

These loyal Englishmen bared their heads (and there were three women among them) and sang, with a pathos that surely the old hymn had never expressed before, their national anthem: "God Save the King."

The effect was immense. Every head aboard the Ark was immediately uncovered. De Beauxchamps removed his cap, and one or two bared heads could be seen peering out of the interior of the submersible below him. As the king was steadied across to the bottom of the companion-ladder, the voices of the singers rose louder, and many of the other passengers, moved by sympathy, or carried away by epidemic feeling, joined in the singing. Never had any monarch a greeting like that! Its recipient was moved to the depths of his soul, and but for the aid given him would have been unable to ascend the swaying steps.

As he was assisted upon the deck, the song ceased

and a great cheer broke forth. There were tears in his eyes, and he trembled in every limb, when he returned the welcoming pressure of Cosmo Versál's hand.

The moment he saw that the king was safely aboard the Ark, De Beauxchamps, with a farewell salutation, disappeared into the interior of the *Jules Verne,* and the submersible sank out of sight as gently as if it had been a huge fish that had come to the top of the sea to take a look about.

After the sensation caused by the arrival of the English monarch aboard the Ark had somewhat quieted down, and after his majesty had had an opportunity to recover himself, Cosmo Versál invited his new guest to tell the story of his escape. They were seated in Cosmo's cabin, and there were present Joseph Smith, Professor Jeremiah Moses, Professor Abel Able, and Amos Blank, beside several other members of the ship's company, including two of the loyal Englishmen who quite naturally had been the first to strike up the national anthem on seeing their rescued king.

Richard Edward, or Richard IV as he was officially entitled, was one of the best kings England ever had. He was popular not only because of his almost democratic manners and the simplicity of his life, but more because he was a great lover of peace. We have already seen how he was chosen, solely on that account, to be of the number of the rulers invited to go in the Ark. He had not even replied to Cosmo's invitation, but that was simply because, like everybody about him in whom he placed confidence, he regarded Cosmo Versál as a mere mountebank, and thought that there was no more danger of a flood that would cover the earth than of the fall of the moon out of the sky.

Before responding to Cosmo's request he made a gracious reference to the indifference with which he had formerly treated his present host.

" I am sorry, Mr. Versál," he said, with a deprecatory smile, " that I did not sooner recognize the fact that your knowledge surpassed that of my scientific advisers."

" Your majesty was not alone," replied Cosmo gravely, turning with his finger a small globe that stood on his desk. " From all these deep-sunken continents " (waving his hand toward the globe), "if the voices once heard there could now speak, there would arise a mighty sound of lament for that great error."

The king looked at him with an expression of surprise. He glanced from Cosmo's diminutive figure to his great overhanging brow, marked with the lines of thought, and a look of instinctive deference came into his eyes.

" But," continued Cosmo Versál, " it is bootless to speak of these things now. I beg that your majesty will condescend to enlighten us concerning the fate of that great kingdom, of ancient renown, over which you so worthily reigned."

An expression of deepest pain passed across the face of Richard Edward. For some moments he remained buried in a mournful silence, and many sighs came from his breast. All looked at him with profound commiseration. At last he raised his head, and said, sorrowfully and brokenly:

" My kingdom is drowned—my subjects have perished, almost to the last soul—my family, my gracious consort, my children—all, all—gone! "

Here he broke down, and could speak no more. Not a word was heard, for a time in the room, and the two Englishmen present wept with their unfortunate king.

Cosmo Versál was no less deeply moved than the others. He sat, for a while, in complete silence. Then he arose and, going to the king, put his hand upon his shoulder, and talked to him long, in a low, consoling voice. At last the broken-spirited monarch was able to suppress his emotions sufficiently to recite, but with many interruptions while he remastered his feelings, the story of his woes and of his marvelous escape.

" Sir Francis Brook," he said, " prepared a barge, when the water invaded London, and in that barge we escaped—her royal majesty, our children, and a number of members of the royal household. The barge was the only vessel of levium that existed in

England. Sir Francis had furnished and provisioned it well, and we did not think that it would be necessary to go farther than to some high point in the interior. Sir Francis was of the opinion that Wales would afford a secure refuge.

" It was a terrible thing to see the drowning of London, the sweeping of the awful bore that came up the Thames from the sea, the shipping wrecked by the tearing waves, the swirl of the fast-rising water round the immense basin in which the city lay, the downfall of the great buildings—Westminster Abbey was one of the first that succumbed—the overturned boats, and even great vessels floating on their sides, or bottom up, the awful spectacle of the bodies of the drowned tossing in the waves—all these sights were before our horrified eyes while the vast eddy swept us round and round until the water rose so high that we were driven off toward the southwest.

" That we should have escaped at all was a miracle of miracles. It was the wonderful buoyancy of the levium barge that saved us. But the terrors of that scene can never fade from my memory. And the fearful sufferings of the queen! And our children —but I *cannot* go on with this! "

" Calm yourself, your majesty," said Cosmo sympathetically. " The whole world has suffered with you. If we are spared and are yet alive, it is through the hand of Providence—to which all of us must bow."

"We must have passed over Surrey and Hampshire," the king resumed, "the invasion of the sea having buried the hills."

"I am surprised at that," said Cosmo. "I did not think that the sea had anywhere attained so great an elevation before the nebula condensed. At New York the complete drowning of the city did not occur until the downpour from the sky began."

"Oh! that deluge from the heavens!" cried the king. "What we had suffered before seemed but little in comparison. It came upon us after night; and the absolute darkness, the awful roaring, the terrific force of the falling water, the sense of suffocation, the rapid filling of the barge until the water was about our necks—these things drove us wild with despair.

"I tried to sustain my poor queen in my arms, but she struggled to seize the children and hold them above the water, and in her efforts she escaped from my hands, and henceforth I could find her no more. I stumbled about, but it was impossible to see; it was impossible to hear. At last I fell unconscious face downward, as it afterward appeared, upon a kind of bench at the rear end of the barge, which was covered with a narrow metallic roofing, and raised above the level of the bulwarks. It was there that I had tried to shelter the queen and the children.

"In some way I must have become lodged there, under the awning, in such a position that the pitching of the barge failed to throw me off. I never regained consciousness until I heard a voice shouting in my ear, and felt some one pulling me, and when I had recovered my senses, I found myself in the submersible."

"And all your companions were gone?" asked Cosmo, in a voice shaking with pity.

"Yes, oh, Lord! All! They had been swept overboard by the waves—and would that I had gone with them!"

The poor king broke down again and sobbed. After a long pause Cosmo asked gently:

"Did the Frenchman tell you how he came upon the barge?"

"He said that in rising to the surface to find out the state of things there the submersible came up directly under the barge, canting it in such a way that I was rolled out and he caught me as I was swept close to the opening."

"But how was it that the downpour, entering the submersible, when the cover was removed, did not fill it with water?"

"He had the cover so arranged that it served as an almost complete protection from the rain. Some water did enter, but not much."

"A wonderful man, that Frenchman," said Cosmo. "He would be an acquisition for me. What did he say his name was? Oh, yes, De Beauxchamps—I'll make a note of that. I shouldn't wonder if we heard of him again."

Cosmo Versál was destined to encounter Yves de Beauxchamps and his wonderful submersible *Jules Verne* sooner, and under more dramatic circumstances than he probably anticipated.

CHAPTER XVIII

NAVIGATING OVER DROWNED EUROPE

AFTER the English king had so strangely become a member of its company the Ark resumed its course in the direction of what had once been Europe. The spot where the meeting with the *Jules Verne* had occurred was west of Cape Finisterre and, according to the calculations of Captain Arms, in longitude fifteen degrees four minutes west; latitude forty-four degrees nine minutes north.

Cosmo decided to run into the Bay of Biscay, skirting its southern coast in order to get a view of the Cantabrian Mountains, many of whose peaks, he thought, ought still to lie well above the level of the water.

"There are the Peaks of Europa," said Captain Arms, "which lie less than twenty miles directly back from the coast. The highest point is eight thousand six hundred and seventy feet above sea level, or what used to be sea level. We could get near enough to it, without any danger, to see how high the water goes."

"Do you know the locality?" demanded Cosmo.

" As well as I know a compass-card! " exclaimed
the captain. " I've seen the Europa peaks a hundred times. I was wrecked once on that coast, and
being of an inquiring disposition, I took the opportunity to go up into the range and see the old mines—
and a curious sight it was, too. But the most curious
sight of all was the shepherdesses of Tresvido, dressed
just like the men, in homespun breeches that never
wore out. You'd meet 'em anywhere on the slopes
of the Pico del Ferro, cruising about with their flocks.
And the cheese that they made! There never was any
such cheese! "

" Well, if you know the place so well," said Cosmo,
" steer for it as fast as you can. I'm curious to find
out just how high this flood has gone, up to the
present moment."

" Maybe we can rescue a shepherdess," returned
the captain, chuckling. " She'd be an ornament to
your new Garden of Eden."

They kept on until, as they approached longitude
five degrees west, they began to get glimpses of the
mountains of northern Spain. The coast was all under deep water, and also the foothills and lower
ranges, but some of the peaks could be made out far
inland. At length, by cautious navigation, Captain
Arms got the vessel quite close to the old shore line
of the Asturias, and then he recognized the Europa
peaks.

" There they are," he cried. " I'd know 'em if

they'd emigrated to the middle of Africa. There's the old Torre de Cerredo and the Peña Santa."

" How high did you say the main peak is? " asked Cosmo.

" She's eight thousand six hundred and seventy feet."

" From your knowledge of the coast, do you think it safe to run in closer? "

" Yes, if you're sure the water is not less than two thousand four hundred feet above the old level we can get near enough to see the water-line on the peaks, from the cro'nest, which is two hundred feet high."

" Go ahead, then."

They got closer than they had imagined possible, so close that, from the highest lookout on the Ark, they were able with their telescopes to see very clearly where the water washed the barren mountainsides at what seemed to be a stupendous elevation.

" I'm sorry about your shepherdesses," said Cosmo, smiling. " I don't think you'd find any there to rescue if you could get to them. They must all have been lost in the torrents that poured down those mountains."

" More's the pity," said Captain Arms. " That was a fine lot of women. There'll be no more cheese like what they made at Tresvido."

Cosmo inquired if the captain's acquaintance with the topography of the range enabled him to say how high that water was. The captain, after long inspection, declared that he felt sure that it was not less than four thousand feet above the old coast line.

"Then," said Cosmo, "if you're right about the elevation of what you call the Torre de Cerredo there must be four thousand six hundred and seventy feet of its upper part still out of water. We'll see if that is so."

Cosmo made the measurements with instruments, and announced that the result showed the substantial accuracy of Captain Arms's guess.

"I suspected as much," he muttered. "Those tremendous downpours, which may have been worse elsewhere than where we encountered them, have increased the rise nearly seventy per cent. above what my gages indicated. Now that I know this," he continued, addressing the captain: "I'll change the course of the Ark. I'm anxious to get into the Indian Ocean as soon as possible. It would be a great waste of time to go back in order to cross the Sahara, and with this increase of level it isn't necessary. We'll just set out across southern France, keeping along north of the Pyrenees, and so down into the region of the Mediterranean."

Captain Arms was astonished by the boldness of this suggestion, and at first he strongly objected to their taking such a course.

"There's some pretty high ground in southern France," he said. "There's the Cevennes Mountains, which approach a good long way toward the

Pyrenees. Are`you sure the depth of water is the same everywhere?"

"What a question for an old mariner to ask!" returned Cosmo. "Don't you know that the level of the sea is the same everywhere? The flood doesn't make any difference. It seeks its level like any other water."

"But it may be risky steering between those mountains," persisted the captain.

"Nonsense! As long as the sky is clear you can get good observations, and you ought to be navigator enough not to run on a mountain."

Cosmo Versál, as usual, was unalterable in his resolution—he only changed when he had reasons of his own—and the course of the Ark was laid, accordingly, for the old French coast of the Landes, so low that it was now covered with nearly four thousand feet of water. The feelings of the passengers were deeply stirred when they learned that they were actually sailing over buried Europe, and they gazed in astonishment at the water beneath them, peering down into it as if they sought to discover the dreadful secrets that it hid, and talking excitedly in a dozen languages.

The Ark progressed slowly, making not more than five or six knots, and on the second day after they dropped the Peñas de Europa they were passing along the northern flank of the Pyrenees and over the basin in which had lain the beautiful city of Pau. The view of the Pyrenees from this point had always been celebrated before the deluge as one of the most remarkable in the world.

Now it had lost its beauty, but gained in spectacular grandeur. All of France, as far as the eye extended, was a sea, with long oceanic swells slowly undulating its surface. This sea abruptly came to an end where it met the mountains, which formed for it a coast unlike any that the hundreds of eyes which wonderingly surveyed it from the Ark had ever beheld.

Beyond the drowned vales and submerged ranges, which they knew lay beneath the watery floor, before them, rose the heads of the Pic du Midi, the Pic de Ger, the Pic de Bigorre, the Massif du Gabizos, the Pic Monné, and dozens of other famous eminences, towering in broken ranks like the bearskins of a " forlorn hope," resisting to the last, in pictures of old-time battles.

Here, owing to the configuration of the drowned land it was possible for the Ark to approach quite close to some of the wading mountains, and Cosmo seized the opportunity to make a new measure of the height of the flood, which he found to be surely not less than his former estimates had shown.

Surveying with telescopes the immense shoulders of the Monné, the Viscos, the d'Ardiden, and the nearer heights, when they were floating above the valley of Lourdes, Cosmo and the captain saw the terrible effects that had been produced by the torrents of rain, which had stripped off the vegetation whose green robe had been the glory of the high Pyrenees on the French side.

Presently their attention was arrested by some moving objects, and at a second glance they perceived that these were human beings.

"Good Heaven!" exclaimed Cosmo Versál. "There are survivors here. They have climbed the mountains, and found shelter among the rocks. I should not have thought it possible."

"And there are women among them," said Captain Arms, lowering his telescope. "You will not leave them there!"

"But what can I do?"

"Lower away the boats," replied the captain. "We've got plenty of them."

"There may be thousands there," returned Cosmo, musing. "I can't take them all."

"Then take as many as you can. By gad, sir, *I'll* not leave 'em!"

By this time some of the passengers who had powerful glasses had discovered the refugees on the distant heights, and great excitement spread throughout the Ark. Cries arose from all parts of the vessel: "Rescue them!" "Go to their aid!" "Don't let them perish!"

Cosmo Versál was in a terrible quandary. He was by no means without humanity, and was capable of deep and sympathetic feeling, as we have seen, but

he already had as many persons in the Ark as he
thought ought to be taken, considering the provision
that had been made, and, besides, he could not throw
off, at once, his original conviction of the necessity
of carefully choosing his companions. He remained
for a long time buried in thought, while the captain
fumed with impatience and at last declared that if
Cosmo did not give the order to lower away the boats
he would do it himself.

At length Cosmo, yielding rather to his own humane feelings than to the urging of others, consented
to make the experiment. Half a dozen levium
launches were quickly lowered and sent off, while the
Ark, with slowed engines, remained describing a circle
as near the mountains as it was safe to go. Cosmo
himself embarked in the leading boat.

The powerful motors of the launches carried them
rapidly to the high slopes where the unfortunates
had sought refuge, and as they approached, and the
poor fugitives saw that deliverance was at hand, they
began to shout, and cheer, and cry, and many of them
fell on their knees upon the rocks and stretched their
hands toward the heavens.

The launches were compelled to move with great
caution when they got near the ragged sides of the
submerged mountains (it was the Peyre Dufau on
which the people had taken refuge), but the men
aboard them were determined to effect the rescue, and
they regarded no peril too closely. At last Cosmo's

launch found a safe landing, and the others quickly
followed it.

When Cosmo sprang out on a flat rock a crowd
of men, women, and children, weeping, crying, sob-
bing, and uttering prayers and blessings, instantly surrounded him. Some wrung his hands in an ecstasy
of joy, some embraced him, some dropped on their
knees before him and sought to kiss his hands. Cosmo
could not restrain his tears, and the crews of the
launches were equally affected.

Many of these people could only speak the patois
of the mountains, but some were refugees from the
resorts in the valleys below, and among these were
two English tourists who had been caught among the
mountains by the sudden rising of the flood. They
exhibited comparative *sang froid,* and served as
spokesmen for the others.

" Bah Jove! " exclaimed one of them, " but you're
welcome, you know! This has been a demnition close
call! But what kind of a craft have you got out
there? "

" I'm Cosmo Versál."

" Then that's the Ark we've heard about! 'Pon
honor, I should have recognized you, for I've seen
your picture often enough. You've come to take us
off, I suppose? "

" Certainly," replied Cosmo. " How many are
there? "

" All that you see here; about a hundred, I should

say. No doubt there are others on the mountains round. There must have been a thousand of us when we started, but most of them perished, overcome by the downpour, or swept away by the torrents. Lord Swansdown (indicating his companion, who bowed gravely and stiffly) and myself—I'm Edward Whistlington—set out to walk over the Pyrenees from end to end, after the excitement about the great darkness died out, and we got as far as the Marboré, and then running down to Gavarnie we heard news of the sea rising, but we didn't give too much credit to that, and afterward, keeping up in the heights, we didn't hear even a rumor from the world below.

" The sky opened on us like a broadside from an aerial squadron, and how we ever managed to get here I'm sure I can hardly tell. We were actually *carried* down the mountainsides by the water, and how it failed to drown us will be an everlasting mystery. Somehow, we found ourselves among these people, who were trying to go *up*, assuring us that there was nothing but water below. And at last we discovered some sort of shelter here—and here we've been ever since."

" You cannot have had much to eat," said Cosmo.

" Not *too* much, I assure you," replied the Englishman, with a melancholy smile. " But these people shared with us what little they had, or could find— anything and everything that was eatable. They're a devilish fine lot, I tell you!

"When the terrible rain suddenly ceased and the sky cleared," he resumed, "we managed to get dry, after a day or two, and since then we've been chewing leather until there isn't a shoe or a belt left. We thought at first of trying to build rafts—but then where could we go? It wasn't any use to sail out over a drowned country, with nothing in sight but the mountains around us, which looked no better than the one we were barely existing on."

"Then I must get you aboard the Ark before you starve," said Cosmo.

"Many have died of starvation already," returned Whistlington. "You can't get us off a moment too quick."

Cosmo Versál had by this time freed himself of every trace of the reluctance which he had at first felt to increasing the size of his ship's company by adding recruits picked up at random. His sympathies were thoroughly aroused, and while he hastened the loading and departure of the launches, he asked the Englishmen who, with the impassive endurance of their race, stayed behind to the last, whether they thought that there were other refugees on the mountains whom they could reach.

"I dare say there are thousands of the poor devils on these peaks around us, wandering among the rocks," replied Edward Whistlington, "but I fancy you couldn't reach 'em."

"If I see any I'll try," returned Cosmo, sweeping

with his powerful telescope all the mountain flanks within view.

At last, on the slopes of the lofty Mont Aigu across the submerged valley toward the south, he caught sight of several human figures, one of which was plainly trying to make signals, probably to attract attention from the Ark. Immediately, with the Englishmen and the remainder of those who had been found on the Peyre Dufau, he hastened in his launch to the rescue.

They found four men and three women, who had escaped from the narrow valley containing the *bains de Gazost,* and who were in the last stages of starvation. These were taken aboard, and then, no more being in sight, Cosmo returned to the Ark, where the other launches had already arrived.

And these were the last that were rescued from the mighty range of the Pyrenees, in whose deep valleys had lain the famous resorts of Cauterets, the Eaux Bonnes, the Eaux Chaudes, the Bagnières de Luchon, the Bagnières de Bigorre, and a score of others. No doubt, as the Englishmen had said, thousands had managed to climb the mountains, but none could now be seen, and those who may have been there were left to perish.

There was great excitement in the Ark on the arrival of the refugees. The passengers overwhelmed them with kind attentions, and when they had sufficiently recovered, listened with wonder and the deepest sympathy to their exciting tales of suffering and terror.

Lord Swansdown and Edward Whistlington were amazed to find their king aboard the Ark, and the English members of the company soon formed a sort of family party, presided over by the unfortunate monarch. The rescued persons numbered, in all, one hundred and six.

The voyage of the Ark was now resumed, skirting the Pyrenees, but at an increasing distance. Finally Captain Arms announced that, according to his observations, they were passing over the site of the ancient and populous city of Toulouse. This recalled to Cosmo Versál's memory the beautiful scenes of the fair and rich land that lay so deep under the Ark, and he began to talk with the captain about the glories of its history.

He spoke of the last great conqueror that the world had known, Napoleon, and was discussing his marvelous career, and referring to the fact that he had died on a rock in the midst of that very ocean which had now swallowed up all the scenes of his conquests, when the lookout telephoned down that there was something visible on the water ahead.

In a little while they saw it—a small moving object, which rapidly approached the Ark. As it drew nearer both exclaimed at once:

" The *Jules Verne!* "

There could be no mistaking it. It was riding with

its back just above the level of the sea; the French flag was fluttering from a small mast, and already they could perceive the form of De Beauxchamps, standing in his old attitude, with his feet below the rim of the circular opening at the top. Cosmo ordered the Stars and Stripes to be displayed in salute, and, greatly pleased over the encounter, hurried below and had the companion-ladder made ready.

"He's got to come aboard this time, anyhow!" he exclaimed. "I'll take no refusal. I want to know that fellow better."

But this time De Beauxchamps had no thought of refusing the hospitalities of the Ark. As soon as he was within hearing he called out :

"My salutations to M. Versál and his charming fellow-voyagers. May I be permitted to come aboard and present myself in person? I have something deeply interesting to tell."

Everybody in the Ark who could find a standing-place was watching the *Jules Verne* and trying to catch a glimpse of its gallant captain, and to hear what he said; and the moment his request was preferred a babel of voices arose, amid which could be distinguished such exclamations as:

"Let him come!"   "A fine fellow!"   "Welcome, De Beauxchamps!"   "Hurrah for the *Jules Verne!*"

King Richard was in the fore rank of the spectators, waving his hand to his preserver.

" Certainly you can come aboard," cried Cosmo heartily, at the same time hastening the preparations for lowering the ladder. " We are all glad to see you. And bring your companions along with you."

CHAPTER XIX

TO PARIS UNDER THE SEA

DE BEAUXCHAMPS accepted Cosmo Versál's invitation to bring his companions with him into the Ark. The submersible was safely moored alongside, where she rode easily in company with the larger vessel, and all mounted the companion-ladder. The Frenchman's six companions were dressed, like himself, in the uniform of the army.

"Curious," muttered Captain Arms in Cosmo's ear, "that these *soldiers* should be the only ones to get off—and in a vessel, too. What were the seamen about?"

"What were *our* seamen about?" returned Cosmo. "How many of *them* got off? I warned them that ships would not do. But it was a bright idea of this De Beauxchamps and his friends to build a submersible. It didn't occur to me, or I would have advised their construction everywhere for small parties. But it would never have done for us. A submersible would not have been capacious enough for the party I wanted to take."

By this time the visitors were aboard, and Cosmo

and the others who could get near enough to grasp them by the hand greeted them effusively. King Richard received De Beauxchamps with emotion, and thanked him again and again for having saved his life; but, in the end, he covered his face and said in a broken voice:

" M. De Beauxchamps, my gratitude to you is very deep—but, oh, the queen—the queen—and the children! I should have done better to perish with them."

Cosmo and De Beauxchamps soothed him as well as they could, and the former led the way into the grand saloon, in order that as many as possible might see and greet their visitors, who had come so mysteriously up out of the sea.

All of the Frenchmen were as affable as their leader, and he presented them in turn. De Beauxchamps conversed almost gaily with such of the ladies as had sufficient command of their feelings to join the throng that pressed about him and his companions. He was deeply touched by the story of the recent rescue of his countrymen from the Pyrenees, and he went among them, trying to cheer them up, with the *élan* that no misfortune can eradicate from the Gallic nature.

At length Cosmo reminded him that he had said that he had some interesting news to communicate.

" Yes," said De Beauxchamps, " I have just come from a visit to Paris."

Exclamations of amazement and incredulity were heard on all sides.

"It is true," resumed the Frenchman, though now his voice lost all its gayety. "I had conceived the project of such a visit before I met the Ark and transferred His Majesty, the King of England, to your care. As soon as that was done I set out to make the attempt."

"But tell me first," interrupted Cosmo, "how you succeeded in finding the Ark again."

"That was not very difficult," replied De Beauxchamps, smiling. "Of course, it was to some extent accidental, for I didn't *know* that you would be here, navigating over France; but I had an idea that you *might* come this way if you had an intention of seeing what had happened to Europe. It is my regular custom to rise frequently to the surface to take a look around and make sure of my bearings, and you know that the Ark makes a pretty large point on the waters. I saw it long before you caught sight of me."

"Very well," said Cosmo. "Please go on with your story. It must, indeed, be an extraordinary one."

"I was particularly desirous of seeing Paris again, deep as I knew her to lie under the waves," resumed De Beauxchamps, "because it was my home, and I had a house in the Champs Elysées. You cannot divorce the heart of a Frenchman from his home, though you should bury it under twenty oceans."

" Your family were lost? "

" Thank God, I had no family. If I had had they would be with me. My companions are all like myself in that respect. We have lost many friends, but no near relatives. As I was saying, I started for France, poor drowned France, as soon as I left you. With the powerful searchlight of the *Jules Verne* I could feel confident of avoiding obstructions; and, besides, I knew very closely the height to which the flood had risen, and having the topography of my country at my fingers' ends, as does every officer of the army, I was able to calculate the depth at which we should run in order to avoid the hilltops."

" But surely," said Cosmo, " it is impossible—at least, it seems so to me—that you can descend to any great depth—the pressure must be tremendous a few hundred feet down, to say nothing of possible thousands."

" All that," replied the Frenchman, " has been provided for. You probably do not know to what extent we had carried experiments in France on the deep submersion of submarines before their general abandonment when they were prohibited by international agreement in war. I was myself perhaps the leader in those investigations, and in the construction of the *Jules Verne* I took pains to improve on all that had hitherto been done.

" Without going into any description of my devices, I may simply remind you nature has pointed out ways of avoiding the consequences of the inconceivable pressures which calculation indicates at depths of a kilometer, or more, in her construction of the deep-sea fishes. It was by a study of them that I arrived at the secret of both penetrating to depths that would theoretically have seemed entirely impossible and of remaining at such depths."

" Marvelous! " exclaimed Cosmo; " marvelous beyond belief! "

" I may add," continued De Beauxchamps, smiling at the effect that his words had had upon the mind of the renowned Cosmo Versál, " that the peculiar properties of levium, which you so wisely chose for your Ark, aided *me* in quite a different way. But I must return to my story.

" We passed over the coast of France near the point where I knew lay the mouth of the Loire. I could have found my way by means of the compass sufficiently well; but since the sky was clear I frequently came to the surface in order, for greater certainty, to obtain sights of the sun and stars.

" I dropped down at Tours and at Blois, and we plainly saw the walls of the old châteaux in the gleam of the searchlight below us. There were monsters of the deep, such as the eye of man never beheld, swimming slowly about them, many of them throwing a strange luminosity into the water from their phosphorescent organs, as if they were inspecting these novelties of the sea-bottom.

" Arrived over Orleans, we turned in the direction of Paris. As we approached the site of the city I sank the submersible until we almost touched the higher hills. My searchlight is so arranged that it can be directed almost every way—up, down, to this side, and to that—and we swept it round us in every direction.

" The light readily penetrated the water and revealed sights which I have no power to describe, and some—reminders of the immense population of human beings which had there met its end—which I would not describe if I could. To see a drowned face suddenly appear outside the window, almost within touch—ah, that was too horrible!

" We passed over Versailles, with the old palace still almost intact; over Sèvres, with its porcelain manufactory yet in part standing—the tidal waves that had come up the river from the sea evidently caused much destruction just before the downpour began—and finally we ' entered ' Paris.

" We could see the embankments of the Seine beneath us as we passed up its course from the Point du Jour. From the site of the Champ de Mars I turned northward in search of the older part of the Champs Élysées, where my house was, and we came upon the great Arc de Triomphe, which, you remember, dates from the time of Napoleon.

" It was apparently uninjured, even the huge bronze groups remaining in their places, and the searchlight, traversing its face, fell upon the heroic group on the east façade of the Marseillaise. You must have seen that, M. Versál? "

" Yes, many a time," Cosmo replied. " The fury in the face of the female figure representing the spirit of war, chanting the ' Marseillaise,' and, sword in hand, sweeping over the heads of the soldiers, is the most terrrible thing of human making that I ever looked upon."

" It was not so terrible as another thing that our startled eyes beheld there," said De Beauxchamps. " Coiled round the upper part of the arch, with its head resting directly upon that of the figure of which you speak, was a monstrous, ribbon-shaped creature, whose flat, reddish body, at least a meter in width and apparently thirty meters long, and bordered with a sort of floating frill of a pinkish color, undulated with a motion that turned us sick at heart.

" But the head was the most awful object that the fancy of a madman could conceive. There were two great round, projecting eyes, encircled with what I suppose must have been phosphorescent organs, which spread around in the water a green light that was absolutely horrifying.

" I turned away the searchlight, and the eyes of that creature stared straight at us with a dreadful, stony look; and then the effect of the phosphorescence, heightened by the absence of the greater light, became more terrible than before. We were unmanned, and I hardly had nerve enough to turn the submersible away and hurry from the neighborhood."

" I had not supposed," said Cosmo, " that creatures of such a size could live in the deeper parts of the sea."

" I know," returned De Beauxchamps, " that many have thought that the abysmal creatures were generally of small size, but they knew nothing about it. What could one have expected to learn of the secrets of life in the ocean depths from the small creatures which alone the trawls brought to the surface? The great monsters could not be captured in that way. But we have *seen* them—seen them taking possession of beautiful, drowned Paris—and we know what they are."

The fascinated hearers who had crowded about to listen to the narrative of De Beauxchamps shuddered at this part of it, and some of the women turned away with exclamations of horror.

" I see that I am drawing my picture in too fearful colors," he said, " and I shall refrain from telling of the other inhabitants of the abyss that we found in possession of what I, as a Frenchman, must call the most splendid capital that the world contained.

" Oh, to think that all that beauty, all those great palaces filled with the master-works of art, all those proud architectural piles, all that scene of the most joyous life that the earth contained, is now become the dwelling-place of the terrible *fauna* of the deep, creatures that never saw the sun; that never felt the transforming force of the evolution which had made the face of the globe so glorious; that never quitted their abysmal homes until this awful flood spread their empire over the whole earth! "

There was a period of profound silence while De Beauxchamps's face worked spasmodically under the influence of emotions, the sight of which would alone have sufficed to convince his hearers of the truth of what he had been telling. Finally Cosmo Versál, breaking the silence, asked:

" Did you find your home? "

" Yes. It was there. I found it out. I illuminated it with the searchlight. I gazed into the broken windows, trying to peer through the watery medium that filled and darkened the interior. The roof was broken, but the walls were intact. I thought of the happy, happy years that I had passed there when I *had* a family, and when Paris was an Eden, the sunshine of the world. And then I wished to see no more, and we rose out of the midst of that sunken city and sought the daylight far above.

" I had thought to tell you," he continued, after a pause, " of the condition in which we found the great monuments of the city—of the Pantheon, yet standing on its hill with its roof crushed in; of Nôtre Dame—a wreck, but the towers still standing proudly; of the old palace of the Louvre, through whose broken roofs and walls we caught glimpses of the treasures washed by the water within—but I find that I have not courage to go on. I had imagined that it would be a relief to speak of these things, but I do not find it so."

" After leaving Paris, then you made no other explorations? " said Cosmo.

" None. I should have had no heart for more. I had seen enough. And yet I do not regret that I went there. I should never have been content not to have seen my beautiful city once more, even lying in her watery shroud. I loved her living; I have seen her dead. It is finished. What more is there, M. Versál? " With a sudden change of manner: " You have predicted all this, and perhaps you know more. Where do *we* go to die? "

" We shall *not* die," replied Cosmo Versál forcefully. " The Ark and your *Jules Verne* will save us."

" To what purpose? " demanded the Frenchman, his animation all gone. " Can there be any pleasure in floating upon or beneath the waves that cover a lost world? Is a brief prolongation of such a life worth the effort of grasping for? "

" Yes," said Cosmo with still greater energy. " We may still *save the race*. I have chosen most of my companions in the Ark for that purpose. Not only may we save the race of man, but we may lead it up upon a higher plane; we may apply the principles of eugenics as they have never yet been applied. You,

M. De Beauxchamps, have shown that you are of the stock that is required for the regeneration of the world."

" But where can the world be regenerated? " asked De Beauxchamps with a bitter laugh. " There is nothing left but mountain-tops."

" Even they will be covered," said Cosmo.

" Do you mean that the deluge has not yet reached its height? "

" Certainly it has not. We are in an open space in the enveloping nebula. After a little we shall enter the nucleus, and then will come the worst."

" And yet you talk of saving the race! " exclaimed the Frenchman with another bitter laugh.

" I do," replied Cosmo, " and it will be done."

" But how? "

" Through the re-emergence of land."

" That recalls our former conversation," put in Professor Abel Able. " It appears to me impossible that, when the earth is once covered with a universal ocean, it can ever disappear or materially lower its level. Geological ages would be required for the level of the water to be lowered even· a few feet by the escape of vapor into space."

" No," returned Cosmo Versál, " I have demonstrated that that idea is wrong. Under the immense pressure of an ocean rising six miles above the ancient sea level the water will rapidly be forced into the interstices of the crust, and thus a material reduction of level will be produced within a few years—five at the most. That will give us a foothold. I have no doubt that even now the water around us is slightly lowering through that cause.

"But in itself that will not be sufficient. I have gone all over this ground in my original calculations. The intrusion of the immense mass of ocean water into the interior of the crust of the earth will result in a grand geological upheaval. The lands will re-emerge above the new sea level as they emerged above the former one through the internal stresses of the globe."

The scientific men present listened with breathless interest, but some of them with many incredulous shakings of the head.

"You must be aware," continued Cosmo, addressing them particularly, "that it has been demonstrated that the continents and the great mountain ranges are buoyed up, and, as it were, are floating somewhat like slags on the internal magma. The mean density of the crust is less under the land and the mountains than under the old sea-beds. This is especially true of the Himalayan region.

"That uplift is probably the most recent of all, and it is there, where at present the highest land of the globe exists, that I expect that the new upheaval will be most strongly manifested. It is for that reason, and not merely because it is now the highest part of the earth, that I am going with the Ark to Asia."

"But," said Professor Jeremiah Moses, "the upheaval of which you speak may produce a complete revolution in the surface of the earth, and if new lands are upthrust they may appear at unexpected points."

" Not at all," returned Cosmo. " The tectonic features of the globe were fixed at the beginning. As Asia has hitherto been the highest and the greatest mass of land, it will continue to be so in the future. It is there, believe me, that we shall replant the seed of humanity."

" Do you not think," asked Professor Alexander Jones, " that there will be a tremendous outburst of volcanic energy, if such upheavals occur, and may not that render the re-emerging lands uninhabitable? "

" No doubt," Cosmo replied, " every form of plutonic energy will be immensely re-enforced. You remember the recent outburst of all the volcanoes when the sea burst over the borders of the continents. But these forces will be mainly expended in an effort of uplifting. Unquestionably there will be great volcanic spasms, but they will not prevent the occupation of the broadening areas of land which will not be thus affected."

" Upon these lands," exclaimed Sir Wilfrid Athelstone, in a loud voice, " I will develop life from the barren minerals of the crust. The age of chemical parthenogenesis will then have dawned upon the earth, and man will have become a creator."

" Will the Sir Englishman give me room for a

word!" cried Costaké Theriade, raising his tall form on his toes and agitating his arms in the air. "He will create not anything! It is *I* that will unloose the energies of the atoms of matter and make of the new man a new god."

Cosmo Versál quieted the incipient outbreak of his jealous "speculative geniuses," and the discussion of his theory was continued for some time. At length De Beauxchamps, shrugging his shoulders, exclaimed, with a return of his habitual gayety:

"*Très bien! Vive* the world of Cosmo Versál! I salute the new Eve that is to come!"

CHAPTER XX

THE ADVENTURES IN COLORADO

WHEN Professor Pludder, the President, and their companions on the aero-raft, saw the three men on the bluff motioning and shouting to them, they immediately sought the means of bringing their craft to land. This did not prove to be exceedingly difficult, for there was a convenient rock with deep water around it on which they could disembark.

The men ran down to meet them, and to help them ashore, exhibiting the utmost astonishment at seeing them there.

"Whar in creation did *you* come from?" exclaimed one, giving the professor a pull up the bank. "Mebbe you're Cosmo Versál, and that's yer Ark."

"I'm Professor Pludder, and this is the President of the United States."

"The President of the Un—— See here, stranger, I'll take considerable from you, considering the fix yer in, but you don't want to go too fur."

"It's true," asseverated the professor. "This gentleman is the President, and we've escaped from Washington. Please help the ladies."

"I'll help the ladies all right, but I'm blamed if

I believe yer yarn. How'd you *git* here? You couldn't hev floated across the continent on that thing."

" We came on the raft that you see," interrupted Mr. Samson. " We left the Appalachian Mountains two weeks ago."

" Well, by—it must be true! " muttered the man. " They couldn't hev come from anywhar else in that direction. I reckon the hull blamed continent is under water."

" So it is," said Professor Pludder, " and we made for Colorado, knowing that it was the only land left above the flood."

All finally got upon the bluff, rejoiced to feel solid ground once more beneath their feet. But it was a desolate prospect that they saw before them. The face of the land had been scoured and gullied by the pouring waters, the vegetation had been stripped off, except where in hollows it had been covered with new-formed lakes, some of which had drained off after the downpour ceased, the water finding its way into the enveloping sea.

They asked the three men what had become of the other inhabitants, and whether there was any shelter at hand.

" We've be'n wiped out," said the original spokes-man. " Cosmo Versál has done a pretty clean job with his flood. There's a kind of a cover that we three hev built, a ways back yonder, out o' timber o' one kind and another that was lodged about. But it wouldn't amount to much if there was another cloudburst. It wouldn't stand a minute. It's good to sleep in."

" Are you the only survivors in this region? " asked the President.

" I reckon you see all thet's left of us. The' ain't one out o' a hundred that's left alive in these parts."

" What became of them? "

" Swept off! " replied the man, with an expressive gesture—" and drownded right out under the sky."

" And how did you and your companions escape? "

" By gitting up amongst some rocks that was higher'n the average."

" How did you manage to live—what did you have to eat? "

" We didn't eat much—we didn't hev much time to think o' eatin'. We had one hoss with us, and he served, when his time come. After the sky cleared we skirmished about and dug up something that we could manage to eat, lodged in gullies where the water had washed together what had been in houses and cellars. We've got a gun and a little ammunition, and once in a while we could kill an animal that had contrived to escape somehow."

" And you think that there are no other human beings left alive anywhere around here? "

" I *know* th' ain't. The's probably some up in the foothills, and around the Pike. They had a better chance to git among rocks. We hed jest made up our minds to go hunting for 'em when we ketched sight o' you, and then we concluded to stay and see who you was."

"I'm surprised that you didn't go sooner."

"We couldn't. There was a roarin' torrent coming down from the mountains that cut us off. It's only last night that it stopped."

"Well, it's evident that we cannot stay here," said Professor Pludder. "We must go with these men toward the mountains. Let us take what's left of the compressed provisions out of the raft, and then we'll eat a good meal and be off."

The three men were invited to share the repast, and they ate with an appetite that would have amused their hosts if they had not been so anxious to reserve as much as possible of their provisions for future necessities.

The meal finished, they started off, their new friends aiding to carry provisions, and what little extra clothing there was. The aspect of the country they traversed affrighted them. Here and there were partially demolished houses or farm structures, or cellars, choked with débris of what had once been houses.

Farm implements and machinery were scattered about and half buried in the torrent-furrowed land. In the wreck of one considerable village through which they passed they found a stone church, and several stone houses of considerable pretensions, standing almost intact as to walls, but with roofs, doors, and windows smashed and torn off.

It was evident that this place, which lay in a depression of the land, had been buried by the rushing water as high as the top stories of the buildings. From some of the sights that they saw they shrank away, and afterward tried to forget them.

Owing to the presence of the women and children their progress was slower than it might overwise have been. They had great difficulty in crossing the course of the torrent which their companions had described as cutting them off from the foothills of the Pike's Peak range.

The water had washed out a veritable cañon, a hundred or more feet deep in places, and with ragged, precipitous walls and banks, which they had to descend on one side and ascend on the other. Here the skill and local knowledge of their three new-found friends stood them in good stead. There was yet enough water in the bottom of the great gully to compel them to wade, carrying the women and children.

But, just before nightfall, they succeeded in reaching a range of rocky heights, where they determined to pass the night. They managed to make a fire with brush that had been swept down the mountain flanks and had remained wedged in the rocks, and thus they dried their soaked garments, and were able to do some cooking, and to have a blaze to give them a little heat during the night, for the air turned cold after the disappearance of the sun.

When the others had sunk into an uneasy slumber, the President and Professor Pludder sat long, replenishing the fire, and talking of what would be their future course.

" I think," said the professor, " that we shall find a considerable population alive among the mountains. There is nothing in Colorado below four thousand feet elevation, and not much below five thousand. The great inner ' parks ' were probably turned into lakes, but they will drain off, as the land around us here has done already.

" Those who managed to find places of comparative shelter will now descend into the level lands and try to hunt up the sites of their homes. If only some plants and grain have been preserved they can, after a fashion, begin to cultivate the soil."

" But there *is* no soil," said the President, shuddering at the recollection of the devastation he had witnessed. " It has all been washed off."

" No," replied the professor, " there's yet a good deal in the low places, where the water rested."

" But it is now the middle of winter."

" Reckoned by the almanac it is, but you see that the temperature is that of summer, and has been such for months. I think that this is due in some way to the influence of the nebula, although I cannot account for it. At any rate it will be possible to plant and sow.

" The whole body of the atmosphere having been raised four thousand feet, the atmospheric conditions here now are virtually the same as at the former sea-level. If we can find the people and reassure them, we must take the lead in restoring the land to fertility, and also in the reconstruction of homes."

" Suppose the flood should recommence? "

" There is no likelihood of it."

" Then," said the President, putting his face between his hands and gazing sadly into the fire, " here is all that remains of the mightiest nation of the world, the richest, the most populous—and we are to build up out of this remnant a new fatherland."

" This is not the only remnant," said Professor Pludder. " One-quarter, at least, of the area of the United States is still above sea-level. Think of Arizona, New Mexico, Utah, Nevada, the larger part of California, Wyoming, a part of Montana, two-thirds of Idaho, a half of Oregon and Washington— all above the critical level of four thousand feet, and all except the steepest moutainsides can be reclaimed.

" There is hope for our country yet. Remember that the climate of this entire region will now be changed, since the barometric isobars have been lifted up, and the line of thirty inches pressure now meets the edge of the Colorado plateau. There may be a corresponding change in the rainfall and in all the conditions of culture and fertility."

"Yes," sighed the President, "but I cannot, I cannot withdraw my mind from the thought of the *millions, millions, millions* who have perished!"

"I do not say that we should forget them," replied Professor Pludder; "Heaven forbid! But I do say that we must give our attention to those that remain, and turn our faces steadily toward the future."

"Abiel," returned the President, pressing the professor's hand, "you are right. My confidence in you was shaken, but now I follow you again."

Thus they talked until midnight, and then got a little rest with the others. They were up and off at break of day, and as they mounted higher they began to encounter immense rocks that had come tumbling down from above.

"How can you talk of people escaping toward the mountains if they had to encounter these?" demanded the President.

"Some of these rocks have undoubtedly been brought down by the torrents," Professor Pludder replied, "but I believe that the greater number fell earlier, during the earthquakes that accompanied the first invasions of the sea."

"But those earthquakes may have continued all through."

"I do not think so. We have felt no trembling of the earth. I believe that the convulsions lasted

only for a brief period, while the rocks were yielding
to the pressure along the old sea-coast. After a little
the crust below adjusted itself to the new conditions.
And even if the rocks fell while people were trying
to escape from the flood below, they must, like the
water, have followed the gorges and hollow places,
while the fugitives would, of course, keep upon the
ridges."

Whatever perils they may have encountered, people
had certainly escaped as the professor had averred.
When the party, in the middle of the day, were seated
at their lunch, on an elevated point from which they
could see far over the strange ocean that they had
left behind them, while the southern buttresses of
Pike's Peak rose steeply toward the north, they discovered the first evidence of the existence of refugees
in the mountains. This was a smoke rising over an
intervening ridge, which their new companions declared could be due to nothing less than a large camp-
fire.

They hastened to finish their meal, and then
climbed the ridge. As soon as they were upon it they
found themselves looking down into a broad, shallow
cañon, where there were nearly twenty rudely constructed cabins, with a huge fire blazing in the midst
of the place, and half a dozen red-shirted men busy
about it, evidently occupied in the preparation of the
dinner of a large party.

Their friends recognized an acquaintance in one

of the men below and hailed him with delight. Instantly men, women, and children came running out of the huts to look at them, and as they descended into this improvised village they were received with a hospitality that was almost hilarious.

The refugees consisted of persons who had escaped from the lower lands in the immediate vicinity, and they were struck dumb when told that they were entertaining the President of the United States and his family.

The entire history of their adventures was related on both sides. The refugees told how, at the commencement of the great rain, when it became evident that the water would inundate their farms and buildings, they loaded themselves with as many provisions as they could carry, and, in spite of the suffocating downpour that filled the air, managed to fight their way to the ridge overhanging the deep cut in which they were now encamped.

Hardly a quarter of those who started arrived in safety. They sheltered themselves to the number of about thirty, in a huge cavern, which faced down the mountain, and had a slightly upward sloping floor, so that the water did not enter. Here, by careful economy, they were able to eke out their provisions until the sky cleared, after which the men, being used to outdoor labor and hunting, contrived to supply the wants of the forlorn little community.

They managed to kill a few animals, and found the

bodies of others recently killed, or drowned. Later they descended into the lowlands, as the water ran off, and searching among the ruins of their houses found some remnants of supplies in the cellars and about the foundations of the barns. They were preparing to go down in a body and seek to re-establish themselves on the sites of their old homes, when the President's party came upon them.

The meeting with these refugees was but the first of a series of similar encounters on the way along the eastern face of the Pike's Peak range. In the aggregate they met several hundred survivors who had established themselves on the site of Colorado Springs, where a large number of houses, standing on the higher ground, had escaped.

They had been soaked with water, descending through the shattered roofs and broken windows, and pouring into the basements and cellars. The fugitives came from all directions, some from the caverns on the mountains, and some from the rocks toward the north and east. A considerable number asserted that they had found refuge in the Garden of the Gods.

As near as could be estimated, about a quarter of the population remained alive.

The strong points of Professor Pludder now, once more, came out conspicuously. He proved himself an admirable organizer. He explored all the country round, and enheartened everybody, setting them to work to repair the damage as much as possible.

Some horses and cattle were found which, following their instincts, had managed to escape the flood. In the houses and other buildings yet standing a great deal of food and other supplies were discovered, so that there was no danger of a famine. As he had anticipated, the soil had not all been washed away from the flat land, and he advised the inhabitants to plant quick-growing seeds at once.

He utilized the horses to send couriers in all directions, some going even as far as Denver. Everywhere virtually the same conditions were found—many had escaped and were alive, only needing the guidance of a quicker intelligence, and this was supplied by the advice which the professor instructed his envoys to spread among the people. He sought to cheer them still more by the information that the President was among them, and looking out for their welfare.

One thing which his couriers at last began to report to him was a cause of surprise. They said that the level of the water was rapidly falling. Some who had gone far toward the east declared that it had gone down hundreds of feet. But the professor reflected that this was impossible, because evaporation could not account for it, and he could not persuade himself that so much water could have found its way into the interior of the crust.

He concluded that his informants had allowed their hopes to affect their eyesight, and, strong as usual in his professional dogmas, he made no personal examination. Besides, Professor Pludder was beginning to be shaken in his first belief that all trouble from the nebula was at an end. Once having been forced to accept the hypothesis that a watery nebula had met the earth, he began to reflect that they might not be through with it.

In any event, he deemed it wise to prepare for it if it *should* come back. Accordingly he advised that the population that remained should concentrate in the stronger houses, built of stone, and that every effort should be made to strengthen them further and to make the roofs as solid as possible. He also directed that no houses should be occupied that were not situated on high ground, surrounded with slopes that would give ready flow to the water in case the deluging rain should recommence.

He had no fixed conviction that it would recommence, but he was uneasy, owing to his reflections, and wished to be on the safe side. He sent similar instructions as far as his horsemen could reach.

The wisdom of his doubts became manifest about two weeks after the arrival of the President's party. Without warning the sky, which had been perfectly blue and cloudless for a month, turned a sickly yellow. Then mists hid the head, and in a little while the entire outline of Pike's Peak, and after that a heavy rain began.

Terror instantly seized the people, and at first nobody ventured out of doors. But as time went on and the rain did not assume the proportions of the former *débâcle,* although it was very heavy and continuous, hope revived. Everybody was on the watch for a sudden clearing up.

Instead of clearing, however, the rain became very irregular, gushing at times in torrents which were even worse than the original downpour, but these tremendous gushes were of brief duration, so that the water had an opportunity to run off the higher ground before the next downpour occurred.

This went on for a week, and then the people were terrified at finding that water was pouring up through all the depressions of the land, cutting off the highlands from Pike's Peak with an arm of the sea. It was evident that the flood had been rapidly rising, and if it should rise but little higher they would be caught in a trap. The inland sea, it was clear, had now invaded the whole of Colorado to the feet of the mountains, and was creeping up on them.

Just at this time a series of earthquakes began. They were not severe, but were continuous. The ground cracked open in places, and some houses were overturned, but there were no wall-shattering shocks —only a continual and dreadful trembling, accompanied by awful subterranean sounds.

This terrible state of affairs had lasted for a day before a remarkable discovery was made, which filled many hearts with joy, although it seemed to puzzle Professor Pludder as much as it rejoiced him.

The new advance of the sea was arrested! There could be no question of that, for too many had anxiously noted the points to which the water had attained.

We have said that Professor Pludder was puzzled. He was seeking, in his mind, a connection between the seismic tremors and the cessation of the advance of the sea. Inasmuch as the downpour continued, the flood ought still to rise.

He rejected as soon as it occurred to him the idea that the earth could be drinking up the waters as fast as they fell, and that the trembling was an accompaniment of this gigantic deglutition.

Sitting in a room with the President and other members of the party from Washington, he remained buried in his thoughts, answering inquiries only in monosyllables. Presently he opened his eyes very wide and a long-drawn " A-ah! " came from his mouth. Then he sprang to his feet and cried out, but only as if uttering a thought aloud to himself, the strange word:

" *Batholite!* "

CHAPTER XXI

"THE FATHER OF HORROR"

AT the time when the President of the United States and his companions were beginning to discover the refugees around Pike's Peak, Cosmo Versál's Ark accompanied by the *Jules Verne,* whose commander had decided to remain in touch with his friends, was crossing the submerged hills and valleys of Languedoc under a sun as brilliant as that which had once made them a land of gold.

De Beauxchamps remained aboard the Ark much of the time. Cosmo liked to have him, with himself and Captain Arms, on the bridge, because there they could talk freely about their plans and prospects, and the Frenchman was a most entertaining companion.

Meanwhile, the passengers in the saloons and on the promenade decks formed little knots and coteries for conversation, for reading, and for mutual diversion, or strolled about from side to side, watching the endless expanse of waters for the occasional appearance of some inhabitant of the deep that had wandered over the new ocean's bottom.

These animals seemed to be coming to the sur-

face to get bearings. Every such incident reminded
the spectators of what lay beneath the waves, and
led them to think and talk of the awful fate that
had overwhelmed their fellow men, until the spirits
of the most careless were subdued by the pervading
melancholy.

King Richard, strangely enough, had taken a lik-
ing for Amos Blank, who was frequently asked to
join the small and somewhat exclusive circle of com-
patriots that continually surrounded the fallen monarch. The billionaire and the king often leaned
elbow to elbow over the rail, and put their heads
companionably together while pointing out some
object on the sea. Lord Swansdown felt painfully
cut by this, but, of course, he could offer no objection.

Finally Cosmo invited the king to come upon the
bridge, from which passengers were generally ex-
cluded, and the king insisted that Blank should go,
too. Cosmo consented, for Blank seemed to him
to have become quite a changed man, and he found
him sometimes full of practical suggestions.

So it happened that when Captain Arms announced
that the Ark was passing over the ancient city of
Carcassonne, Cosmo, the king, De Beauxchamps,
Amos Blank, and the captain were all together on
the bridge. When Captain Arms mentioned their
location, King Richard became very thoughtful.
After a time he said musingly:

" Ah! how all these names, Toulouse, Carcassonne, Languedoc, bring back to me the memory of my namesake of olden times, Richard I. of England. This, over which we are floating, was the land of the Troubadours, and Richard was the very Prince of Troubadours. With all his faults England never had a king like him!"

" Knowing your devotion to peace, which was the reason why I wished you to be of the original company in the Ark, I am surprised to hear you say that," said Cosmo.

" Ah!" returned the King, " But Cœur de Lion was a true Englishman, even in his love of fighting. What would he say if he knew where England lies to-day? What would he say if he knew the awful fate that has come upon this fair and pleasant land, from whose poets and singers he learned the art of minstrelsy?"

" He would say, ' Do not despair,' " replied Cosmo. " ' Show the courage of an Englishman, and fight for your race if you cannot for your country.' "

" But may not England, may not all these lands, emerge again from the floods?" asked the king.

" Not in our time, not in our children's time," said Cosmo Versál, thoughtfully shaking his head. " In the remote future, yes—but I cannot tell how remote. Tibet was once an appanage of your crown, before China taught the West what war meant, and in Tibet you may help to found a new empire, but I must tell you that it will not resemble the empires of the past. Democracy will be its corner stone, and science its law."

"Then I devote myself to democracy and science," responded King Richard.

"Good! Admirable!" exclaimed Amos Blank and De Beauxchamps simultaneously, while Captain Arms would probably have patted the king on the back had not his attention, together with that of the others, been distracted by a huge whale blowing almost directly in the course of the Ark.

"Blessed if I ever expected to see a sight like that in these parts!" exclaimed the captain. "This lifting the ocean up into the sky is upsetting the order of nature. I'd as soon expect to sight a cachalot on top of the Rocky Mountains."

"They'll be there, too, before long," said Cosmo.

"I wonder what he's looking for," continued Captain Arms. "He must have come down from the north. He couldn't have got in through the Pyrenees or the Sierra Nevadas. He's just navigated right over the whole country straight down from the English Channel."

The whale sounded at the approach of the Ark, but in a little while he was blowing again off toward the south, and then the passengers caught sight of him, and there was great excitement.

He seemed to be of enormous size, and he sent

his fountain to an extraordinary height in the air. On he went, appearing and disappearing, steering direct for Africa, until, with glasses, they could see his white plume blowing on the very edge of the horizon.

Not even the reflection that they themselves were sailing over Europe impressed some of the passengers with so vivid a sense of their situation as the sight of this monstrous inhabitant of the ocean taking a view of his new domain.

At night Cosmo continued the concerts and the presentation of the Shakespearian dramas, and for an hour each afternoon he had a " conference " in the saloon, at which Theriade and Sir Athelstone were almost the sole performers.

Their disputes, and Cosmo's efforts to keep the peace, amused for a while, but at length the audiences diminished until Cosmo, with his constant companions, the Frenchman, the king, Amos Blank, the three professors from Washington, and a few other savants were the only listeners.

But the music and the plays always drew immensely.

Joseph Smith was kept busy most of the time in Cosmo's cabin, copying plans for the regeneration of mankind.

When they knew that they had finally left the borders of France and were sailing above the Mediterranean Sea, it became necessary to lay their course

with considerable care. Cosmo decided that the only
safe plan would be to run south of Sardinia, and then
keep along between Sicily and Tunis, and so on toward lower Egypt.

There he intended to seek a way over the mountains north of the Sinai peninsula into the Syrian
desert, from which he could reach the ancient valley
of the Euphrates and the Persian Gulf. He would
then pass down the Arabian Sea, swing round India
and Ceylon, and, by way of the Bay of Bengal and
the plains of the Ganges and Brahmaputra, approach
the Himalayas.

Captain Arms was rather inclined to follow the
Gulf of Suez and the depression of the Red Sea,
but Cosmo was afraid that they would have difficulty
in getting the Ark safely through between the Mt.
Sinai peaks and the Jebel Gharib range.

"Well, you're the commodore," said the captain
at the end of the discussion, "but hang me if I'd
not rather follow a sea, where I know the courses,
than go navigating over mountains and deserts in the
land of Shinar. We'll land on top of Jerusalem
yet, you'll see!"

Feeling sure of plenty of water under keel, they
now made better speed and De Beauxchamps retired
into the *Jules Verne,* and detached it from the Ark,
finding that he could distance the latter easily with
the submersible running just beneath the surface of
the water.

" Come up to blow, and take a look around from the bridge, once in a while," the captain called out to him as he disappeared and the cover closed over him. The *Jules Verne* immediately sank out of sight.

They passed round Sardinia, and between the old African coast and Sicily, and were approaching the Malta Channel when their attention was drawn to a vast smoke far off toward the north.

" It's Etna in eruption," said Cosmo to the captain.

" A magnificent sight! " exclaimed King Richard, who happened to be on the bridge.

" Yes, and I'd like to see it nearer," remarked Cosmo, as a wonderful column of smoke, as black as ink, seemed to shoot up to the very zenith.

" You'd better keep away," Captain Arms said warningly. " There's no good comes of fooling round volcanoes in a ship."

" Oh, it's safe enough," returned Cosmo. " We can run right over the southeastern corner of Sicily and get as near as we like. There is nothing higher than about three thousand feet in that part of the island, so we'll have a thousand feet to spare."

" But maybe the water has lowered."

" Not more than a foot or two," said Cosmo. " Go ahead."

The captain plainly didn't fancy the adventure, but he obeyed orders, and the Ark's nose was turned northward, to the delight of many of the passengers who had become greatly interested when they learned that the tremendous smoke that they saw came from Mount Etna.

Some of them were nervous, but the more adventurous spirits heartily applauded Cosmo Versál's design to give them a closer view of so extraordinary a spectacle. Even from their present distance the sight was one that might have filled them with terror if they had not already been through adventures which had hardened their nerves. The smoke was truly terrific in appearance.

It did not spread low over the sea, but rose in an almost vertical column, widening out at a height of several miles, until it seemed to canopy the whole sky toward the north.

It could be seen spinning in immense rolling masses, the outer parts of which were turned by the sunshine to a dingy brown color, while the main stem of the column, rising directly from the great crater, was of pitchy blackness.

An awful roaring was audible, sending a shiver through the Ark. At the bottom of the mass of smoke, through which gleams of fire were seen to shoot as they drew nearer, appeared the huge conical form of the mountain, whose dark bulk still rose nearly seven thousand feet above the sea that covered the great, beautiful, and historic island beneath it.

They had got within about twenty miles of the

base of the mountain, when a shout was heard by those on the bridge, and Cosmo and the captain, looking for its source, saw the *Jules Verne,* risen to the surface a little to starboard, and De Beauxchamps excitedly signaling to them. They just made out the words, " Sheer off! " when the Ark, with a groaning sound, took ground, and they were almost precipitated over the rail of the bridge.

" Aground again, by——! " exclaimed Captain Arms, instantly signaling all astern. " I told you not to go fooling round a volcano."

" This beats me! " cried Cosmo Versál. " I wonder if the island has begun to rise."

" More likely the sea has begun to fall," growled Captain Arms.

" Do you know where we are? " asked Cosmo.

" We can't be anywhere but on the top of Monte Lauro," replied the captain.

" But that's only three thousand feet high."

" It's exactly three thousand two hundred and thirty feet," said the captain. " I haven't navigated the old Mediterranean a hundred times for nothing."

" But even then we should have near seven hundred and fifty feet to spare, allowing for the draft of the Ark, and a slight subsidence of the water."

" Well, you haven't allowed enough, that's plain," said the captain.

" But it's impossible that the flood can have subsided more than seven hundred feet already."

"I don't care how impossible it is—here we are!
We're stuck on a mountain-top, and if we don't leave
our bones on it I'm a porpoise."

By this time the *Jules Verne* was alongside, and
De Beauxchamps shouted up:

"I was running twenty feet under water, keeping
along with the Ark, when my light suddenly revealed
the mountain ahead. I hurried up and tried to warn
you, but it was too late."

"Can't you go down and see where we're fast?"
asked Cosmo.

"Certainly; that's just what I was about to pro-
pose," replied the Frenchman, and immediately the
submersible disappeared.

After a long time, during which Cosmo succeeded
in allaying the fears of his passengers, the submersible reappeared, and De Beauxchamps made his report. He said that the Ark was fast near the bow
on a bed of shelly limestone.

He thought that by using the utmost force of the
Jules Verne, whose engines were very powerful, in
pushing the Ark, combined with the backing of her
own engines, she might be got off.

"Hurry up, then, and get to work," cried Captain
Arms. "This flood is on the ebb, and a few hours
more will find us stuck here like a ray with his saw
in a whale's back."

De Beauxchamps's plan was immediately adopted.
The *Jules Verne* descended, and pushed with all her

force, while the engines of the Ark were reversed, and within fifteen minutes they were once more afloat.

Without waiting for a suggestion from Cosmo Versál, the Frenchman carefully inspected with his searchlight the bottom of the Ark where she had struck, and when he came to the surface he was able to report that no serious damage had resulted.

" There's no hole," he said, " only a slight denting of one of the plates, which will not amount to anything."

Cosmo, however, was not content until he had made a careful inspection by opening some of the manholes in the inner skin of the vessel. He found no cause for anxiety, and in an hour the Ark resumed its voyage eastward, passing over the site of ancient Syracuse.

By this time a change of the wind had sent the smoke from Etna in their direction, and now it lay thick upon the water, and rendered it, for a while, impossible to see twenty fathoms from the bridge.

" It's old Etna's dying salute," said Cosmo. " He won't have his head above water much longer."

" But the flood is going down," exclaimed Captain Arms.

" Yes, and that puzzles me. There must have been an enormous absorption of water into the interior, far greater than I ever imagined possible. But wait until the nucleus of the nebula strikes us! In the meantime, this lowering of the water renders it necessary for us to make haste, or we may not get over the mountains round Suez before the downpour recommences."

As soon as they escaped from the smoke of Etna they ran full speed ahead again, and, keeping well south of Crete, at length, one morning they found themselves in the latitude and longitude of Alexandria.

The weather was still superb, and Cosmo was very desirous of getting a line on the present height of the water. He thought that he could make a fair estimate of this from the known elevation of the mountains about Sinai. Accordingly they steered in that direction, and on the way passed directly over the site of Cairo.

Then the thought of the pyramids came to them all, and De Beauxchamps, who had come aboard the Ark, and who was always moved by sentimental considerations, proposed that they should spend a few hours here, while he descended to inspect the condition in which the flood had left those mighty monuments.

Cosmo not only consented to this, but he even offered to be a member of the party. The Frenchman was only too glad to have his company. Cosmo Versál descended into the submersible after instructing Captain Arms to hover in the neighborhood.

The passengers and crew of the Ark, with expressions of anxiety that would have pleased their subject if he had heard them, watched the *Jules Verne* disappear into the depths beneath.

The submersible was gone so long that the anxiety of those aboard the Ark deepened into alarm, and finally became almost panic. They had never before known how much they depended upon Cosmo Versál. He was their only reliance, their only hope. He alone had known how to keep up their spirits, and when he had assured them, as he so often did, that the flooding would surely recommence, they had hardly been terrified because of their unexpressed confidence that, let come what would, his great brain would find a way out for them.

Now he was gone, down into the depths of this awful sea, where their imaginations pictured a thousand unheard-of perils, and perhaps they would never see him again! Without him they knew themselves to be helpless. Even Captain Arms almost lost his nerve.

The strong good sense of Amos Blank alone saved them from the utter despair that began to seize upon them as hour after hour passed without the reappearance of the *Jules Verne*.

His experience had taught him how to keep a level head in an emergency, and how to control panics. With King Richard always at his side, he went about among the passengers and fairly laughed them out of their fears.

Without discussing the matter at all, he convinced them, by the simple force of his own apparent confidence, that they were worrying themselves about nothing.

He was, in fact, as much alarmed as any of the others, but he never showed it. He started a rumor, after six hours had elapsed, that Cosmo himself had said that they would probably require ten or twelve hours for their exploration.

Cosmo had said nothing of the kind, but Blank's prevarication had its intended effect, and fortunately, before the lapse of another six hours, there was news from under the sea.

And what was happening in the mysterious depths below the Ark? What had so long detained the submersible?

The point where the descent was made had been so well chosen that the *Jules Verne* almost struck the apex of the Great Pyramid as it approached the bottom. The water was somewhat muddy from the sands of the desert, and the searchlight streamed through a yellowish medium, recalling the " golden atmosphere " for which Egypt had been celebrated. But, nevertheless, the light was so powerful that they could see distinctly at a distance of several rods.

The pyramid appeared to have been but little injured, although the tremendous tidal wave that had swept up the Nile during the invasion of the sea before the downpour began had scooped out the sand down to the bed-rock on all sides.

Finding nothing of particular interest in a circuit of the pyramid, they turned in the direction of the Great Sphinx.

This, too, had been excavated to its base, and it now stood up to its full height, and a terrible expression seemed to have come into its enigmatic features.

Cosmo wished to get a close look at it, and they ran the submersible into actual contact with the forepart of the gigantic statue, just under the mighty chin.

While they paused there, gazing out of the front window of the vessel, a bursting sound was heard, followed by a loud crash, and the *Jules Verne* was shaken from stem to stern. Every man of them threw himself against the sides of the vessel, for the sound came from overhead, and they had an instinctive notion that the roof was being crushed down upon them.

A second resounding crash was heard, shaking them like an earthquake, and the little vessel rolled partly over upon its side.

"We are lost!" cried De Beauxchamps. "The Sphinx is falling upon us! We shall be buried alive here!"

A third crash came over their heads, and the submersible seemed to sink beneath them as if seeking

to avoid the fearful blows that were rained upon its
roof.

Still, the stout curved ceiling, strongly braced
within, did not yield, although they saw, with af-
fright, that it was bulged inward, and some of the
braces were torn from their places. But no water
came in.

Stunned by the suddenness of the accident, for a
few moments they did nothing but cling to such supports as were within their reach, expecting that another blow would either force the vessel completely
over or break the roof in.

But complete silence now reigned, and the missiles from above ceased to strike the submersible.
The searchlight continued to beam out of the fore
end of the vessel, and following its broad ray with
their eyes, they uttered one cry of mingled amazement and fear, and then stared without a word at
such a spectacle as the wildest imagination could not
have pictured.

The front of the Sphinx had disappeared, and the
light, penetrating beyond the place where it had
stood, streamed upon the face and breast of an
enormous black figure, seated on a kind of throne,
and staring into their faces with flaming eyes which
at once fascinated and terrified them.

To their startled imaginations the eyes seemed
to roll in their sockets, and flashes of fire to dart
from them. Their expression was menacing and

terrifying beyond belief. At the same time the aspect
of the face was so majestic that they cowered before
it.

The cheekbones were high, massive, and polished
until they shone in the light; the nose and chin were
powerful in their contours; and the brow wore an
intimidating frown. It seemed to the awed onlookers as if they had sacrilegiously burst into the
sanctuary of an offended god.

But, after a minute or two of stupefaction, they
thought again of the desperateness of their situation,
and turned from staring at the strange idol to consider what they should do.

The fact that no water was finding its way into
the submersible somewhat reassured them, but the
question now arose whether it could be withdrawn
from its position.

They had no doubt that the front of the Sphinx,
saturated by the water after the thousands of years
that it had stood there, exposed to the desiccating
influences of the sun and the desert sands, had suddenly disintegrated, and fallen upon them, pinning
their vessel fast under the fragments of the huge head.

De Beauxchamps tried the engines and found that
they had no effect in moving the *Jules Verne*. He
tried again and again by reversing to disengage the
vessel, but it would not stir. Then they debated the
only other means of escape.

"Although I have levium life-suits," said the

"IT IS A PROPHECY OF THE SECOND DELUGE"

Frenchman, "and although the top of the *Jules Verne* can probably be opened, for the door seems not to have been touched, yet the instant it is removed the water will rush in, and it will be impossible to pump out the vessel."

"Are your life-suits so arranged that they will permit of moving the limbs?" demanded Cosmo.

"Certainly they are."

"And can they be weighted so as to remain at the bottom?"

"They are arranged for that," responded De Beauxchamps.

"And can the weights be detached by the inmates without permitting the entrance of water?"

"It can be done, although a very little water might enter during the operation."

"Then," said Cosmo, "let us put on the suits, open the door, take out the ballast so that, if released, the submersible will rise to the surface through its own buoyancy, and then see if we cannot loosen the vessel from outside."

It was a suggestion whose boldness made even the owner and constructor of the *Jules Verne* stare for a moment, but evidently it was the only possible way in which the vessel might be saved; and knowing that, in case of failure, they could themselves float to the surface after removing the weights from the bottom of the suits, they unanimously decided to try Cosmo Versál's plan.

It was terribly hard work getting the ballast out of the submersible, working as they had to do under water, which rushed in as soon as the door was opened, and in their awkward suits, which were provided with apparatus for renewing the supply of oxygen; but at last they succeeded.

Then they clambered outside, and labored desperately to release the vessel from the huge fragments of stone that pinned it down. Finally, exhausted by their efforts, and unable to make any impression, they gave up.

De Beauxchamps approached Cosmo and motioned to him that it was time to ascend to the surface and leave the *Jules Verne* to her fate. But Cosmo signaled back that he wished first to examine more closely the strange statue that was gazing upon them in the still unextinguished beam of the searchlight with what they might now have regarded as a look of mockery.

The others, accordingly, waited while Cosmo Versál, greatly impeded by his extraordinary garment, clambered up to the front of the figure. There he saw something which redoubled his amazement.

On the broad breast he saw a representation of a world overwhelmed with a deluge and encircling it was what he instantly concluded to be the picture of a nebula. Underneath, in ancient Egyptian hieroglyphics, with which Cosmo was familiar, was

an inscription in letters of gold, which could only
be translated thus:

I Come Again—
At the End of Time.

" Great Heavens! " he said to himself. " It is a
prophecy of the Second Deluge! "

He continued to gaze, amazed, at the figure and
the inscription, until De Beauxchamps clambered to
his side and indicated to him that it was necessary
that they should ascend without further delay, showing him by signs that the air-renewing apparatus
would give out.

With a last lingering look at the figure, Cosmo
imitated the others by detaching the weights from
below his feet, and a minute later they were all shooting rapidly toward the surface of the sea, De Beauxchamps, as he afterwards declared, uttering a prayer
for the repose of the *Jules Verne.*

The imaginary time which Amos Blank had fixed
as the limit set by Cosmo for the return from the
depths was nearly gone, and he was beginning to
cast about for some other invention to quiet the rising
fears of the passengers, when a form became visible
which made the eyes of Captain Arms, the first to
catch sight of it, start from their sockets. He rubbed
them, and looked again—but there it was!

A huge head, human in outline, with bulging,

glassy eyes, popped suddenly out of the depths, followed by the upper part of a gigantic form which was no less suggestive of a monstrous man, and which immediately began to wave its arms!

Before the captain could collect his senses another shot to the surface, and then another and another, until there were seven of them floating and awkwardly gesticulating within a radius of a hundred fathoms on the starboard side of the vessel.

The whole series of apparitions did not occupy more than a quarter of a minute in making their appearance.

By the time the last had sprung into sight Captain Arms had recovered his wits, and he shouted an order to lower a boat, at the same time running down from the bridge to superintend the operation. Many of the crew and passengers had in the meantime seen the strange objects, and they were thrown into a state of uncontrollable excitement.

" It's them! " shouted the captain over his shoulder, in response to a hundred inquiries all put at once, and forgetting his grammar in the excitement. " They've come up in diving-suits."

Amos Blank comprehended the situation at once; and while the captain was getting out the boat, he explained matters to the crowd.

" The submersible must be lost," he said quietly, " but the men have escaped, so there is no great harm done. It does great credit to that Frenchman that he should have been prepared for such an emergency. Those are levium suits, and I've no doubt that he has got hydrogen somewhere inside to increase their buoyancy."

Within a quarter of an hour all the seven had been picked up by the boat, and it returned to the Ark. The strange forms were lifted aboard with tackle to save time; and as the first one reached the deck, it staggered about on its big limbs for a moment.

Then the metallic head opened, and the features of De Beauxchamps were revealed.

Before anybody could assist him he had freed himself from the suit, and immediately he began to aid the others. In ten minutes they all stood safe and sound before the astonished eyes of the spectators. Cosmo had suffered from the confinement, and he sank upon a seat, but De Beauxchamps seemed to be the most affected. With downcast look he said, sadly shaking his head:

"The poor *Jules Verne!* I shall never see her again."

"What has happened?" demanded Captain Arms.

"It was the Father of Horror," muttered Cosmo Versál.

"The Father of Horror—what's that?"

"Why, the Great Sphinx," returned Cosmo, gradually recovering his breath. "Didn't you know that that was what the Arabs always called the Sphinx?

"It was that which fell upon the submersible—split right open and dropped its great chin upon us as we were sailing round it, and pinned us fast. But the sight that we saw when the Sphinx fell apart! Tell them, De Beauxchamps."

The Frenchman took up the narrative, while, with breathless attention, passengers and crew crowded about to listen to his tale.

"When we got to the bottom," he said, "we first inspected the Great Pyramid, going all round it with our searchlight. It was in good condition, although the tide that had come up the Nile with the invasion of the sea had washed away the sands to a great depth all about. When we had completed the circuit of the pyramid, we saw the Sphinx, which had been excavated by the water so that it stood up to its full height.

"We ran close around it, and when we were under the chin the whole thing, saturated by the water, which no doubt caused an expansion within—you know how many thousand years the gigantic idol had been sun-dried—dropped apart.

"The submersible was caught by the falling mass, and partly crushed. We labored for hours and hours to release the vessel, but there was little that we could do. It almost broke my heart to think of leaving the *Jules Verne* there, but it had to be done.

"At last we put on the levium floating-suits, opened the cover at the top, and came to the surface. The last thing I saw was the searchlight, still burning, and illuminating the most marvelous spectacle that human eyes ever gazed upon."

"Oh, what was it? What was it?" demanded a score of voices in chorus.

"It is impossible to describe it. It was the secret of old Egypt revealed at last—at the end of the world!"

"But what was it like?"

"Like a glimpse into the remotest corridors of time," interposed Cosmo Versál, with a curious look in his eyes.

"Some of you may have heard that long ago holes were driven through the Sphinx in the hope of discovering something hidden inside, but they missed the secret. The old god kept it well until his form fell apart. We were pinned so close to it that we could not help seeing it, even in the excitement of our situation.

"It had always been supposed that the Sphinx was the symbol of something—it *was,* and more than a symbol! The explorers away back in the nineteenth century who thought that they had found something mysterious in the Great Pyramid went wide of the mark when they neglected the Sphinx."

"But what did you see?"

"*We saw the prophecy of the Second Deluge,*"

said Cosmo, rising to his feet, his piercing eyes aflame. " In the heart of the huge mass, approachable, no doubt, by some concealed passage in the rock beneath, known only to the priests, stood a gigantic idol, carved out of black marble.

" It had enormous eyes of some gem that blazed in the electric beam from the searchlight, with huge golden ears and beard, and on its breast was a representation of a drowning world, with a great nebula sweeping over it."

" It might have been a history instead of a prophecy," suggested one of the listening savants. " Perhaps it only told what had once happened."

" No," replied Cosmo, shaking his big head. " It was a prophecy. Under it, in ancient Egyptian hieroglyphics, which I recognized, was an inscription which could only be translated by the words, ' I come again—at the end of time! ' "

There was a quality in Cosmo Versál's voice which made the hearers shudder with horror.

" Yes," he added. " It comes again! The prophecy was hidden, but science had its means of revelation, too, if the world would but have listened to its voice. Even without the prophecy I have saved the flower of mankind."

CHAPTER XXII

THE TERRIBLE NUCLEUS ARRIVES

WHEN the company in the Ark had recovered from the astonishment produced by the narratives of De Beauxchamps and Cosmo Versál, and particularly the vivid description given by the latter of the strange idol concealed in the breast of the " Father of Horror," and the inferences which he drew concerning its prophetic character, the question again arose as to their future course.

Captain Arms was still for undertaking to follow the trough of the Red Sea, but Cosmo declared that this course would be doubly dangerous now that the water had lowered and that they no longer had the *Jules Verne* to act as a submarine scout, warning them of hidden perils.

They must now go by their own soundings, and this would be especially dangerous in the close neighborhood of half-submerged mountains, whose buttresses and foothills might rise suddenly out of the depths with slopes so steep that the lead would afford no certain guidance.

It was first necessary to learn if possible the actual height of the water, and whether it was still subsiding. It was partly for this purpose that they had passed over Egypt instead of keeping directly on toward the coast of lower Palestine.

But now Cosmo abandoned his purpose of taking his measurement by the aid of Mount Sinai or some of its neighboring peaks, on account of the dangerous character of that rugged region. If they had been furnished with deep-sea sounding apparatus they might have made a direct measurement of the depth in Egypt, but that was one of the few things which Cosmo Versál had overlooked in furnishing the Ark, and such an operation could not be undertaken.

He discovered that there was a mountain north of the Gulf of Akaba having an elevation of 3,450 feet, and since this was 220 feet higher than Monte Lauro, in Sicily, on which the Ark had grounded, he counted on it as a gage which would serve his purpose.

So they passed almost directly over Suez, and about 120 miles farther east they found the mountain they sought, rising to the west of the Wadi el Arabia, a continuation of the depression at whose deepest point lay the famous " Dead Sea," so often spoken of in the books of former times.

Here Cosmo was able to make a very accurate estimate from the height of the peak above the water, and he was gratified to find that the recession had not continued. The level of the water appeared to be exactly the same as when they made their unfortunate excursion in the direction of smoking Etna.

"It's all right," he said to Captain Arms. "We can get over into the Syrian desert without much danger, although we must go slowly and carefully until we are well past these ranges that come down from the direction of the Dead Sea. After that I do not see that there is anything in our way until we reach the ancient plains of Babylon."

King Richard, who was full of the history of the Crusades, as well as of Bible narratives, wished to have the Ark turn northward, so that they might sail over Jerusalem, and up the Valley of the Jordan within sight of Mount Hermon and the Lebanon range.

Cosmo had had enough of that kind of adventure, while Captain Arms declared that he would resign on the spot if there was to be any more "fool navigating on mountain tops." But there were many persons in the Ark who would have been very glad if King Richard's suggestion had been carried out.

The feelings of some were deeply stirred when they learned that they were now crossing the lower end of Palestine, and that the scenes of so many incidents in the history of Abraham, Moses, and Joshua lay buried beneath the blue water, whose almost motionless surface was marked with a broad trail of foaming bubbles in the wake of the immense vessel.

Cosmo greatly regretted the absence of the submersible when they were picking their way over this perilous region, but they encountered no real difficulty, and at length found, by celestial observations, that they were beyond all dangers and safely arrived over the deeply submerged desert.

They kept on for several days toward the rising sun, and then Captain Arms announced that the observations showed that they were over the site of Babylon.

This happened just at the time of the midday dinner, and over the dessert Cosmo seized the opportunity to make a little speech, which could be heard by all in the saloon.

"We are now arrived," he said, "over the very spot where the descendants of Noah are said to have erected a tower, known as the Tower of Babel, and which they intended to build so high that it would afford a secure refuge in case there should be another deluge.

"How vain were such expectations, if they were ever entertained, is sufficiently shown by the fact that, at this moment, the water rolls more than three thousand feet deep over the place where they put their tower, and before the present deluge is over it will be thirty thousand feet deep.

"More than half a mile beneath our feet lie the broad plains of Chaldea, where tradition asserts that the study of astronomy began. It was Berosus, a Chaldean, who predicted that there would come a second deluge.

"It occurs to me, since seeing the astounding spectacle disclosed by the falling apart of the Sphinx, that these people may have had an infinitely more profound knowledge of the secrets of the heavens than tradition has assigned to them.

"On the breast of the statue in the Sphinx was the figure of a crowned man, encircled by a huge ring, and having behind him the form of a boat containing two other human figures. The boat was represented as floating in a flood of waters.

"Now, this corresponds exactly with figures that have been found among the most ancient ruins in Chaldea. I regard that ring as symbolical of a nebula enveloping the earth, and I think that the second deluge, which we have lived to see, was foretold here thousands of years ago."

"Who foretold it first, then, the people who placed the statue in the Sphinx, or these astronomers of Chaldea?" asked Professor Abel Able.

"I believe," Cosmo replied, "that the knowledge originated here, beneath us, and that it was afterward conveyed to the Egyptians, who embodied it in their great symbolical god."

"Are we to understand," demanded Professor Jeremiah Moses, "that this figure was all that you saw on the breast of the statue, and that you simply *inferred* that the ring represented a nebula?"

"Not at all," Cosmo replied. "The principal representation was that of a world overwhelmed with a flood, and of a nebula descending upon it."

"How do you know that it was intended for a nebula?"

"Because it had the aspect of one, and it was clearly shown to be descending from the high heavens."

"A cloud," suggested Professor Moses.

"No, not a cloud. Mark this, which is a marvel in itself: It had *the form of a spiral nebula*. It was unmistakable."

At this point the discussion was interrupted by a call to Cosmo Versál from Captain Arms on the bridge. He hastily left the table and ascended to the captain's side.

He did not need to be told what to look for. Off in the north the sky had become a solid black mass, veined with the fiercest lightning. The pealing of the thunder came in a continuous roll, which soon grew so loud as to shake the Ark.

"Up with the side-plates!" shouted Cosmo, setting twenty bells ringing at once. "Close tight every opening! Screw down the port shutters!"

The crew of the Ark was, in a few seconds, running to and fro, executing the orders that came in swift succession from the commander's bridge, and the passengers were thrown into wild commotion. But nobody had time to attend to them.

"It is upon us!" yelled Cosmo in the captain's ear, for the uproar had become deafening. "The nucleus is here!"

The open promenade decks had not yet all been turned into inner corridors when the downpour began upon the Ark. A great deal of water found its way aboard, but the men worked with a will, as fearful for their own safety as for that of others, and in a little while everything had been made snug and tight.

In a short time a tremendous tempest was blowing, the wind coming from the north, and the Ark, notwithstanding her immense breadth of beam, was canted over to leeward at an alarming angle. On the larboard side the waves washed to the top of the great elliptical dome and broke over it, and their thundering blows shook the vessel to her center, causing many to believe that she was about to founder.

The disorder was frightful. Men and women were flung about like tops, and no one could keep his feet. Crash after crash, that could be heard amid the howling of the storm, the battering of the waves, and the awful roar of the deluge descending on the roof, told the fate of the tableware and dishes that had been hastily left in the big dining saloon.

Chairs recently occupied by the passengers on what had been the promenade decks, and from which they had so serenely, if often sorrowfully, looked over the broad, peaceful surface of the waters, were now darting, rolling, tumbling, and banging about, intermingled with rugs, hats, coats, and other abandoned articles of clothing.

The pitching and rolling of the Ark were so much worse than they had been during the first days of the cataclysm, that Cosmo became very solicitous about his collection of animals.

He hurried down to the animal deck, and found, indeed, that things were in a lamentable shape. The trained keepers were themselves so much at the mercy of the storm that they had had all they could do to save themselves from being trampled to death by the frightened beasts.

The animals had been furnished with separate pens, but during the long continued calm the keepers, for the sake of giving their charges greater freedom and better air, had allowed many of them to go at large in the broad central space around which the pens were placed, and the tempest had come so unexpectedly that there had been no time to separate them and get them back into their lodgings.

When Cosmo descended the scene that met his eyes caused him to cry out in dismay, but he could not have been heard if he had spoken through a trumpet. The noise and uproar were stunning, and the spectacle was indescribable. The keepers had taken refuge on a kind of gallery running round the central space, and were hanging on there for their lives.

Around them, on the railings, clinging with their claws, wildly flapping their wings, and swinging with every roll of the vessel, were all the fowls and every winged creature in the Ark except the giant turkeys, whose power of wing was insufficient to lift them out of the mêlée.

But all the four-footed beasts were rolling, tumbling, and struggling in the open space below. With every lurch of the Ark they were swept across the floor in an indistinguishable mass.

The elephants wisely did not attempt to get upon their feet, but allowed themselves to slide from side to side, sometimes crushing the smaller animals, and sometimes, in spite of all their efforts, rolling upon their backs, with their titanic limbs swaying above them, and their trunks wildly grasping whatever came within their reach.

The huge Californian cattle were in no better case, and the poor sheep presented a pitiable spectacle as they were tumbled in woolly heaps from side to side.

Strangest sight of all was that of the great Astoria turtles. They had been pitched upon their backs and were unable to turn themselves over, and their big carapaces served admirably for sliders.

They glided with the speed of logs in a chute, now this way, now that, shooting like immense projectiles through the throng of struggling beasts, cutting down those that happened to be upon their feet, and not ending their course until they had crashed against the nearest wall.

As one of the turtles slid toward the bottom of the steps on which Cosmo was clinging it cut under the legs of one of the giant turkeys, and the latter, making a superphasianidæan effort, half leaped, half flapped its way upon the steps to the side of Cosmo Versál, embracing him with one of its stumpy wings, while its red neck and head, with bloodshot eyes, swayed high above his bald dome.

The keepers gradually made their way round the gallery to Cosmo's side, and he indicated to them by signs that they must quit the place with him, and wait for a lull of the tempest before trying to do anything for their charges.

A few hours later the wind died down, and then they collected all that remained alive of the animals in their pens and secured them as best they could against the consequences of another period of rolling and pitching.

The experiences of the passengers had been hardly less severe, and panic reigned throughout the Ark. After the lull came, however, some degree of order was restored, and Cosmo had all who were in a condition to leave their rooms assemble in the grand saloon, where he informed them of the situation of affairs, and tried to restore their confidence. The roar on the roof, in spite of the sound-absorbing cover which had been re-erected, compelled him to use a trumpet.

" I do not conceal from you," he said in conclusion, " that the worst has now arrived. I do not look for any cessation of the flood from the sky until we shall have passed through the nucleus of the nebula. But the Ark is a stout vessel, we are fully provisioned, and we shall get through.

" All your chambers have been specially padded, as you may have remarked, and I wish you to remain in them, only issuing when summoned for assembly here.

" I shall call you out whenever the condition of the sea renders it safe for you to leave your rooms. Food will be regularly served in your quarters, and I beg you to have perfect confidence in me and my assistants."

But the confidence which Cosmo Versál recommended to the others was hardly shared by himself and Captain Arms. The fury of the blast which had just left them had exceeded everything that Cosmo had anticipated, and he saw that, in the face of such hurricanes, the Ark would be practically unmanageable.

One of his first cares was to ascertain the rate at which the downpour was raising the level of the water. This, too, surprised him. His gages showed, time after time, that the rainfall was at the rate of about four inches per minute. Sometimes it amounted to as much as six!

" The central part of the nebula," he said to the captain, through the speaking-tube which they had arranged for their intercommunications on the bridge, " is denser than I had supposed. The condensation is enormous, but it is irregular, and I think it very likely that it is more rapid in the north, where the front of the globe is plunging most directly into the nebulous mass.

" From this we should anticipate a tremendous flow southward, which may sweep us away in that direction. This will not be a bad thing for a while, since it is southward that we must go in order to reach the region of the Indian Ocean. But, in order not to be carried too rapidly that way, I think it would be the best thing to point the Ark toward the northeast."

" How am I to know anything about the points in this blackness? " growled the captain.

" You must go the best you can by the compass," said Cosmo.

Cosmo Versál, as subsequently appeared, was right in supposing that the nucleus of the nebula was exceedingly irregular in density. The condensation was not only much heavier in the north, but it was very erratic.

Some parts of the earth received a great deal more water from the opened flood-gates above than others, and this difference, for some reason that has never been entirely explained, was especially marked between the eastern and western hemispheres.

We have already seen that when the downpour recommenced in Colorado it was much less severe than during the first days of the flood. This difference continued. It seems that all the denser parts of the nucleus happened to encounter the planet on its eastern side.

This may have been partly due to the fact that as the rotating earth moved on in its eastward motion round the sun the comparatively dense masses of the nebula were always encountered at the times when the eastern hemisphere was in advance. The fact, which soon became apparent to Cosmo, that the downpour was always the most severe in the morning hours, bears out this hypothesis.

It accords with what has been observed with respect to meteors, viz., that they are more abundant in the early morning. But then it must be supposed that the condensed masses in the nebula were relatively so small that they became successively exhausted, so to speak, before the western hemisphere had come fairly into the line of fire.

Of course the irregularity in the arrival of the water did not, in the end, affect the general level of the flood, which became the same all over the globe, but it caused immense currents, as Cosmo had foreseen.

But there was one consequence which he had overlooked. The currents, instead of sweeping the Ark continually southward, as he had anticipated, formed a gigantic whirl, set up unquestionably by the great ranges of the Himalayas, the Hindoo Koosh, and the Caucasus.

This tremendous maelstrom formed directly over

Persia and Arabia, and, turning in the direction of the hands of a watch, its influence extended westward beyond the place where the Ark now was.

The consequence was that, in spite of all their efforts, Cosmo and the captain found their vessel swept resistlessly up the course of the valley containing the Euphrates and the Tigris.

They were unable to form an opinion of their precise location, but they knew the general direction of the movement, and by persistent logging got some idea of the rate of progress.

Fortunately the wind seldom blew with its first violence, but the effects of the whirling current could be but little counteracted by the utmost engine power of the Ark.

Day after day passed in this manner, although, owing to the density of the rain, the difference between day and night was only perceptible by the periodical changes from absolute blackness to a very faint illumination when the sun was above the horizon.

The rise of the flood, which could not have been at a less rate than six hundred feet every twenty-four hours, lifted the Ark above the level of the mountains of Kurdistan by the time that they arrived over the upper part of the Mesopotamian plain, and the uncertain observations which they occasionally obtained of the location of the sun, combined with such dead reckoning as they were able to make, finally convinced them that they must certainly be approaching the location of the Black Sea and the Caucasus range.

"I'll tell you what you're going to do," yelled Captain Arms. "You're going to make a smash on old Ararat, where your predecessor, Noah, made his landfall."

"*Très bien!*" shouted De Beauxchamps, who was frequently on the bridge, and whose Gallic spirits nothing could daunt. "That's a good omen! M. Versál should send out one of his turkeys to spy a landing place."

They were really nearer Ararat than they imagined, and Captain Arms's prediction narrowly missed fulfillment. Within a couple of hours after he had spoken a dark mass suddenly loomed through the dense air directly in their track.

Almost at the same time, and while the captain was making desperate efforts to sheer off, the sky lightened a little, and they saw an immense heap of rock within a hundred fathoms of the vessel.

"Ararat, by all that's good!" yelled the captain. "Sta'board! Sta'board, I tell you! Full power ahead!"

The Ark yielded slowly to her helm, and the screws whirled madly, driving her rapidly past the rocks, so close that they might have tossed a biscuit upon them. The set of the current also aided them, and they got past the danger.

"Mountain navigation again!" yelled the captain. "Here we are in a nest of these sky-shoals! What are you going to do now?"

"It is impossible to tell," returned Cosmo, "whether this is Great or Little Ararat. The former is over 17,000 feet high, and the latter at least 13,000. It is now twelve days since the flooding recommenced.

"If we assume a rise of 600 feet in twenty-four hours, that makes a total of 7,200 feet, which, added to the 3,300 that we had before, gives 10,500 feet for the present elevation. This estimate may be considerably out of the way.

"I feel sure that both the Ararats are yet well above the water line. We must get out of this region as quickly as possible. Luckily the swirl of the current is now setting us eastward. We are on its northern edge. It will carry the Ark down south of Mount Demavend, and the Elburz range, and over the Persian plateau, and if we can escape from it, as I hope, by getting away over Beluchistan, we can go directly over India and skirt the southern side of the Himalayas. Then we shall be near the goal which we have had in mind."

"Bless me!" said the captain, staring with mingled admiration and doubt at Cosmo Versál, "if you couldn't beat old Noah round the world, and give him half the longitude. But I'd rather *you'd* navigate this hooker. The ghost of Captain Sumner itself couldn't work a traverse over Beluchistan."

" You'll do it all right," returned Cosmo, " and the next time you drop your anchor it will probably be on the head of Mount Everest."

CHAPTER XXIII

ROBBING THE CROWN OF THE WORLD

NOW that they were going with the current instead of striving to stem it, the Ark made much more rapid way than during the time that it was drifting toward the Black Sea.

They averaged at least six knots, and, with the aid of the current, could have done much better, but they thought it well to be cautious, especially as they had so little means of guessing at their exact location from day to day. The water was rough.

There was, most of the time, little wind, and often a large number of the passengers assembled in the saloon.

The noise of the deluge on the roof was so much greater than it had been at the start that it was difficult to converse, but there was plenty of light, and they could, at least, see one another, and communicate by signs if not very easily by the voice. Cosmo's library was well selected, and many passed hours in reading stories of the world they were to see no more!

King Richard and Amos Blank imitated Cosmo and the captain by furnishing themselves with a speaking-tube, which they put alternately to their lips and their ears, and thus held long conversations, presumably exchanging with one another the secrets of high finance and kingly government.

Both of them had enough historical knowledge and sufficient imagination to be greatly impressed by the fact that they were drifting, amidst this terrible storm, over the vast empire that Alexander the Great had conquered.

They mused over the events of the great Macedonian's long marches through deserts and over mountains, and the king, who loved the story of these glories of the past, though he had cultivated peace in his own dominions, often sighed while they recalled them to one another. Lord Swansdown and the other Englishmen aboard seldom joined their king since he had preferred the company of an untitled American to theirs.

The first named could not often have made a member of the party if he had wished, for he kept his room most of the time, declaring that he had never been so beastly seasick in his life. He thought that such an abominable roller as the Ark should never have been permitted to go into commission, don't you know.

On the morning of the twelfth day after they left the neighborhood of Mount Ararat Captain Arms averred that their position must be somewhere near longitude 69 degrees east, latitude 26 degrees north.

" Then you have worked your traverse over Beluchistan very well," said Cosmo, " and we are now afloat above the valley of the River Indus. We have the desert of northwestern India ahead, and from that locality we can continue right down the course of the 'Ganges. In fact it would be perfectly safe to turn northward and skirt the Himalayas within reach of the high peaks. I think that's what I'll do."

" If you go fooling round any more peaks," shouted Captain Arms, in a fog-horn voice, " you'll have to do your own steering! I've had enough of that kind of navigation! "

Nevertheless when Cosmo Versál gave the order the captain turned the prow of the Ark toward the presumable location of the great Himalayan range, although the rebellion of his spirit showed in the erect set of his whiskers. They were now entirely beyond the influence of the whirl that had at first got them into trouble, and then helped them out of it, in western Asia.

Behind the barrier of the ancient " Roof of the World " the sea was relatively calm, although, at times, they felt the effect of currents pouring down from the north, which had made their way through the lofty passes from the Tibetan side.

Cosmo calculated from his estimate of the probable rate of rise of the flood and from the direction and force of the currents that all but the very highest of the Pamirs must already be submerged.

It was probable, he thought, that the water had attained a level of between seventeen and eighteen thousand feet. This, as subsequent events indicated, was undoubtedly an underestimate. The downpour in the north must have been far greater than Cosmo thought, and the real height of the flood was considerably in excess of what he supposed.

If they could have seen some of the gigantic peaks as they approached the mountains in the eastern Punjab, south of Cashmere, they would have been aware of the error.

As it was, owing to the impossibility of seeing more than a short distance even when the light was brightest, they kept farther south than was really necessary, and after passing, as they believed, over Delhi, steered south by east, following substantially the course that Cosmo had originally named along the line of the Ganges valley.

They were voyaging much slower now, and after another ten days had passed an unexpected change came on. The downpour diminished in severity, and at times the sun broke forth, and for an hour or two the rain would cease entirely, although the sky had a coppery tinge, and at night small stars were not clearly visible.

Cosmo was greatly surprised at this. He could only conclude that the central part of the nebula had been less extensive, though more dense, than he had estimated. It was only thirty-four days since the deluge had recommenced, and unless present appearances were deceptive, its end might be close at hand.

Captain Arms seized the opportunity to make celestial and solar observations which delighted his seaman's heart, and with great glee he informed Cosmo that they were in longitude 88 degrees 20 minutes east, latitude 24 degrees 15 minutes north, and he would stake his reputation as a navigator upon it.

"Almost exactly the location of Moorshedabad, in Bengal," said Cosmo, consulting his chart. "The mighty peak of Kunchingunga is hardly more than two hundred miles toward the north, and Mount Everest, the highest point in the world, is within a hundred miles of that!"

"But you're not going skimming around *them!*" cried the captain with some alarm.

"I shall, if the sky continues in its present condition, go as far as Darjeeling," replied Cosmo. "Then we can turn eastward and get over upper Burmah and so on into China. From there we can turn north again.

"I think we can manage to get into Tibet somewhere between the ranges. It all depends upon the height of the water, and that I can ascertain exactly by getting a close look at Kunchingunga. I would follow the line of the Brahmaputra River if I dared, but the way is too beset with perils."

"I think you've made a big mistake," said the captain. "Why didn't you come directly across Russia, after first running up to the Black Sea from the Mediterranean, and so straight into Tibet?"

"I begin to think that that's what I ought to have done," responded Cosmo, thoughtfully, "but when we started the water was not high enough to make me sure of that route, and after we got down into Egypt I didn't want to run back. But I guess it would have been better."

"Better a sight than steering among these five-mile peaks," growled Captain Arms. "How high does Darjeeling lie? I don't want to run aground again."

"Oh, that's perfectly safe," responded Cosmo. "Darjeeling is only about 7,350 feet above the old sea-level. I think we can go almost to the foot of Kunchingunga without any danger."

"Well, the name sounds dangerous enough in itself," said the captain, "but I suppose you'll have your way. Give me the bearings and we'll be off."

They took two days to get to the location of Darjeeling, for at times the sky darkened and the rain came down again in tremendous torrents. But these spells did not last more than two or three hours, and the weather cleared between them.

As soon as they advanced beyond Darjeeling, keeping a sharp outlook for Kunchingunga, Cosmo began to perceive the error of his calculation of the height of the flood.

The mountain should still have projected more than three thousand feet above the waves, allowing that the average rise during the thirty-six days since the recommencement of the flood had been six hundred feet a day.

But, in fact, they did not see it at all, and thought at first that it had been totally submerged. At last they found it, a little rocky island, less than two hundred feet above the water, according to Cosmo's careful measure, made from a distance of a quarter of a mile.

" ,This is great news for us," he exclaimed, as soon as he had completed the work. " This will save us a long journey round. The water must now stand at about 27,900 feet, and although there are a considerable number of peaks in the Himalayas approaching such an elevation, there are only three or four known to reach or exceed it, of which Kunchingunga is one.

" We can, then, run right over the roof of the world, and there· we'll be, in Tibet. Then we can determine from what side it is safest to approach Mount Everest, for I am very desirous to get near that celebrated peak, and, if possible, see it go under."

" But the weather isn't safe yet," objected Captain Arms. " Suppose we should be caught in another downpour, and everything black about us! I'm not going to navigate this ship by searchlight among mountains twenty-eight thousand feet tall, when the best beam that ever shot from a mirror won't show an object a hundred fathoms away."

" Very well," Cosmo replied, " we'll circle around south for a few days and see what will happen. I think myself that it's not quite over yet. The fact is, I hope it isn't, for now that it has gone so far, I'd like to see the top-knot of the earth covered."

" Well, it certainly couldn't do any more harm if it got up as high as the moon," responded the captain.

They spent four days sailing to and fro over India, and during the first three of those days there were intermittent downpours. But the whole of the last period of twenty-four hours was entirely without rain, and the color of the sky changed so much that Cosmo declared he would wait no longer.

" Everest," he said, " is only 940 feet higher than Kunchingunga, and it may be sunk out of sight before we can get there."

" Do you think the water is still rising? " asked De Beauxchamps, while King Richard and Amos Blank listened eagerly for the reply, for now that the weather had cleared, the old company was all assembled on the bridge.

" Yes, slowly," said Cosmo. " There is a perceptible current from the north which indicates that condensation is still going on there. You'll see that it'll come extremely close to the six miles I predicted before it's all over."

By the time they had returned to the neighborhood of the mountains the sky had become blue, with only occasionally a passing sunshower, and Cosmo ordered the promenades to be thrown open, and the passengers, with great rejoicings, resumed their daily lounging and walking on deck.

It required a little effort of thought to make them realize their situation, but when they did it grew upon them until they could not sufficiently express their wonder.

Here they were, on an almost placid sea, with tepid airs blowing gently in their faces, and a scorching sun overhead, whose rays had to be shielded off, floating over the highest pinnacles of the roof of the world, the traditional " Abode of Snow! "

All around them, beneath the rippled blue surface, lined here and there with little white windrows of foam, stood submerged peaks, 24,000, 25,000, 26,000, 27,000, 28,000 feet in elevation! They sailed over their summits and saw them not.

All began now to sympathize with Cosmo's desire to find Everest before it should have disappeared with its giant brothers. Its location was accurately known from the Indian government surveys, and Captain Arms had every facility for finding the exact position of the Ark. They advanced slowly toward the northwest, a hundred glasses eagerly scanning the horizon ahead.

Finally, at noon on the third day of their search, the welcome cry of " Land ho! " came down from the cro'nest. Captain Arms immediately set his course for the landfall, and in the course of a little more than an hour had it broad abeam.

"It's Everest, without question," said Cosmo. "It's the crown of the world."

But how strange was its appearance! A reddish-brown mass of rock, rising abruptly out of the blue water, really a kind of crown in form, but not more than a couple of square rods in extent, and about three feet high at its loftiest point.

There was no snow, of course, for that had long since disappeared, owing to the rise of temperature, and no snow would have fallen in that latitude now, even in mid-winter, because the whole base of the atmosphere had been lifted up nearly six miles.

Sea-level pressures were prevailing where the barometric column would once have dropped almost to the bottom of its tube. It was all that was left of the world!

North of them, under the all-concealing ocean, lay the mighty plateau of Tibet; far toward the east was China, deeply buried with its 500,000,000 of inhabitants; toward the south lay India, over which they had so long been sailing; northwestward the tremendous heights of the Pamir region and of the Hindu-Kush were sunk beneath the sea.

"When this enormous peak was covered with snow," said Cosmo, "its height was estimated at 29,002 feet, or almost five and three-quarter miles. The removal of the snow has, of course, lowered it, but I think it probable that this point, being evidently steep on all sides, and of very small area, was so swept by the wind that the snow was never very deep upon it.

"If we allow ten, or even twenty feet for the snow, the height of this rock cannot be much less than 29,000 feet above the former sea-level. But I do not dare to approach closer, because Everest had a broad summit, and we might possibly ground upon a sharp ridge."

"And you are sure that the water is still rising?" asked De Beauxchamps again.

"Watch and you will see," Cosmo responded.

The Ark was kept circling very slowly within a furlong of the rocky crown, and everybody who had a glass fixed his eyes upon it.

"The peak is certainly sinking," said De Beauxchamps at last. "I believe it has gone down three inches in the last fifteen minutes."

"Keep your eyes fixed on some definite point," said Cosmo to the others who were looking, "and you will easily note the rise of the water."

They watched it until nobody felt any doubt. Inch by inch the crown of the world was going under. In an hour Cosmo's instruments showed that the highest point had settled to a height of but two feet above the sea.

"But when will the elevation that you have predicted begin?" asked one.

" Its effects will not become evident immediately,"
Cosmo replied. " It may possibly already have begun, but if so, it is masked by the continued rise of
the water."

" And how long shall we have to wait for the re-
emergence of Tibet? "

" I cannot tell, but it will be a long time. But do
not worry about that. We have plenty of provisions,
and the weather will continue fine after the departure
of the nebula."

They circled about until only a foot or so of the
rock remained above the reach of the gently washing
waves. Suddenly struck by a happy thought, De
Beauxchamps exclaimed:

" I must have a souvenir from the crown of the
disappearing world. M. Versál, will you permit me
to land upon it with one of your boats? "

De Beauxchamps's suggestion was greeted with
cheers, and twenty others immediately expressed a
desire to go.

" No," said Cosmo to the eager applicants, " it is
M. De Beauxchamps's idea; let him go alone. Yes,"
he continued, addressing the Frenchman, " you can
have a boat, and I will send two men with you to
manage it. You'd better hurry, or there will be
nothing left to land upon."

The necessary orders were quickly given, and in
five minutes De Beauxchamps, watched by envious
eyes, was rapidly approaching the disappearing rock.

They saw him scramble out upon it, and they gave a mighty cheer as he waved his hand at them.

He had taken a hammer with him, and with breathless interest they watched him pounding and prying about the rock. They could see that he selected the very highest point for his operations.

While he worked away, evidently filling his pockets, the interest of the onlookers became more and more intense.

" Look out ! " they presently began to shout at him, " you will be caught by the water."

But he paid no attention, working with feverish rapidity. Suddenly the watchers saw a little ripple break over the last speck of dry land on the globe, and De Beauxchamps standing up to his shoe-laces in water. Cries of dismay came from the Ark. De Beauxchamps now gave over his work, and, with apparent reluctance, entered the boat, which was rowed close up to the place where he was standing.

As the returning boat approached the Ark, another volley of cheers broke forth, and the Frenchman, standing up to his full height, waved with a triumphant air something that sparkled brilliantly in the sunshine.

" I congratulate you, M. De Beauxchamps," cried Cosmo, as the adventurer scrambled aboard. " You have stood where no human foot has ever been before, and I see that you have secured your souvenir of the world that was."

"Yes," responded De Beauxchamps exultantly, "and see what it is—a worthy decoration for such a coronet."

He held up his prize, amid exclamations of astonishment and admiration from those who were near enough to see it.

"The most beautiful specimen of amethyst I ever beheld!" cried a mineralogist enthusiastically, taking it from De Beauxchamps's hand. "What was the rock?"

"Unfortunately, I am no mineralogist," replied the Frenchman, "and I cannot tell you, but these gems were abundant. I could have almost filled the boat if I had had time.

"The amethyst," he added gayly, "is the traditional talisman against intoxication, but, although these adorned her tiara, the poor old world has drunk her fill."

"But it is only water," said Cosmo, smiling.

"Too much, at any rate," returned the Frenchman.

"I should say," continued the mineralogist, "that the rock was some variety of syenite, from its general appearance."

"I know nothing of that," replied De Beauxchamps, "but I have the jewels of the terrestrial queen, and," he continued gallantly, "I shall have the pleasure of bestowing them upon the ladies."

He emptied his pockets, and found that he had

enough to give every woman aboard the Ark a specimen, with several left over for some of the men, Cosmo, of course, being one of the recipients.

" There," said De Beauxchamps, as he handed the stone to Cosmo, " there is a memento from the Gaurisankar."

" I beg your pardon—Mount Everest, if you please," interposed Edward Whistlington.

" No," responded the Frenchman stoutly, " it is the Gaurisankar. Why will you English persist in renaming everything in the world? Gaurisankar is the native name, and, in my opinion, far more appropriate and euphonious than Everest."

This discussion was not continued, for now everybody became interested in the movements of the Ark. Cosmo had decided that it would be safe to approach close to the point where the last peak of the mountain had disappeared.

Cautiously they drew nearer and nearer, until, looking through the wonderfully transparent water, they caught sight of a vast precipice descending with frightful steepness, down and down, until all was lost in the profundity beneath.

The point on which De Beauxchamps had landed was now covered so deep that the water had ceased to swirl about it, but lay everywhere in an unbroken sheet, which was every moment becoming more placid and refulgent in the sunshine.

The world was drowned at last! As they looked

abroad over the convex surface, they thought, with a shudder, that now the earth, seen from space, was only a great, glassy ball, mirroring the sun and the stars.

But they were ignorant of what had happened far in the west!

CHAPTER XXIV

THE FRENCHMAN'S NEW SCHEME

AFTER the disappearance of Mt. Everest, Cosmo Versál made a careful measurement of the depth of water on the peak, which he found to be forty feet, and then decided to cruise eastward with the Ark, sailing slowly, and returning after a month to see whether by that time there would be any indications of the reappearance of land.

No part of his extraordinary theory of the deluge was more revolutionary, or scientifically incredible, than this idea that the continents would gradually emerge again, owing to internal stresses set up in the crust of the earth.

This, he anticipated, would be caused by the tremendous pressure of the water, which must be ten or twelve miles deep over the greatest depressions of the old ocean-bottoms. He expected that geological movements would attend the intrusion of the water into subterranean cavities and into the heated magma under volcanic regions.

He often debated the question with the savants aboard the Ark, and, despite their incredulity, he persisted in his opinion. He could not be shaken, either, in his belief that the first land to emerge would be the Himalayas, the Pamirs, and the plateau of Tibet.

"We may have to wait some years before any considerable area is exposed," he admitted, "but it must not be forgotten that what land does first appear above the water will lie at the existing sea-level, and will have an oceanic climate, suitable for the rapid development of plants.

"We have aboard all things needed for quick cultivation, and in one season we could begin to raise crops."

"But at first," said Professor Jeremiah Moses, "only mountain tops will emerge, and how can you expect to cultivate them?"

"There is every probability," replied Cosmo, "that even the rocks of a mountain will be sufficiently friable after their submergence to be readily reduced to the state of soil, especially with the aid of the chemical agents which I have brought along, and I have no fear that I could not, in a few weeks, make even the top of Everest fertile.

"I anticipate, in fact, that it will be on that very summit that we shall begin the re-establishment of the race. Then, as the plateaus below come to the surface, we can gradually descend and enlarge the field of our operations."

"Suppose Everest should be turned into a volcano?"

"That cannot happen," said Cosmo. "A volcano is built up by the extrusion of lava and cinders from below, and these cannot break forth at the top of a mountain already formed, especially when that mountain has no volcanic chimney and no crater, and Everest had neither."

"If the lowering of the flood that caused our stranding on a mountain top in Sicily was due to the absorption of water into the interior of the crust, why may not that occur again, and thus bring the Himalayas into view, without any rising on their part?" demanded Professor Moses.

"I think," said Cosmo, "that all the water that could enter the crust has already done so, during the time that the depression of level which so surprised us was going on. Now we must wait for geologic changes, resulting from the gradual yielding of the internal mass to the new forces brought to bear upon it.

"As the whole earth has gained in *weight* by the condensation of the nebula upon it, its plastic crust will proportionally gain in *girth* by internal expansion, which will finally bring all the old continents to the surface, but Asia first of all."

Whether Cosmo Versál's hypotheses were right or wrong, he always had a reply to any objection, and the prestige which he had gained by his disastrously correct theory about the watery nebula gave him an advantage so enormous that nobody felt enough confidence in himself to stand long against anything that he might advance.

Accordingly, everybody in the Ark found himself looking forward to the re-emergence of Mount Everest almost as confidently as did their leader, Cosmo Versál.

They began their waiting voyage by sailing across the plateau of Tibet and the lofty chain of the Yungling Mountains out over China.

The interest of all aboard was excited to the highest degree when they found themselves sailing over the mighty domains of the Chinese President-Emperor, who had developed an enormous power, making him the ruler of the whole eastern world.

He, with his half-billion or more of subjects, now reposed at the bottom of an ocean varying from three to five or six miles in depth. Deep beneath the Ark lay the broad and once populous valleys of the Yangtse-Kiang and the Hoang-Ho, the "Scourge of China."

Finally they swung round northward and re-entered the region of Tibet, seeking once more the drowned crown of the world. In the meantime Cosmo had had the theatrical exhibitions and the concerts resumed in the evenings, and sometimes there was music, and even dancing on the long promenades, open to the outer air.

Let not that be a matter of surprise or blame, for the spirit of joy in life is unconquerable, as it should be if life is worth while. So it happened that, not infrequently, and not with any blameworthy intention, or in any spirit of heartless forgetfulness, this remarkable company of world-wanderers drifted, in the moonlight, above the universal watery grave of the drowned millions, with the harmonies of stringed instruments stealing out upon the rippling waves, and the soft sound of swiftly shuffling feet tripping over the smooth decks.

Costaké Theriade and Sir Wilfrid Athelstone resumed their stormy efforts to talk each other down, but now even Cosmo was seldom a listener, except when he had to interfere to keep the peace.

King Richard and Amos Blank, however, usually heard them out, but it was evident from their expressions that they enjoyed the prospective fisticuffs rather more than the exposition of strange scientific doctrines.

Perhaps the happiest man aboard was Captain Arms. At last he could make as many and as certain observations as he chose, and he studied the charts of Asia until he declared that now he knew the latitude and longitude of the mountains better than he did those of the seaports of the old oceans.

He had not the least difficulty in finding the location of Mount Everest again, and when he announced that they were floating over it, Cosmo immediately prepared to make another measurement of the depth of water on the peak. The result was hardly gratifying. He found that it had diminished but four inches. He said to Captain Arms:

" The range is rising, but less rapidly than I hoped. Even if the present rate should be doubled it would require five years for the emergence of the highest point. Instead of remaining in this part of the world we shall have an abundance of time to voyage round the earth, going leisurely, and when we get back again perhaps there will be enough land visible to give us a good start."

" Mr. Versál," said the captain, " you remember that you promised me that I should drop my anchor on the head of Mount Everest if I worked a traverse across Beluchistan."

" Certainly I remember it; and also that you were not much disposed to undertake the task. However, you did it well, and I suppose that now you want me to fulfill the bargain? "

" Exactly," replied the captain. " I'd just like to get a mud-hook in the top-knot of the earth. I reckon that that'll lay over all the sea yarns ever spun."

" Very well," returned Cosmo. " Try it, if you've got cable enough."

" Enough and to spare," cried the captain, " and I'll have the Gaurisankar, as the Frenchman calls it, hooked in a jiffy."

This was an operation which called everybody to to the rails to watch it. Hundreds of eyes tried to follow the anchor as it descended perpendicularly upon the mountain-top, nearly forty feet beneath. Through the clear water they could dimly see the dark outline of the summit below, and they gazed at it with wonder, and a sort of terror.

Somehow they felt that never before had they fully appreciated the awful depths over which they had been floating. The anchor steadily dropped until it rested on the rock.

It got a hold finally, and in a few minutes the great vessel was swinging slowly round, held by a cable whose grasp was upon the top of the world! When the sensation had been sufficiently enjoyed the anchor was tripped, and the nose of the Ark was turned northwestward. Cosmo Versál announced his intention to circumnavigate the drowned globe.

The news of what they were about to do was both welcome and saddening to the inmates of the vessel. They wished to pass once more over the lands where they had first seen the light, and at the same time they dreaded the memories that such a voyage would inevitably bring back with overwhelming force. But, at any rate, it would be better than drifting for years over Tibet and China.

While everybody else was discussing the prospects of the new voyage, and wondering how long it would last, Yves de Beauxchamps was concentrating all his attention upon a new project which had sprung up in his active mind as soon as Cosmo's intention was

announced. He took Cosmo aside and said to him:
" M. Versál, the dearest memory that I have treasured in my heart is that of the last sight of my
drowned home, my beautiful dead Paris. It may be
that the home-loving instincts of my race arouse in
me a melancholy pleasure over such a sight which
would not be shared by you, of a different blood; but
if, perchance, you do share my feelings on this subject I believe that I can promise you a similar visit
to the great metropolis where your life began, and
where you executed those labors whose result has
been to preserve a remnant of humanity to repeople
the earth."

Cosmo Versál's quick intelligence instantly comprehended the Frenchman's design, but it startled him,
and apparently insuperable difficulties at once occurred to his mind.

" M. De Beauxchamps," he responded, grasping
his friend warmly by the hand, " I thank you from
the bottom of my heart for your amiable intention,
and I assure you that nothing could afford me greater
satisfaction than to see once more that mighty city,
even though it can now be but an awful ruin, tenanted
by no life except the terrible creatures of the deep.
But, while I foresee what your plan must be, I can
hardly conceive that its execution could be possible.
You are thinking, of course, of constructing a diving
apparatus capable of penetrating to a depth of nearly
six miles in the sea. Setting aside the question

whether we could find in the stores of the Ark the materials that would be needed, it appears to me most improbable that we could make the apparatus of sufficient strength to withstand the pressure, and could then cause it to sink to so great a depth, and afterward bring it safely to the surface."

The Frenchman smiled.

" M. Versál," he replied, " I have taken the liberty to look over the stock of materials which you have so wisely prepared for possible repairs to the Ark and for use after the Ark lands, and I know that among them I can find all that I shall need. You yourself know how completely you are provided with engineering tools and machines of all kinds. You have even an electric foundry aboard. With the aid of your mechanical genius, and the skill of your assistants, together with that of my own men, who are accustomed to work of this kind, I have not the faintest doubt that I can design and construct a diving-bell, large enough to contain a half-dozen persons, and perfectly capable of penetrating to any depth. Of course I cannot make it of levium, but you have a sufficient supply of herculeum steel, the strength of which is so immense that the walls of the bell can be made to remit the pressure even at a depth of six miles. From my previous experiments I am confident that there will be no difficulty in sinking and afterward raising this apparatus. It is only necessary that the mean specific gravity of the bell shall be greater than that of the water at a given depth, and you know that as far back as the end of the nineteenth century your own countrymen sent down sounding apparatus more than six miles in the Pacific Ocean, near the island of Guam."

" But the air inside the bell——" Cosmo began.

" Excuse me," interrupted De Beauxchamps, " but that air need be under no greater pressure than at the surface. I shall know how to provide for that. Remember the *Jules Verne*. Simply give me *carte blanche* in this matter, let me have the materials to work with, afford me the advantage of your advice and assistance whenever I shall need them, and I promise you that by the time we have arrived over the site of New York we shall be prepared for the descent."

Cosmo was deeply impressed by the Frenchman's enthusiastic self-confidence. He had a great admiration for the constructor of the *Jules Verne*, and, besides, the proposed adventure was exactly after his own heart. After meditating a while, he said heartily:

" Well, M. De Beauxchamps, I give my consent. Everything you wish shall be at your disposal, and you can begin as soon as you choose. Only, let the thing be kept a secret between us and the workmen who are employed. If it should turn out a failure it would not do that the people in the Ark should be aware of it. I can give you a working room on one of the lower decks, where there will be no interference with your proceedings, and no knowledge of what you are about can leak out."

" That is exactly what I should wish," returned De Beauxchamps, smiling with delight, " and I renew my promise that you shall not be disappointed."

So, without a suspicion of what was going on entering the minds of any person in the great company outside the small company of men who were actually employed in the work, the construction of De Beauxchamps's great diving-bell was begun, and pushed with all possible speed, consistent with the proper execution of the work. In the meantime the Ark continued its course toward the west.

They ran slowly, for there was no hurry, and the Ark had now become to its inhabitants as a house and a home—their only foothold on the whole round earth, and that but a little floating island of buoyant metal. They crossed the Pamirs and the Hindu-Kush, the place where the Caspian Sea had been swallowed up in the universal ocean, and ran over Ararat, which three months before had put them into such fearful danger, but whose loftiest summit now lay twelve thousand feet beneath their keel.

At length, after many excursions toward the north and toward the south, in the halcyon weather that had seldom failed since the withdrawal of the nebula, they arrived at the place (or above it) which had stood during centuries for a noon-mark on the globe.

It was midday when Captain Arms, having made his observations, said to Cosmo and the others on the bridge:

" Noon at Greenwich, and noon on the Ark. Latitude, fifty-one degrees thirty minutes. That brings you as nearly plumb over the place as you'd be likely to hit it. Right down there lies the old observatory that set the chronometers of the world, and kept the clocks and watches up to their work."

King Richard turned aside upon hearing the captain's words. They brought a too vivid picture of the great capital, six miles under their feet, and a too poignant recollection of the disastrous escape of the royal family from overwhelmed London seven months before.

As reckoned by the almanac, it was the 15th of September, more than sixteen months since Cosmo had sent out his first warning to the public, when the Ark crossed the meridian of seventy-four degrees west, in about forty-one degrees north latitude, and the adventurers knew that New York was once more beneath them.

There was great emotion among both passengers and crew, for the majority of them had either dwelt in New York or been in some way associated with its enterprises and its people, and, vain as must be the hope of seeing any relic of the buried metropolis, every eye was on the alert.

They looked off across the boundless sea in every

direction, interrogating every suspicious object on the far horizon, and even peering curiously into the blue abyss, as if something might suddenly appear there which would speak to them like a voice from the past.

But they saw only shafts of sunlight running into bottomless depths, and occasionally some oceanic creature floating lazily far below. The color of the sea was wonderful. It had attracted their attention after the submergence of Mount Everest, but at that time it had not yet assumed its full splendor.

At first, no doubt, there was considerable dissolved matter in the water, but gradually this settled, and the sea became bluer and bluer—not the deep indigo of the old ocean, but a much lighter and more brilliant hue—and here, over the site of New York, the waters were of a bright, luminous sapphire, that dazzled the eye.

Cosmo declared that the change of the sea-color was undoubtedly due to some quality in the nebula from whose condensation the water had been produced, but neither his own analyses, nor those of the chemists aboard the Ark, were able to detect the subtle element to whose presence the peculiar tint was due.

But whatever it may have been, it imparted to the ocean an ethereal, imponderous look, which was sometimes startling. There were moments when they almost expected to see it expand back into the nebulous form and fly away.

CHAPTER XXV

NEW YORK IN HER OCEAN TOMB

DURING the long voyage from the sunken Himalayas to still deeper sunken New York, De Beauxchamps, with his fellow-countrymen and the skilled mechanics assigned by Cosmo Versál to aid them, had finished the construction of the huge diving-bell. No one not in the secret had the slightest idea of what had been done, owing to the remote situation of the deck on which the construction was carried out.

Now, while a thousand pairs of eyes were interrogating the smooth surface of the sea, and striving to penetrate its cerulean depths, a great surprise was sprung upon the passengers. The rear gangway of the lowest deck was cleared, a heavy crane-like beam was set projecting over the water, and men began to rig a flexible cable, which had been specially prepared for the purpose of lowering the bell into the depths, and of raising it again when the adventurers should wish to return to the surface. Everybody's attention was immediately attracted to these strange preparations, and the utmost curiosity was aroused. A chorus of wondering exclamations broke out when a metallic globe, twenty feet in diameter, and polished until it shone like a giant thermometer bulb, was rolled out and carefully attached to the cable by means of a strong ring set in one side of the bell. The excitement of the passengers would soon have become uncontrollable if Cosmo had not at this point summoned the entire ship's company into the great saloon. As soon as all were assembled he mounted his dais and began to speak.

"My fellow-citizens of the old world, which has perished, and of the new, which is to take its place," he said, "we owe to the genius of M. De Beauxchamps an apparatus which is about to enable us to inspect, by an actual visit, the remains of the vast metropolis, which we saw in all its majesty and beauty but so few months ago, and which now lies forever silent at the bottom of this universal ocean.

"If it were practicable I should wish to afford to every one of you a farewell glimpse of that mighty city, to which the hearts of so many here are bound, but you can readily understand that that would be impossible. Only six persons can go in this exploring bell, and they have been chosen; but a faithful account will be brought back to you of all that they see and learn. The adventuring company will consist of M. De Beauxchamps, M. Pujol, his first assistant, Mr. Amos Blank, King Richard, Professor Abel Able, and myself. Captain Arms has ascertained the location of the center of Manhattan Island, over which we are now floating. The quietness of the sea, the absence of any apparent current, and the serenity of the heavens are favoring circumstances, which may be relied upon to enable Captain Arms to keep the Ark constantly poised almost precisely over our point of descent. It is not possible to predict the exact duration of our absence in the depths, but it will not, in any case, exceed about twenty hours.

" Once arrived at the bottom, nearly six miles down, we shall attach the cable to some secure anchorage, by means of a radio-control, operated from within the bell, and then, with the bell free, we shall make explorations, as extensive as possible. The radio-control of which I have spoken governs also the attachment of the cable to the bell. This appliance has been prepared and tested with such care that we have no doubt of its entire efficiency. I mention these things in order to remove from your minds any fear as to the success of our enterprise.

" The bell being once detached, we shall be able to move it from point to point by means of a pair of small propellers, which you will perceive on the outside of the bell, and which are also controlled from within. These will be used to increase our speed of descent. From a calculation of the density of the sea-water at the depth to which we shall descend, we estimate that the bell with its contents will press upon the bottom with a gravitational force of only five pounds, so that it will move with very slight effort, and may even, when in motion, float like a fish.

" For the purposes of observation we have provided, on four sides of the bell, a series of circular windows, with glass of immense thickness and strength, but of extraordinary transparency. Through these windows we shall be able to see in almost all directions. It was our intention to provide wireless telephone apparatus with which we might have kept you informed of all our doings and discoveries, but unfortunately we have found it impracticable to utilize our control for that purpose. We shall, however, be able to send and receive signals as long as we are connected with the cable.

" I should add that the construction of the bell, although suggested by M. De Beauxchamps immediately after our departure from Mount Everest, has been carried on in secret simply because we did not wish to subject you to the immense disappointment which you would certainly have experienced if this brilliant conception of our gifted friend, after being once made known to you, had proved to be a failure. Our preparations have all been made, and within an hour we shall begin the descent."

It is quite impossible to describe the excitement of the passengers while they lisened to this extraordinary communication. When Cosmo Versál had finished speaking he stood for some minutes looking at his audience with a triumphant smile. First a murmur of excited voices arose, and then somebody proposed three cheers, which were given and repeated until the levium dome rang with the reverberations. Nobody knew exactly why he was cheering, but the infectious enthusiasm carried everything before it. Then the crowd began to ask questions, addressed not to Cosmo but to one another. The wildest suggestions were made. One woman who had left some treasured heirlooms in a Fifth Avenue mansion demanded of her husband that he should commission Cosmo Versál to recover them.

" I'm sure they're there," she insisted. " They were locked in the safe."

" But, don't you see," protested the poor man, " he can't get outside of that bell to get 'em."

" I don't see *why* he can't, if he should really try. I think it's too mean! They were my grandmother's jewels."

" But, my dear, how could he get out? "

" Well, *how does he get in?* What's his radio-control good for; won't that help him? What is he going down there for if he can't do a little thing like that, to oblige? "

She pouted at her husband because he persistently refused to present her request to Cosmo, and declared that she would do it herself, then, for she must have those jewels, now that they were so near.

But Cosmo was saved from this, and other equally unreasonable demands, by a warning from De Beauxchamps that all was ready, and that no time should be lost. Then everybody hastened out on the decks to watch the departure of the adventurers. Many thoughtfully shook their heads, predicting that they would never be seen again. As soon as this feeling began to prevail the enthusiasm quickly evaporated, and efforts were made to dissuade Cosmo and De Beauxchamps from making the attempt. But they were deaf to all remonstrance, and pushing out of the chattering crowd, Cosmo ordered the gangway about the bell to be cleared of all bystanders. The opposition heated his blood a little, and he began to bear himself with an air which recalled his aspect when he quelled and punished the mutiny. This was enough to silence instantly every objector to his proceedings. Henceforth they kept their thoughts to themselves, although some muttered, under their breath such epithets as " fool " and " harebrain."

In about half an hour after Cosmo's speech the bell, with its hardy explorers safely inclosed within, was lowered away, and a minute later hundreds were craning their necks over the rails to watch the shining globe engulf itself swiftly in the sapphire depths. It was about nine o'clock in the morning when the descent was begun, and for a long time, so remarkable was the transparency of the water, they could see the bell sinking, and becoming smaller until it resembled a blue pearl. Sometimes a metallic flash shot from its polished sides like a gleam of violet lightning. But at length it passed from view, swallowed up in the tremendous watery chasm.

We turn now to trace the adventures of the bell and its inmates as they entered the awful twilight of the ocean, and, sinking deeper, passed gradually into a profundity which the sun's most powerful rays were unable to penetrate. Fortunately every one of the adventurers left a description of his experiences and sensations, so that there is no lack of authentic information to guide us.

The windows, as Cosmo had said, were so arranged that they afforded views on all sides. These views were, of course, restricted by the combined effects of the smallness of the windows and their great thickness; the inmates were somewhat like prisoners looking out of round ports cut through massive walls, but the range of view was much widened when they placed themselves close to the glasses, because the latter were in the form of truncated cones with the base outward.

Glancing through the ports on the upper side of the bell Cosmo and his companions could perceive the huge form of the Ark, hanging like a cloud above them, but rapidly receding, while from the side ports they saw great shafts of azure sunlight, thrown into wonderful undulations by the disturbance of the water. These soon became fainter and gradually disappeared, but before the gloom of the depths settled about them they were thrilled by the spectacle of sharks and other huge fishes nosing about the outer side of the transparent cones, and sometimes opening their jaws as if trying to seize them. Most of the cone-shaped windows had flat surfaces, but a few were of spherical outline both without and within, and the radius of curvature had been so calculated that these particular windows served as huge magnifying lenses for an eye placed at a given distance. Once or twice a marine monster happened to place himself in the field of one of these magnifying windows, startling the observers almost out of their senses with his frightful appearance.

There were also four windows reserved for projecting a searchlight into the outer darkness. The inner side of the bell corresponded in curvature with the outer, so that the adventurers had no flat flooring on any side to stand upon, but this caused little inconvenience, since the walls were abundantly provided with hand and foot holds, enabling the inmates to maintain themselves in almost any position they could wish.

After a while they passed below the range of daylight, and then they turned on the searchlight. The storage batteries which supplied energy for the searchlight and the propellers served also to operate an apparatus for clearing the air of carbonic acid, and De Beauxchamps had carefully calculated the limit of time that the air could be kept in a breathable condition. This did not exceed forty-eight hours— but as we have seen they had no intention of remaining under water longer than twenty hours at the utmost.

When the bell entered the night of the sea-depths they passed into an apparently lifeless zone, where the searchlight, projected now on one side and now on another, revealed no more of the living forms which they had encountered above, but showed only a desert of solid transparent water. Here, amid this awful isolation, they experienced for the first time a feeling of dread and terror. An overpowering sense of loneliness and helplessness came over them, and only the stout heart of Cosmo Versál, and his reassuring words, kept the others from making the signal which would have caused the bell to be hastily drawn back to the Ark.

" M. De Beauxchamps," said Cosmo, breaking the impressive silence, " to what depth have we now descended ? "

" A thousand fathoms," replied the Frenchman, consulting his automatic register.

" Good! We have been only thirty minutes in reaching this depth. We shall sink more slowly as we get deeper, but I think we can count upon reaching the bottom in not more than four hours from the moment of our departure. It will require only two hours for them to draw us back again with the powerful engines of the Ark, especially when aided by our propellers. This will leave fourteen hours for our explorations, if we stay out the limit that we have fixed."

There was such an air of confidence in Cosmo's

manner and words that this simple statement did much to enhearten the others.

"The absence of life in this part of the sea," Cosmo continued cheerfully, "does not surprise me. It has long been known that the life of the ocean is confined to regions near the surface and the bottom. We shall certaintly find plenty of wonderful creatures below."

When they knew that they must be near the bottom they turned the light downward, and every available window was occupied by an eager watcher. Presently a cry of "Look! Look there!" broke from several voices at once.

The searchlight, penetrating far through the clear water beneath the bell, fell in a circle round a most remarkable object—tall, gaunt, and spectral, with huge black ribs.

"Why, it's the Metropolitan tower, still standing!" cried Amos Blank. "Who would have believed it possible?"

"No doubt there was some lucky circumstance about its anchorage," returned Cosmo. "Although it was built so long ago, it was made immensely strong, and well braced, and as the water did not undermine it at the start, it has been favored by the very density of that which now surrounds it, and which tends to buoy it up and hold it steady. But you observe that it has been stripped of the covering of stone."

"Would it not be well to utilize it for anchoring the cable?" asked De Beauxchamps.

"We could have nothing better," said Cosmo.

De Beauxchamps immediately called to the Ark, and directed the movements of those in charge of the drum of the cable so nicely that the descent ceased at the exact moment when the bell came to rest upon a group of beams at the top of the tower. The radio-control, which is so familiar in its thousand applications to-day, was then a new thing, having been invented only a year or so before the deluge, and De Beauxchamps's form of the apparatus was crude. The underlying principle, however, was the same as that now employed—transmission through a metallic wall of impulses capable of being turned into mechanic energy. With its aid they had no difficulty in detaching the cable from the bell, but it required some careful maneuvering to secure a satisfactory attachment to the beams of the tower. At last, however, this was effected, and immediately they set out for their exploration of drowned New York.

They began with the skeleton tower itself, which had only once or twice been exceeded in height by the famous structures of the era of skyscrapers. In some places they found the granite skin yet *in situ*, but almost everywhere it had been stripped off, probably by the tremendous waves which swept over it as the flood attained its first thousand feet of elevation. They saw no living forms, except a few curiously shaped phosphorescent creatures of no great size, which scurried away out of the beam of the search-light. They saw no trace of the millions of their fellow-beings who had been swallowed up in this vast grave, and for this all secretly gave thanks. The soil of Madison Square had evidently been washed away, for no signs of the trees which had once shaded it were seen, and a reddish ooze had begun to collect upon the exposed rocks. All around were the shattered ruins of other great buildings, some, like the Metropolitan tower, yet retaining their steel skeletons, others tumbled down, and lying half-buried in the ooze.

Finding nothing of great interest in this neighborhood they turned the course of the bell northward, passing everywhere over interminable ruins, and as soon as they began to skirt the ridge of Morningside Heights the huge form of the cathedral of St. John fell within the circle of projected light. It was un-roofed, and some of the walls had fallen, but some of the immense arches yet retained their upright position. Here, for the first time, they encountered the real giants of the submarine depths. De Beaux-champs, who had seen some of these creatures during his visit to Paris in the *Jules Verne*, declared that nothing which he had seen there was so terrifying as what they now beheld. One creature, which seemed to be the unresisted master of this kingdom of phosphorescent life, appears to have exceeded in strange-

"AND THEN THEY FLOATED NEAR THE MONUMENTAL
TOMB OF GENERAL GRANT"

ness the utmost descriptive powers of all those who looked upon it, for their written accounts are filled with ejaculations, and are more or less inconsistent with one another. The reader gathers from them, however, the general impression that it made upon their astonished minds.

The creatures were of a livid hue, and had the form of a globe, as large as the bell itself, with a valvular opening on one side which was evidently a mouth, surrounded with a circle of eyelike disks, projecting shafts of self-evolved light into the water. They moved about with surprising ease, rising and sinking at will, sometimes rolling along the curve of an arch, emitting flashes of green fire, and occasionally darting across the intervening spaces in pursuit of their prey, which consisted of smaller prosphorescent animals that fled in the utmost consternation. When the adventurers in the bell saw one of the globular monsters seize its victim they were filled with horror. It had driven its prey into a corner of the wrecked choir, and suddenly it flattened itself like a rubber bulb pressed against the wall, completely covering the creature that was to be devoured, although the effect of its struggles could be perceived; and then, to the amazement of the onlookers, the living globe slowly turned itself inside out, engulfing the victim in the process.

" Great heavens," exclaimed Professor Abel Able, " it is a gigantic *hydroid polyps!* That is precisely the way in which those little creatures swallow their prey; outside becomes inside, what was the surface of the body is turned into the lining of the digestive cavity, and every time they take a meal the process of introversion is repeated. This monster is nothing but a huge self-sustaining maw!"

"*Très bien,*" exclaimed De Beauxchamps, with a slight laugh, "and he finds himself in New York, quite *chez soi.*"

Nobody appeared to notice the sarcasm, and, in any case they would quickly have forgotten it, for no sooner had the tragic spectacle which they had witnessed been finished than they suddenly found the bell surrounded by a crowd of the globe-shaped creatures, jostling one another, and flattening themselves against its metallic walls. They pushed the bell about, rolling themselves all over it, and apparently finding nothing terrifying in the searchlight, which was hardly brighter than the phosphorescent gleams which shot from their own luminescent organs. One of them got one of its luminous disks exactly in the field of a magnifying window, and King Richard, who happened to have his eye in the focus, started back with a cry of alarm.

"I cannot describe what I saw," the king wrote in his notebook. "It was a glimpse of fiery cones, triangles, and circles, ranged in tier behind tier with a piercing eye in the center, and the light that came from them resembled nothing that I have ever seen.

It seemed to be a *living emanation,* and almost paralyzed me."

"We must get away from them," cried De Beauxchamps, as soon as the first overwhelming effect of the attack upon the bell had passed. And immediately he set the propellers at their highest speed.

The bell shook and half rolled over, there was a scurrying among the monsters outside, and two or three of them floated away partly in collapse, as if they had been seriously wounded by the short propeller blades.

The direction of flight chanced to carry them past the dome of the Columbia University Library, which was standing almost intact, and then they floated near the monumental tomb of General Grant, which had crowned a noble elevation overlooking the Hudson River. A portion of the upper part of this structure had been carried away, but the larger part remained in position. They saw no more of the globular creatures which had haunted the ruins of the cathedral, but, instead, there appeared around the bell an immense multitude of small luminescent animals, many of them most beautifully formed, and emitting from their light-producing organs various exquisite colors which turned the surrounding water into an all-embracing rainbow.

But a more marvelous phenomenon quickly made its appearance, causing them to gasp with astonishment. As they drew near the dismantled dome a brilliant gleam suddenly streamed into the ports on the side turned toward the monument—a gush of light so bright that the air inside the bell seemed to have been illuminated with a golden sunrise. They glanced toward the monument, and saw that it was surmounted by some vibrating object which seemed instinct with blinding fire. The colors that sprang from it changed rapidly from gold to purple, and then, through shimmering hues of bronze, to a deep rich orange. It looked like a sun, poised on the horizon. The spectacle was so dazzling, so unexpected, so beautiful, and, associated with the architectural memorial of one of the greatest characters in American history, so strangely suggestive, that even King Richard and the two Frenchmen were strongly moved, while Cosmo and his fellow-countrymen grasped each other by the hand, and the former said, in solemn tones:

"My friends, to my mind, this scene, however accidental, has something of prophecy about it. It changes the current of my thought—America is not dead; in some way she yet survives upon the earth."

Long they gazed and wondered, but at last, partly recovering from their astonishment, at the suggestion of De Beauxchamps, they drew nearer the monument. But when they had arrived within a few yards of it, the blinding light disappeared as if snuffed out, and they saw nothing but the broken gray walls of the dome. The moving object, which had been dimly visible at the beginning, and had evidently been the source of the light, had vanished.

"The creature that produced the illumination," said Professor Abel Able, "has been alarmed by our approach, and has withdrawn into the interior."

This was, no doubt, the true explanation, but they could perceive no signs of life about the place, and they finally turned away from it with strange sensations.

Avoiding the neighborhood of the cathedral, they steered the bell down the former course of the Hudson, but afterward ventured once more over the drowned city until they arrived at the site of the great station of the Pennsylvania Railroad, which they found completely unroofed. They sank the bell into the vast space where the tunnels entered from underneath the old river bed, and again they had a startling experience. Something huge, elongated, and spotted, and provided with expanding claw-like limbs, slowly withdrew as their light streamed upon the reddish ooze covering the great floor. The nondescript retreated backward into the mouth of a tunnel. They endeavored, cautiously, to follow it, turning a magnifying window in its direction, and obtaining a startling view of glaring eyes, but the creature hastened its retreat, and the last glimpse they had was of a grotesque head, which threw out piercing rays of green fire as it passed deeper into the tunnel.

"This is too terrrible," exclaimed King Richard,

shuddering. "In Heaven's name, let us go no farther."

"We must visit Wall Street," said Amos Blank. "We must see what the former financial center of the world now looks like."

Accordingly they issued from the ruined station, and, resuming their course southward, arrived at length over the great money center. The tall buildings which had shouldered each other in that wonderful district, turning the streets into immense gorges, had, to a certain extent, protected one another against the effects of the waves, and the skeletons of many were yet standing. In the midst of them the dark spire of old Trinity still pointed stoutly upward, as if continuing its hopeless struggle against the spirit of worldly grandeur whose aspiring creations, though in ruins, yet dwarfed this symbol of immortality. At the intersection of the Wall and Broad Street cañons they found an enormous steel edifice, which had been completed a short time before the deluge, tumbled in ruins upon the classic form of the old Stock Exchange, the main features of whose front were yet recognizable. The weight of the fallen building had been so great that it had crushed the roof of the treasure vaults which had occupied its ground floor, and the fragments of safes with their contents had been hurled over the northern expanse of Broad Street. The red ooze had covered most of the wasted wealth there heaped up, but in places piles of gold showed through the covering. Amos Blank became greatly excited at this. His old proclivities seemed to resume their sway and his former madness to return, and he buried his finger nails in his clenched palms as he pressed his face against a window, exclaiming:

"*My gold!* My GOLD! Let me out of this! I must have it!"

"Nobody can get out of the bell, Mr. Blank," said Cosmo soothingly. "And the gold is now of no use to anybody."

"I tell you," cried Blank, "that that is *my* gold. It comes from *my* vaults, and I *must* get out!" And he dashed his fists wildly against the glass until his knuckles were covered with blood. Then he sought about for some implement with which to break the glass. They were compelled to seize him, and a dreadful struggle followed in the restricted space within the bell. In the midst of it Blank's face became set, and his eyes stared wildly out of a window.

The others followed the direction of his gaze, and they were almost frozen into statues. Close beside the bell, which had, during the struggle, floated near to the principal heap of mingled treasure and ruin, heavily squatted on the very summit of the pile, was such a creature as no words could depict—of a ghastly color, bulky and malformed, furnished with three burning eyes that turned now green, now red with lambent flame, and great shapeless limbs, which it uplifted one after the other, striking awkward, pawing blows at the bell! It seemed to the horrified on-lookers to be the very demon of greed defending its spoil. Blank sank helpless on the bottom side of the bell, and the others remained for a time petrified, and unable to speak. Suddenly the dreadful creature, making a forward lunge from its perch, struck the bell a mighty blow that sent it spinning in a partly upward direction. The inmates were tumbled over one another, bruised and cut by the projections that served for hand and foot holds. So great had been the impact of the blow that the bell continued to revolve for several minutes, and they could do nothing to help themselves, except to seize the holds as they came within their grasp, and hang on for dear life. The violent shaking up roused Blank from his trance, and he hung on desperately with the others.

After a while the bell ceased to spin, and began to sink again toward the bottom. De Beauxchamps, who had recovered some degree of self-command, instantly began to operate the control governing the propellers, and in a few minutes he had the bell moving in a fixed direction.

" This way, this way," cried Cosmo, glancing out of the windows to orient himself. " We have seen enough! We must get back to the cable, and return to the Ark! "

They were terror-stricken now, and pushing the propellers to their utmost, they fled toward the site of the Metropolitan tower. On their way, although for a time they passed over the course of the East River, they saw no signs of the great bridges except the partly demolished but yet beautiful towers of the oldest of them, which had been constructed of heavy granite blocks. They found the cable attached as they had left it, and, although they were yet nervous from their recent experience, they had no great difficulty in re-attaching it to the bell. Then, with a sigh of relief, they signaled, and shouted through the telephone to the Ark.

But no answer came, and there was no responsive movement of the cable! They signaled and called again, but without result.

"My God!" said Cosmo, in a faltering voice. "Can anything have happened to the cable?"

They looked at each other with blanched cheeks, and no man found a word to reply.

CHAPTER XXVI

THERE had been great excitement on the Ark when the first communication from the bell was received, announcing the arrival of the adventurers at the Metropolitan tower. The news spread everywhere in a few seconds, and the man in charge of the signaling apparatus and telephone would have been mobbed if Captain Arms had not rigorously shut off all communication with him, compelling the eager inquirers to be content with such information as he himself saw fit to give them. When the announcement was made that the bell had been cut loose, and the exploration begun, the excitement was intensified, and a Babel of voices resounded all over the great ship.

As hour after hour passed with no further communication from below the anxiety of the multitude became almost unbearable. Some declared that the adventurers would never be able to re-attach the bell to the cable, and the fear rapidly spread that they would never be seen again. Captain Arms strove in vain to reassure the excited passengers, but they grew every moment more demoralized, and he was nearly

380

driven out of his senses by the insistent questioning to which he was subjected. It was almost a relief to him when the lookout announced an impending change of weather—although he well new the peril which such a change might bring.

It came on more rapidly than anybody could have anticipated. The sky, in the middle of the afternoon, became clouded, the sun was quickly hidden, and a cold blast arose, quickly strengthening into a regular blow. The Ark began to drift as the rising waves assailed its vast flanks.

"Pay out the cable!" roared Captain Arms through his trumpet.

If he had not been instantly obeyed it is probable that the cable would have been dragged from its precarious fastening below. Then he instantly set the engines at work, and strove to turn the Ark so as to keep it near the point of descent. At first they succeeded very well, but the captain knew that the wind was swiftly increasing in force, and that he could not long continue to hold his place. It was a terrible emergency, but he proved himself equal to it.

"We must float the cable," he shouted to his first assistant. "Over with the big buoy."

This buoy of levium had been prepared for other possible emergencies. It was flat, presenting little surface to the wind, and when, working with feverish speed, aided by an electric launch, they had attached the cable to it, it sank so low that its place on the sea was indicated only by the short mast, capped with a streamer, which rose above it.

When this work was completed a sigh of relief whistled through Captain Arms's huge whiskers.

"May Davy Jones hold that cable tight!" he exclaimed. "Now for navigating the Ark. If I had my old *Maria Jane* under my feet I'd defy Boreas himself to blow me away from here—but this whale!"

The wind increased fast, and in spite of every effort the Ark was driven farther and farther toward the southwest, until the captain's telescope no longer showed the least glimpse of the streamer on the buoy. Then night came on, and yet the wind continued to blow. The captain compelled all the passengers to go to their rooms. It would be useless to undertake to describe the terror and despair of that night. When the sun rose again the captain found that they had been driven seventy-five miles from the site of New York, and yet, although the sky had now partly cleared, the violence of the wind had not diminished.

Captain Arms had the passengers' breakfast served in their rooms, simply sending them word that all would be well in the end. But in his secret heart he doubted if he could find the buoy again. He feared that it would be torn loose with the cable.

About noon the wind lulled, and at last the Ark could be effectively driven in the direction of the buoy. But their progress was slow, and night came on once more. During the hours of darkness the wind ceased entirely, and the sea became calm. With the sunrise the search for the buoy was begun in earnest. The passengers were now allowed to go upon some of the decks, and to assemble in the grand saloon, but no interference was permitted with the navigators of the Ark. Never had Captain Arms so fully exhibited his qualities as a seaman.

"We'll find that porpoise if it's still afloat," he declared.

About half after eight o'clock a cry ran through the ship, bringing everybody out on the decks.

The captain had discovered the buoy through his glass!

It lay away to the nor'ard, about a mile, and as they approached all could see the streamer, hanging down its pole, a red streak in the sunshine.

"Hurrah! Hurrah! Hurrah!" The Ark echoed with glad cries from stem to stern. A thousand questions were shouted at the captain on his bridge, but he was imperturbable. He only glanced at his watch, and then said, in an undertone, to Joseph Smith, who stood beside him:

"Forty-seven hours and twenty minutes. By the time we can get the cable back on the drum it will be full forty-eight hours since they started, and the air in the bell could be kept in condition no longer than that. It may take as much as two hours more to draw it up."

" Can you do it so rapidly as that? " asked Smith, his voice trembling.

" I'll do it or bust," returned the captain. " Perhaps they may yet be alive."

Smith turned his eyes upward and clasped his hands. The Ark was put to its utmost speed, and within the time estimated by the captain the cable was once more on the great drum. Before starting it the captain attached the telephone and shouted down. There was no reply.

" Start gently, and then, if she draws, drive for your lubberly lives," he said to the men in charge of the big donkey engine.

The moment it began to turn he inspected the indicator.

" Hurrah! " he exclaimed. " She pulls; the bell is attached."

The crowded decks broke into a cheer. In a few minutes the Ark was vibrating with the strokes of the engine. Within five minutes the strong, slender cable was issuing out of the depths at the rate of 250 feet a minute. But there were six miles of it! The engineer controlling the drum shook his head.

" We may break the cable," he said.

" Go on! " shouted Captain Arms. " It's their only chance. Every second of delay means sure death."

Within forty minutes the cable was coming up 300 feet a minute. The speed increased as the bell rose

out of the depths. It was just one hour and forty-
five minutes after the drum began to revolve when
the anxious watchers were thrown into a furore of
excitement by the appearance of a shining blue point
deep beneath. It was the bell! Again there broke
forth a tempest of cheers.

Rapidly the rising bell grew larger under their
eyes, until at last it burst the surface of the sea. The
engine had been skillfully slowed at the last moment,
and the rescued bell stopped at the level of the deck
open to receive it. With mad haste it was drawn
aboard and the hermetic door was opened. Those
who were near enough glanced inside and turned pale.
Tumbled in a heap at the bottom lay the six men,
with yellow faces and blank, staring eyes. In an instant they were lifted out and two doctors sprang to
the side of each. Were they dead? Could any skill
revive them? A hush as of death spread over the
great vessel.

They were not dead. The skill of the physicians
brought them, one after another, slowly back to consciousness. But it was two full days before they
could rise from their beds, and three before they could
begin to tell their story—the story of the wonders
they had seen, and of the dreadful struggle for breath
in the imprisoned bell before they had sunk into un-
consciousness. Not a word was ever spoken about
the strange outbreak of Blank at the sight of the

gold, although the others all recorded it in their note-books. He himself never referred to it, and it seemed to have faded from his mind.

As soon as it was evident that the rescued men would recover, Captain Arms, acting on his own re-sponsibility, had started the Ark on its westward course. It was a long and tedious journey that they had yet before them, but the monotony was broken by the undying interest in the marvelous story of the adventures of the bell.

Three weeks after they left the vicinity of New York, the observations showed that they must be nearing the eastern border of the Colorado plateau. Then one day a bird alighted on the railing of the bridge, close beside Cosmo and Captain Arms.

"A bird!" cried Cosmo. "But it is incredible that a bird should be here! How can it ever have kept itself afloat? It surely could not have remained in the air all this time, and it could not have rested on the waves during the downpour from the sky! Its presence here is absolutely miraculous!"

The poor bird, evidently exhausted by a long jour-ney, remained upon the rail, and permitted Cosmo to approach closely before taking flight to another part of the Ark. Cosmo at first thought that it might have escaped from his aviary below.

But close inspection satisfied him that it was of a different species from any that he had taken into the Ark, and the more he thought of the strangeness of its appearance here the greater was his bewilderment.

While he was puzzling over the subject the bird was seen by many of the passengers, flitting from one part of the vessel to another, and they were as much astonished as Cosmo had been, and all sorts of conjectures were made to account for the little creature's escape from the flood.

But within an hour or two Cosmo and the captain, who were now much oftener alone upon the bridge than they had been during their passage over the eastern continents, had another, and an incomparably greater, surprise.

It was the call of " Land, ho! " from the lookout.

" Land! " exclaimed Cosmo. " Land! How can there be any land? "

Captain Arms was no less incredulous, and he called the lookout down, accused him of having mistaken a sleeping whale for a landfall, and sent another man aloft in his place. But in a few minutes the same call of " Land, ho! " was repeated.

The captain got the bearings of the mysterious object this time, and the Ark was sent for it at her highest speed. It rose steadily out of the water until there could be no possibility of not recognizing it as the top of a mountain.

When it had risen still higher, until its form seemed gigantic against the horizon, Captain Arms, throwing away his tobacco with an emphatic gesture, and striking his palm on the rail, fairly shouted:

"The Pike! By—the old Pike! There she blows!"

"Do you mean Pike's Peak?" demanded Cosmo.

"Do I mean Pike's Peak?" cried the captain, whose excitement had become uncontrollable. "Yes, I mean Pike's Peak, and the deuce to him! Wasn't I born at his foot? Didn't I play ball in the Garden of the Gods? And look at him, Mr. Versál! There he stands! No water-squirting pirate of a nebula could down the old Pike!"

The excitement of everybody else was almost equal to the captain's, when the grand mass of the mountain, with its characteristic profile, came into view from the promenade-decks.

De Beauxchamps, King Richard, and Amos Blank hurried to the bridge, which they were still privileged to invade, and the two former in particular asked questions faster than they could be answered. Meanwhile, they were swiftly approaching the mountain.

King Richard seemed to be under the impression that they had completed the circuit of the world ahead of time, and his first remark was to the effect that Mount Everest appeared to be rising faster than they had anticipated.

"That's none of your pagodas!" exclaimed the captain disdainfully; "that's old Pike; and if you can find a better crown for the world, I'd like to see it."

The king looked puzzled, and Cosmo explained

that they were still near the center of the American continent, and that the great peak before them was the sentinel of the Rocky Mountains.

" But," replied the king, " I understood you that the whole world was covered, and that the Himalayas would be the first to emerge."

" That's what I believed," said Cosmo, " but the facts are against me."

" So you thought you were going to run over the Rockies! " exclaimed the captain gleefully. " They're no Gaurisankars, hey, M. De Beauxchamps? "

"*Vive les Rockies! Vive le Pike!*" cried the Frenchman, catching the captain's enthusiasm.

" But how do you explain it? " asked King Richard.

" It's the batholite," responded Cosmo, using exactly the same phrase that Professor Pludder had employed some months before.

" And pray explain to me what is a batholite? "

Before Cosmo Versál could reply there was a terrific crash, and the Ark, for the third time in her brief career, had made an unexpected landing. But this time the accident was disastrous.

All on the bridge, including Captain Arms, who should surely have known the lay of the land about his childhood's home, had been so interested in their talk that before they were aware of the danger the great vessèl had run her nose upon a projecting buttress of the mountain.

She was going at full speed, too. Not a person aboard but was thrown from his feet, and several were severely injured.

The prow of the Ark was driven high upon a sloping surface of rock, and the tearing sounds showed only too clearly that this time both bottoms had been penetrated, and that there could be no hope of saving the huge ship or getting her off.

Perhaps at no time in all their adventures had the passengers of the Ark been so completely terrorized and demoralized, and many members of the crew were in no better state. Cosmo and the captain shouted orders, and ran down into the hold to see the extent of the damage. Water was pouring in through the big rents in torrents.

There was plainly nothing to be done but to get everybody out of the vessel and upon the rocks as rapidly as possible.

The forward parts of the promenade-deck directly overhung the rock upon which the Ark had forced itself, and it was possible for many to be let down that way. At the same time boats were set afloat, and dozens got ashore in them.

While everybody was thus occupied with things immediately concerning their safety, nobody paid any attention to the approach of a boat, which had set out from a kind of bight in the face of the mountain.

Cosmo was at the head of the accommodation-ladder that was being let down on the starboard side, when he heard a shout, and, lifting his eyes from his work, was startled to see a boat containing, beside the rowers, two men whom he instantly recognized—they were President Samson and Professor Pludder.

Their sudden appearance here astonished him as much as that of Pike's Peak itself had done. He dropped his hands and stared at them as their boat swiftly approached. The ladder had just been got ready, and the moment the boat touched its foot Professor Pludder mounted to the deck of the Ark as rapidly as his great weight would permit.

He stretched out his hand as his foot met the deck, and smilingly said:

" Versál, you were right about the nebula."

" Pludder," responded Cosmo, immediately recovering his aplomb, and taking the extended hand of the professor, " you certainly know the truth when you see it."

Not another word was exchanged between them for the time, and Professor Pludder instantly set to work aiding the passengers to descend the ladder. Cosmo waved his hand in greeting to the President, who remained in the boat, and politely lifted his tall, but sadly battered hat in response.

The Ark had become so firmly lodged that, after the passengers had all got ashore, Cosmo decided to open a way through the forward end of the vessel by removing some of the plates, so that the animals

could be taken ashore direct from their deck by simply descending a slightly sloping gangway.

This was a work that required a whole day, and
while it was going forward under Cosmo's directions
the passengers, and such of the crew as were not
needed, found their way, led by the professor and
the President, round a bluff into a kind of mountain
lap, where they were astonished to see many rough
cottages, situated picturesquely among the rocks, and
small cultivated spaces, with grass and flowers, surrounding them.

Here dwelt some hundreds of people, who received
the shipwrecked company with Western hospitality,
after the first effects of their astonishment had worn
off.   It appears that, owing to its concealment by
a projecting part of the mountain, the Ark had not
been seen until just at the moment when it went
ashore.

Although it was now the early part of September,
the air was warm and balmy, and barn-yard fowls
were clucking and scratching about the rather meager
soil around the houses and outbuildings.

There was not room in this place for all the new-
comers, but Professor Pludder assured them that in
many of the neighboring hollows, which had formerly
been mountain gorges, there were similar settlements,
and that room would be found for all.

Parties were sent off under the lead of guides, and
great was the amazement, and, it may be added, joy,

with which they were received in the little communities that clustered about the flanks of the mountain.

About half of Cosmo's animals had perished, most of them during the terrible experiences attending the arrival of the nucleus, which have already been described, but those that remained were in fairly good condition, and with the possible exception of the elephants, they seemed glad to feel solid ground once more under their feet.

The elephants had considerable difficulty in making their way over the rocks to the little village, but finally all were got to a place of security. The great Californian cattle caused hardly less trouble than the elephants, but the Astorian turtles appeared to feel themselves at home at once.

Cosmo, with King Richard, De Beauxchamps, Amos Blank, Captain Arms, and Joseph Smith, became the guests of Professor Pludder and the President in their modest dwellings, and as soon as a little order had been established explanations began. Professor Pludder was the first spokesman, the scene being the President's " parlor."

He told of their escape from Washington and of their arrival on the Colorado plateau.

" When the storm recommenced," he said, " I recognized the complete truth of your theory, Mr. Versál—I had partially recognized it before—and I made every preparation for the emergency.

" The downfall, upon the whole, was not as severe

here as it had been during the earlier days of the deluge, but it must have been far more severe elsewhere.

"The sea around us began to rise, and then suddenly the rise ceased. After studying the matter I concluded that a batholite was rising under this region, and that there was a chance that we might escape submergence through its influence."

"Pardon me," interrupted King Richard, "but Mr. Versál has already spoken of a 'batholite.' What does that mean?"

"I imagine," replied the professor, smiling, "that neither Mr. Versál nor I have used the term in a strictly technical sense. At least we have vastly extended and modified its meaning in order to meet the circumstances of our case.

"Batholite is a word of the old geology, derived from a language which was once widely cultivated, Greek, and meaning, in substance, stone, or rock, 'from the depths.'

"The conception underlying it is that of an immense mass of plastic rock rising under the effects of pressure from the interior of the globe, forcing, and in part melting its way to the surface, or lifting up the superincumbent crust.

"Geologists had discovered the existence of many great batholites that had risen in former ages, and there were some gigantic ones known in this part of America."

" That," interposed Cosmo, " was the basis of my idea that the continents would rise again, only I supposed that the rise would first manifest itself in the Himalayan region.

" However, since it has resulted in the saving of so many lives here, I cannot say that my disappointment goes beyond the natural mortification of a man of science upon discovering that he has been in error."

" I believe," said Professor Pludder, " that at least a million have survived here in the heart of the continent through the uprising of the crust. We have made explorations in many directions, and have found that through all the Coloradan region people have succeeded in escaping to the heights.

" Since the water, although it began to rise again after the first arrest of the advance of the sea, never attained a greater elevation than about 7,500 feet as measured from the old sea-level contours, there must be millions of acres, not to say square miles, that are still habitable.

" I even hope that the uprising has extended far through the Rocky Mountain region."

Professor Pludder then went on to tell how they had escaped from the neighborhood of Colorado Springs when the readvance of the sea began, and how at last it became evident that the influence of the underlying " batholite " would save them from submergence.

In some places, he said, violent phenomena had been manifested, and severe earthquakes had been felt, but upon the whole, he thought, not many had perished through that cause.

As soon as some degree of confidence that they were, after all, to escape the flood, had been established, they had begun to cultivate such soil as they could find, and now, after months of fair weather, they had become fairly established in their new homes.

When Cosmo, on his side, had told of the adventures of the Ark, and of the disappearance of the crown of the world in Asia, and when De Beauxchamps had entertained the wondering listeners with his account of the submarine explorations of the *Jules Verne* and the diving bell, the company at last broke up.

From this point—the arrival of the Ark in Colorado, and its wreck on Pike's Peak—the literature of our subject becomes abundant, but we cannot pause to review it in detail.

The re-emergence of the Colorado mountain region continued slowly, and without any disastrous convulsions, and the level of the water receded year by year as the land rose, and the sea lost by evaporation into space and by chemical absorption in the crust.

In some other parts of the Rockies, as Professor

Pludder had anticipated, an uprising had occurred, and it was finally estimated that as many as three million persons survived the deluge.

It was not the selected band with which Cosmo Versál had intended to regenerate mankind, but from the Ark he spread a leaven which had its effect on the succeeding generations.

He taught his principles of eugenics, and implanted deep the germs of science, in which he was greatly aided by Professor Pludder, and, as all readers of this narrative know, we have every reason to believe that our new world, although its population has not yet grown to ten millions, is far superior, in every respect, to the old world that was drowned.

As the dry land spread wider extensive farms were developed, and for a long time there was almost no other occupation than that of cultivating the rich soil.

President Samson was, by unanimous vote, elected President of the republic of New America, and King Richard became his Secretary of State, an office, he declared, of which he was prouder than he had been of his kingship, when the sound of the British drum-beat accompanied the sun around the world.

Amos Blank, returning to his old methods, soon became the leading farmer, buying out the others until the government sternly interfered and compelled him to relinquish everything but five hundred acres of ground.

But on this Blank developed a most surprising collection of domestic animals, principally from the stocks that Cosmo had saved in the Ark.

The elephants died, and the Astorian turtles did not reproduce their kind, but the gigantic turkeys and the big cattle and sheep did exceedingly well, and many other varieties previously unknown were gradually developed with the aid of Sir Wilfrid Athelstone, who found every opportunity to apply his theories in practice.

Of Costaké Theriade, and the inter-atomic force, it is only necessary to remind the reader that the marvelous mechanical powers which we possess to-day, and which we draw directly from the hidden stores of the electrons, trace their origin to the brain of the "speculative genius" from Roumania, whom Cosmo Versál had the insight to save from the great second deluge.

All of these actors long ago passed from the scene, President Samson being the last survivor, after winning by his able administration the title of the second father of his country. But to the last he showed his magnanimity by honoring Cosmo Versál, and upon the latter's death he caused to be carved, high on the brow of the great mountain on which his voyage ended, in gigantic letters, cut deep in the living rock, and covered with shining, incorrodible levium, an inscription that will transmit his fame to the remotest posterity:

HERE RESTED THE ARK OF
COSMO VERSAL!
He Foresaw and Prepared for the Second Deluge,
And Although Nature
Aided Him in Unexpected Ways,
Yet, but for Him, His Warnings, and His Example
The World of Man Would Have Ceased
To Exist.

It would be unjust to Mr. Samson to suppose that any ironical intention was in his mind when he composed this lofty inscription.

Postscriptum

While these words are being written, news comes of the return of an aero, driven by inter-atomic energy, from a voyage of exploration round the earth.

It appears that the Alps are yet deeply buried, but that Mount Everest now lifts its head more than ten thousand feet above the sea, and that some of the loftiest plains of Tibet are beginning to re-emerge.

Thus Cosmo Versál's prediction is fulfilled, though he has not lived to see it.

THE END

Chapter 8

1. *China White Paper*, p. 469 (Cf. chapter 5, note 2).
2. Barbara W. Tuckman, *Stilwell and the American Experience in China 1911–1945* (New York: Macmillan, 1971), p. 288.
3. Ibid., p. 266 and p. 288.
4. Ibid., p. 285.
5. *China White Paper*, p. 66.
6. During the seven-year period, 1937–1944, the area under Communist control was estimated to have increased from 35,000 to 155,000 square miles, the population from 1.5 million to 54 million, and the armed forces from 100,000 to 495,000.
7. *China White Paper*, p. 71.
8. *Foreign Relations of the United States, China*, vol. 6 (1944), p. 689.
9. *China White Paper*, p. 76.
10. Ibid., p. 582.
11. Tuckman, *Stilwell*, pp. 525–26.
12. *China White Paper*, p. 607.
13. Lloyd C. Gardener, *Architects of Illusion: Men and Ideas in American Foreign Policy 1941–1949* (Chicago: Quadrangle Books, 1970), pp. 161–62.
14. *China White Paper*, p. 153.
15. Ibid., p. 652.
16. The difference of one seat had critical importance because the Council was to consist of forty members, one half of whom would be nominated by the Kuomintang and the other half by the other parties and independents, and its decisions involving a change in the resolutions of the Political Consultative Conference (PCC) would require two-thirds votes; hence any party or group that could muster one-third votes—fourteen to be exact—would enjoy a veto power. Specifically, the Communists with their fourteen votes could block any Kuomintang attempt at revision.
17. *China White Paper*, p. 189.
18. Ibid., p. 685.
19. Ibid., pp. 773–74.
20. Ibid., pp. 318–19.
21. Ibid., p. 279.
22. For further study, see Mao Tse-tung, *On New Democracy* (Peking: Foreign Language Press, 1954).
23. This treaty and the accompanying exchange of notes had provided for: (1) mutual economic assistance in the postwar period, (2) recognition by China of the independence of Outer Mongolia if the people of that area confirm this desire in a plebiscite, (3) the status of Dairen as a free port, (4) joint control of Port

Arthur and the establishment of a Sino-Soviet military commission, (5) reaffirmation by the Soviet government of the Three Eastern Provinces (Manchuria) as part of China, and (6) non-interference by the Soviet government in the internal affairs of Sinkiang, it being part of China.

Chapter 9

1. *Occupation of Japan,* p. 21 (Cf. chapter 7, note 10).
2. Internationally there had been a similar attempt in 1928 when the Kellogg-Briand Pact (the Pact of Paris) was signed by many sovereign states, including Japan, China, and the United States.
3. Douglas MacArthur, *Reminiscence* (New York: McGraw-Hill, 1964), p. 288.
4. Those sentenced to death were: General Tojo Hideki, wartime premier and war minister; Hirota Koki, premier and foreign minister; General Itagaki, Kwantung Army Chief of Staff and war minister (1938–39); General Doihara, chief of Kwantung Army Secret Service; General Kimura, Chief of Staff Kwantung Army and commander of the Burma Expeditionary Force; General Matsui, commander of the Japanese Army in China during the "rape of Nanking"; and General Muto, army commander.
5. *Occupation of Japan,* pp. 78–79.
6. The four major *zaibatsu* were: Mitsui, Mitsubishi, Sumitomo. and Yasuda. One of the most significant features of the *zaibatsu* power control was their strong personal ties that enabled them to wield their power and influence not only in Japan's economy but also in its politics and government. They intermarried with the families of the peerage, ranking bureaucrats, politicians, generals, admirals, and diplomats.
7. By 1952 the *zaibatsu* consolidated their system and structure, facilitating once more a close alliance between the government and the leading industrialists and financiers.
8. For the complete text, see *Congressional Record,* 93 (March 12, 1947), pp. 1999–2000.
9. Peter Duns, *The Rise of Modern Japan* (New York: Houghton Mifflin, 1976), p. 252, citing Kosaka Masatake, *100 Million Japanese: The Postwar Experience* (Tokyo, 1972), pp. 106–7.
10. Comparative figures for other countries' growth were: West Germany, 6.1 percent; France, 5.3 percent; England, 2.4 percent; and the United States, 2.3 percent.
11. *New York Times,* October 12, 1954.
12. See *Girard* v. *Wilson* et al. (United States, Supreme Court, 1957, 35 U.S. 524).

Chapter 10

1. The Koreans believed the crew of the *General Sherman* to be the tomb robbers of the imperials' cemetery which had been looted a month earlier. In fact, even to this day the stage play reenacting this incident has been an officially sanctioned, patriotic manifestation of the North Korean Communists. A century later when the American spy ship *Pueblo* was captured by the North Korean Navy, the world was reminded of the historic parallel. The *Pueblo* incident is discussed in the following chapter.

2. Compare this thirty-ninth parallel with the thirty-eighth parallel dividing Korea into two zones, north and south, after World War II.

3. More than thirty years later U.S. troops were still stationed in Korea and President Carter's plan of troop withdrawal was unpopular among the majority of the South Korean people.

4. Strobe Talbott, trans. and ed., *Khrushchev Remembers* (Boston: Little, Brown and Co., 1970), p. 368.

5. Talbott, *Khrushchev Remembers,* p. 368.

6. Ibid., p. 369.

7. "Crisis in Asia—An Examination of U.S. Policy," Department of State *Bulletin* (June 23, 1950), p. 116.

8. Harry S. Truman, *Memoirs; Years of Trial and Hope,* vol. 1 (Garden City, N.Y.: Doubleday, 1956), p. 333.

9. John W. Spanier, *The Truman-MacArthur Controversy and The Korean War* (New York: W. W. Norton, 1965), pp. 202–3.

10. *United Nations Bulletin,* August 15, 1953, p. 135.

11. For the complete text, see Department of State *Bulletin,* October 12, 1953, p. 484.

12. Geographically, Vietnam consists of three regions: northern Tonkin, central Annam, and southern Cochin China.

13. The Organization of Strategic Services (OSS) was America's wartime intelligence agency, the forerunner of the Central Intelligence Agency (CIA).

14. Allan B. Cole, *Conflict in Indochina and International Repercussions: A Documentary History, 1945–1955* (Ithaca: Cornell University Press, 1956), pp. 19–21.

15. Neil Sheehan and others, *The Pentagon Papers* (New York: Bantam Books, 1971), p. 26. Cited hereafter as *The Pentagon Papers.*

16. Marvin E. Gettleman, ed., *Vietnam* (New York: Fawcett Publications, 1965), p. 79.

17. Department of State *Bulletin,* May 22, 1950, p. 821.

18. Ibid., June 5, 1950, p. 5.

19. *New York Times,* April 17, 1954.
20. According to Georges Bidault, Secretary Dulles had twice offered him the use of the American atomic bomb. Fearing the consequences of such a move, M. Bidault endorsed only General Ely's (Paul Ely, French chief of staff and later commander in Indochina) request for American nonatomic air strikes at Dienbienphu. See Roscoe Drummond and Gaston Coblentz, *Duel at the Brink* (New York: Doubleday, 1960), pp. 116–23.
21. *Pentagon Papers,* p. 10.
22. At one point during the conference, Secretary Dulles turned his back on the outstretched hand of Chou En-lai, the premier of the People's Republic of China. See Edgar Snow, *Red China Today: The Other Side of the River* (New York: Vintage Books, 1970), p. 660.
23. For the complete text of the Geneva agreements, see Gettleman, *Vietnam,* pp. 137–59.
24. *Pentagon Papers,* p. 14.
25. This was a statement of General Bedell Smith in his response to congressional critics of the Geneva agreements.
26. The first was during the Boxer Rebellion in China in 1900–1901; the second, the Siberian Intervention in 1918–1919; and the third, World War II against Japan in 1941–1945.
27. *Pentagon Papers,* p. 27.
28. Ibid., p. 46.
29. This was the term used in a memorandum by Robert Cutler, special assistant to President Eisenhower, May 7, 1954.
30. Robert Shaplen, *The Lost Revolution* (New York: Harper, 1966), p. 95.
31. *Pentagon Papers,* p. 25.

Chapter 11

1. *Public Papers of the Presidents, John F. Kennedy, 1961* (Washington, D.C.: Government Printing Office, 1962), pp. 1–3.
2. U.S. Senate, Committee on Foreign Relations, *Vietnam and Southeast Asia,* Report of Senator Mike Mansfield, et al., 88th Congress 1st Session (Washington, D.C.: Government Printing Office, 1963), p. 5.
3. Roger Hillsman, *To Move the Nation* (Garden City, N.Y.: Doubleday, 1967), p. 420.
4. Ibid., p. 420.
5. U.S. Senate, Committee on Foreign Relations, *Background Information Relating to Southeast Asia and Vietnam,* 89th Congress 2nd Session (Washington, D.C.: Government Printing Office, 1966), p. 87.

6. David Halberstam, *The Best and the Brightest* (New York: Random House, 1972), p. 172.
7. Arthur M. Schlesinger, Jr., *A Thousand Days* (Boston: Houghton Mifflin, 1965), p. 549.
8. Allan Nevins, ed., *The Burden and the Glory* (New York: Harper and Row, 1964), p. 22 and p. 28.
9. Department of State *Bulletin*, May 11, 1963, p. 730.
10. Hillsman, *To Move the Nation*, p. 497.
11. Ibid., p. 502.
12. U.S. Senate, Committee on Foreign Relations, *U.S. Involvement in the Overthrow of Diem*, 92nd Congress, 2nd Session (Washington, D.C.: Government Printing Office, 1972), p. 25.
13. In an eighteen-month period, from November 1963 to June 1965, there were no less than ten government changes by coups.
14. *Public Papers of the Presidents, Lyndon B. Johnson, 1963–1964*, p. 8.
15. Shaplen, *Lost Revolution*, p. 214.
16. Halberstam, *The Best and the Brightest*, p. 350.
17. *New York Times*, July 25, 1964.
18. "Why Our Foreign Policy Is Failing," *Look*, May 3, 1966, pp. 25–26.
19. He first made this statement, which he was to repeat in numerous election speeches, to a crowd at an outdoor barbecue on August 29 in a belated celebration of his fifty-sixth birthday at his ranch in Texas.
20. David Kraslow and Stuart H. Loory, *The Secret Search for Peace in Vietnam* (New York: Random House, 1968) is a readable, revealing, investigative account of the behind-the-scenes maneuvers for a negotiated peace in Vietnam from the late spring of 1966 to early summer of 1968.
21. *United Nations Press Service Note 3075*, February 24, 1965.
22. Kraslow and Loory, *Search for Peace*, pp. 120–21.
23. *Pentagon Papers*, p. 592.
24. The Phoenix program was aimed at destroying the Vietcong political and administrative apparatus through the assassination or capture of Vietcong cadres. It was reported that 20,587 persons had been counted as killed in Phoenix operations from 1968 to May 1971, with $80 million provided by the U.S. Department of Defense and the CIA. Several hundred American military personnel were engaged as advisors to the program. One report said "Phoenix operations have been a disappointment to many officials and military men because they have failed thus far to result in the capture of anything more than a very small percentage of the highest-level members of the Vietcong political underground." See *Christian Science Monitor*, August 3, 1971.

25. *Public Papers of the Presidents, Richard M. Nixon, 1969*, p. 370.
26. The following episode was interesting and revealing: In November 1969, Henry Kissinger, Nixon's national security advisor, was asked if the Nixon administration was going to repeat the same mistakes of its predecessor. He replied, "No"; then with a sense of humor he added, "We will not make their mistakes. We will not send 500,000 men. We will make our own mistakes and they will be completely our own." Indeed, through repeated misconceptions, mistakes, and miscalculations, the tragedy in Vietnam resulted from, in the words of Russell Baker, "the reign of President Lyndon B. Nixonger." See, David Halberstam, *The Best and the Brightest*, p. 664.
27. *U.S. Foreign Policy for the 1970's: Building for Peace*, A Report to the Congress by Richard Nixon, President of the United States (Washington, D.C.: Government Printing Office), February 25, 1971, p. 14.
28. Ibid., p. 13.
29. *Public Papers of the Presidents, Richard Nixon, 1969*, p. 909.
30. There was a dissenting voice within the Nixon cabinet. In a private letter to President Nixon, Secretary of Interior Walter J. Hickel wrote: "I believe this Administration finds itself, today, embracing a philosophy which appears to lack appropriate concern for the attitude of a great mass of Americans—our young people. Addressing either politically or philosophically, I believe we are in error if we set out consciously to alienate those who could be our friends. Today, our young people, or at least a vast segment of them, believe they have no opportunity to communicate with government, regardless of administration, other than through violent confrontation. . . . I believe the Vice-President initially has answered a deep seated mood of America in his public statements. However, a continued attack on the young—not on their attitudes so much as on their motives—can serve little purpose other than to further cement those attitudes to a solidarity impossible to penetrate with reason." Shortly thereafter Secretary Hickle was relieved of his post.
31. See Robert Haldeman, *The Ends of Power* (New York: Harper and Row, 1978).
32. *New York Times*, November 21, 1971.
33. Ibid.
34. For a succinct discussion of the backgrounds of Sino-American and Soviet-American relations, see John G. Stoessinger, *Nations in Darkness: China, Russia and America* (New York: Random House, 1971).
35. During the medieval church-state struggle for supremacy over investiture, in 1076, Emperor Henry IV of Germany declared

that Pope Gregory VII was unworthy of the papal throne. Thereupon, the pope excommunicated Henry and deposed him, absolving his subjects from oaths of allegiance. Facing a revolt of the German nobles, Henry was compelled to journey to Canossa where the pope was staying and begged, garbed as a penitent, for papal forgiveness for three days until it was granted.

36. It was first enunciated as a military concept in October 1969 by Defense Secretary Melvin R. Laird, authorizing American bomber-fighters to escort unarmed reconnaissance flights over North Vietnam and to attack enemy antiaircraft gun positions and SAM sites if the enemy initiated offensive action.

37. He was subsequently relieved and ordered to return to Washington, where he became the first four-star general in modern U.S. military history to be demoted upon retirement.

38. U.S. Senate, Committee on Foreign Relations, *Economic and Political Developments in the Far East,* Report by Senator Charles H. Percy, 93rd Congress, 1st Session (Washington, D.C.: Government Printing Office, 1973), p. 6.

39. For the complete text of the agreement, see Department of State *Bulletin,* February 12, 1973, pp. 169–88.

40. *Congressional Record,* vol. 119, part 24, 93rd Congress, 1st Session, September 20–27, 1973, p. 31764.

41. Ibid., vol. 118, part 2, 92nd Congress, 2nd Session, Jan. 26–February 2, 1972, p. 1634.

42. See John Sirica, *To Set the Record Straight* (New York: W. W. Norton, 1979).

43. *New York Times,* March 21, 1975.

44. During the retreat, "a Vietnamese sailor saw six high-ranking Army officers load refrigerators, television sets, and air conditioners onto a boat at a beach east of Hue. They did not take any troops or military equipment with them, only personal effects, as they made their escape." *Christian Science Monitor,* March 31, 1975.

45. British Foreign Office, *Documents Relating to the Discussion of Korea and Indochina at the Geneva Conference April 29–June 15, 1954* (London, 1954), pp. 100–101.

46. In May 1960, on the eve of the Paris Summit Conference, Premier Khrushchev demanded President Eisenhower's public apology for the U-2 intrusion of Soviet air space. As Eisenhower refused to comply with his demand, Khrushchev torpedoed the conference.

47. See the United States "admission" of espionage signed to obtain the release of the crew, and related documents, *8 International Legal Materials* (1969), pp. 198–99.

48. For the complete text of the New South Korean Constitution, see

Journal of Korean Affairs, vol. 3, no. 1 (April 1973), pp. 39–53.

49. For the complete text of the New North Korean Constitution, see Ibid., vol. 2, no. 3 (January 1973), pp. 46–57.

50. For the complete text of the communiqué, see Ibid., vol. 2, no. 2 (July 1972), p. 48. See also U.S., Senate, Committee on Foreign Relations, *Korea and the Philippines: November 1972,* 93rd Congress, 2nd Session (Washington, D.C.: Government Printing Office, 1973), pp. 11–12.

51. Department of State *Bulletin,* July 10, 1961, pp. 57–58.

52. Mr. Kishi Nobusuke, born a Sato, adopted the surname of his wife's family, *Kishi,* following a common practice in Japan to perpetuate the succession of her family name.

53. On November 10, 1971, the U.S. Senate approved the Okinawa Reversion Agreement by a vote of 84–6 and Okinawa was returned to Japan on May 15, 1972.

54. In 1969 the per capita income was: United States, $3,800; France, $2,100; West Germany, $1,900; Great Britain, $1,500; the Philippines, $280; Taiwan, $270; South Korea, $160; Thailand, $120; and India, $70.

55. Edwin O. Reischauer, *Japan: The Story of a Nation* (New York: Alfred A. Knopf, 1970), p. 289.

56. Japan's GNP in 1950 was about $10 billion; it grew to $200 billion in 1970. In comparison with that of the United States, Japan's GNP in 1950 was 1/28 and 1/5 in 1970.

57. *U.S. Foreign Policy for the 1970's: The Emerging Structure of Peace,* A Report to the Congress by Richard Nixon, President of the United States (Washington, D.C.: Government Printing Office), February 9, 1972, p. 57.

58. Takeuchi Yasuo, "A Fable About Security," *Japan Echo,* vol. 4, no. 1 (Tokyo: Toppan Printing Co., 1977), p. 22.

59. Well-known examples, at this time, of Japanese firms owning factories in the United States were Sony in California, Kikkoman soy sauce manufacturer in Wisconsin, and zipper maker YKK in Georgia.

60. Formed in August 1967 by the Philippines, Indonesia, Singapore, Malaysia, and Thailand, the Association of Southeast Asian Nations (ASEAN) was designed primarily to promote economic and cultural cooperation among member nations.

61. For the complete text, see Department of State *Bulletin* September 8, 1958, pp. 385–90.

62. James C. Thomson, Jr., "How Could Vietnam Happen?" *Atlantic Monthly* (April 1968), p. 47.

63. Arthur Schlesinger, Jr., *A Thousand Days* (Cambridge, Mass.: Houghton Mifflin, 1965), pp. 479–80. The immediately preceding quotation was from the same source.

64. For a brief discussion on each of these issues, see Young Hum

Kim, comp., *Twenty Years of Crises: The Cold War Era* (Engle-wood Cliffs, N.J.: Prentice-Hall, 1968), pp. 181–82.
65. Robert A. Diamond, ed., *China and U.S. Foreign Policy* (Washington: Congressional Quarterly, 1971), p. 42.
66. Among the prominent ones were Lin Piao, then the heir-apparent to Mao; Chiang Ching, Mao's wife; Wang Hung-wen; Chang Chun-chiao, and Wang Hung-wen—all Politburo members. Lin Piao was reported killed in 1972, together with fellow conspirators, in a plane crash while attempting to escape the country after an abortive plot against Mao's life. The other four were arrested in October 1976, only a month after the death of Mao, labelled as the "gang of four," and charged with usurpation of power and distortion of Mao's instructions.
67. Congressional Quarterly, *China and U.S. Foreign Policy*, p. 14.
68. *U.S. Foreign Policy for the 1970's: Building for Peace*, pp. 105–6.
69. For a discussion on possible Sino-American "military ties," see Kenneth A. Oye et al., ed., *Eagle Entangled: Foreign Policy in a Complex World* (New York: Longman, 1979), pp. 231–33.
70. For the complete text of the Shanghai communique, see U.S. Senate, Committee on Foreign Relations, *The United States and China*, 94th Congress, 2nd Session (Washington, D.C.: Government Printing Office, 1976), pp. 53–55.

Bibliography

General

Anderson, Irvine H., Jr. *The Standard-Vacuum Oil Company and United States East Asian Policy, 1933–1941.* Princeton: Princeton University Press, 1974.

Beckman, George. *Modernization of China and Japan.* New York: Harper and Row, 1962.

Beloff, Max. *Soviet Policy in the Far East, 1944–51.* London: Oxford University Press, 1951.

Bisson, T. A. *American Policy in the Far East, 1931–1941,* rev. ed. New York: Institute of Pacific Relations, 1941.

Bohlen, Charles E. *The Transformation of American Foreign Policy.* New York: W. W. Norton and Company, 1970.

Borg, Dorothy. *The United States and the Far Eastern Crisis of 1933–1938.* Cambridge: Harvard University Press, 1968.

Buell, R. L. *The Washington Conference.* New York: Appleton-Century-Crofts, 1922.

Burns, Richard Dean, and Bennett, Edward M. *Diplomats in Crisis: United States-Chinese-Japanese Relations 1919–1941.* Santa Barbara: ABC-Clio, 1974.

Buss, Claude A. *War and Diplomacy in Eastern Asia.* New York: Macmillan, 1941.

————. *Asia in the Modern World.* New York: Macmillan, 1964.

Cameron, Meribeth E., et al. *China, Japan and the Powers,* 2nd ed. New York: Ronald Press, 1960.

Chen, King C., ed. *China and the Three Worlds, A Foreign Policy Reader.* White Plains, N.Y.: M. E. Sharpe, 1978.

Christopher, J. W. *Conflict in the Far East: American Diplomacy in China from 1928–33.* Leiden: Arno Press, 1950.

Currey, Roy W. *Woodrow Wilson and Far Eastern Policy 1913–1921.* New York: Bookman Associates, 1957.

Dallin, David. *The Rise of Russia in Asia.* New Haven: Yale University Press, 1949.

Daniels, Roger. *The Politics of Prejudice.* Berkeley: University of California Press, 1978.

Dennett, Tyler. *Americans in Eastern Asia.* New York: Barnes Company, 1941.

Endicott, John E., and Heaton, William R. *The Politics of East Asia: China, Japan, Korea.* Boulder, Colo.: Westview, 1977.

Eudin, X. J., and North, Robert. *Soviet Russia and the East, 1920–1927: A Documentary Survey.* Stanford: Stanford University Press, 1957.

Fairbank, John K. *The United States and China.* Cambridge: Viking Press, 1958.

———— et al. *East Asia: Tradition and Transformation.* Boston: Houghton Mifflin, 1973.

Fifield, Russell H. *Woodrow Wilson and the Far East: The Diplomacy of the Shantung Issue.* New York: Crowell, 1952.

Friedman, Edward, and Selden, Mark, eds. *American's Asia: Dissenting Essays on Asian-American Relations.* New York: Pantheon, 1971.

Gates, John M. *Schoolbooks and Krags: The United States Army in the Philippines, 1898–1902.* Westport, Conn.: Greenwood, 1973.

Griswold, Whitney. *The Far Eastern Policy of the United States.* New Haven: Yale University Press, 1964.

Harrison, Selig S. *The Widening Gulf: Asian Nationalism and American Policy.* New York: Free Press, 1978.

Hay, Stephen N. *Asian Ideas of East and West: Tagore and His Critics in Japan, China, and India.* Cambridge: Harvard University Press, 1970.

Hellmann, Donald C., ed. *China and Japan: A New Balance of Power.* New York: Lexington Books, 1976.

Hoopes, Townsend. *The Limits of Intervention.* New York: McKay, 1969.

Hundley, Norris, Jr., ed. *The Asian-American: The Historical Experience.* Santa Barbara: ABC-Clio Press. 1976.

Hunsberger, Warren S. *Japan and the United States in World Trade.* New York: Harper and Row, 1964.

Isaacs, Harold R. *New Cycle in Asia, Selected Documents.* New York: Day Company, 1947.

Jaffe, Philip. *New Frontiers in Asia: A Challenge to the West.* New York: Knopf, 1945.

Jo, Yung-hwan. *U.S. Foreign Policy in Asia.* Santa Barbara: ABC-Clio Press, 1978.

Kennan, George F. *American Diplomacy, 1900–1950.* Chicago: University of Chicago Press, 1951.

Kim, C. I. Eugene, and Ziring, Lawrence. *An Introduction to Asian Politics.* Englewood Cliffs, N.J.: Prentice-Hall, 1977.

Kim, Samuel S. *China, the United Nations, and World Order.* Princeton: Princeton University Press, 1979.

Kim, Young Hum. *East Asia's Turbulent Century: With American Diplomatic Documents.* New York: Appleton-Century-Crofts, 1966.

————, ed. *Twenty Years of Crises: The Cold War Era.* Englewood Cliffs, N.J.: Prentice-Hall, 1968.

Lach, Donald F., and Wehrle, Edmund S. *International Politics in East Asia Since World War II.* New York: Praeger, 1975.

Langer, Robert. *Seizure of Territory, the Stimson Doctrine and Related Principles in Legal Theory and Diplomatic Practice.* Princeton: Princeton University Press, 1947.

Langer, William L. *The Diplomacy of Imperialism, 1890–1902.* New York: A. A. Knopf, 1935.

Latourette, Kenneth S. *The American Record in the Far East, 1945–1951.* New York: Macmillan, 1952.

Lattimore, Owen. *Manchuria, Cradle of Conflict,* rev. ed. New York: Macmillan, 1935.

Li, Tien-yi. *Woodrow Wilson's China Policy, 1913–1917.* New York: Twayne, 1952.

Lyman, Stanford M. *The Asian in North America.* Santa Barbara: ABC-Clio Press, 1977.

MacArthur, Douglas. *Reminiscence.* New York: McGraw-Hill, 1964.

MacNair, H. F. *The Real Conflict Between China and Japan.* Chicago: University of Chicago Press, 1938.

Maki, John M. *Conflict and Tension in the Far East: Key Documents, 1894–1940.* Seattle: University of Washington Press, 1961.

Mandel, William, ed. *Soviet Source Materials on USSR Relations with East Asia, 1945–1950.* New York: Institute of Pacific Relations, 1950.

Matthew, Helen G., ed. *Asia in the Modern World.* New York: New American Library, 1963.

McKenzie R. D. *Oriental Exclusion.* Chicago: University of Chicago Press, 1928.

Michael, Franz, and Taylor, George. *The Far East in the Modern World,* 3rd ed. New York: Holt, Rinehart and Winston, 1975.

Moore, H. L. *Soviet Far Eastern Policy, 1931–1945.* Princeton: Princeton University Press, 1945.

Mueller, Peter G. *China and Japan—Emerging Global Powers.* New York: Praeger, 1975.

Nagai, Yonosuke, and Iriye, Akira, eds. *The Origins of the Cold War in Asia.* New York: Columbia University Press, 1977.

Panikkar, K. M. *Asia and Western Dominance*. New York: Allen and Unwin, 1954.

Pasvolsky, L. *Russia in the Far East*. New York: Macmillan, 1922.

Paterson, Thomas G., ed. *Cold War Critics: Alternatives to American Foreign Policy in the Truman Years*. New York: New Viewpoints, 1971.

Pratt, Sir John T. *The Expansion of Europe into the Far East*. London: Caxton Company Ltd., 1947.

Price, E. B. *The Russo-Japanese Treaties of 1907–1916 Concerning Manchuria and Mongolia*. Baltimore: Johns Hopkins University Press, 1933.

Quigley, Harold S. *Far Eastern War, 1937–1941*. Boston: World Peace Foundation, 1942.

Quigley, Harold S., and Turner, John E. *The New Japan Government and Politics*. Minneapolis: University of Minnesota Press, 1956.

Reischauer, Edwin O. *Wanted: An Asian Policy*. New York: Knopf, 1955.

_____. *Beyond Vietnam: The United States and Asia*. New York: Knopf, 1967.

Reischauer, Edwin O., and Fairbank, John K. *East Asia: The Great Tradition*. Boston: Houghton Mifflin, 1960.

Romanov, B. A. *Russia in Manchuria, 1892–1906*, tr. Susan W. Jones. Ann Arbor: J. W. Edwards, 1952.

Romein, Jan. *Asian Century*. Berkeley: University of California Press, 1962.

Scalapino, Robert A. *Asia and the Road Ahead*. Berkeley: University of California Press, 1975.

Smith, Sara R. *The Manchurian Crisis, 1931–1932: A Tragedy in International Relations*. New York: Columbia University Press, 1948.

Stettinius, E. R. *Roosevelt and the Russians: The Yalta Conference*, ed. Walter Johnson. New York: Doubleday Company, 1949.

Stimson, Henry L. *The Far Eastern Crisis: Recollections and Observations*. New York: Harper, 1936.

Stoessinger, John G. *Nations in Darkness: China, Russia, and America*. New York: Random House, 1971.

Tamagna, Frank M. *Italy's Interests and Policies in the Far East*. New York: Institute of Pacific Relations, 1941.

Taylor, Jay. *China and Southeast Asia: Peking's Relations with Revolutionary Movements*. New York: Praeger, 1976.

Teng Ssu-yu, and Fairbank, John K. *China's Response to the West*, 2 vols. Cambridge: Atheneum Press, 1954.

Tompkins, Pauline. *American-Russian Relations in the Far East*. New York: Macmillan, 1949.

Vinacke, Harold M. *History of the Far East in Modern Times*, 6th ed. New York: Appleton-Century-Crofts, 1956.

Weinstein, Franklin B., ed. *U.S.-Japan Relations and the Security of East Asia: The Next Decade.* Boulder, Colo.: Westview, 1977.

Whetten, Lawrence L. *Contemporary American Foreign Policy.* New York: Lexington Books, 1974.

Whiting, Allen S. *Soviet Policies in China, 1917–1924.* Stanford: Stanford University Press, 1954.

Wilbur, C. Martin, and Lien-ying How, Julie, eds. *Documents on Communism, Nationalism, and Soviet Advisors in China, 1918–1927: Papers Seized in the 1927 Peking Raid.* New York: Columbia University Press, 1956.

Willoughby, W. W. *The Sino-Japanese Controversy and the League of Nations.* Baltimore: Johns Hopkins University Press, 1935.

Wright, Quincy, et al. *Legal Problems in the Far Eastern Conflict.* New York: Institute of Pacific Relations, 1941.

Ying-mao Kau, Michael. *The People's Liberation Army and China's Nation-Building.* White Plains, N.Y.: M. E. Sharpe, 1978.

Young, Kenneth T. *Diplomacy and Power in Washington-Peking Dealings: 1953–1967.* Chicago: University of Chicago Press, 1967.

Zabriskie, Edward H. *American-Russian Rivalry in the Far East: A Study in Diplomacy and Power Politics.* Philadelphia: University of Pennsylvania Press, 1946.

Zinkin, Maurice. *Asia and the West.* London: Institute of Pacific Relations, 1951.

China

Armstrong, J. D. *Revolutionary Diplomacy: Chinese Foreign Policy and the United Front Doctrine.* Berkeley: University of California Press, 1977.

Bachrack, Stanley D. *The Committee of One Million: "China Lobby" Politics.* New York: Columbia University Press, 1976.

Barnett, A. D. *Communist China and Asia: Challenge to American Policy.* New York: Harper and Row, 1960.

Brandt, Conrad, et al. *A Documentary History of Chinese Communism.* Cambridge: Atheneum Press, 1952.

Buss, Claude A. *The People's Republic of China.* Princeton: Van Nostrand, 1962.

Chan, F. Gilbert, and Etzold, T. H. *History of Modern China.* New York: New Viewpoints, 1976.

Cheng, Tien-fang. *A History of Sino-Russian Relations.* Washington, D.C.: Public Affairs Press, 1957.

Choudhury, Golam W., ed. *Sino-American Relations in the Post-Mao Era.* Washington, D.C.: University Press of America, 1977.

Clements, P. H. *The Boxer Rebellion.* New York: Columbia University Press, 1915.

Clubb, O. Edmund. *China and Russia: The "Great Game."* New York: Columbia University Press, 1971.

————. *20th Century China*, 3rd ed. New York: Columbia University Press, 1978.

Clyde, Paul H. *International Rivalries in Manchuria*, rev. ed. Columbus: Ohio State University Press, 1928.

Cohen, Warren I. *The Chinese Connection, Roger S. Greene, Thomas W. Lamont, George E. Sokolsky and American-East Asian Relations.* New York: Columbia University Press, 1978.

Domes, Jurgen. *China after the Cultural Revolution.* Berkeley: University of California Press, 1977.

Eberhard, Wolfram. *A History of China*, 4th ed. Berkeley: University of California Press, 1977.

Feis, Herbert. *The China Triangle.* Princeton: Princeton University Press, 1953.

Gentzler, J. Mason, ed. *Changing China.* New York: Holt, Rinehart and Winston, 1977.

Gray, Jack, ed. *Modern China's Search for a Political Form.* London: Oxford University Press, 1969.

Harrison, Selig S. *China, Oil, and Asia: Conflict Ahead?* New York: Columbia University Press, 1977.

Hinton, Harold C. *Communist China in World Politics.* Boston: Houghton Mifflin, 1966.

Hsueh, Chun-tu. *Chinese Communist Movement.* Stanford: Stanford University Press, 1960.

————, ed. *Dimensions of China's Foreign Relations.* New York: Praeger, 1976.

Hudson, G. F. *Europe and China.* Boston: Beacon Press, 1961.

Israel, John. *Student Nationalism in China, 1927–1937.* Stanford: Hoover Institution Press, 1966.

Kataoka, Tetsuya. *Resistance and Revolution in China.* Berkeley: University of California Press, 1974.

Katnow, Stanley. *Mao and China: From Revolution.* New York: Viking, 1972.

Kau, Michael Y. M. *The Lin Piao Affair: Power Politics and Military Coup.* White Plains, N.Y.: M. E. Sharpe, 1978.

Lee, Hong Yung. *The Politics of the Chinese Cultural Revolution.* Berkeley: University of California Press, 1978.

Lerman, Arthur Jay. *Taiwan's Politics: The Provincial Assemblyman's World.* Washington, D.C.: University Press of America, 1978.

Li, Chien-nung. *The Political History of China.* Princeton: Van Nostrand Company, 1956.

McLane, Charles. *Soviet Policy and the Chinese Communists, 1931–1946.* New York: Columbia University Press, 1958.

Metzger, Thomas A. *Escape from Predicament: Neo-Confucianism and*

China's Evolving Political Culture. New York: Columbia University Press, 1977.

Morley, James William. *Japan, Germany, and the U.S.S.R., 1935–1940.* New York: Columbia University Press, 1976.

Morse, H. B. *The International Relations of the Chinese Empire, 1910–1918,* 3 vols. New York: Longmans, Green and Company, n.d.

North, Robert. *Moscow and the Chinese Communists,* 2nd ed. Stanford: Stanford University Press, 1963.

Pepper, Suzanne. *Civil War in China: The Political Struggle, 1945–1949.* Berkeley: University of California Press, 1978.

Pollard, Robert T. *China's Foreign Relations, 1917–1931.* New York: Macmillan, 1933.

Reinsch, Paul S. *An American Diplomat in China.* Garden City and Toronto: Doubleday, Page and Company, 1922.

Schwartz, Benjamin I. *Chinese Communism and the Rise of Mao.* Cambridge: Harvard University Press, 1961.

Tang, Peter S. H. *Communist China Today: Domestic and Foreign Policies.* New York: Seton Hall University Press, 1957.

Tsou, Tang. *America's Failure in China, 1941–1950.* Chicago: University of Chicago Press, 1963.

Wei, Henry. *China and Soviet Russia.* Princeton: Princeton University Press, 1956.

White, John Albert. *The Siberian Intervention.* Princeton: Princeton University Press, 1950.

Young, C. Walter. *International Relations of Manchuria.* Chicago: University of Chicago Press, 1929.

Japan

Asakawa, K. *The Russo-Japanese Conflict.* Boston and New York: Houghton Mifflin, 1904.

Beasley, W. G. *The Modern History of Japan.* 2nd ed. New York: Holt, Rinehart and Winston, 1973.

_____. *Selected Documents on Japanese Foreign Policy, 1853–1868.* London: Oxford University Press, 1955.

Bisson, T. A. *Japan in China.* New York: Macmillan, 1938.

Blaker, Michael. *Japanese International Negotiating Style.* New York: Columbia University Press, 1977.

Blakeslee, G. H. *Japan and Japanese-American Relations.* New York: G. E. Stechert and Company, 1912.

Borton, Hugh. *Japan's Modern Century.* New York: Ronald Press, 1955.

Borton, Hugh, et al. *Japan Between East and West.* New York: Harper and Row, 1957.

Brooks, Lester. *Behind Japan's Surrender: The Secret Struggle that Ended an Empire*. New York: McGraw, 1968.

Butow, R. J. C. *Tojo and the Coming of War*. Princeton: Princeton University Press, 1962.

Bywater, Hector C. *The Great Pacific War: A History of the American-Japanese Campaign of 1931–1933*. Boston: Houghton, 1932.

Causton, E. N. *Militarism and Foreign Policy in Japan*. London: Allen and Unwin, 1936.

Cohen, Bernard C. *The Political Process and Foreign Policy: The Making of the Japanese Settlement*. Princeton: Princeton University Press, 1957.

Cohen, Jerome B., ed. *Pacific Partnership: U.S.-Japan Trade*. New York: Lexington Books, 1973.

Endicott, John E. *Japan's Nuclear Option*. New York: Praeger, 1975.

Falk, Edwin A. *From Perry to Pearl Harbor: The Struggle for Supremacy in the Pacific*. Garden City: Doubleday, 1943.

Feis, Herbert. *Japan Subdued: The Atomic Bomb and the End of the War in the Pacific*. Princeton: Princeton University, 1961.

————. *The Road to Pearl Harbor*. Princeton: Princeton University Press, 1950.

Hall, Robert B., Jr. *Japan, Industrial Power of Asia*. Princeton: Van Nostrand, 1963.

James, David H. *The Rise and Fall of the Japanese Empire*. New York: Allen and Unwin, 1951.

Kawai, Kazue. *Japan's American Interlude*. Chicago: University of Chicago Press, 1960.

Kuno, Y. S. *Japanese Expansion on the Asiatic Continent*, 2 vols. Berkeley: California State University Press, 1937.

Lockwood, William W. *The State and Economic Enterprise in Japan*. Princeton: Princeton University Press, 1965.

Lu, David J. *Sources of Japanese History*, 2 vols. New York: McGraw-Hill, 1974.

Mendel, D. H., Jr. *Japanese People and Foreign Policy*. Berkeley: University of California Press, 1961.

Mineler, E., *Victor's Justice: Tokyo War Crime Trials*. Princeton: Princeton University Press, 1971.

Morley, James W. *The Japanese Thrust into Siberia, 1918*. New York: Columbia University Press, 1957.

Mosley, Leonard. *Hirohito, Emperor of Japan*. Englewood Cliffs, N.J.: Prentice-Hall, 1966.

Neumann, William L. *America Encounters Japan: From Perry to MacArthur*. Baltimore: Johns Hopkins University Press, 1963.

Nish, Ian Hill. *The Anglo-Japanese Alliance: The Diplomacy of Two Island Empires, 1894–1907*. London: Greenwood, 1968.

Okazaki, Hisahiko. *Japanese View of Détente*. New York: Lexington Books, 1974.

Patrick, Hugh, ed. *Japanese Industrialization and Its Social Consequences.* Berkeley: University of California Press, 1976.

Reischauer, Edwin O. *The United States and Japan,* rev. ed. Cambridge, Mass.: Howard University Press, 1965.

Sansom, G. B. *The Western World and Japan.* New York: Knopf, 1949.

————. *Japan: A Short Cultural History,* rev. ed. New York: Appleton-Century-Crofts, 1962.

Scalapino, Robert A. *The Foreign Policy of Modern Japan.* Berkeley: University of California Press, 1977.

Schroeder, Paul W. *The Axis Alliance and Japanese-American Relations.* New York: Cornell University Press, 1958.

Schwantes, Robert S. *Japanese and Americans: A Century of Cultural Relations.* New York: Greenwood, 1955.

Shillony, B. A. *Revolt in Japan: The February 26, 1936 Incident.* Princeton: Princeton University Press, 1974.

Takeuchi, Tatsuji. *War and Diplomacy in the Japanese Empire.* Garden City, N.Y.: Doubleday, Doran and Company, 1935.

Togo, Shigenori. *The Cause of Japan.* New York: Simon and Schuster, 1956.

Treat, Payson J. *Diplomatic Relations Between the United States and Japan, 1853–1905,* 3 vols. Stanford: Stanford University Press, 1938.

Varley, H. Paul. *Japanese Culture.* New York: Holt, Rinehart and Winston, 1977.

Walworth, Arthur. *Black Ships off Japan: The Story of Commodore Perry's Expedition.* New York: Plates Company, 1946.

Ward, Robert E. *Japan's Political System,* 2nd ed. Englewood Cliffs, N.J.: Prentice-Hall, 1978.

Weinstein, Martin E. *Japan's Postwar Defense Policy, 1947–1968.* New York: Columbia University Press, 1971.

White, John A. *The Diplomacy of the Russo-Japanese War.* Princeton: Princeton University Press, 1964.

Yoshida, Shigeru. *The Yoshida Memoirs: The Story of Japan in Crisis.* Boston: Houghton Mifflin, 1962.

Yoshihashi, Takehiko. *Conspiracy at Mukden: The Rise of the Japanese Military.* New Haven: Yale University Press, 1963.

Korea

Acheson, Dean. *The Korean War.* New York: W. W. Norton, 1971.

Berger, Carl. *The Korea Knot: A Military-Political History,* rev. ed. Philadelphia: University of Pennsylvania Press, 1964.

Cho, Soon-sung. *Korea in World Politics, 1940–1950: An Evaluation of American Responsibility.* Berkeley: University of California Press, 1967.

Conroy, Hilary. *The Japanese Seizure of Korea*. Philadelphia: University of Pennsylvania Press, 1961.

George, Alexander L. *The Chinese Communist Army in Action: The Korean War and Its Aftermath*. New York: Columbia University Press, 1967.

Han, Sungjoo, *The Failure of Democracy in South Korea*. Berkeley: University of California Press, 1974.

Hatada, Takashi. *A History of Korea*. Santa Barbara: ABC-Clio Press, 1969.

Heller, Francis H., ed. *The Korean War: A 25-year Perspective*. Kansas: Regents Press, 1977.

Henderson, Gregory. *Korea: The Politics of the Vortex*. Cambridge: Harvard University Press, 1968.

Kim, C. I., and Kim, Han-Kyo. *Korea and the Politics of Imperialism: 1876–1910*. Berkeley: University of California Press, 1968.

Kim, Jai-Hyup. *The Garrison State in Pre-War Japan and Post-War Korea: A Comparative Analysis of Military Politics*. Washington, D.C.: University Press of America, 1978.

Kiyosaki, Wayne S. *North Korea's Foreign Relations: The Politics of Accommodation*. New York: Praeger, 1976.

Lee, Chong-sik. *The Politics of Korean Nationalism*. Berkeley: University of California Press, 1963.

McCune, G. M., and Harrison, John A., eds. *Korean-American Relations: Documents Pertaining to the Far Eastern Diplomacy of the United States*. Vol. 1: *The Initial Period, 1883–1886*. Berkeley: University of California Press, 1951.

Meade, E. Grant. *American Military Government in Korea*. New York: King's Crown, 1951.

Noble, Harold H., ed. *Embassy at War*. Seattle: University of Washington Press, 1975.

Oliver, Robert T. *Why War Came to Korea*. New York: Fordham University Press, 1950.

————. *Syngman Rhee: The Man Behind the Myth*. New York: Dodd, 1954.

Osgood, Cornelius. *The Koreans and Their Culture*. New York: Ronald, 1951.

Paige, Glenn D. *The Korean Decision: June 24–30, 1950*. New York: Free Press, 1968.

Park, Chung Hee. *Major Speeches by Korea's Park Chung Hee*. Seoul: Hallym, 1970.

Reeve, W. D. *The Republic of Korea: A Political and Economic Study*. London: Oxford University Press, 1963.

Scalapino, Robert A., and Lee, Chong-sik. *Communism in Korea*. Berkeley: University of California Press, 1974.

Simmons, Robert R. *The Strained Alliance: Peking, Pyungyang, Moscow, and the Politics of the Korean Civil War*. Riverside, N.J.: Free Press, 1974.

Tewksbury, Donald G., ed. *Source Book on Korean Politics and Ideologies.* New York: Institute of Pacific Relations, 1950.
Wade, L. L. *Economic Development of South Korea. The Political Economy of Success.* New York: Praeger, 1978.
White, Nathan. *U.S. Policy Toward Korea: Analysis, Alternatives, and Recommendations.* Boulder, Colo.: Westview, 1979.
Whiting, Allen S. *China Crosses the Yalu: The Decision to Enter the Korean War.* New York: Macmillan, 1960.

Vietnam

Armbruster, Frank E., et al. *Can We Win in Vietnam?* New York: Praeger, 1968.
Bloodworth, Dennis. *An Eye for the Dragon: Southeast Asia Observed, 1954–1970.* New York: Farrar, 1970.
Chau, Phan Thien. *Vietnamese Communism: A Research Bibliography.* Westport, Conn.: Greenwood, 1975.
Chen, K. C. *Vietnam and China, 1938–1954.* Princeton: Princeton University Press, 1969.
Coedes, G. *The Making of Southeast Asia.* Berkeley: University of California Press, 1967.
Fall, Bernard B. *Street Without Joy,* 3rd ed. Harrisburg, Pennsylvania: Stackpole Company, 1963.
————. *Viet-Nam Witness, 1953–66.* New York: Praeger, 1966.
————. *The Two Viet-Nams,* 2nd rev. ed. New York: Praeger, 1967.
Garrett, Stephen A. *Ideals and Reality: An Analysis of the Debate Over Vietnam.* Washington, D.C.: University Press of America, 1978.
Giap, Vo Nguyen. *People's War, People's Army: The Viet Cong Insurrection Manual for Underdeveloped Countries.* New York: Praeger, 1965.
Gurtov, Melvin. *The First Vietnam Crisis.* New York: Columbia University Press, 1967.
Lansdale, Edward Geary. *In the Midst of Wars: An American's Mission to Southeast Asia.* New York: Harper and Row, 1972.
Oberdorfer, Don. *Tet.* Garden City, N.Y.: Doubleday, 1971.
The Pentagon Papers. Chicago: Quadrangle, 1971. Paperback ed., Bantam.
Pfeffer, Richard M., ed. *No More Vietnams?* New York: Harper and Row, 1968.
Pike, Douglas. *Viet Cong.* Cambridge: MIT Press, 1966.
Race, Jeffrey. *War Comes to Long An: Revolutionary Conflict in a Vietnamese Province.* Berkeley: University of California Press, 1972.
Schlesinger, Arthur M., Jr. *Bitter Heritage.* Boston: Houghton Mifflin, 1967.
Schoenbrun, David. *Vietnam.* New York: Atheneum, 1968.

Schurmann, Franz, et al. *The Politics of Escalation in Vietnam.* Boston: Beacon Press, 1966.

Shaplen, Robert. *The Lost Revolution.* New York: Harper and Row, 1966.

Tanham, George K. *Communist Revolutionary Warfare;* rev. ed. New York: Praeger, 1967.

Thompson, Sir Robert. *No Exit from Vietnam.* New York: McKay, 1969.

Zasloff, Joseph J., and Goodman, Allan E., eds. *Indochina in Conflict.* New York: Lexington Books, 1971.

Zasloff, Joseph J., and Brown, MacAllister. *Communist Indochina and U.S. Foreign Policy: Postwar Realities.* Boulder, Colo.: Westview, 1978.

Index

DATE DUE			
GAYLORD			PRINTED IN U.S A